*P*ink is the color of universal love of oneself. It represents inner peace and affection. It's thought to be a calming color associated with flirtation, love, and kindness. Pink is both feminine and vibrant. Lake learned early on that she wanted to kiss girls, and from that point forward, her eyes and thoughts naturally gravitated to women's mouths and their soft, pink, kissable lips. And then the reality of the social construct that girls were meant to kiss only boys set in, creating an internal rift that would take decades for Lake to conquer. This story is about honoring the clumsy discontent of childhood and early adulthood and embracing the precipice of peace and happiness from where Lake now perches. The words that appear on these pages were nudged into being and landed exactly as they should, here for those who choose to read them. May they help to inspire and shine a light on your own most scrumptious story.

Robee Berry

The Pink Divide

Robee Berry

Halo
PUBLISHING
INTERNATIONAL

ISBN: 978-1-63765-209-1
LCCN: 2022904430

Halo Publishing International, LLC
www.halopublishing.com

Printed and bound in the United States of America

For Grams, a fierce and faithful woman whose indelible impression made this book a reality. To love yourself is to live your truth...an incredibly important lesson.

"If you're always trying to be normal, you will never know how amazing you can be."

~ Maya Angelou

The majority of locales and historical events within this book are factual, such as the Great Blizzard of 1978, yet much of this story and many of the characters are a product of the author's imagination.

Preface

Lounging comfortably in her daughter's oversized beanbag chair, Lake arches her back, stretching every muscle in her body, before sinking farther into the squishy orange sack. On a whim, she'd planned a day off work in the middle of the week. The night before, a strong storm had passed through, leaving everything outside wet, fully hydrated, and gleaming. She couldn't have picked a better day to be alone in the house. Feeling relaxed and content, she closes her eyes, inhaling deeply through her nose. Lake opens her mouth, pushing the air slowly through her lips, exhaling completely before repeating the process. The house is refreshingly quiet. She had entered Paige's room for one reason, to grab her dirty laundry and start a load of wash before her morning workout, but the chair beckoned and here she is. A rare moment of solitude in a customarily busy family abode. From this vantage point, Lake feels as if she's in a treehouse, with nothing but the large maple tree branches visible from the laid-back beanbag. As she allows her body to fully settle, her eyes fixate on the contrast of golden sunbeams piercing through the vivid green of the leaves. The naturally slow picture show driven by the light breeze is captivating. As she stares blankly, fleeting thoughts of Carly, her childhood crush, float softly into her mind, perhaps triggered by the beanbag. She releases the memories, and sweet thoughts of Kiki move in to replace the images of Carly. Appreciating her current circumstance and the timing of this pleasantry, Lake smiles to herself.

Admittedly, she has always possessed an indiscriminate love for the ladies, regardless of age, shape, color, size, or personality. She finds certain comfort in the sound of their voices, the way they smell, feel, and move. This discovery didn't occur magically one day but was rather gracefully and lovingly enticed into being by her beloved grandma Kiki. It is she whom Lake credits with helping her understand and accept who she is through the course of an awkward and confusing time in her life. And to this day, Lake draws from Kiki's depth of emotion when seeking to calm and placate any sporadic feelings of unsettledness. The fundamental constants from her early years were Kiki's gentle voice, the story of how she came to be, and their time together at the ranch.

Chapter 1

Kristina Adele Myers, aka Kiki, is Lake's heart, and she loves her more than any other person. Kiki, her first great love, her biggest advocate, and her fiercest protector, always one step ahead, silently laying the groundwork for Lake's discovery of her true self. At just five feet tall, including the added height from her dark-chestnut bouffant, her body radiates warmth, understanding, and a beauty that far surpasses the physical. Kiki's customary approach is to come at you with arms wide open, and the lucky recipient of her embrace is first struck by an invisible wave of Avon's Hawaiian White Ginger perfume. Her signature scent is an energetic and delicate combination of jasmine, rose, grass, and, of course, ginger. The exact notes detected depend on the time of year, but one thing's for certain: It's a warm, endless aroma of tropical loveliness, just like Kiki. Everyone and everything are naturally attracted to who and what she is, and to see her effortlessly hold court to all in her circle is a thing of wonder. Like everyone else, Kiki must have dressed for each of the four distinct Ohio seasons, but in Lake's mind, she's forever clad in brightly colored culotte shorts; a wide, terry-cloth tube top; and tastefully bedazzled flip-flops. Her bouncy, beautiful hair is held firmly in place by one of her many floral-print headbands. Hands on her hips, breasts pushed forward, she smiles down at Lake, a slight wrinkle in her forehead.

#

In the mid-forties, the Myers clan settled on a nondescript stretch of road just a couple of miles outside of town. As the family grew, more and more houses were filled by their people. Grandpa Kevin's horse ranch occupies most of the land on the east side of the two lanes between Main Street and the railroad tracks just north of the farm. We live directly across the street from Grandma Kiki and Grandpa Kevin's house. To the right is Uncle Rick and Aunt Joe, short for Josephine, and on the other side of them is Cousin Danny's place. Dad works with Grandpa and Uncle Rick on the ranch, and Mom stays home to take care of us kids. Our modern, midcentury home was built in 1953, with lots of windows and a floor-to-ceiling fireplace. Mom despises clutter, and so the house is sparsely furnished, each piece of furniture and décor deliberately placed. Every few months, she rearranges everything, hellbent on mixing things up and keeping it fresh. Lake finds this annoying, because it makes her feel as if she's a guest in her own home, so she escapes to her grandparents' house as often as possible. Their place is bigger, older, and has lots of nooks and crannies to call her own, a home with true character. Standing near the picture window admiring her summer blooms, her mom asks, "Lake, you haven't finished your breakfast, young lady, where do you think you're going?"

"I'm just not that hungry today. I want to go visit Grams," she says.

"Okay, but before you do, I need you to march right back into the kitchen, rinse your plate, and set it in the sink before you leave. And be sure to look both ways before you cross the street. I swear, no one pays attention to the speed limit signs. If it weren't for the railroad tracks slowing folks down, they'd go even faster!"

Perturbed, Lake stops short, does an about-face, and clears her plate from the table. Sprinting for the door, she yells in her mom's direction, "Bye, Mom. I'll be careful!"

Lake pushes the screen door open and jumps from the top stair of the porch to the bottom in one leap. Just as the door slams behind her, she hears her mom say, "And don't let the screen door slam shut!" Chuckling to herself, she says, "Too late for that!"

With summer in full swing, Lake makes the mindless jaunt to Gram's, which takes all of five minutes if you count the time it takes to stop, look left, look right, and then look left again before sprinting across the narrow road.

Walking around to the back of the house, she pulls the screen door open and steps inside. The air is heavy with the scent of bacon, and her mouth immediately begins to water. "Hey, Grams, it's Lake. Where are you?"

Kiki responds with a yell, "Lake, is that you?"

Lake passes through the kitchen and dining room and is halfway down the back hall when she sees Gram's head pop out of the door to her bedroom. "I thought I heard you come in. What are you up to today? Anything fun?"

"Not sure yet. What are you doing?"

"I've spent the better part of the morning looking for my favorite pair of Dr. Scholl's, with no luck. I'm glad you're here! My legs are feeling all stiff today. Would you mind going upstairs and looking for them in the bedroom? I think they might be in the closet. Just open the door and check the pockets of that hanging shoe organizer. It's clear plastic, so you can see everything without having to rummage through it all."

Always eager to please Kiki, Lake turns and starts up the stairs. Halfway up, she hears Kiki call out, "They're kind of a cream-color sandal with a big silver buckle on top." Lake easily finds the shoes right where Kiki said they'd be. Shutting the closet door, she turns and slowly looks around. The room is stuffy, and a thin layer of dust sits atop everything in sight. Across from the only set of windows in the room is a bed, neatly made, with lots of pillows. With just the one option to shine, it's hard to ignore the bright beam of sunlight coming through, and the billions of dust particles dancing and floating in the air.

The room is seldom used for anything other than storage. On the floor around the bed are boxes filled with clothes, more shoes, boots, old photos, and Gramps's fishing gear. Once, Lake and her older sister, Jeannie, had snuck up here and sifted through a few of the boxes. Lake hit the jackpot with the first one she opened. She remembers it being filled with fancy gowns; long, silk gloves; lacy pajama-looking things; fishnet pantyhose; and spiky high-heeled shoes. "What the heck is all this stuff?" Lake asked. Jeannie laughed and said, "I think we found Grandma Kiki's 'entertainment box.' She wore these things when she danced for money." It was Lake's first real glimpse into Kiki's former self, and it made her feel justified for having agreed to snoop. She and Jeannie tried on a few things, laughing and acting silly, before Grams started up the stairs. Halfway up, she stopped and yelled, "What are you two doing up there? Get on down here now, girls!" Hurriedly, they shoved the stuff back in the box and left the room. Lake doubted

Grams would have been too mad if she'd caught them trying on her old clothes, but they never did it again.

"Lake, what's taking you so long, child? Did you find my Dr. Scholl's?"

"Yeah, Grams, I'm coming down now." Walking into the downstairs bedroom, Lake hands Kiki the shoes and picks up a photo of her grandparents from the nightstand. Cradling it in her hands, she stares at the picture of the two, willing it to speak and share details of the moment it was captured. Grandpa Kevin's right arm was draped across Kiki's shoulders. In his left hand is a bottle of beer. He's holding it out as if toasting the camera. Ear-to-ear grins stretch across both faces as they look at each other. Palm trees behind them blow in the breeze. "That's my favorite picture of us," says Grams. Carefully placing it back where she found it, Lake nods and says, "I know. Mine too."

Before she was my grams, Kiki used to do burlesque, which is a kind of sexy dance. That's how she met Grandpa Kevin. She was a schoolteacher by day and a moonlight performer at a popular club in Cleveland by night. Gramps was in town on business for just one night. After dinner, a few of his buddies suggested they check out the local hotspot. Grandpa Kevin walked in, and there she was, up on stage shaking her booby tassels, big brown eyes staring directly at him. He fell in love with her, right then and there.

Grams interrupted Lake's thoughts. "Your grandpa Kevin has always been a rugged, handsome man who could stop my heart with just one look. He came into my life at exactly the right time, and it was love at first sight for the both of us." The story melts Lake's heart every time; she's aware of how truly rare their love is.

Their home is filled with pictures of the two of them, and even though she's old now, Lake can see that Grams has always been a beautiful woman, especially when she was younger. It's no wonder Grandpa Kevin fell head over heels for her. She still wears her dark-red hair stacked high on her head, headband framing her sweet, freckled face. And with each smile formed, her expressive eyes and lips say, *I love you* without ever speaking a word. Lake adores her.

#

The ranch house has been the same for more years than Lake's been alive. Grandma Kiki's content with the way things are, and so is Lake. The continuous arrangement is comfortable and reassuring,

14

an unconventional paradise. There are three things Lake can always count on at Gram's place: one, a fridge full of Orange Crush, her favorite soda—forbidden in her own house because of all the sugar and preservatives; two, Gram's cobalt-blue sea-glass candy dish filled to the brim with the chewy, peppermint goodness of Brach's Christmas Nougats—equally pleasing to the eyes and mouth, the center of each piece containing the outline of a perfect little pine tree surrounded by a wheel of deep red lines; and three, maybe the best thing of all, the joy Lake feels when out of the blue, Grams stops whatever it is she's doing and says to her in that sweet, singsong voice, "Ooooch, Lake…I believe it's time." The phrase is always followed by a wink and, "I have a story for you, little one. Are you ready?" The thought of what's about to happen makes Lake perk up, and she can't help but smile. "Of course, I am!"

Lake is always ready to hear the story, their favorite, and today is no exception. With her Dr. Scholl's now on her feet, Grams makes her way to the kitchen, Lake close behind. Grams grabs Lake an orange soda and pours herself a fresh cup of coffee. Easing into the corner banquette, she adds two teaspoons of sugar, blows on her cup a few times, and takes a sip. She pats the space next to her and says, "Sit down here beside me so I can tell your story."

#

Grandma Kiki thoroughly enjoys revisiting the day Lake was born, when Mother Nature whipped up one helluva of a wicked winter storm and she became Lake Elisabeth Myers. Sitting up straight, Grams rubs her hands together and pushes them straight out, fingers spread wide open like a magician who's just performed an amazing trick. In her best storytelling voice, she begins.

"The Great Blizzard of 'Seventy-Eight struck the Ohio Valley and the Great Lakes regions, bringing record snowfall and cold the likes of which few had ever seen before. The storm of the century initially started as rain, quickly turned to snow in the early morning hours, and over three days, dumped nearly fifty inches of the fluffy stuff on our little town. High winds helped to pick it up, swirl it around, and leave it covering all the houses on our road in a blanket of white. Like a snow globe, Nature's expansive hand gave Geneva a good shake, and when all was said and done, the air was still and quiet, the ground covered so completely that nothing appeared the same as it had just one day earlier. Cars left parked on the street disappeared overnight, nondescript mounds of wintery flakes. Tree limbs heaved and cracked from the weight of it. Electric lines snapped in an instant, stealing the inside light from homes already dark from their cold encasements. A state of emergency was declared. Classes in every school in the county were canceled, and authorities warned citizens to stay off the icy roads unless it was an absolute emergency. Travel of any kind, even in a vehicle equipped with four-wheel drive, was nearly impossible.

"Your mom was beyond pregnant, eight days overdue, and she woke up that morning feeling out of sorts and anxious. She was miserable there at the end. She looked like she'd stumbled upon a hornets' nest and spun 'em up something fierce. Every part of her body that you could see was swollen. Luckily, I'd treated her to a special moms' day of beauty just before you arrived, even though she'd totally lost sight of her toes. Poor thing, the only shoes that still fit were her flip-flops, so there she was, in the dead of winter, walking around with her gorgeously manicured, chubby toes fully exposed to the harsh winter elements.

After breakfast that morning, I layered up and braved the short walk over to check in and see how she was feeling. She was just cleaning up after making breakfast for your brother and sister, and I told her to take a load off and go lie down for a bit, just to rest her eyes. She shuffled down the hallway, and right as she heaved her enormous-bellied body onto the bed, she felt the gush of liquid between her legs. I was cleaning the countertops when I heard her. 'Kiki, can you come in here?' I traipsed down the hallway and into the bedroom to see her staring down at the floor. Naturally, I looked down, too, and realized she was standing in a puddle. 'Hot damn, Sylvia, it's time! I'll go fetch Jack. It's going to take me a while in this storm. But I'll hurry as fast as I can.'

Doing my best not to waste time, I pull on the least number of layers possible to keep warm and head for the barn, my mind troubled by the condition of the roads. It wasn't an ideal day for travel, but considering the alternative, your parents knew they had to venture out. Your dad and I did our best to follow the path I'd made earlier and hightailed it back to the house. Your mom was a sight, sitting on the couch waiting for us dressed in a pair of old sweatpants, one of your dad's faded hooded sweatshirts, and that long, black mink coat, the one she inherited from her mom. 'You ready, Sylvia?' I asked. Without answering, she edged forward and stood, struggling to free the hood of her sweatshirt and get it over her head. Completing her colorful ensemble that day were those awful, bright yellow wool mittens she'd knit—you know the ones? Says she picked the color on purpose to avoid losing them. Got to give it to her, though, they haven't gone missing yet!

I grabbed your mom's overnight bag and held one of her hands tight while your dad held on to the other. We were both scared to death she might take a tumble in the snow, her flip-flops wet and slippery. Clinging to her elbows and hands, we slowly got her settled in the car. I can still see your dad sitting firmly in the driver's seat, clutching the steering wheel, eyes glancing up in the rearview mirror as he slowly began backing his truck out of the driveway. Told us later, he white-knuckled it all the way into town! As luck would have it, he made it to the hospital just in time for your appearance.

I was so disappointed, Lake! I wanted nothing more than to be there, scoop you up, and blow raspberries on your cheeks, but not one single person in the family, aside from your mom and dad, got to see you 'til five days later, all on account of the Great Blizzard!

I stayed with your brother and sister until you came home. Those two were so preoccupied with sledding and enjoying the snow days away from school they didn't fuss too much about losing power or not being able to visit their new little sister in the hospital. After a few days, the snow tapered off and the winds died down. With the roads all plowed and salted, it was finally safe to bring you home. I was so anxious to get ahold of you, I nearly peed my pants waiting for your dad to come through the door."

It's always at this point in the story that Kiki becomes more animated. Glancing over to make sure Lake is listening, she says, "I nearly knocked poor Jack over trying to get at you!" For emphasis, she sticks her arms out, opens her hands, fingers stretching out, then closes them quickly. She does this several times, as if desperately trying to grasp something. A gesture of impatience that makes Lake smile.

"The first time I held you, I was sitting in your dad's easy chair. You fit perfectly in the crook of my arm, snug as a bug, and you smelled heavenly! There you were all bundled up, perfectly still and precious. Instantly smitten, I pushed the blanket back, carefully revealing your tiny pink face for the first time. Your big blue eyes locked on mine. 'Look at this little bundle of sweetness! Don't you just want to kiss her face right off?' I said. Your sister, Jeannie, took one look and replied, 'That little runt ain't my sister. They obviously gave us someone else's baby.' Keep in mind, we had just experienced the biggest blizzard of her life, and she's five years older than you. I think it was the combination of an abundance of snow and freedom from no kindergarten classes that made her indifferent. And besides, you know she's just ornery!"

Lake was eight years old now and knew this to be true. Seemed like Jeannie had woken up crabby every day since the day she arrived, acting as if Lake was some sort of alien being she was forced to share a bedroom with. Their older brother, Pete, is a quiet sort. Jeannie bosses him nonstop and swears she'll sock him in the eye if she ever catches him even looking at Lake. Rather than endure her wrath, he stays clear and spends most of the time in his room reading or studying.

"It's a good thing your dad's a patient man with nerves of steel. Many drivers failed to make it to their destination during the Great Blizzard of 'Seventy-Eight, abandoned cars and trucks littered the streets and ditches of Ashtabula County for days, but your dad was determined to get you and your mom to the hospital safely, and that's just what he did. I see so much of him in you. You know, it was his idea to name you Lake. Lord knows, the man enjoys the challenge of a good storm, and the one that hit the day before you came into this world was all because of the lake. They call it a lake-effect snow when cold air from Canada pushes across the warm waters of Lake Erie, picking up moisture and spreading snow across the land." Grams zeroes in on Lake's eyes and takes hold of her face with both hands. "That blizzard was a force to be reckoned with, and so are you, Miss

Lake Myers. Always believe in yourself. You're a strong, exceptional young lady who was born to do great things. Don't ever let anyone tell you otherwise. Now, just don't go spilling the beans to your dad that it was the mightiest of all mothers who stirred up his inspiration. He likes to think he came to the decision on all his own. It's not a family name, but it suits you!"

Feeling inspired, Lake takes the last sip of her Orange Crush, wondering how she'll spend the rest of her day. Before she has a chance to figure it out, she feels Kiki's hand resting on her knee. "How about you help me beat the dust out of those old bears in the living room?"

Chapter 2

The Myers men rely heavily on the *Old Farmer's Almanac*, planning each fishing and hunting trip based on the long-range weather forecasts and full-moon dates and times. Moving as one, fully in-sync masculine unit, Dad and his brother, Rick, had traveled with Grandpa Kevin across the country and around the world to fish the open waters and hunt wild game of all sizes. Those worthy of keeping are proudly preserved and displayed, symbols of the sport, a shared bond, and respect for the animal.

Sylvia doesn't like seeing the stuffed and mounted heads of dead creatures in our house, so Dad's prize trophies are confined to the basement, where only he can enjoy and appreciate them. Aunt Joe feels the same as Mom, but she and Uncle Rick don't have a basement, so his are out in the horse barn, where all the Myers men can talk and reminisce about them whenever they want. Grandma Kiki is a supportive, progressive woman who occasionally enjoys walking alongside Gramps on a hunting trip and dipping her rod in the water wherever they may be. Adventurous types, the two have adopted a snowbird lifestyle in their old age, spending a few months each winter on their boat in Key West, aptly named *Kiki's Keep*.

Gram and Gramps's house is tastefully decorated with creatures of all types. The walls of their dining room are dedicated solely to those pulled from the waters. Arching gracefully over the large picture window is a colorful, nine-foot sailfish. Upstaging the handmade teak dining table that comfortably seats ten, the fish appears to have just taken flight and is headed for the other side of the windows, where it can once again be back where it belongs, safe amid the blue-green waters of the Atlantic. The remaining walls of the dining room are draped with nets full of shells, crustaceans, sponges, and starfish. A deep-sea fishing pole rests in brackets, spanning the length of the transom window over the doorway leading into the area. A sight to see, the room is both breathtaking and calming.

The formal living space of the house is wall-to-wall animals taken from the land, air, and den—from a full-scale pheasant in midflight to a beautiful red fox in a leaping position, rear feet suspended in midair, front feet resting on a brilliant piece of weathered wood. It's fun to watch new visitors to the house amble through these areas of the home for the first time. The more-than-fifty mounts cover nearly every inch of wall and floor space, each silently vying for one's undivided attention. It's like visiting a museum for the first time, and it can be overwhelming. When Lake was little, she'd run from room to room, never stopping to appreciate the beauty of the mounts, terrified by their snarling teeth and glossy eyes that are always open, tracking her every movement. She's since grown accustomed to them and considers each to be a friend of sorts. The years provided Lake ample time to study them all individually and collectively, as a group, giving each the best name possible based on the type of animal they were and how they look now. Her grandparents' house was built to resemble a barn, complete with high, pitched ceilings, rustic beams, and plenty of exposed wood. It looks nothing like her own house. It's one of a kind, inspired, and different from any place in the whole town. The structure is filled with cozy little spots perfect for hiding or reading books. The floors are wood, and it smells like a barn, which, to her, is one of the best smells ever, a combination of hay, leather, and saddle oil. Almost all the furniture is dark brown leather with metal studs in the seams, and she never has to fight anyone for a throw pillow to rest her head.

A typical third grader, Lake is no longer in awe of the house or her grandparents, but deep down, she knows the couple is different. Their love is the envy of all who know them, and the two are legends in the town, mostly on account of the ranch, their prizewinning quarter horses, and the taxidermy business they run on the side. The art of stuffing and mounting the skins of dead animals is an acquired skill, one that only a select few choose to pursue. But just like everything else, the pair excels at it.

As she and her grams carefully maneuver the biggest bear over the door frame and out to the front porch, Kiki uses her foot to push it back against the railing and says, "I knew the moment I met your grandpa that we'd end up together." Kiki raises her right hand to her chest, placing it over her heart as if she's about to recite the Pledge of Allegiance, then brings her left hand up to cover her right. "It's hard to explain, Lake, but one day, when you meet the person who makes your heart beat so fast, like it's about to explode, you'll know what I'm talking about. One minute, I'm up on stage dancing, and the next, I can hardly breathe. Seeing your grandpa for the first time was a truly moving experience. After my dance ended, I went to the bar for some cold water and realized I was sweating uncontrollably. I tried taking some deep breaths to calm myself down, but it wasn't working. When I turned to look for your grandpa, he was there at my side, smiling. It was as if I'd lost the ability to speak. He was calm and incredibly handsome. He introduced himself and smiled. I thought he had the most incredible gray eyes I'd ever seen. My words came out in a jumble, and I had to repeat myself to make any sense at all. He asked if I'd like to take a walk with him, and I said yes, just like that! We've been together ever since. I've never questioned my life with your grandpa because I've never doubted it. Each day is fresh, and I almost always learn something new. Life on this ranch is raw and real. It's multidimensional. Everywhere I look, I see something I want to touch and feel. It's incredible."

Lake looks at Kiki and notices the hint of a tear in her eye. It is moments like this that make their relationship special. Kiki is the only adult who speaks to her like this. Completely honest and vulnerable. Blinking back tears, Kiki looks up at the sky. There isn't a cloud in sight.

#

Kiki says all creatures deserve respect, even the dead ones, so she takes extra care to position them just right and give them the eyes that best suits them. "It's the eyes that tell the story, Lake, especially in these creatures. If we don't give them just the right eyes, we're missing the mark, and they're stuck like that for all eternity, somewhere in the middle of their story."

At first, Kiki just watched Grandpa Kevin, carefully taking it all in, occasionally asking questions. Over time, she began working on small birds and animals, Gramps's keen eyes watching her develop her own technique and appreciating her tender approach.

The bearskin rugs are Kiki's pride and joy. Gramps made most of them himself. A couple, he inherited from the men in his family. The big grizzly was a special gift from his dad, my great-grandpa Myers. Story has it, he was out hunting elk and was ambushed by the mammoth. Several shots later, the big guy finally fell, and now he rests forever on the living room floor.

Kiki has the black and brown bear rugs hung over the front porch railings, their glass eyeballs shining in the sun, enormous teeth gleaming. And as if that's not scary enough, she insists on rolling the nine-foot-tall stuffed and mounted polar bear out here, too. Perched on its hind legs, the polar bear towers over us, commanding the attention of anyone who happens to drive by.

As much as she loves spending time with Grandma Kiki, Lake doesn't enjoy bear-cleaning days. Grams's attachment to the dead grumblers is beyond Lake's comprehension. In a purely selfish attempt to divert Kiki's attention, she begins to drop not-so-subtle hints of ice cream as she inches closer to the door. She knows if she persists, she'll wear Kiki down and be granted a temporary reprieve from the bears and the glaring sun. As if on cue, Grams says, "I believe these guys are as clean as they're going to get. Help me roll 'em all back in the house, and we'll see what kind of ice cream we have in the freezer. Kevin's sweet tooth has been acting up lately, and we may be running low on your favorites."

Lake gladly helps Kiki move the bears back inside and into their respective spots. They lay the final rug in front of the fireplace and head for the fridge. Reaching into the freezer, Kiki pulls out two containers. "We have rocky road and vanilla, your favorite. Must be your lucky day!"

With her bowl of ice cream in hand, Lake decides to enjoy it from the dining room window seat. It's the perfect spot to keep an eye on the barn and watch Kiki, who's on her way over to the stereo to play on an old Motown record. At the opening note, Kiki spins around once and begins shaking her behind, humming and moving about the dining room with the feather duster. Lake takes another bite of ice cream and chuckles, feet tapping to the beat of "Tears of a Clown." Scattered among the never-ending pictures on display throughout the house are a few of Grams with her own mom and dad. A time of her life she rarely speaks of but one that obviously was important to her.

Before claiming her space on the ranch with Grandpa Kevin, Kiki's life was the opposite of what it is now. Born in Beachwood, she grew up in a big house on Cedar Road, living a life of privilege, attending private schools, and graduating with honors from an all-girls college. As was expected, she earned a teaching degree, like her mother.

She had a job outside the home, an occupation she was good at, and she was fiercely independent. "I needed a change of scenery, Lake, so I decided to take a part-time job at the Roxy. Dancing a couple nights each week added color to my life, and I met so many interesting and fun people."

Kiki lived under her parents' roof until the day she met Grandpa Kevin. Successful in his own right, he was never good enough for Grams's parents. When he proposed, they pitched a fit. She and Gramps drove straight to city hall and got married. Kiki left behind everything she'd ever known to move to our small, rural town. A true leap of faith. Grandpa Kevin treats her like a queen, never forgetting where she comes from or what she gave up for him. Every few years, he whisks Kiki off to a big, fancy city for an impromptu shopping spree. In the winter months, the excursions focus on warmer climates like Atlanta, Miami, or Houston. In the summer, it's Boston, New York, or San Francisco. They live an enchanted life of mutual respect, free of judgment. No regrets, never looking back.

It's barely mid-July, and Lake feels as if she's already done everything she planned to do during her summer vacation. She's spent every day for the past forty-one days with Grandma Kiki. Her daily routine consists of waking up early, getting dressed, and walking across the street to hang out with Kiki. Sometimes she goes to the horse barn, depending on what's happening that day. Most of the time, she eats breakfast at Kiki's and settles into a spot to read or watch a show. At some point during the day, a few of her neighborhood friends show up to hang out.

It's 9 a.m., and she's already bored. Lake is lying on a bearskin rug, the back of her head resting against the back of the bear's head. She's watching a repeat episode of some kids' show and decides to go through the beat-up wicker movie basket next to the TV. Kiki picks up old movies and videos on sale at the library, and sometimes Lake comes across a good one. This morning, she finds a videotape of an old TV show called *The Courtship of Eddie's Father*. On the cover, there's a picture of a cute little boy with black hair and a silly grin. To herself, Lake thinks, *He looks nice.*

Grams is making a pass through the living room on her way to putting away a stack of folded laundry. "Hey, Lake, you should watch that video. I think you'd really like it!" Popping the tape into the player, Lake resumes her position on the black bearskin rug in front of the television. She is hooked from the first episode. The show is about a kid named Eddie who's always on the search for his dad's next wife. He and his dad live in Los Angeles, where all the movie stars are, and they have a Japanese housekeeper named Mrs. Livingston. Lake is fascinated by Eddie and his schemes to pair his dad with a woman. Relaxed in her cool spot on the living room floor, she watches five episodes of the show before noticing Grams standing next to her. "I knew you'd like that show. Have you even peed since you started watching it?"

"No, but I haven't had anything to drink either!"

"Let's get you some lunch. How's a fried bologna sandwich with chips sound?"

That sounds good to Lake. She follows Kiki to the kitchen, then continues down the short hall to the guest bath. Come to think of it, she *does* have to pee. After finishing up in the bathroom, she skips back to the kitchen. Grams is standing at the stove. "You toast the bread, and I'll finish frying the bologna. It smells so yummy, I think I'll have a sandwich, too. Toast a couple extra slices for me."

Lake pushes the rolltop of the breadbox open, then grabs four slices from the loaf and puts it back. "Do you want chips, Grams?"

"No sweetie, just a sandwich. And maybe one of my special drinks," she says with a wink. Grams's "special drink" is a dirty martini, with extra olive juice and two olives stuffed with blue cheese. Most days, Grams sips sweet tea from a tall glass. But sometimes she enjoys one of her "special drinks" with lunch.

Lake finishes toasting the bread, grabs a couple of paper plates from the cabinet, and places two slices on each. Dumping a handful of chips on her plate, Lake takes a seat at the banquette.

"So, tell me about the show you've been watching all morning." While they eat lunch, Lake runs through each of the five episodes she's watched.

"That Eddie sounds like a real character. I'm glad you're enjoying it. I wish I had a Mrs. Livingston to help me around the house." Kiki raises her glass and smiles. "There's more work to do here today. I'll be down in the basement finishing up the laundry if you need me."

"Okay, Grams." Tossing her plate in the trash, Lake returns to the living room to watch a few more episodes.

Lake pushes PLAY on the VCR, grabs a couple pillows from the couch, and uses them to prop herself up on the rug. The next two episodes are more of the same shenanigans from Eddie. Grams was right, he is a cute little guy. A real character!

Then, just like that, the last episode on the tape changes Lake's life forever. In season one, episode eight, Eddie gets punched by an adorable little blond girl named Joey. But he's hesitant to tell his dad who hit him, because he's got a crush on Joey and he's embarrassed that he's being bullied by a girl, who's a "little rough around the edges."

Joey Kelly is a slugger with sass, and Lake falls hard the moment she lays eyes on her. She is literally obsessed with this one episode and immediately watches it a second time when the tape ends. Joey has the prettiest blond hair Lake has ever seen, and the way she scrunches her face up when she talks makes Lake want to kiss her.

Lake can hear the water running in the kitchen sink and realizes Grams is washing dishes. The kitchen sink faces the back of the house with no clear line of sight to where she is in the living room. Even if she finishes the dishes, it will take at least a couple of minute for her to dry her hands and get to a place where she can see Lake.

Having walked through the logic, Lake feels the coast is clear to go about her business. She snuggles up to the TV, declares her undying love, and lays a big, wet kiss right on Joey's lips. Well, her lips on the television. She has no idea Grams is standing in the archway until she hears her clear her throat and ask, "So, you got any plans for the rest of the day?"

Letting go of the TV, Lake spins around as if she hadn't just been making out with the television. "Um, I'm not sure. Why?"

"I could use your help hanging the sheets on the line outside. Unless, of course, you have something better to do," says Grams.

"Sure, I can help. I think the gang will be here soon. I'll just play outside when we're done."

Grams smiles, winks at Lake, and walks back to the kitchen. Lake's face feels like it's on fire, and she's worried Kiki will ask questions about what she just saw, or worse yet, tell her mom or dad she was kissing the TV and telling Joey that she loved her. Lake quickly turns the TV and VCR off and goes to help Kiki. Grams is upbeat, whistling and humming while they hang the sheets. No questions are asked, and she never says a word to anyone.

For the next few days, Lake thinks about Joey nonstop. She's never really had a crush on anyone before, and it's a strange thing to suddenly be infatuated with another person, let alone a girl! Her feelings for Joey are genuine, and she imagines what it would be like to actually kiss her. The thought makes her smile, and she gets butterflies in her belly.

#

Grandpa Kevin owns the biggest horse ranch in all northeast Ohio. When he was young, he was a champion barrel racer, but now he mostly just oversees the ranch and stuffs dead animals. Today's horseshoeing day, and normally Lake would be out there watching, but it's hot as blazes, and she doesn't feel like playing outside, so she wanders off to the living room for some alone time with Joey. She hears a knock at the back door and Grams yells, "Lake, can you see who's at the door?"

"Sure, Kiki." Lake pauses the tape and makes her way to the back door. "Hi, Mrs. Scott. Come on in. Grandma's in the kitchen."

"Thank you, Lake. Please, call me Veronica. How's your summer going?"

"It's pretty good. I passed the third grade, no problem, and I hope I get Mrs. Spence for my teacher this fall. Jeannie says she's nice and doesn't give a lot of homework."

"I'll keep my fingers crossed for you. Nice seeing you, Lake." Veronica walks toward the kitchen, and Lake returns to her spot in front of the TV. She must be careful not to get caught kissing Joey again. She gets up and peeks around the corner to make sure Grams and Veronica are sitting down in the kitchen. She can't see Kiki's face, but she can hear her talking. "Kevin and the boys are headed over to Kentucky this weekend to look at a mare they're interested in. You and I should get together if you're not busy." Tiptoeing back to her spot, Lake makes out with Joey on the television for a few minutes, and the episode ends. The natural light in the living room has all but disappeared as the clouds roll in. Lake feels like going outside now. She mouths the words, *"Bye, Joey,"* then walks through the kitchen unnoticed and heads for the barn, carrying her secret love for Joey with her.

Chapter 3

onathon Sunburst. What the heck kind of name is that anyways? Lake doesn't like Jonathon much. He's a snot, and his clothes always match his socks and shoes. He's just too well put together for a kid their age. Of all the kids who live on her road, he lives the closest, and for some reason, Lake's mom thinks he's as cute as a button, so Lake has to be somewhat pleasant. "Why can't you be sweet and polite like Jonathon?"

Lake rolls her eyes and says, "I don't know, Mom, maybe 'cause I'm not a crybaby 'little cupcake'?" Geez, she hates it when Sylvia says stuff like this to her.

Standing in front of the fireplace, rearranging the items on the mantle, Sylvia ignores Lake's response completely. "Jonathon comes from a good family. He has excellent manners, and he gets good marks in school. You really should be nicer to him."

Jonathon and his family own a historic house that's at least three times the size of Lake's house. It reminds Lake of the plantation homes they learned about in American history class. It's white, perfectly square, and has lots of windows and a big front porch. Jonathon lives with his mom and dad in the upstairs part of the house. His grandmother, aunt, and uncle live there too. They all work in the family restaurant, which takes up the entire first floor. The Grand Derby Tavern is really old, and it costs a lot of money to eat there. It's a "special occasion" kind of place, with real china and crystal drinking glasses. Lake has never once had a meal there. Her dad took her mom there a long time ago, to celebrate their ten-year wedding anniversary, and Sylvia still talks about how terrific it was.

Because he lives on the same side of the road as the ranch, Jonathon doesn't have to cross the street to come over. He's at the ranch so often, he's worn a path alongside the road all the way from the restaurant to Kiki's house. Jonathan, the pain in her butt, just follows the path through the fields and ends up at the ranch almost every day.

Since discovering *The Courtship of Eddie's Father*, Lake has taken to beating Jonathon's ass on a semi-regular basis. As far as she's concerned, he's basically useless as a boy. He's afraid of the horses and refuses to go frogging with her 'cause the frogs make weird noises and squirt pee when you squeeze them. Worst of all, he can't kick a ball or run fast.

It's the summer before fourth grade, and they play outside from the time they get up until it gets dark. Down her road, in the opposite direction of Jonathon's house, is a small mobile-home park that sits back off the road. Lake swears half the kids in her school live there. A bunch of them ride their bikes to the ranch, and that's where they hang out all day. The ranch is the perfect gathering spot because it has woods and fields to play in, a pond for frogging, and lots of yard space for kickball. A couple of years ago, Gramps put up an outdoor light on a pole near the side yard so they could see when it got dark, but they don't have to turn it on much. In the summer, the sun stays out 'til it's almost time for bed.

With this many kids, they have to compromise on what they do, but Lake's number-one favorite thing to do is to play kickball, so whenever it's her turn to pick, she always chooses that. She practices kicking a lot and is a pretty good kickball player, if she does say so herself. Besides Lake, Gretchen is the only other girl who plays at the ranch. Jonathon gets picked on a lot because he cries all the time and is terrible at sports. Gretchen feels bad and tries to include him whenever she can.

The days of summer vacation are almost over. Lake is kicking a ball against the side of the barn not paying attention when Gretchen turns and says, "Hey, Jonathon, you want to jump rope or play hopscotch?"

He looks over at her, eyes pleading for her to lower her voice. "Are you trying to get me killed? I mean, sure, I want to do those things, Gretchen, but Lake or one of the boys will beat me up if I go off to jump rope or play hopscotch with you." Jonathon grins as if he's about to reveal some juicy secret. "You know Lake. She thinks she's hot shit on a silver platter, but really, she's just cold poop on a paper plate!"

He giggles like a girl and slaps his knee. Jonathon is convinced he's the first person to have ever spoken this phrase, and it's his favorite thing to say about her. Never mind. Lake's older brother, Pete, has been saying the exact same thing about her sister, Jeannie, for the past two years.

Gretchen rolls her eyes. "What about clover picking? You wanna look for four-leaf clovers in the grass?"

"I guess that'd be alright," says Jonathon. They sit a few feet away from Lake, looking for four-leaf clovers, and she goes back to kicking the ball. Just a few minutes into it, Gretchen's already spotted a couple lucky clovers. Jonathon is zero for her two. Lake can sense a fit coming on when all of a sudden, he jumps up screaming like his ass is on fire. "Holy shit on a stick! There're ants all over my balls and my din-galing. They're biting me everywhere, and it hurts! Gretchen, help me. You got to help me get 'em off!"

Lake stops kicking the ball and turns to look. In one swift move, Jonathon pulls down his shorts and kicks them completely off, revealing the fact that he's not wearing any underwear. Who wears shorts without underwear and then sits in the grass? He's got little black dots all over his peter, his balls, and his butt. Jonathon is spinning around, bouncing from one foot to the other, and Lake can see they're crawling on his legs, too. "Gretchen, help! They're biting me in my butthole. You got to get 'em out!"

Gretchen looks over at Lake, her eyes as big as saucers, and Lake says, "I'm not touching his butthole." By this time, most of the other boys have gathered around due to all the commotion, and they're laughing like crazy and pointing at Jonathon's scrawny wiener and tiny balls. It's obvious no one wants to go digging ants out of his backside.

Gretchen looks at him, drops her head, and gets out a barely audible, "Sorry, Jon." So, what does the little turd do? He drops right down on his butt and starts dragging it across the grass like a damn dog. He's practically hysterical, crying harder than she's ever seen him cry, and Lake feels a little sorry for him, but just for a minute. After a few good swipes across the lawn, Jonathon struggles to stand, tears streaming down his face. He picks a few stragglers off his legs, turns to look at Gretchen, and says, "Thanks a lot, Gretchen, thanks for nothing! You're not my friend anymore." And to Lake, "You never were! Cold poop! Cold poop!" Leaning down to pick up his shorts, he shakes them off, puts them on inside out, and limps away like an injured stray. It will be weeks before they see Jonathon again.

#

It's another uneventful day at the ranch, drama-free without Jonathon. Chilling on the porch, Lake says, "Hey, Gretch, you wanna play kick-ball with us? We could use another girl out there. You can play any position you want. What do you say?"

Gretchen looks up, happy to focus on something else besides solving the Rubik's cube mystery she's been twisting away on for more than an hour. "Okay. I'll try, but I want to pitch." Turns out Gretchen is a pretty good pitcher! She likes the game almost as much as Lake does, and their team wins by four runs.

Gretchen is quiet in school, and Lake never paid much attention to her until the summer of kickball. Her mom died when she was four, and Gretchen went to live with her aunt and uncle in Michigan for a year. Before that, Gretchen and her brother, Josh, lived on a farm a few miles away from the ranch. Her dad grew corn and soybeans and let Gretchen ride on the tractor with him. When she lived on the farm, she had three dogs and a cat. Then her mom got sick with the cancer, and the doctors and hospital took all their money. Her dad had to sell the farm to pay the bills. Now her family lives in the mobile-home park with just the cat, and her dad works at the feed and seed store up on Route 84.

#

On rainy days, when they can't play kickball, Gretchen rides her bike over, and the girls read books up in the hayloft. Kiki makes peanut-butter-and-jelly sandwiches with plain potato chips for lunch, and sometimes, she surprises them with an orange soda. Today is an orange soda day, and they each get a cold Orange Crush.

The summer is almost over. It's late August and raining like crazy outside. Thunder and lightning are all around the farm, and neither Gretchen nor Lake wants to leave the barn. The horses don't like the storms and have all come into the barn for shelter. When they look down through the cracks of the floorboards, they can see them stomping around, whinnying, and huddling together. Luckily, they had just finished eating lunch in the hayloft when the rain started. There's nowhere they have to be now. Lake is feeling a little sleepy when Gretchen turns to her and says, "Hey, Lake, you wanna play Spin the Bottle?"

She has no idea what that is, but it sounds fun. "Sure, how do we play?"

"I've never actually played before. I just heard Josh talking about it with his friends. He went to Susie Bradley's house last Friday for her thirteenth birthday party, and they played Spin the Bottle in her basement. They had more people and were able to sit in a circle, but we can just sit like this. Scooch back a little." Gretchen picks up her Orange Crush bottle and lays it on the wood floor of the hayloft between them. She shifts her weight and says, "I'll spin it, and if it lands on you, I get to give you a kiss."

Picturing this in her head, Lake looks at her and says, "What happens if it doesn't land on me?"

Gretchen smiles and says, "I'll spin until it does."

Up to this moment, Joey had been Lake's one true love. But now, she's looking at Gretchen in a whole new light. Everyone in Lake's family has brown or blue eyes. Her own eyes are light blue. Gretchen has twinkly green eyes. Lake's hair is light-colored, blond. Not as light as Joey's, but still pretty light. Gretchen has long, shiny dark hair. Grandpa Kevin would call it chestnut brown. At school, she wears it down, but here on the ranch, Gretchen wears it in one perfect braid that falls halfway down her back. Her red Converse tennis shoes are worn, the left one has a hole in it, but they look good with her cutoff shorts and ringer T-shirts. Most important, she's really awesome at kickball.

When Gretchen smiles at Lake, her nose scrunches up a little. Her lips are full and sort of pink, but Lake knows she's not wearing lip gloss. Maybe it's the orange soda that makes them look that color? Whatever it is, she finds herself wanting the bottle to stop so it's pointing right at her. On the first spin, the bottle stops and lands so that it's pointing between them and a bale of hay. The same thing happens on her second and third try. Just when Lake thinks she won't get her kiss, Gretchen spins the bottle hard. When it stops, it's pointing directly at her. Without so much as a warning, Gretchen leans over the bottle, places her hands on Lake's shoulders, and pulls her over toward her, landing a solid kiss on her waiting lips. "Lake, you're supposed to close your eyes when you kiss."

"Oh, sorry. I thought I was closing my eyes."

"Let's try again. It's your turn to spin." Lake nervously gives the bottle a spin. It hits her shoe and ends up pointing back at her. On her second try, it lands a little to the left of Gretchen, but they decide it's close enough. This time, they both lean in and put their hands on each other's shoulders. The second kiss is much better than the first and lasts longer. Lake is just getting the hang of it when she hears Grandma Kiki calling out from down below. "Lake, you and Gretchen need to come down out of the loft. Her dad wants her home now."

"Okay, Kiki, we're on our way."

#

The next two days are warm and sunny. The kids pass the time with marathon kickball tournaments, exploring the woods, and the occasional dip in the pond. Lake secretly longs for rain and more time with Gretchen in the hayloft. To make sure she's prepared for the next time, she hides an Orange Crush bottle way back behind a row of hay. Finally, on Labor Day, her wish comes true.

It's dark and raining when she wakes up and walks across the street to Kiki's house. Grams never locks the doors, and she never knocks. She's been coming here almost every day for as long as she's been alive. She throws open the back door, take off her rain boots, and makes her way to the kitchen.

Veronica and Grandma Kiki are sitting at the table drinking coffee. Each is wearing one of Kiki's shiny, satin robes. Veronica turns to Lake and says, "Good morning. Nice to see you again, Lake. Your grandma and I were just talking about what we should have for breakfast. Any suggestions?"

Lake doesn't even have to think about this one. "Eggs are always good. I like them scrambled. Grams likes them with hot sauce, but

I like them plain, nothing on them. I also like toast with butter and grape jelly to go with my eggs."

Veronica looks over at Grams. "That sounds like a wonderful breakfast. Would you agree, Kiki?"

"I'm in total agreement. I'll get it started," says Grams as she starts to get up.

Reaching for Gram's arm, Veronica looks at her and says, "No, let me make breakfast this morning. You sit with Lake and enjoy your coffee." She gives the two of them a wink. When she gets up to make breakfast, Lake can see that Veronica isn't wearing a bra under the robe. She's obviously spent the night with Grams. Her hair is all messed up, and she isn't wearing any makeup.

Lake has to go to the bathroom, so she excuses herself and says she'll be right back. The guest bedroom in Grandma Kiki's house is right off the kitchen by the bathroom. Lake is there so often, she thinks of the room as her own. She feels a twinge of jealousy, thinking Veronica might have slept in the guest bed, *her* guest bed. But as she goes into the bathroom, she glances sideways and can see the bed is made and there are no clothes anywhere. It's just as neat as always, waiting for Lake to come and spend the night. The only other spare bedroom in the house is upstairs, but it's hot, dusty, and used for storage. No one ever sleeps in it. Lake heads back to the table, lost in thought about the situation.

"I hope you're hungry." Veronica is sitting next to her at the banquette. Lake is completely absorbed in thought and doesn't hear Veronica until she says, "Earth to Lake…are you ready for your eggs, darlin'?"

"Oh, yeah. Thank you."

Grams takes a sip of her coffee and looks over at Lake. "So, what are you up to today?"

She stops midbite and responds, "I was thinking maybe I'd read up in the hayloft for a while."

"That sounds like a nice morning. Is Gretchen coming over?"

Lake can feel her face getting hot, and she wonders why Grams is asking about Gretchen. Does she know the real reason why she wants to be in the hayloft? Lake stares down at her eggs, pushing them around on her plate. "I don't know. She might."

"Veronica and I are going out to do some shopping after breakfast, but I'll be back before lunch. I can make your favorite peanut butter and jelly with some chips and maybe even a bottle of orange soda. It's your last day of fun before you have to think about going back to school." Grams reaches out, squeezes Lake's hand, and smiles, letting her know she's loved without actually saying the words.

Lake hears a faint knock at the back door followed by a familiar voice. "Mrs. Myers? Hello?"

It's Gretchen. She's here! Lake's heart skips a beat, and she jumps up, walking to the back door. Gretchen sees her coming and opens it before she gets there. She looks so cute in her cutoff shorts and rain jacket. Holding onto the doorknob, Gretchen uses the toe of each foot to pry off her rain-soaked tennis shoes and follows Lake to the kitchen. Grams smiles at Gretchen and says, "You're just in time for breakfast. Would you like some eggs?"

Gretchen glances over at Veronica and then looks back at Grams. "No, thank you, Mrs. Myers. My dad made bacon and eggs this morning. He's always talking about breakfast being the most important meal. He won't let me leave the house without eating something. He says a rainy day like this requires a hot breakfast, one that'll stick to your guts. He calls it fuel for riding bikes and playing."

Lake realizes she's grinning wide and is staring at Gretchen. Looking away, she finally says, "Are you sure you don't want anything? We have toast with butter and grape jelly.""I could eat a piece a toast. Thanks, Lake."

Lake pops a couple slices in the toaster and stands with her back to everyone waiting for it to pop up. *Be cool, Lake.* She breathes in and out. The toast pops up, and she places it on a paper towel and slides into the corner banquette alongside Gretchen. Their legs touch, and Lake pulls her leg away.

Kiki looks across the table at them and says, "How do you two young ladies feel about starting school this week?"

They both groan and kick each other under the table. Gretchen says, "I think it's going to be a lot harder than third grade. Josh says

I can expect more homework and less time for play. Lake is lucky she got Mrs. Spence. Everyone says she's the best."

Veronica used to be a teacher before she retired. From her place at the table, she says, "Kiki tells me you two enjoy reading. That's really quite good. Fourth grade is a lot more reading than you're used to, but you'll both do well if you continue to read on your own. I have a whole library full of books at my house. If you ever want to come take a look, I'm sure Kiki wouldn't mind bringing you by. You're welcome to take any book on my shelves." Smiling, she says, "Think of it as your very own bookmobile, without the wheels."

"That would be great! Thanks, Veronica." Lake turns to Gretchen. "Maybe after we're done eating, we can read up in the hayloft? I mean, at least until the rain stops. I have this month's *Highlights* magazine, and Jeannie gave me the latest *Bops*."

Taking the last bite of her toast, Gretchen says, "Yeah, cool. Okay, Lake."

She's come prepared. Lake has the magazines and two other books in her backpack ready to go. When she saw that it was raining this morning, she had a vision of how the day would go, and now it's happening. They finish eating and start for the back door. They're halfway to the barn when Lake hears Gretchen ask, "Did Mrs. Scott sleep over at your grandma's last night?"

Lake is walking fast to get out of the rain. She stops, pulls the hood down to shield her eyes, and says, "Yeah, I think so. Her husband died in a car accident a long time ago, and her kids are all grown up. She likes spending time with Kiki now when Gramps is away on business, says her house is too quiet. I think they get a little loopy from the wine they drink, and it's more 'responsible' if Veronica stays over instead of driving home."

The rain is hitting Lake's face. It stings a little. Gretchen says, "I guess that makes sense. Sometimes my dad has guys over to play cards on Friday nights. They drink beer, cuss, and act dumb. Some of them are so drunk when they leave, they can hardly stand. They definitely shouldn't be driving home like that. Its good Veronica sleeps over when your grandma and her are drinking wine. And your grandma has a nice guest room. We don't have a guest room in our house."

Lake doesn't say anything about where Veronica may have slept last night. They're in the hayloft now, and she wants to get started with how she sees the rest of the morning going. They settle in and start to read their magazines, but Lake is fidgety and can't concentrate. She's read the same paragraph three times when Gretchen says, "You want to play Spin the Bottle again?"

One hundred percent! "Yes, I do."

Gretchen is looking around the hayloft. "We need a bottle." Lake gets up and walks over to the place where she'd hidden the Orange Crush bottle they'd used the last time. "Good thinking, Lake. You're so smart!"

This time, there's no awkwardness or hesitation. They assume the same positions they were in the last time, and Lake decides it's her turn to go first. Her luck is for shit today, and she's on her fourth spin when Gretchen says, "For Pete's sake!" She turns the bottle so it's directly facing her and leans in. Using her fingers, Lake raises up a little and leans forward toward Gretchen, closing her eyes just as their lips touch. They stay like that for a while, pressing their lips tighter together. Lake still has her eyes closed when Gretchen pulls back and says, "I think you're ready now."

Lake isn't sure what she means by this. "Ready for what?"

"For your first kiss with a boy."

Wait, what? Lake wants to tell her that she doesn't want to kiss boys, that she only wants to kiss Gretchen, but she stops herself. Gretchen's view of how it's supposed to be is the same as everyone else's. Girls kiss boys. They hold their hands, dance with them, and eventually marry them. That's how the world sees it, and that's how Gretchen sees the world. It's simple, black and white. Lake isn't ready for that world right now. She much prefers the cozy safety of the hayloft, where she can hear the rain hitting the metal roof and the horses stamping their hooves below. Where she can catch a whiff of Pert shampoo when Gretchen leans in to kiss her, and how it mixes with the smell of the barn when she pulls away. Lake loves everything about this time, and she doesn't want it to end.

38

Bringing herself back to the moment, Lake says, "I think I need just a little more practice. I want to be perfect when the time comes."

Gretchen says, "Okay, just one more, and then I wanna finish my *Highlights* magazine."

Knowing it's the last time she'll ever kiss Gretchen, Lake moves closer to her. She looks into her eyes, and just as she's about to kiss Gretchen, a piece of her hair falls across her face, covering her left eye. Lake moves it away, tucking it behind her ear, Lake's eyes never leaving Gretchen's. When they kiss, Lake's heart is beating fast, and she has butterflies in her belly. She gets a weird, tingly feeling "down there."

When the kiss ends, Gretchen is looking proudly at Lake. "You're a really good kisser. Let's promise we'll tell each other as soon as we have our first boy kisses." Lake glances up at the ceiling and slowly nods her head, the heady feelings all but knocked out of her.

Lake moves back to her spot in the loft and resumes reading the same boring magazine. She likes how it feels to kiss Gretchen, and she wonders how she can go about only kissing girls. She's thinking about the future when Gretchen says, "I have to pee. Can we go back to your grandma's house now?"

Two days later, they are fourth graders.

#

At eight, Lake sincerely doubts she's fully grasped the concept of fate, but she now believes there are people who come into our lives for reasons we can't explain. Some know things about us long before we do, and they welcome the responsibility of helping us find our way. How else to explain the bond with her beloved grandma Kiki? At the time, she was too young to realize how her presence would deeply impact and shape her world, yet she still managed to teach Lake so much during those extremely formative years. Secret life lessons learned through modest conversation, passive action, and all-consuming observance. Occurrences she couldn't begin to understand or absorb in any deep and meaningful way. A naïve girl, doing her best to wrap her head around not-so-ordinary sights, feelings, and desires.

Chapter 4

*L*ake is thankful to have Mrs. Spence as her teacher. Jeannie was right about her. So far, she hasn't hit the class too hard with homework, which is good because weekends at the ranch are busier than ever. Since Gretchen put the kibosh on any more kissing, Lake practices kickball every day after school so she can be the best player on the field every weekend.

Another consideration is Halloween. It's just around the corner, a completely unpredictable holiday weather-wise. Two years ago, it was so hot, Lake felt as though she'd melt in her costume. Last year, the houses were covered in frost on Halloween Eve. She should have taken that as a clue to dress as something other than Mountain Fiji, woman wrestler extraordinaire from the TV show *Glow, Gorgeous Ladies of Wresting*. Regrettably, she had no backup plan, and the thin leotard wasn't practical for a typical fall night in northeast Ohio. Once the sun went down, it was cold and breezy, and Lake had to wear her puffy coat, the one that went all the way down to her knees. It completely covered her costume and made her appear to be a regular kid walking the neighborhood, exploiting one of her favorite days just for the sake of candy. Halloween 1986 had been an epic failure. It left such a bad taste in her mouth that she hasn't given a single thought to this year's costume. Just to be safe, she'll need a plan A and B. This year, Halloween planning and costume execution will take time.

The point of this entire rant is that once Halloween comes and goes, the weather will turn cold, the gang will stop coming over as much, and Lake will seek refuge in a warm spot to read. Lake enjoys reading more than watching TV because using her imagination is easier and more exciting to explore new places and situations as the stories unfold.

In the winter, time slows, and the air becomes thin and quiet. Until the cold becomes unbearable, Lake will climb the ladder that takes her to the hayloft, but she misses being there with Gretchen and frankly, she finds those memories a distraction. A lot has happened since the summer, and she no longer finds herself wanting to steal away with Joey as much. She's almost nine, but Joey's still a little kid. Lake's romantic desires and attraction have moved from television pipe dreams to real-life, breathing girls of the same age.

#

It's Friday afternoon, and as Lake steps off the bus, she can hear Kiki calling her name, but she can't see her. She waits for the bus to pull away and turns to see Grams standing on the front porch, waiving her arms. "Hey, Lake, put your things in the house and come over. We're going to visit Veronica."

Lake runs up the driveway to her house, opens the storm door, and throws her bookbag on the floor. Sylvia is standing just inside the door. "Lake, you know better than to toss your bag in here like that. Pick it up and walk it to your room, please."

Lake sighs loudly and rolls her eyes. "Mom, Grandma Kiki is waiting for me. We're going to Veronica's house so I can take a look at her books."

"I'm well aware of the plan, Lake. Kiki called to ask if she could take you. Go and have fun."

Running back from her room, Lake says, "Thanks, Mom."

"Wait a minute, young lady." *What now?* "You forgot to give me a kiss good-bye." Lake backs up a few feet and kisses her mom on the cheek. "Love you, Lake."

"Love you too, Mom. Can I please go now?"

"Yes. Be careful crossing the street." Sylvia reaches out and pats Lake on the behind as she steps out the door. "Left, right, and left again!"

"I know!"

It's been a couple days since Lake has seen Grams, and she's busting with the news!

"Grams, guess what!" Lake says excitedly.

Kiki looks over at Lake, smiling, and quickly turns back toward the road while saying,

"You're amazing?"

"No, that's not it," says Lake.

"You said to guess, and that was my guess. What else could it be?"

"I won the first spelling bee contest in our class today!"

"See, Lake, you *are* amazing and smart. I knew it! Congratulations," says Kiki.

"Thanks, Grams. I was a little nervous when my winning word came up because I wasn't sure I could spell it. I had to close my eyes and picture it in my mind. I knew there was only one *L*, and then I remembered the ending was special. My word was *although*, and I got it right! I get to be line leader all next week."

Grams smiles and says, "That's terrific, Lake. How fitting that we're driving to Veronica's this afternoon so you can pick out some books. She has a lot of them."

Feeling proud about her win, Lake nods to no one in particular while watching the familiar landscape of her childhood town whiz by.

#

It's an understatement to say that Veronica downplayed the size of her book collection. It would take Lake a week to look at all the books she has! She spends more than an hour pulling books from the shelf, reading the covers of the most interesting ones, and setting some aside in a stack to take home. When it's time to go, Lake has two neatly stacked piles of books next to her. She can hear Grams and Veronica laughing as they walk toward the study.

"How'd you do, Lake? Did you find some good books to take home?" Veronica asks.

"Yes, ma'am, I have seventeen, if that's okay?" Lake asks.

"Of course! I promised it would be just like the library, except you don't have to return these books. They're yours to keep. Have you ever heard the phrase 'knowledge is power'?" asks Veronica.

"Of course! Mrs. Spence told us that just last week."

Lake is still thinking about the question when Veronica says, "Reading expands your vocabulary, helps foster your imagination, and fills your head with knowledge. That's a powerful thing. You never know when that knowledge will be useful, but if you take the time to read and think about the words you take in, it's easier to recall that information when you need it. Does that make sense?

"It sure does! Lake says, "I know exactly what you mean, Veronica. I did that today during the spelling bee. We learned a new word just a couple days ago, and I saw it in my head when I spelled it. I won, too!"

"That's exactly right. And congratulations! Kiki was just telling me about the spelling bee. I see you have a few books by Judy Blume. My daughter, Cheryl, loved her books—she read them all. You'll have to tell me what you think after you've read them."

"I will, Veronica. Thank you."

Grams gives Veronica's shoulder a squeeze, and Veronica smiles sweetly at Grams, an understated show of affection that once again warms Lake's heart. She doesn't actually know if there's anything more to the relationship, but she likes to think so. The discreet gestures, both physical and nonphysical, happen only on occasion and never when anyone else is present. It makes Lake feel special, trustworthy, and one hundred percent loved.

#

Kapow! Reading is the bomb. After careful consideration, Lake has decided the first of Veronica's books she'd read will be *Tales of a Fourth Grade Nothing* by Judy Blume. She thinks it is perfect because she's in the fourth grade, she has an annoying sister, and in spite of it all, she loves her family very much. She can also relate to Sheila Tubman, the know-it-all. Sheila seems to have it all together, but on the inside, she's got a lot of stuff going on. Scary stuff, that she can't admit to. Like Sheila, Lake "keeps her bad points to herself."

Hopeless Jonathon, the brown nose, sits behind Lake in class and calls her a know-it-all at least once a week, so why not pretend she's Sheila when he does? The best part about reading is how Lake can picture herself slipping into someone else's life, in another city, or another state, way cooler than Ohio. Even though she's a know-it-all, Sheila's also smart and fun. Lake enjoys pretending she's Sheila, even if it's just for a few minutes.

Next week is Thanksgiving, and Lake's already read four whole books. When they went to Veronica's house, she was rereading *Black Beauty*, and she had to finish that book before starting a new one, which set her back by at least a week. Otherwise, she'd probably have five of Veronica's new books read by now. Although she doesn't get to ride the horses much, Lake can't help but love and respect them. Quarter horses are powerful, beautiful, and proud creatures who deserve to be treated with respect, kindness, and a gentle hand. It was

Lake's love for horses that helped her talk Jeannie into reading *Black Beauty*, and she doesn't even like animals.

#

Ask any kid Lake's age what their favorite holiday is, and she'll bet nine out of ten will say Christmas, probably because of the presents. Ask Lake, and she'll tell you she likes Thanksgiving the best. All the aunts, uncles, and cousins come to the ranch for a day of food, football, board games, and eventually yelling. Grandma Kiki roasts a turkey and a duck, and everyone brings a covered dish to go with the birds. There's so many Myerses, the boys have to bring extra tables and chairs up from the basement. They set up three small card tables in the living room for the kids, with the dead, wild animals, away from the grown-ups. Lake's dad has three sisters and his brother, Rick. Each of them is married with kids of their own, and when they all get together for the holidays, they're a rowdy bunch. The adults usually drink too much, and after a long day of eating, playing cards, watching football, and more eating, the kids start bickering and a fight or two busts out. It's complete chaos, and Lake loves it. This year is more of the same.

Pete's at the oldest-kid table, Jeannie's at the middle-age kid table, which is a girl-only table, and Lake is stuck at the little-kids table with three annoying boy cousins who do nothing but talk about cartoons and sports. It's not that she doesn't like sports—she does—but she doesn't feel like talking about sports during Thanksgiving dinner. She'd much rather eavesdrop on Jeannie's conversation about boys. Lake finds it interesting and hilarious.

"Have you seen Eddie Boone lately? Girl, he is capital F—*Fine*! I don't remember him filling out his 501s that good last year. His bootie is so beautiful, it's a shame he has to sit on it." The girl cousins laugh and high-five each other. "I know that's right!"

Lake turns her chair to hear the girls behind her better. She hasn't given much thought to butts before and has certainly never thought of one as "beautiful." Maybe she just hasn't come up on the right butt yet? She makes a mental note to remember this discussion before asking for pie. Pumpkin pie with homemade whipped cream. That's what Lake calls beautiful and delicious!

"Lake, I need you to help clear the tables so the boys can fold them up and take them back to the basement with the chairs," says Grams. "Once everything's put away, you kids can go outside while we clean up and plate the leftovers."

"Okay, Grams." Lake does as she's told, and the kids scatter like the wind when they hit the ground outside. Lake's at an awkward age: too young to hang out with the other girls, and too female to enjoy playing with the boy cousins close to her age. They're obsessed with football and insist on tossing the ball around and tackling each other. Lake suggests a game of kickball, and they not-so-politely decline. Her cousin Jeremy snorts and says, "Kickball is lame." *Whatever, Jeremy.*

The other girls have gone back inside to play Monopoly, and the older boys are inside watching football.

Lake heads for the barn and the hayloft. Climbing the ladder, she looks over at the horses who've come to the barn, perhaps anticipating a Thanksgiving treat of their own. On this holiday, everyone on the ranch gets a special dessert, even the horses. They each get one shiny McIntosh apple with their evening oats. "Hey there. It'll be halftime soon, almost time for your apples." The horses perk up at the sound of Lake's voice and whinny loudly. "You all are so beautiful and strong." A couple of the horses shake their heads up and down as though they agree. 'Yeah, you know that, huh?" Lake takes the last two steps up the ladder and turns around, sitting at the hayloft's edge. This place is familiar and all-absorbing. The sights and smells encase her like a cocoon. Thoughts of Gretchen flood her mind, and she closes her eyes, inviting the image of her lips, eyes, and long dark hair to linger. Lake slowly replays their last kiss, thinking how nice it would be if they were real girlfriends and could kiss all the time. In today's fantasy, Gretchen takes charge, using her thick, long eyelashes to form soft butterfly kisses on Lake's cheek before kissing her closed eyelids and the tip of her nose. At last, their lips connect, and both press further into one another. Gretchen takes hold of Lake's hands, and their fingers automatically intertwine. Lake feels helpless excitement. Suspended in this incredible moment, she feels dizzy but unable to move. The tingly feeling is back, stirring lightly in that special place between her legs before progressing upward. Her entire body is on high alert as the tingling settles in her lips and the crown of her head.

"Lake, what are you doing?"

Lake's eyes fly open, and she feels her face turning red. Her brother, Pete, is standing at the foot of the ladder looking up at her.

"Sorry, I was just daydreaming…about the spelling bee."

"You need to come to the house now. Something's happened to Grandpa Kevin."

Climbing down from the hayloft as fast as possible, Lake skips the last three rungs altogether. She jumps from the ladder and hits the ground running. She has a bad feeling all of a sudden, and she pushes her legs to run faster. Pete's ahead of her, holding the back door open. Lake jumps over the threshold and keeps running until she's in the living room. Grandpa Kevin is lying on the couch surrounded by the family.

As Lake makes her way over to Kiki, she says to no one in particular, "What's wrong? What happened?"

The aunts and uncles are standing in a semicircle around the foot of the couch, Aunt Sue answers, "We're not sure, but we think your grandpa Kevin may have had a heart attack. I called nine-one-one, and the ambulance is on the way. We think it's best if he goes to the hospital and gets checked out."

"Is he going to be okay?" Lake can hear the distant wailing of a siren. The ambulance is getting closer to the house. Just then, everyone turns to look in the direction it's coming from.

"Your grandpa's the toughest, most fetching man I ever met, Lake. He's going to be fine!" says Kiki. "But your dad's right. He needs to get checked out by the doctor just to be sure."

The ambulance is pulling in the driveway. The siren is deafening, and then it just stops.Uncle Rick backs up and says, "I'll go let them in. You all make an opening so they can get to your grandpa." Everyone backs up and makes space for the men with the stretcher. One of them kneels next to Gramps and asks how he is feeling.

When Gramps answers, he sounds old and frail. "Better now. We were just sitting here watching the game. Green Bay was playing a hell of a game, and Stanley had just scored again. We were all up on our feet, yelling and cheering, when I felt a pain in the left side of my chest. I got lightheaded and sweaty, and I moved my hand to my chest when Rick looked over. He and Jack had to help me sit back down on the couch. My breath got short, and the pain stayed for maybe a minute or two."

The men are checking Gramps's pulse and blood pressure. "Your heart rate is elevated, and your color hasn't returned to normal yet."

"We'll take you to the hospital for an exam and possibly some tests. Your doctor can determine next steps."

The men gently lift Gramps up on the stretcher and wheel him out of the house. Once he is safely loaded in the back of the ambulance, Grams climbs in to be with Gramps on the short ride to the hospital.

"Kevin Myers, you scared the bejesus out of me in there! Promise me you'll slow down a little and never leave me. We have a lot more years of love to give to one another."

Smiling up at Grams, Kevin attempts to respond with an "Okay," but he is challenged by the oxygen mask covering his mouth. Instead, he gives her hand a squeeze and blinks.

Laying her head softly on his arm, she squeezes his hand right back.

#

Before the ambulance has even left the driveway, Mom and the aunts are back in the kitchen barking orders at the men. Tension in the house is high, and someone needs to restore order. Sylvia turns to Jack and says, "Honey, can you please make sure the kids are okay?"
Anxious to be out of the kitchen, Jack says, "Yeah, I'll check on them," as he walks toward the living room.

"Joe, can you pack an overnight bag for Kiki and throw in a clean outfit for Kevin?" asks Sylvia.

"Of course. I know she keeps a basket of travel-size shampoos, soaps, and stuff in their bathroom. I'll gather as much as I can. Just give me a few minutes."

Glancing over at Aunt Sue, Mom says, "Sue, can you or Sean take Kiki's overnight bag to the hospital? Maybe after you drop the kids off at your house?"

Aunt Sue works nights at the nursing and rehabilitation center in town. She looks tired, but says, "I'm sure that won't be a problem. I'll let Sean know."

Marching orders in hand, the aunts take off in opposite directions, leaving only Lake and her mom in the kitchen. "You doing okay, sweetie?" asks her mom.

Tears form in the corners of her eyes, and Lake says, "I'm scared, Mom. What if Grandpa Kevin dies?"

"You heard your grandma Kiki. He's going to be fine. He just needs to get the okay from his doctor and take it easy for a few days. He'll be okay, Lake. I promise."

Taking a deep breath, Lake lets it go and says, "I just love Gram and Gramps so much."

Sylvia strokes Lake's hair and says, "I know. We all do. And no one's going anywhere. How about another piece of pie?"

Never one to pass on pumpkin pie, Lake says, "Sure. Will you sit with me while I eat it? We could play rummy."

"You betcha. Go get the cards, and I'll get your pie. You want whipped cream on it?"

Looking back at her mom, Lake says, "Do you even have to ask?"

#

It doesn't take long for Doctor Jeremy to confirm that Gramps has suffered a mild heart attack. They want to keep him in the hospital for observation and tests. Kiki stays with him the first night, sleeping restlessly in the chair next to his bed. When she wakes up, her body is stiff and sore, but she's still holding his hand. Clearing the sleep from her eyes, she stretches and looks over at Kevin. He's awake, smiling at her. "Good morning, love of my life," says Kiki.

"Good morning, sleeping beauty. How'd you sleep?"

"I slept okay. How do you feel, hon?"

"Like I need more sleep. My whole body is tired." Gramps presses his lower and upper lips together to suppress a giggle before adding, "Your hair is lopsided."

"Kevin Myers! I slept in a chair with one eye open all night because you had me worried sick, and that's all you have to say?"

Gramps squeezes her hand, and they both laugh. A little humor always lightens the mood.

Pushing the chair back, Kiki stands and stretches again before walking to the bathroom.

Flipping the switch, she looks at her reflection in the mirror and laughs out loud. Damn Aqua Net didn't hold up at all last night. Completely flat on the right side, her 'do' is saying 'don't' and is screaming for a little TLC. She does her best to push it back into place before shrugging and throwing her hands up in defeat. Knowing she has more work to do on her appearance than she can manage at the moment, she leaves the bathroom for now.

"I'm going to get some coffee before I come back to freshen up. The kids dropped off a bag with a change of clothes and some toiletries. Don't go anywhere while I'm gone," she says.

"Not a chance," says Gramps.

When Kiki returns, the doctor is standing next to Kevin's bed. "Good morning, Kristina."

"Good morning, Doctor Jeremy. How's he doing?"

"His test results look good. The only concern is his blood sugar level, which is a little high. We'll keep him here for another night and continue to monitor it. If it comes down on its own and everything else continues to go well, we may release him tomorrow afternoon. If it doesn't begin to improve by this evening, we may need to treat him with insulin. He needs to eat a little something and rest. Sleep will do wonders."

Grams sighs a breath of relief. "Thank you, doctor. Appreciate you coming by first thing this morning."

"No problem. Kevin and I have known each other a long time. I'll be back to check on him again after lunch."

Grams steps closer to the bed and kisses Gramps's forehead. "Be back in just a little bit."

Returning to the bathroom, Kiki washes up, changes her clothes, and fixes her hair. Somewhat satisfied with the results, she settles into the chair next to Kevin to drink her coffee and watch the morning news.

After a few minutes, she glances over at Kevin. He's fast asleep, and his body looks relaxed.

Tiptoeing out of the room, she returns to the cafeteria in search of a muffin and more coffee. On her way back to the room, Kiki picks up the latest issue of *Ladies Home Journal*.

Back in the room, she grabs a blanket from the closet and gets comfortable in the chair, flipping mindlessly through the magazine while eating her muffin and drinking her coffee. Even though she's had two cups, she still feels exhausted. She checks to make sure Kevin's okay before allowing herself to fall asleep again.

She and Kevin both wake up when Doctor Jeremy comes back into the room. It's nearly one o'clock in the afternoon.

"It's nice to see you both resting. You needed it! I'm going to check your heart rate, Kevin, while the nurse draws some blood. We'll check your blood sugar level again. We should have the results back later this evening, after dinner."

The two finish up and leave the room. As they leave, an attendee delivers lunch. Lifting the lid off the plate, Kiki makes a grand sweeping gesture with her hand and says, "Lunch is served, my love. Today's selection includes a boneless, skinless chicken breast, steamed broccoli, and a cup of fresh fruit."

Kiki sets the tray on the rolling table and positions it in front of Kevin as he raises his bed.

"Not what I would have ordered, but I guess I don't get to choose."

"It's healthy and not too heavy. Just eat what you can."

Switching channels, Gramps is annoyed with the lack of decent daytime programs. He eats almost everything on the plate and drinks a full glass of water.

The two watch PBS for a while before Kevin falls asleep once again. Suddenly, the phone rings. Kiki jumps up to answer it before it wakes Gramps.

"Hello?"

"Hi, Mom, how's Dad doing?" Jack's voice comes over the phone.

"He's fine, Jack. He's been sleeping off and on, and he ate most of his lunch this afternoon. The doctor said his tests look good. The only concern is his blood sugar, which is just a little high. They drew blood again this afternoon. We should know more tonight. How's everyone at home doing?"

"We're all doing well. Just checking in to make sure everything there is good. Do you need anything?"

"I may need a change of clothes later on. Depends on what the doctor says."

"Let us know if you need one of us to bring you anything. Tell dad we love him."

"Okay, son, I sure will."

Kiki gently sets the handset on the phone base and returns to her chair.

"You don't have to tiptoe. I'm awake," says Kevin.

"I'm sorry, darlin', did the phone wake you?"

"Yes, but that's okay. Who was it?"

"It was Jack, calling to check on you. I let him know we're doing fine."

"Kiki, if my blood sugar comes back okay, why don't you go home this evening and get a good night's sleep in our bed? I'll probably get released tomorrow afternoon."

Looking at Kevin, Kiki says, "If it's just one more night, I can stay. I don't want to leave you here alone."

Kevin replies, "It's fine. We could both use a good night's sleep. Just think about it. We'll both be in better shape when I'm released if we get a solid eight hours."

"Let's see what Doc has to say. If your tests are better, I'll call Jack to come get me. You're a pushy old man, you know that?" says Kiki.

"Yeah, but you love me," says Kevin.

"That I do!"

The two sit quietly watching TV the rest of the afternoon. Kevin dozes occasionally, but he has a hard time sleeping for any length of time. Around five thirty, a young candy striper pushes open the door and peeks in. "Hi there. I'm Kelly. I have dinner here if you're hungry. I have some extra this evening, so you can each have a plate, if you want."

"Sure, Kelly," Kiki says, "that sounds great. It'll save me a trip to the cafeteria."

Kelly leaves two plates on the desk and says, "Have a good night," before leaving the room.

Dinner looks a lot like lunch. The boneless, skinless chicken breast is sliced on the diagonal and served with a leafy, green salad, vinaigrette dressing on the side, and a fruit cup.

"I hope this isn't a sign of things to come," says Kevin.

"I think it is, hon. After what's happened, we'll need to make some changes to your diet and how much sleep you get, and the smoking needs to stop."

Groaning, Kevin says, "Baby steps, Kiki. Let's not get all worked up. A man can only handle so much change at once."

"We'll see."

After dinner, Kevin flips the TV to the evening news. While watching the footage of President Reagan, Kiki looks at Kevin and back at the television. The physical similarities between her husband and the president are uncanny, but Kevin is undoubtedly more handsome. The next news story contains images of the hordes of people out shopping the day after Thanksgiving. Glad to have dodged the crowds, Kiki grows restless waiting for the doctor to return. The news ends, and the program changes to *Wheel of Fortune*. Just as the final puzzle is being solved, Doctor Jeremy returns.

"Good evening, folks. I have great news. Kevin's blood sugar levels have returned to normal, and everything looks excellent. You'll stay another night with us, but you should be able to go home tomorrow afternoon."

"That's terrific news, Doctor Jeremy!"

"I'll have the nurses prepare for your checkout tomorrow. We have several pamphlets and recommendations for changes to your diet and work hours. I don't need to tell you, Kevin, but you need to quit smoking to reduce your risk of another heart attack."

"I know. Kiki's already mentioned it."

"Well, she makes a good point. We all want the best for you. Try and get some sleep this evening. I'll be back tomorrow morning."

After Doctor Jeremy leaves, Kevin says, "Please call Jack so you can go home now. I'm ready to get some sleep so I can go home tomorrow."

"Fine, but I'm coming back first thing in the morning!"

#

It feels like more than just one day had passed since Lake has seen Grandma Kiki. When she calls looking for Jack, Lake answers the phone. "Hi, Grams! It's so great to hear your voice. How's Gramps?"

"He's doing well, Lake. He's coming home tomorrow. Hey, is your dad home?"

"Sure, Grams, hold on... Daaaaad, Grandma Kiki is on the phone. She wants to talk to you."

Hearing her dad coming up the basement steps, Lake begs to stay the night with Grandma Kiki. "I miss you, Grams. Pleeeeeease..."

Not wanting to spend the night alone, Kiki relents. "You can stay over, but no fidgeting or TV. It's lights-out early. Understood?"

"Yes, Grams. I understand."

That night, Grams cries herself to sleep. She doesn't make any sound, but Lake can tell by the way she's breathing next to her in bed that she's crying. Lake hates to see Grams sad, and she isn't able to fall asleep, so she lies there, still as a statue. When Kiki's breathing finally slows, Lake feels her own body relax and her muscles begin to twitch. She opens her eyes slowly, allowing her vision to adjust to the dark room. The streetlamp outside provides just enough light for Lake to see Kiki's face. Her round cheeks are wet with tears, and a Virginia Slim dangles precariously from her slender fingers, resting on the edge of the ashtray still perched on her chest. The cigarette is burned down to the filter, a silhouette of what was once a long, slender roll reduced to nothing more than ashes. Grams wastes more cigarettes than she smokes. An attentive wife, mother, and grand-mother, she had a constant need to multitask that probably saved her from having a heart attack, too.

Earlier that night, Kiki told Lake she would quit smoking when Grandpa Kevin came home from the hospital. She can't expect him to quit while she continues to smoke. It wouldn't be fair, and besides, she has wanted to quit for ages. Now she has the motivation she needs.

Moving as slowly as a sloth, Lake gets out of bed, walks around to Grams's side, and wedges the cigarette butt and ashtray free from Kiki's hand, then places it on the nightstand, just out of reach. She returns to bed as slowly as she got up and is soon fast asleep.

#

After Gramps's heart attack, life at the ranch is different for everyone. When Gramps is discharged from the hospital, Doctor Jeremy sends him home with a list of rules to follow, none of which Grandpa Kevin likes. The people at the hospital have said the lifestyle changes they recommended are necessary to help improve Gramps's heart health, but he only sees them as restrictive and bothersome.

"Kevin, the doctor said you need to take it easy for a few weeks. Jack and Rick can manage the farm while you rest. You can still oversee the day-to-day work. But you need to be comfortable letting them do more."

"I've worked this ranch more than forty years, building one of the biggest, most well-respected horse farms in the state. I can't just stop tomorrow."

"Kevin, it's time to let the boys take more responsibility. No one is saying you have to step away completely, but just take a step or two back. Can you please try?"

"I'll start my day a little later and end it a little earlier. That's all I can promise for now," says Gramps.

"That's a fair compromise. I'll make sure your meals are healthy and tasty. And I'll get some of that nicotine gum to help you quit smoking," Grams says.

Gramps shakes his head. "I'll be in the barn if you need me."

As the days go by, noticeable and necessary changes are wedged in, creating tension and unwelcome concessions. Kiki throws herself into being the supportive, post–heart attack wife. She's overly attentive to Gramps and means well, but her efforts make him angry, and he snaps at her several times a day.

Before Thanksgiving and the heart attack, Grandpa Kevin's unflappable strength had been like a blanket of warmth on a cold day. No matter what the situation, he alone had the power to make Grams feel whole, safe, and comfortable. He was the peanut butter to her jelly, and together they were the best thing Lake had ever seen. Now everything is different. With Gramps spending more time closer to the house, Lake feels less compelled to be there as often.

Treading lightly, Sylvia also gives Kevin and Kiki space to work through the new changes in their lives. She had wanted to surprise Jack with a new recliner for Christmas, but with all the extra hours he's putting in at the ranch, she decides to give it to him early. Lake loves the chair and the way it smells like her dad. It becomes her new favorite place to read, and she spends hours in it, chipping away at the stack of books Veronica gave her.

Chapter 5 - Claire

*C*hristmas is next week, but it doesn't feel like it. Lake's house is decorated and there's snow on the ground, but she's not as excited this year as she as usually is. Things at the ranch are getting better, but Kiki is still undecided about hosting Christmas dinner. On the Sunday before Christmas, Kiki stops by the house on her way to run errands. As usual, Lake is the last to finish her breakfast, her eggs gone cold while she sits reading at the table. Dad, Uncle Rick, and Grandpa Kevin are out checking fox traps this morning, and Kiki seems relaxed and chatty. Standing in the kitchen, Kiki says, "I'm just not sure Kevin's up to all the excitement this year. Doc Jeremy says he's doing better, but I'm still worried. Thank goodness he's stopped smoking, and he doesn't complain as much about the healthy meals, but I just don't know. I did manage to get the Christmas tree up in the living room, but the house isn't as festive as usual."

Mom takes a sip of her coffee and says, "No one is expecting the house to be fully decorated. The last few weeks have been stressful. If you're up to having the family over, Joe and I can cook the birds and bring them over with us. You and Kevin can just relax and enjoy the day."

"I hate to put all that work on you girls, but it would be nice not to have to worry about cooking. We'd love to have the family over. Christmas dinner at the ranch house is a tradition. Let's do it."

Mom claps her hands and says, "We'll take care of everything. It'll be lovely."

Christmas Day goes off without a hitch. After breakfast, Lake and her family open presents. She gets some clothes, a few new books, and a Speak & Spell, just like she asked for. Dinner with Kiki and Grandpa Kevin is later in the day, and they only stay for a few hours. Lake feels a twinge of sadness as they put on their winter layers and say their good-byes. She hugs her grandparents and holds on to Kiki for a few extra moments.

Leaning down to whisper in her ear, Kiki says, "Bye, little one. Come back soon, and I'll tell you the story of the Great Blizzard and the day you were born. It's been so long since I told that story, I hope I can remember it all."

"It hasn't been that long, Grams. And besides, I know it by heart. I can help with any parts you forget."

"I bet you can, Lake. Merry Christmas. I love you."

"Love you, too, Grams. Bye."

A few minutes later, Lake is shedding the winter layers she'd painstakingly put on for the walk back to her house. Unwrapping the scarf from her neck, she gets a whiff of Kiki's signature scent, Hawaiian White Ginger. She decides to keep the scarf close and snuggles up with it while watching television with the family.

#

When the holidays are over, Lake is happy to be back in school. During the winter break, she was able to finish two more books, and all that time spent reading is beginning to pay off. So far, she's undefeated in her school spelling bees. A few days into the new year, she's given the opportunity to prove to everyone just how amazing she really is. Today in class, Mrs. Spence announces the upcoming fourth-grade spelling bee, a super-big deal at her school.

"Okay, kids, for the first time in the history of our school, the winner of this year's final spelling bee will go on to compete with the winners from each of the other elementary schools in our county. And the winner of *that* competition will compete in the state finals—in Columbus."

Oh my gosh! If I can make it to state, I'll be the most popular girl in the entire fourth grade—and then maybe I'll meet someone interesting.

Lake can't wait to get home. The ten-minute ride to her house feels much longer, and the bus driver barely has time to open the accordion doors fully before Lake is off and running full-speed up the driveway. "Mom! Where are you? *Mom!*"

"I'm right here, Lake, in the dining room. What's happened?"

"Just the most exciting thing ever! Mrs. Spence told us the winner of the final spelling bee gets to go to Columbus to compete in the state finals. Mom, I have to get new index cards. Can you take me to the store? Please, Mom!"

"Right this minute, Lake?"

"Yes, right this minute. I have to start making flashcards today. The state finals are the first week of March!"

Sylvia hasn't seen Lake this excited since she'd won the first spelling bee. "Okay, let's go. I need a few things from the store anyway."

As soon as they get home, Lake begins making flashcards with all kinds of words. She vows to practice every day, realizing she has only seven weeks to prepare for her victory in Columbus.

She's going to win the whole thing. She can feel it!

#

Things are going exactly as planned. Lake is killing it in her weekly practice bees and is out-spelling girls in all the other classes. One week until the final bee in her school. She's ready, and she knows it. No one can stump her on the flashcards she made, so Jeannie made new ones with words from her sixth-grade spelling list. It takes her a while to master the bigger, harder words, but she does it. Mom and Dad go off-script at dinner and throw out words she's never seen or heard before. Lake breaks them down into smaller, bite-sized words in her head before attempting to spell them, and then she gives it a go. It's a good strategy and works most every time.

The day of the spelling bee, Mom gets up early to make Lake's favorite breakfast: eggs, bacon, toast with grape jelly, and fresh strawberries. The strawberries aren't in season, but Sylvia has splurged and bought them anyway because she knows how important this day is to Lake. Dad has a few things to pick up in town this morning and offers to give Lake and Jeanne a ride to school after breakfast.

It's really not far at all to the school. Only one song on the radio has played before they're pulling in the driveway, waiting in the drop-off line. Lake feels good, confident. She grabs the door handle and is about to get out when her dad says, "We all know how important this day is to you, Lake, but I want you to know, your mom and I are proud of you no matter what. Just do your best, okay?" Reaching into his jacket pocket, he adds, "Here's some extra lunch money so you can treat yourself to an ice cream after you win." Lake loves her dad. He always knows just what to say.

"Thanks, Dad!" Lake jumps down from the truck, then strolls into school, passing the trophy case that one day will hold her state spelling bee champion trophy. Smiling, she heads for her classroom, takes her seat, and waits patiently for the contest to begin. After the longest roll call ever, the class finally lines up for the walk to the auditorium. Lake has done an awesome job preparing for this day.

Two hours later, she wins the bee by correctly spelling the word *straight*. One day when things start to "click," Lake will look back at this moment and laugh at how unbelievably ironic it is. And better yet, the girl she beats, Claire, has lost because she misspells the word *experience*. She couldn't make this stuff up if she tried!

#

Claire Long is a fourth-grade hipster. She's in the same class as Gretchen, and Lake doesn't really know her that well. Claire's family lives in a house overlooking Lake Erie, and they own, like, twenty cottages they rent out during the summer. Her dad's the school superintendent, and her mom used to be a teacher, but she quit to run the cottage rental business full-time.In awe of actually winning the school's final spelling bee, Lake is still standing in her spot onstage when she hears someone say, "Congratulations on winning the bee."

She turns to see Claire standing next to her, her hand out. "Thank you, Claire." Shaking her hand, Lake says, "I'm sorry you lost. That was a hard word, *experience*."

"I gave it my best shot. I went with an *i-a* when I should have gone with an *i-e*. That's just the way it goes, I guess. Hey, do you want to come over and spend the night on Friday?"

Wait. What's happening? Did Claire Long just ask Lake to spend the night at her house? Be cool, Lake. "Yeah, sure. I mean, I have to ask my parents first, but I'm sure it'll be okay."

"Cool. See ya later, Lake."

#

Lake and Claire's dads have known each other a long time. They both belong to the Masonic Temple and attend the super-secret meetings every month. Mom's not so sure about letting Lake spend the night away from home for the first time, but good old dad saves the day. "Hon, we can't keep her home with us forever. Her brother and sister don't pay much attention to her, and she's always holed up in her room reading a book. Maybe this will be good for her? Ever since Dad's heart attack, she's been so closed off."

Lake is standing in the hall, just far enough back to think she's undetectable, but her dad knows she's there. "Sylvia, what is it? What's bothering you?"

"I don't know, Jack. It's the first time Lake will spend an entire night away from home with people who aren't her relatives. Are you sure the Longs are good people?"

"Yes! Absolutely. She'll be fine."

Sylvia's still not sold on the idea of Lake spending the night at Claire's house, but she caves anyway, "Okay, but if she calls and wants to come home in the middle of the night, you're going to pick her up."

Way to go, Pops. You got me the green light from Sylvia!

Lake is forced to wait until the next day to tell Claire she's allowed to spend the night on Friday. She should have gotten her phone number, but she was so excited when Claire asked that she didn't even think about it. She makes a mental note to ask for it today. She's sure her mom will want it, anyway.

At school, some girls from Mrs. Carlyle's fourth-grade class invite Lake to sit at their table during lunch, but Claire has already saved her a seat. She and Claire talk nonstop during lunch, becoming fast friends, and they spend the entire time at recess making plans for Friday night.

When Friday comes, Lake has a note to ride the bus home with Claire and eat dinner at her house. Claire's house is the last stop on the route, and when the two girls step off the bus, the piercing cold takes Lake's breath away. The wind is much stronger here by the lake. Shivering, the two girls run to the house.

Claire's house has an enclosed front porch, the perfect place to shake off the snow and hang their coats up before going inside. Just as Claire reaches for the door handle, her mom opens it, urging them to come in from the cold. "You two look positively frozen. Come stand by the fire and warm up!" Leading her through the house,

Mrs. Long says, "Welcome to our home, Lake. Can I get you some hot chocolate?"

Lake looks to her friend for guidance, and Claire says, "Mom, we just walked in the door. We're fine."

"I'm not sure Lake is used to the winter chill here on the lakeshore." Turning to Lake, she says, "Have you been up our way during the winter?"

"No, ma'am, we don't come up here much during the winter. Mostly we come in the summer to eat or get ice cream. Sometimes we walk on the beach at the state park and look for shells and driftwood."

"We don't get much traffic up here until spring, when the donut shop is open on the weekends. That's the start of bringing people back to the strip every year, but during the winter, it's pretty quiet."

There are a few seconds of awkward silence before Mrs. Long says, "Okay. I'll leave you girls to it. I thought we could order a pizza tonight. Dad can pick it up on his way home. Do you like pepperoni, sausage, plain cheese? What's your favorite, Lake?"

"Anything's fine, really. I like all of those things."

"Well, you sure are easy to please. I'll get us a plain cheese and a pepperoni. We'll eat dinner around five thirty or six."

Dinner with Claire's family is different from dinner at Lake's house. Claire's an only child, and her mom and dad make a point to include Lake in the conversation. Firing in rapid succession, Mr. and Mrs. Long take turns asking her questions.

"How do you like the fourth grade, Lake?"

"So far, so good. Mrs. Spence is nice. My sister, Jeannie, had her, too."

"Claire told us all about the spelling bee. Congratulations on winning. Even though Claire lost, she was so happy for you! How are your mom and dad doing?"

"Thank you. They're both good."

"We heard about your grandpa Kevin's heart attack. So sorry."

"Thank you. He's doing much better."

"One more question, and we'll let you get back to your pizza," says Mr. Long. "Claire's mom and I are curious. How did you get the name 'Lake'? It's so clever, especially with our town being right here on the shore of Lake Erie."

Having talked so much already, Lake decides to go with the abbreviated version of Kiki's story. She knows it so well, she can skip a bunch of parts and get through it pretty fast.

"Do you remember the great blizzard of 1978? My mom was pregnant with me, and she went into labor during the worst part of the storm. My dad was nervous to drive in the snow, but he had to get my mom to the hospital. So, he drove her in his truck and made it the hospital just in time! Dad told me he had to dodge abandoned cars on the streets, and it took him half an hour to drive the eight miles to the hospital. He'd never seen so much snow! Grandma Kiki said it was a lake-effect storm and the biggest blizzard of the century. It was Dad's idea to name me Lake after that. Mom was against it at first, but she liked that my name had a good story behind it, so she eventually said yes. And that's how I got my name."

Feeling completely satisfied with her version of the story, Lake leans back in her chair, crosses her arms, and waits for the questions and comments.

"That's a spectacular story, Lake! We remember that blizzard very well," says Mr. Long. "We didn't go anywhere for almost a week. That was one for the history books. With a powerful name like that, no wonder you won the spelling bee."

Lake smiles and thanks him. "Grandma Kiki says the same thing! She tells me always to remember that I'm a strong person. She says I'm a 'force to be reckoned with.' I guess she knows what's she's talking about."

The Longs look at each other and smile.

Talking to Claire's mom and dad isn't too bad. Sharing Kiki's story with everyone at dinner is fun, empowering. Unfolding her arms, Lake takes a bite of her cheese pizza. Since she was little, she has always preferred cold pizza over hot, and now hers is perfectly cold.

The group finishes eating, and Lake offers to help with the dishes. "Thank you for offering, Lake," says Mrs. Long. "It's easy cleanup this evening, and I can handle it. Why don't you two go and relax in the family room? Claire got a couple new board games for Christmas."

"I love board games. Which ones did you get, Claire?"

"I got Operation and the game of Life," says Claire. "Do you want to play one?"

"Sure. How about Operation?"

"Okay. I'll set it up," says Claire. "Dad, can you help me with the card table?"

Claire's dad is sitting in the living room, reading the newspaper. Looking up from the paper, he asks, "You want it near the fireplace?" "Yeah, but not too close." Claire wins the first game and is about to win the second when Sam's nose lights up and the loud buzzer goes off. Both girls have been challenged by the dreaded breadbasket, which is nearly impossible to remove from the patient, but it is the pencil that gets Claire on the second game. "Ugh! The pencil is so hard to get out! You win, Lake. Now what do you want to do?"

"It's almost time for *Full House*. Do you feel like watching TV?"

"Sure. I'll ask Mom to make us some popcorn."

There is a huge TV in Claire's family room, and the girls agree to watch their favorite Friday night programs: *Full House* and *Mr. Belvedere*. "My mom bought these beanbag chairs before Christmas. Pick one and cop a squat," Claire says.

Lake has never sat in a beanbag chair before, but it's surprisingly comfortable! Mrs. Long hands each girl a bowl of buttered popcorn and leaves them to watch their shows. *Mr. Belvedere* is cracking them up, when out of the blue, Claire starts playing footsies with Lake. Lake goes along with it, trying to figure out if Claire's just messing around, but she can't be sure. Lake smiles at Claire and goes back to watching the show. She doesn't think about Claire like she'd thought about Gretchen. Claire is cool and all, but Lake doesn't daydream about kissing her. She's still crushing on Gretchen and is glad they have different teachers. It would be torture to have to see her all day in school.

After the show ends, Lake is kind of tired, but Claire is wide awake. "You wanna listen to records in my room?" she asks.

"Sure, I'm down for some music."

Taking the empty bowl from Lake's hands, Claire says, "Grab your beanbag chair and bring it with you." Lugging the chair up the steps and into Claire's room, Lake positions it in front of the record player near the corner of the room. Wow! Claire's room is exactly the way Lake would decorate her own room if she could do whatever she wanted. She wonders what it's like to be an only child. Claire's room is down the hall from her parents' room, next to the guest bedroom. It's a corner bedroom with a view of the lake from both sides—and she has her own bathroom! The bed is bigger than Lake's twin-sized bed; the headboard is white wicker with a cool design in the middle and a thick braided edging around the top. The comforter is puffy and blue, like the lake, and is covered with pillows and all sorts of stuffed animals. On either side of the bed are two matching white wicker nightstands. Maybe if she was an only child, Lake could have talked Jack and Sylvia into springing for a white wicker bedroom set...

"Lake, did you hear what I said? Hello! Who do you like better? Madonna or Michael Jackson?"

"Huh? Oh, sorry. Either one is good, you pick."

"Okay, then. Madonna it is."

Dang, this room is awesome.

Even though they're only in the fourth grade, Claire's room is like a grown-up's room. Everything matches, right down to the white wicker mirror hanging above the white wicker dresser. Yeah, Lake could brave the cold winds coming off Lake Erie to have a bedroom like this.

Kicking back, the girls tap their feet to Madonna, listening to music until they're both falling asleep in their beanbag chairs. Too stubborn to give in to the night, Lake wakes to a faint knock on the door. The door opens a crack, and Mr. Long pokes his head in. "It's past eleven... Claire, you two should probably get ready for bed."

"Okay, Dad. Can we at least finish the song?"

"Yes, but then it's time for bed. Good night, Lake. I'll see you girls in the morning."

"Good night, Mr. Long."

Pushing the beanbag chairs to the corner, Claire turns to Lake and says, "You can use the bathroom first if you want to brush your teeth and stuff."

"Okay, thanks." Lake grabs her bag and walks into the bathroom to change and get ready for bed. She has packed her best pajamas—red plaid with a satin bow just above the top button. After she's done getting ready, Lake takes a seat on the edge of Claire's bed while she's in the bathroom.

Opening the door, Claire says to her, "You wanna sleep on the side by the bathroom or the side by the window?"

Lake chooses the side closest to the bathroom just in case she has to go during the night.

#

The next morning, Lake wakes up to the smell of pancakes. Claire is already awake, staring up at the ceiling.

"What time is it?" asks Lake.

Rolling over to look at her alarm clock, Claire says, "It's eight twenty. I'm glad you're awake. My dad always cooks breakfast on Saturday mornings. Smells like pancakes. Let's go see."

After breakfast, the girls lounge in their pajamas until it's time for Lake's dad to come pick her up. She is having such a good time, and she isn't ready to leave. When her dad arrives, she thanks the Longs for having her over. "I had a really fun night. Thanks for inviting me, Claire."

Claire looks at her and says, "I had a fun time, too. Call me later."

Chapter 6

"Lake, your grandma's on the phone. She wants to know what kind of cake you want for your birthday."

"Same as every year, strawberry cake with chocolate frosting."

"Did you catch that, Kiki? Yes, same as last year, strawberry cake with chocolate frosting. Okay, I'll let her know."

Sylvia is standing next to the recliner Lake is lounging in. "Kiki said she'll bring your cake over Friday before you get home from school. It will be here when she and Kevin come for dinner. We're making your favorite meal, spaghetti with homemade meatballs and fresh-baked Italian bread. I can't believe you're turning nine already. My baby girl is going to be nine!"

Rolling her eyes, Lake says, "Mom, all your kids are growing up. It's not just me."

"I know, Lake, but you're my baby. I want you to stay little."

"Mom, please, I'm trying to read."

Kissing her on the forehead, Lake's mom says, "Fine. I have things to do anyway!"

Lake wishes her birthday wasn't this Friday. She wants to ask Claire over to spend the night, but she can't because she has to spend the evening with her family. After her night at Claire's, Lake told her mom she wants a white wicker bedroom set for her birthday, and Sylvia laughed at her. "The bedroom furniture you have now is fine. You don't need a new bedroom set."

"Can I at least have my own record player?"

#

On Friday night, Grams and Gramps walk over to Lake's house for dinner. Grams had dropped the cake off earlier in the day, and it looks delicious! Grandpa Kevin is back to his old self and is excited to eat a dinner that doesn't consist of baked chicken and salad. "Thank goodness for birthdays! The perfect excuse to get out, spend time with family, and eat *real food*," says Gramps.

"You look good, Kevin," says Lake's mom. "How are you feeling?"

"Doing great, Sylvia. I'm working less on the farm, so the boys have had to step up, but we're getting things done and are in a good place. Doc says I can do most everything I did before the heart attack—in moderation, of course!"

As she lovingly glances over at her husband, Kiki says, "We were going to wait until after dinner to tell everyone, but now is as good a time as any. We've decided to make the trip to Key West this year after all. Kevin has been cleared for travel, and we'll take our time driving down. We're leaving early Sunday morning."

"Did you know about this, Jack?" asks Mom.

"Yes, I heard a couple days ago, but it wasn't for sure yet, and I promised not to say anything." Dad turned to his parents. "You two deserve some downtime. And who wouldn't jump at the chance to get away to sunny Florida? One of these days, we're going to join you."

Clearing his throat, Grandpa Kevin says, "We're only going for a couple months. I want to be back by mid-April to get ready for foaling season, even though I have complete confidence in the boys to take care of the ranch until we get back." Exaggerating the words in an overly dramatic way, Gramps ends with, "Now, can we pleeeeeease eat?"

This elicits a good laugh from everyone while Mom and Kiki begin dishing up the spaghetti. Much to Gramps's chagrin, the meal does include a small side salad. After dinner, the family rallies for an off-key rendition of "Happy Birthday" before cake and ice cream. Closing her eyes tight, Lake makes the wish to meet a girl who is like her. Someone she can talk to and confide in. Inhaling deeply, she opens her eyes and easily blows out all nine candles, hoping her wish will come true.

Feeling happy and full, they all make their way to the living room for the ceremonial opening of the presents. Acting as the grand marshal of gift opening, Sylvia insists on handing each present to Lake one at a time. *Great.* "Now, this one's from Jeanne… And this one's from Pete… These are from all of us…" The opening of the gifts reveals new pajamas, clothes, and books from Pete and Jeannie.

"And this one is from your dad and me."

Now we're talking, Lake says to herself while pulling back the wrapping on the biggest gift. Lake sees the image of a turntable and immediately knows her parents had actually listened to what she wanted. They'd bought her the one gift she wanted most—aside from new bedroom furniture—a record player of her very own!

As she carefully begins to open the box, Pete steps forward to help her pull the aqua-blue record player out. She loves it!

"Thanks, Mom and Dad! It's exactly what I wanted, and you picked the best color. I love it!" "You're welcome, sweetheart. We're glad you like it," says Sylvia.

Reaching back behind his chair, Grandpa Kevin pulls out a large basket with several wrapped items in it. "Happy birthday, Lake. This is from your grandma and me. We hope it's enough to keep you busy until we get back from Key West."

Tearing into the basket, Lake has everything unwrapped in no time flat. Among the crinkled-up paper are several .45s, a couple of record albums, two more books, and a new soccer ball. She can't wait to play her new records on the record player!

Blinking back a tear, Lake says, "Thanks, everyone. The presents are great, and so are all of you!" It isn't like Lake to get sentimental with her family, but tonight feels different. They had all come together to celebrate her, and in just a couple of days, her grandparents will be off to Key West.

Grams is up and out of her chair hugging Lake and whispering in her ear. "Hey, Lake. I do believe we have time for a story. Do you want to hear it?"

Hugging her sweet grandma Kiki, Lake takes in her scent, her face pressed against Grams's bosom. "Yes, I do want to hear a story."

Letting go, Kiki straightens and says, "Okay, everyone, I have a tale to tell. The perfect story for this night—on Lake's ninth birthday." Standing in front of the floor-to-ceiling fireplace, the warm glow of the fire illuminating her small figure, Kiki touches her hair, a quick check to make sure all is in place. Then Kiki looks around to make sure she has everyone's full attention before slowly raising her hands up to the ceiling, palms open, fingers spread wide.

"The Great Blizzard of 'Seventy-Eight struck the Ohio Valley and the Great Lakes region bringing record snowfall and cold the likes of which few had ever seen before..." For effect, Kiki lowers her hands while moving each of her fingers to illustrate snow gently falling. And so it went. With several inches of real snow on the ground and the wind whipping up bare branches just outside the window, it's easy to imagine the onset of the Great Blizzard of 1978. The whole family is spellbound by the story, and Kiki tells it better than she ever has before.

Everyone in Lake's family has heard the story at least once or twice, but this evening, each is inspired to the point of chiming in when their part is mentioned. Treating the tale as a fun family game, Dad and Mom even go so far as to act out scenes from the story, like they would in Charades. In the end, Dad delivers a big belly laugh when Kiki references Mother Nature as the true inspiration for Lake's name, but he ultimately gives credit where credit is due.

Seeing her family together like this warms Lake's heart. She is going to miss Kiki and Grandpa Kevin, but she's happy they're able to travel and spend time in a place they love. Lake will be counting the days until they return to the ranch.

#

The next morning, Lake and her father walk across the street to help her grandparents load the car. Although Gramps has been given a clean bill of health, Lake's parents still worry he will unintentionally overexert himself. Living on a small boat can be challenging, and space is at a premium. The weather in Key West is warm enough for shorts and flip-flops most days, so there's not a lot of bulky clothing to pack—not much luggage at all, actually, which is a relief. They are leaving the harsh winter weather behind.

Lake gives both of her grandparents one last kiss and hug before they get into their car and pull away. She stands in the driveway waving good-bye until she can no longer see the car.

On Monday, Lake returns to school and her friends. It's almost February—a short month full of cold days that end too soon. It's dark when Lake walks out to catch the bus in the mornings, and it's pitch-black darkness by the time she and her family sit down to dinner each night. February is easily one of her least-favorite months. The holidays are over, her birthday has come and gone, and her grandparents are now in Key West. It's too cold and snowy outside to practice kickball or soccer, and the only thing left to do is read or watch TV. At least the house is cozy and inviting. Her dad builds a fire in the fireplace most every night this time of year. They don't need the fire to warm the house, but it's nice to have one anyway. The heat radiating from the flames calls to Lake, and she cuddles under a blanket on the couch or in her dad's chair each night after dinner until it's time for her to take a shower and get ready for bed.

"Mom, can I invite Claire over to spend the night this Friday?" asks Lake.

Sylvia is sitting next to Lake on the couch, flipping through a magazine. "Your uncle Rick and Aunt Joe are coming over on Friday to watch the Pro Bowl, and I already told Pete he could have a friend over to spend the night. Next Friday would be better, Lake."

"But Mom, I told Claire she could. Please?"

"It's not a good night, Lake. Jeannie is planning to stay over at a friend's next Friday. Claire can have her bed, so you two won't have to share. I'm sure she won't mind waiting a week to stay over."

"Ugh. Fine! Can we get pizza when she stays over?"

"We'll see. You know your dad doesn't like pizza. If you want takeout, maybe we could order Chinese?"

"I don't even know if Claire likes Chinese. I'll ask."

Lake is upset that Claire can't spend the night this Friday. She wants to see how she'll react to Spin the Bottle. Ever since Claire played footsies with Lake when they were watching TV, she isn't sure what "kind of girl" she is. Suggesting a game of Spin the Bottle is the only thing Lake can think of to find out. Even if the kissing isn't great, knowing she has a friend who is like her would be nice.

#

At school the next day, Lake breaks the bad news to Claire during lunch. "My aunt and uncle are coming over on Friday night to watch football, and Pete is having one of his nerdy friends over to spend the night, so you can't sleep over this week like we planned. But you can come over next Friday night if you want."

"I'm sure that'll be okay. We don't do too much this time of year. I'll ask Mom and Dad tonight, just to make sure."

"Hey, do you like Chinese food?"

"I love it. We hardly ever order it because my dad has a reaction to something in it, but Mom and I get it sometimes when he has his lodge meetings, and she doesn't feel like cooking."

"Well, my dad doesn't like pizza, but Mom said we can order Chinese for dinner when you spend the night."

"Your dad doesn't like pizza? I've never heard of anyone who doesn't like pizza."

"I know. He's weird that way."

The girls laugh, and the bell rings. Throwing her leftovers into her lunch box, Claire says, "We have the option of taking recess inside or outside today because of the cold. What do you want to do?"

"I have a deck of cards in my lunchbox. We could stay in and play Crazy Eights."

"Sounds good. Let's go."

#

February is such a crappy month. Claire asks Lake if she will show her the ranch this weekend when she stays over, but it will be too cold and dark to hang out in the hayloft. Lake can show her around on Saturday morning after breakfast, but her Spin the Bottle plans will have to happen in the house. There, she has two options: her bedroom or the basement. The basement is sort of creepy, not to mention damp and cold. With Jeannie at her friend's house, the bedroom will have to do. Mom doesn't let them drink soda, which means there are no bottles in the house, but the ketchup is almost gone. Lake makes a note to ask her mom for it this week. She'll tell her she needs it for a project at school.

The timing couldn't have worked out better.

Mom makes hash browns for breakfast on Thursday morning, and Pete uses the last of the ketchup. Being the mom she is, Sylvia soaks the bottle, removes the label, and washes it before handing it to her. "For your school project, Lake."

Her brother, Pete, looks at her and says, "What kind of project?"

Gosh dang, Pete! Why are you such a nerd? "I'm not sure. Mrs. Spence just asked us to bring an empty soda or ketchup bottle to school for a project she has planned. Mom won't let us drink soda, so I need to bring the ketchup bottle.

"This gets Jeannie worked up. "All my friends drink soda. It's so dumb we aren't allowed to have it."

"It's full of sugar and chemicals. It's—"

Before Mom can finish the sentence, Jeannie interrupts, "Not good for us. I know, you say that all the time. None of my friends have gotten sick or grown an extra limb from drinking soda. I think you're overreacting, Mom."

Telling Sylvia she's overreacting is like telling her to calm down. She doesn't like it one bit! Mom takes a couple steps toward the table and says, "I think it's time for you to finish up, Jeannie. You don't want to miss the bus."

"Whatever, Mom. I still think—"

"Go! *Now*, young lady."

Getting up from the table, Jeannie says, "But—" and Mom loses it. "Say one more word, Jeannie, and you won't be spending the night with Kellie on Friday."

Jeannie clenches her teeth, sets her plate in the sink, and stomps out of the kitchen. Thank goodness she doesn't say anything else. If Jeannie's home this weekend, Lake's whole plan is shot. Getting up from the table, Lake puts her plate in the sink, grabs the bottle from the counter, and says, "Thanks, Mom," as she leaves the kitchen.

Walking down the hallway, she notices the bathroom door is closed. With Jeannie in the bathroom, Lake sprints into their shared bedroom and hides the ketchup bottle in the back of her sock drawer. Just as she's closing the drawer, Jeannie walks in. "Wear warm socks today, runt. It's cold out."

Looking down at her feet, Lake replies, "Way ahead of you, Jeannie." Grabbing her backpack, Lake heads for the door. "C'mon. We don't want to miss the bus."

#

Stepping off the bus on Friday, Claire says, "I'm so excited to stay over tonight. I can't wait to see your room and the horses. You're so lucky to live across the street from your grandparents and their ranch. My grandparents live in Cleveland and Pennsylvania. We usually just see them on holidays. But their places are boring, not like you and the horse ranch."

"Yeah, well, my mom's dad lives in Kentucky, and we hardly ever see him. Grandma Shelly died when Mom was a teenager, so we never got to meet her. Grandpa Noah doesn't like to fly or drive too far, so we don't see him very often at all. He sends cards and stuff for our birthdays and Christmas, but I haven't seen him in a couple of years. We might go visit him this summer when the weather is better."

"Still, I think it's neat to have the ranch and at least one set of grandparents close by. You have the coolest ones right here!"

Lake remembers her birthday dinner and Kiki standing in front of the fireplace telling her story, and she smiles. "Yeah, they're pretty awesome."

With Jeannie gone, Lake's bedroom isn't so bad. She and Jeannie have matching twin beds and dressers. They're wooden and just a boring brown color, but the room is symmetrical, bright, and always tidy, thanks to Sylvia.

"How do you like sharing a room with Jeannie?" asks Claire.

"She ignores me most of the time, and I read in the living room a lot, so it's okay, I guess. We've shared a bedroom since I was born, so I don't know anything different. Dad promised Pete he'd fix up the basement so he can have his own room down there and Jeannie can move into his room. When that happens, I'll finally have my own room."

"Sometimes I wish I had a brother or a sister. Being an only child gets lonely."

"When you're ready to trade lives for a while, let me know!"

Just then, they hear a knock at the door. "Come in."

Sylvia opens the door and says, "I thought I heard you girls. Hello, Claire. We're glad to have you here. Are you two hungry? Would you like a snack?"

"What do we have?" asks Lake.

"We've got apple slices with caramel or peanut butter, trail mix, and Chex mix."

Lake looks at her friend. "Do you like any of those, Claire?"

"Sure. Anything is fine."

"Okay, Mom. We'll have some apple slices and Chex mix. And a couple glasses of water," Lake says.

"I'm headed down to the basement for a few things. I'll put your snacks and water on the kitchen table, and you girls can grab them when you're ready."

As the door is closing, Lake says, "Thanks, Mom."

"These movie posters are so cool. *ET* is one of my all-time favorite movies!" says Claire.

Looking around, Lake replies, "Mine, too. Most of these posters are Jeannie's, but a couple are mine."

"Let me guess. The *Black Beauty* poster is definitely yours, and *The Gremlins*?"

"Close. You're half-right."

Looking around the room, Claire isn't sure which of the other posters belong to Lake. "I don't know. Just tell me."

"It's the one with the palm trees that says, 'Key West'. Grandma Kiki and Grandpa Kevin got it for me last year. They go there in the winter and live on their boat. They're there now."

"That's so cool. I can't wait to meet them someday!"

"I'll introduce you to them when they get back. Let's go get our snacks."

The girls get the apple slices and Chex mix and take them back to Lake's room. "I didn't even notice your record player, Lake. I like the color better than mine," says Claire.

"Yeah, it's great. I'm obsessed with the new Whitney Houston album. Do you want to listen to it?"

"Sure," says Claire.

While the album is playing, Lake decides to ask a question that's on her mind. "Do you like anyone in your class?"

"What do you mean? Like, do I like any of the boys in my class?"

"Yeah, like, do you think any of them are cute?"

"I guess. Craig Bell is sort of cute, and he's nice. He's really smart, too. The other boys in my class are kind of mean."

Interesting, thinks Lake. "I know Craig Bell. His family owns the hardware store. My dad takes me there sometimes. Craig is nice, he helps out at the store on Saturdays."

Now that she knows Claire thinks Craig is cute, she can use that as an excuse later to introduce Spin the Bottle.

After dinner, Lake and Claire sit together on the couch and watch the same Friday night TV shows they'd watched at Claire's. Jack is busy working on something in the basement, but Sylvia is there in the living room, working on a new scarf. Lake's mom learned to knit after Jeannie was born, and during the winter months, she insists on knitting new scarves for everyone in the family. Occasionally, she laughs at something on TV, and the knitting stops momentarily. Lake is restless and bored with the shows. Not wanting to draw attention to herself, she sits next to Claire, waiting patiently for them to end. She knows her mom's Friday night program will be on next, giving her an excuse to take Claire back to her room.

With the closing credits rolling, Lake says, "You want to go hang out in my room?"

"Okay."

Lake turns to her mom and says, "We're going to go hang out in my room."

Sylvia keeps knitting. "Okay. Let me know if you need anything."

Lake refills their water glasses, and they head for the bedroom. "My mom's favorite Friday night show is about to come on. I think she likes watching it by herself sometimes."

"My parents like to watch *Miami Vice* on Friday nights, but it comes on later," says Claire.

Lake puts on an album and each of them flops down on a bed. Sitting across from each other, they talk about the ranch for a while. Lake tells Claire about the barn, the hayloft, and the layout of the farm, promising to give her a tour in the morning. Then she changes the subject. "Hey, Claire. Have you ever kissed a boy?"

"Yeah. Once in first grade. Todd Connor kissed me during recess."

Impressed, Lake asks, "Does he still go to our school?"

"No. I'm not sure where he went. He didn't come back for second grade."

"So, what was it like? The kiss," asks Lake.

"It was wet," says Claire. They both crack up. Sensing it's a good time to press on, Lake asks Claire the one question she's been waiting to ask. "Have you ever played Spin the Bottle?"

Looking at her friend, Claire says, "No. Have you?"

For some reason, Lake tenses. She doesn't want Claire to know about Gretchen, afraid she'll somehow know that she *like* likes Gretchen and dreams of kissing her again. So, she lies. "No. I've never played, but I heard Pete talk about it one time. I think he played it at a birthday party last summer."

The two sit there in silence for a few seconds, until Lake says, "I have an old ketchup bottle if you want to play. We could practice kissing. So we're ready when the time comes to kiss a boy."

"Okay. What do we do?" asks Claire.

Pulling the bottle out of her sock drawer, Lake says, "We sit on the floor facing each other. Hold on. I want to make sure my mom is still watching her show." Walking to the door, Lake slowly opens it and listens. She can hear the TV. Tiptoeing out the door and down the hall, she sees her dad in his chair. Her mom is there next to him, yarn and knitting needle resting in her lap.

Slowly, Lake backs down the hallway and into her room. Shutting the door, she turns to see Claire sitting on the floor in front of Jeannie's bed. The door to her room doesn't have a lock on it, but she feels secure knowing her mom's show is on for at least another half hour.

Taking a seat across from Claire, she places the bottle on the floor between them. Then, spinning it, she says, "The object of the game is to spin the bottle like this. When it stops, you're supposed to kiss whoever the person is that it's pointing at." They both look down to see the bottle slowing. It lands pointing more toward Lake than Claire. "If it's not pointing at anyone when it stops, you get to try again. That was just a practice spin. You want to try it?"

Claire gives the bottle a spin, and it stops pointing almost directly at Lake. The two look at each other, and neither of them moves. Lake says, "Nice spin. We're supposed to kiss now."

Claire looks nervous, so Lake leans in and says, "Are you ready?"

Claire nods yes.

"Okay, then close your eyes." Claire shuts her eyes, and her body is as stiff as a statue. Lake leans closer and kisses Claire on the lips. It's a quick kiss. It feels forced, and Lake doesn't really enjoy it. Pulling back, Claire opens her eyes but doesn't say anything.

Reaching for the bottle, Claire says, "I want to spin again." On her next try, the bottle lands pointing toward the record player. "Can I try one more time?" Lake nods her head, and Claire spins the bottle hard. This time it lands pointing just past Lake. "Close enough," says Claire, and then she's up, leaning toward Lake. The second kiss is better, but it still doesn't feel right.

Bummed, Lake watches Claire return to her spot. "I think you're a good kisser, Claire. If you ever get to play this game with Craig, you'll be ready for him!"

"You think so? It's kind of weird playing with a girl, but we're just playing. It doesn't mean anything," says Claire.

"Right. It doesn't mean anything. What do you want to do now?"

They decide to play rummy but tire out before either reaches 500 points. The next morning, Lake gives Claire the full tour of the ranch after breakfast. She likes spending time with Claire, but now that she knows for sure they're not the same, she finds herself dreaming about finding a new friend. The one she hasn't met yet but hopes to one day.

#

The next weekend is the county spelling bee tournament. There are thirty-two public schools in her county, which means she has to out-spell thirty-one kids to win. She can't imagine not winning the bee. She practices her flashcards all the time, and she can spell every word on her Speak & Spell. At dinner, her family takes turns giving her words to spell, and she is awesome! Still, she's a little nervous. On Friday, the day before the tournament, Mrs. Spence and her class surprise her with a banner and cupcakes when she gets to school. Draped across both chalkboards is a sign that says, "Good Luck, Lake!" It's signed by everyone in the class, including Mrs. Spence, and the principal. Lake is overwhelmed by the support from her class. She hopes she's able to pull out a win and make everyone proud.

On Saturday morning, Lake is awake before her alarm goes off. Worried she's overslept, she squints to read the time. It's 7:24 a.m.—she's fine. She hasn't overslept. She hears her dad's voice and can smell bacon cooking. Careful not to wake Jeannie, Lake gets out of bed.

Fumbling for her slippers, she finds them at the foot of the bed. It's still cold outside, and the floors in her house are always cold, even in the summer, so she likes to keep the slippers close by.

Shutting the bedroom door behind her, Lake pads down the hall and into the kitchen. As soon as Dad sees her, he says, "There she is! Miss Lake Myers, spelling bee champion of her school. How do you feel this morning? Are you excited?"

"Yeah, I guess. A little scared, but excited, too."

"That's perfectly normal, kiddo. Try not to let the nerves get to you. You're going to be great. What does Kiki say? You're a force to be reckoned with!"

Lake smiles at the mention of Kiki. She wishes her grandparents were here to watch her in the bee.

"Your mom and I are so proud of you. Just do your best," says her dad. "I'm going to check in with your uncle Rick, and then I'll be back. Your mom made a big breakfast with all your favorites." He kisses her on the head and says to Sylvia, "We need to leave by nine o'clock. I'll make sure Jeannie and Pete are up before I check in with Rick."

On the way to the tournament, Lake feels sick to her stomach. Wishing she hadn't eaten so much bacon, she closes her eyes and rests her head against the back seat. Dad has the radio on, and everyone is quiet, listening to the local news and dozing. Traffic is light, and they arrive at the high school early. Lake is glued to her seat in the car.

"What are you doing, Lake?" Jeannie is pushing against her leg. "We're here. Are you getting out of the car?"

Lifting her head off the headrest, Lake says, "Yeah, I was waiting for you."

With everyone out of the car, Dad doubles back to make sure he locked it and then is back ahead of them all, holding the door for his family when they get there. He helps Lake sign in, then walks her to the room where the participants are told to wait.

At exactly 9:45, the kids are led into the auditorium and assembled on the stage. Lake doesn't know anyone here, and she's feeling more nervous than ever. She spots her parents in the third row on the right, and her dad gives her a thumbs-up. Seeing them makes her feel better, and she takes several deep breaths, willing herself to stay calm and focused.

The kids here are good spellers, getting their words right even before the timer goes off. Each gets through two rounds of words before the first one misspells a word. It's a boy, named Alex. Not long after he's out, a few more fail to spell their words correctly and are forced out of the competition. Lake is doing well, getting words she knows and can easily spell.

When they break for lunch, there are only fourteen kids remaining. Her family is there waiting and give her words of encouragement during the break. Even Jeannie is positive, telling her she's doing great. "Keep it up!"

Returning to the stage, Lake feels confident and calm. She spells each word correctly while others get the spelling wrong. Soon several more kids are forced out, leaving just five of them on the stage. Lake loses count of the words being given. No one is misspelling a word. And then she hears it, "That is incorrect. The correct spelling of *manageable* is *m-a-n-a-g-e-a-b-l-e*." It's down to just four of them now.

A short while later, the girl next to Lake misspells her word and is out. Lake is unsure of how much time has passed before the boy next to her gets the word *detrimental*. Holding her breath during his try, she hears him say *a* when he should have said *i*. He's out, and Lake spells the word correctly.

Now it's down to just Lake and one other girl. They both spell every word given to them correctly, and the judges finally declare a tie. Both will go to the state final.

Everyone is on their feet clapping and cheering. Lake is exhausted, but happy. She and the other winner each get a fifty-dollar savings bond and a small trophy. What a rush! She can't wait to tell Kiki.

The ride home is much livelier than the ride to the tournament had been. Everyone is chatty and excited for Lake. The trip to Columbus is just three weeks away! Dad treats the family to an early dinner at their favorite burger place, a local spot that's been around for years. When they get back to the house, Lake is antsy. She wants to tell Grams and Gramps about her win, but they won't call to check in until tomorrow,

Sunday. She and Pete play several rounds of Battleship, and she loses two out of three. "You always find my ships, Pete."

"That's because you always put them in the same places," he says. Lake tries to deny this, but she knows she tends to place her ships in basically the same place every time. "I'm going to read for a while. Thanks for playing with me."

"Sure thing, little sister. Good job today!"

A few hours later, Lake falls asleep on the couch and wakes up to discover her dad carrying her to her room. "You're getting too big for this, Lake. Next time I might just wake you up and walk you in here." Pulling the covers back, her dad lays her on the bed and tucks her in. "Sleep tight, spelling bee winner. See you in the morning." Pulling the covers up to her chin, Lake snuggles in deep and falls back to sleep.

The next morning when Lake wakes up, the house is quiet. No breakfast smells, no TV, no voices that she can hear. She looks at her alarm clock. It's after eight o'clock. Maybe everyone is sleeping in? It is Sunday, after all. When she looks over at Jeannie's bed, it's empty. What is going on?

Walking down the hallway, she can hear whispering. It sounds like someone is crying. "Hey, what's going on?" she calls out.

Her whole family is sitting at the kitchen table. She can tell her mom's been crying. Her dad says, "Come sit down, Lake. We need to tell you something."

Swallowing hard, she sits down in her normal seat at the table. "You guys are scaring me. What's wrong?"

Reaching across the table, her mom takes her hand. "Something terrible has happened, Lake."

"What? What happened?"

"Your grandma and grandpa were in the city last night having dinner. As they were walking back to their car, a man with a gun tried to rob them."

"Oh my gosh, are they okay?" Lake asks.

Her dad answers, "The police called this morning. They said the man took all their money and their valuables, including Kiki's jewelry and her wedding ring. They think your grandpa Kevin struggled with the man and was shot. We don't have all the details, but Kiki was also shot."

Lake feels like she's been punched in the stomach. "They're alright, though, right? They're going to be okay?"

Her dad has tears in his eyes. "I'm sorry, Lake. They're not okay. I'm so sorry."

Lake feels like she's going to throw up. "What are you saying, Dad? Dad?"

A tear rolls down her dad's cheek. She's never seen him cry before. Shaking his head, he says, "They both died, Lake. Your grandparents are gone. I'm sorry, honey."

Lake suddenly wants to scream. Instead, she pounds her fists on the table and says, "*No!* You're lying! Grandma and Grandpa are in Key West on their boat. They're coming home next month."

Both of her parents are on their feet, standing next to her. Leaning down, her mom grabs on to her and holds her tight.

This has to be a terrible dream. Kiki and Grandpa Kevin are her two most favorite people in the whole wide world. They can't be dead. They just can't.

The rest of the morning is a blur. Somehow Lake ends up back in her room. Lying on her bed, she stares out the window, watching the dry, bare tree limbs bend with the wind. She hears a knock at the door, but she doesn't move or respond in any way.

Red-eyed and looking exhausted, Sylvia pokes her head in the room and says, "Lake, I made breakfast. Come eat."

Still staring out the window, Lake says, "I'm not hungry, Mom. I just want to stay here in bed."

"Okay, honey, but if you get hungry, there's plenty of food," says Sylvia.

Lake stays in her bed most of the day, napping and reading. Jeannie stays away from the bedroom they share, choosing instead to be close to Mom in the kitchen. Pete keeps to himself in his own room. The only sounds in the house are the muted voices of the living room TV, which no one is watching.

Lake's mom and dad let the kids stay home from school while they make arrangements to get her grandparents back to Ohio. It's all very matter-of-fact. Uncle Rick will fly to Florida and bring their bodies back on Friday. The funeral will take place the following Tuesday—one funeral for the two of them. Together in death, just as they were when they were alive.

Throughout the week, friends of the family stop by all hours of the day to drop off cakes, pies, casseroles, and deli platters. In a house full of people, Lake feels completely alone and totally exhausted. For the most part, she stays in her room and only ventures out to eat when it is absolutely necessary.

Jeannie and Pete return to school on Thursday, but Lake stays home until Friday. When her dad drops her off, she notices some of the kids look away to avoid eye contact. As she walks to her class, voices around Lake are lowered, and some conversations stop altogether. She wants to run to the bathroom and stay there the entire day, but she keeps walking, chin up, and takes her seat in the classroom.

Mrs. Spence comes over as soon as she spots her. The desk in front of Lake is empty, and her teacher sits sideways in the seat so that she can look her in the eye. In a quiet voice, she says, "I'm sorry about your grandparents, Lake. We're all very sorry. Please let me know if you need anything."

"Thank you, Mrs. Spence. I'm fine." But Lake isn't fine. She feels numb and hollow inside, like her heart has been ripped from her chest. She feels absolutely nothing.

At the funeral, Lake is the only one not crying. She stares at her Grams and Gramps lying completely still in their matching caskets and has no tears to shed. After the service, she has no words to offer, nothing to say.

Her parents, along with her aunts and uncles, decide to have everyone over to the ranch after the services. Her grandparents' house is untouched, nothing moved or disturbed since the day they left, still overflowing with objects, photos, and memories of Kevin and Kiki. The family feels it will be comforting to have the gathering there, surrounded by the smiles and spirits of her dead ancestors. Half the town has come out to pay their respects, making the house feel cramped and unfamiliar.

Lake has a hard time catching her breath, and she seeks refuge in her grandparents' bedroom. She's standing next to the bed they shared, looking at her favorite photo of the two of them, when Veronica walks up behind her. She can feel the presence of someone, but she refuses to look away from the photo. With one arm, Veronica hugs the side of Lake that's closest to her and says, "Your grandma Kiki loved you so much, Lake. She always said you were her favorite."

Lake turns toward Veronica, then walks to the other side of the bed. With her back against the wall, she slides down until her butt touches the floor, out of sight of anyone who might walk in. She crosses her legs and fixates on the photo, willing them to come back to her.

Veronica takes a deep breath and exhales slowly, as though she's trying to steady herself. Once composed, she walks quietly out of the room.

No one pushes Lake to speak or cry. She must deal with the death of her grandparents in her own way, in her own time. She wonders if she'll ever feel anything at all, ever again.

#

Lake knows the loss of her grandpa Kevin and grandma Kiki is deep and far reaching. She loved Grandpa Kevin so much, but Kiki was more than a grandmother to her. She was her liberator, her champion, and her strongest ally, long before she fully understood what that meant.

When she closes her eyes, Lake can see Kiki's arms drawing her into her familiar bosom, her line of sight blurred by the breasts squashed against her face. She breathes in the scent of her and feels the warmth radiate from Kiki's body. Lake has always been madly in love with her grams, but not in a weird or inappropriate way. It was nothing more than a profound and pure love. When she is in her grandmother's arms, wrapped in her scent, Lake can't imagine a more safe and beautiful space.

For years to come, Lake will rely heavily on the comfort and safety of the story Kiki insisted on telling her time and time again to keep the memory of her precious Kiki very much alive.

Chapter 7

Settling comfortably within her pit of desolation, Lake is in a deep state of denial and utter emptiness when she wins the state spelling bee championship in Columbus. It isn't enough that her friend Claire made the trip with her family, or that Uncle Rick and Aunt Joe made the long drive down and back just to be there for the day, to love and support her in her time of need. When she looks out at the seats filled by her family and friends, all Lake sees are the two empty seats that should be occupied by her grandparents. She knows they weren't planning to return from Key West in time for the tournament, but if they had still been alive, they would call and ask for a full rundown on how she did. But now, that call will never come.

It sucks going to bed thinking one thing, only to wake up and find your reality is the absolute opposite of what it had been just eight hours earlier. Her grandparents' death was incredibly abrupt and cruel. And no matter how hard she tries, Lake can't wrap her head around the losses. She is angry at the world, and the pain is more than she ever imagined.

Lake needs to move forward and face the terrible truth head-on, but no one in her family is willing to take the first step now that her grandparents are in the ground. Dad and Uncle Kevin work long hours to prepare for foal season while the ranch house sits dark and empty. Mom and the aunts spend hours on the phone talking, but none of them wants to discuss what happened or go inside Grandma and Grandpa's house.

Following their lead, Lake skirts the topic at every turn and avoids looking at the house across the street from hers. School and her bedroom are benign spaces, free of mindless chitchat and tangible reminders of the two grandparents she'd lost. Her reclusive demeanor somehow makes her more appealing to the kids at school, and her grades have never been better. Days roll by, documented by way of light and darkness, and the heavy black mark on a calendar square, another day dead and gone.

Lake graduates from the fourth grade, and her reputation is elevated to superstar status, driven by the misfortune of others. On the last day of school, she passes by the state spelling bee trophy with her name on it, encased in glass under a spotlight in the school's main hall, and thinks she would gladly give it up to have her grandparents back and to feel happiness again.

For weeks, her neighborhood friends drop by every day, aiming to coax her out of the house for a spirited game of kickball or a refreshing dip in the pond, but she has no desire to do the physical things that once brought her such joy. She's been struggling to connect with other kids since the murders. Shut down emotionally, she turns to the characters in her books for strength, support, and a familiar means to an escape.

#

Once the school year was over, the adults in Lake's family decide it's necessary to work through the devastation, confront reality, and sort through all things tangible and real. Her paternal grandparents had left behind a boat in the Keys; a vast horse ranch full of vehicles, trailers, farm equipment, animals, and acreage; their taxidermy trade; and a home filled with memories and keepsakes. To deal with the pain and anger head-on, Lake reluctantly accepts her dad's offer to help organize and box up items in the ranch house.

The walk over is surreal and feels much longer than she remembers. She is flanked by her parents, and the trio arrive at the back door together. Her first instinct is to open the door unannounced and waltz in as usual, but before she is able, her dad reaches in front of her and inserts the key, unlocking the door to a once-lively place that hasn't been lived in for months.

Crossing the threshold, Lake says, "It smells different, kind of like the basement, but not as sour." With his hand on her back, Lake's dad gently nudges her forward, into the stagnant kitchen.

"I check on the place every few days, bring in the mail and double-check the thermostat to make sure the house stays comfortable, but I know what you mean, it does smell different."

Lake glances over at the kitchen table and can see stacks of mail spread from one end to the other. Walking over and reaching up to the cupboard above the dishwasher, her mom says, "I'll make a pot of coffee and work on the mail. If it's anything like ours, most of its junk and can be tossed. Jack, can you bring the garbage can over for me?"

Grabbing the can from under the sink, Lake's dad sets it next to the table and gives his wife a kiss on the top of her head. "Lake and I will see what needs to be done in the dining room."

Flipping on lights as he walks from room to room, her dad makes a sweep of the main level of the house, Lake close behind. "It's weird to be here, Dad. I keep thinking they're still alive and that they'll walk in the back door any minute. Grams will touch her hair, say she's 'had a day' and that she's ready for one of her 'special drinks'."

"I know it's hard, Lake, and I wish that was the case, but they're gone. I'm so sorry," says her dad.

Hugging her dad tight, Lake replies, "I miss them so much. I don't know why I'm here. What are we supposed to do today?"

"I had your uncle Rick order a bunch of boxes. They were delivered to the house this week and should be in the living room up against the far wall. We have newspaper to wrap the dishes in, and I thought you could help with that, and I'll box and label them. Kiki had certain sets she wanted each of her kids to have, and others that will go to the grandchildren or be donated. Do you feel like helping me with that?"

"Sure," Lake agreed.

"Good, I'll go grab a stack of boxes. You get the newspaper and the packing tape in the kitchen. There should be a couple big rolls of clear tape and a round do-hicky thing to use with them. You can't miss it."

Walking back through the living and dining rooms, Lake can't help but notice Grandpa Kevin's handsome face in at least half of the photos showcased throughout the house. He was always looking directly at the camera, cigarette suspended between his lips near the corner of his mouth, always on the right side, never the left. Most of the pictures had been taken during a hunting or fishing trip, with Gramps proudly holding an enormous largemouth bass or some type of animal.

"Lake, you've been standing there staring up at that picture of your grandpa for a while now. I thought maybe you got lost on your way back," says her dad from the other side of the room.

Lake looks back from where she's standing to see him sitting at the banquette, cup of coffee in hand. It was Kiki's favorite spot in the house. Lake steals a quick glance around the dining room, going from picture to picture until she's given each another good look—just enough to keep hold of the images for a day or so until they've faded away again.

#

It's soothing to be back in the ranch house laying hands on things that once belonged to Kiki and Grandpa Kevin. Lake helps her dad in the dining room, systematically working through each of the sideboards and china cabinets until it's time for lunch. "Grams had a lot of dishes. Why would anyone need so many sets of plates and saucers?" asks Lake as she hands the last piece of china over to her dad.

"Your grandma Kiki was big on tradition, and she believed in creating memories and preserving things for the family. She separated from her parents when she met and married your grandpa, and that made her sad for a while. She knew that one day, she and your grandpa would pass on and we would be sad, as well. Saving different sets of china for each of her children was a way for her to help us hold her close now that she's gone. It doesn't take away the pain, but it helps to bring smiles to all of us who are still here. Some traditions are held in stories, like the one about the day you were born. Think about how many times Kiki told that story and you never got tired of hearing it. I bet if you think about the night of your birthday, when she told the story after dinner, it makes you smile. You'll always have that story to help you hold her close."

"That's a really good way of explaining things, Dad. Now I get why she had so much china, and why she told me that story so many times. I'll never forget it—and I'll never forget her."

"I don't imagine you will, Lake. I bet one day you'll even tell the story to your own daughter," he says with a wink.

"Maybe," she says, winking back at him.

#

Over the next few weeks, Lake helps her mom and dad organize nearly all of her grandparents' personal belongings. A lot of the animals and mounts are given to various members of the family, and those of greatest stature are donated to different organizations throughout Northeast Ohio for educational purposes or display. Most of the clothes are donated or sold, along with some of the less-meaningful pieces of furniture. With less than two weeks before the start of the new school year, the house is almost empty. The undertaking of touching, sorting, and boxing the material possessions of her grandparents has been therapeutic and has offered Lake a sense of purpose.

Standing in front of the long, double sinks in the vanity area of the primary bathroom, Lake picks up a bottle of Kiki's signature perfume and removes the brightly colored cap. Pressing down on the gold aerosol top, she releases a stream of spray into the air, then tilts her head back to breathe in a trace of the scented mist. Closing her eyes, the smell immediately summons an image of Kiki in her floral summer shorts, tube top, and hairband. Allowing herself to linger here, Lake enjoys the moment. Opening her eyes, she catches her mom looking at her in the mirror. Holding the bottle up for her mom to see, Lake asks, "Do you think it would be okay if I kept this bottle of perfume?"

"Of course," said her mom. "Is there anything else you'd like to have?"

Gently lifting the cloth ties hanging from the makeup mirror, Lake replies, "Can I have her hairbands, too?"

"I think that would be fine. I'm sure she'd love for you to have them."

Lake pushes the hairbands into her shorts pocket and sets the bottle of perfume aside. It's her family's goal to have the house cleared out and cleaned from top to bottom before Lake and the other kids return to school. She has overheard the adults talk about selling the house, but her mom and the aunts feel strongly that it should stay in the family, so it was decided that they will rent the house out.

There's a young family of four who live in the mobile home park down the road. Albert, the husband, worked at the ranch every summer when he was in high school. He recently graduated from community college with a degree in criminal justice and is now working for the local police department. His wife, Alicia, a hairstylist, just gave birth to the couple's second child and is home on maternity leave. They're busting at the seams of their current home and are looking for a bigger place. Albert stopped to speak with Jack the same day the FOR RENT sign went up in the yard. The Kellers are good people. They'll be respectful tenants, treating the home as if it were their own. By the weekend before school starts, they are completely moved in.

#

Lake didn't expect fifth grade to be much different from the fourth grade, but it is. She likes learning and has always loved school, but this year is a challenge. From struggling with the concepts of prealgebra to conducting research for essays, her fifth-grade year is more intense than she thought it would be. As the year progresses, Lake spends more time doing homework and less reading for pleasure or kicking a soccer ball around. Her studies are prioritized over her social life and free time, to the point that the latter liberties have gone by the wayside. All that remain are passing waves in the halls to people she knows and the random lunchtime chats with old friends. She's still considered a popular girl in her school, but it isn't a standing she works for. The year literally flies by, and in the end, she's earned straight As and a perfect attendance award. Lake has inadvertently prepared herself for an amazing career as a sixth grader.

The summer before the sixth grade, Lake decides to read the books Kiki and Gramps had given her when she turned nine. The day she'd learned of their deaths, Lake had stood on a chair and shoved the entire basket of birthday gifts from them to the very back of her top closet shelf and forgotten about it. Classifying their personal items had consumed the entire summer after they were taken, followed by another year of school, hard work, and the commitment required to earn top grades. Now that she has fully grieved the losses in her own way, she feels less guilty about enjoying life again.

She pushes a chair from the dining room down the hall to her bedroom and uses it to gain access to the far reaches of her top closet shelf. She moves old dolls, stuffed animals, and other junk aside to reveal the hidden basket of treasures. Lake lifts it down gently and realizes one of the books has fallen out of the basket and is lying in the far corner of the shelf. Pulling a hanger from the rod, she uses it to scoot the book toward her. Once satisfied she'd successfully recovered everything, Lake jumps down off the chair and returns it to its place at the table.

Taking a seat on the floor in front of her bed, she leans back against the frame and picks up the book that had fallen out of the basket. On the cover is a picture of a girl in tennis shoes. She's sitting on a suitcase surrounded by more suitcases, with stacks of books and a cat poking its head out from behind the suitcase the girl is sitting on. The book is titled *How Far Is Berkeley?* Lake has never heard of the book or the author before, but she's intrigued.

She flips through the pages, noticing the print is not too small and there are only 122 pages. If she reads twenty-five pages a day, she can get through the book in no time. Lake grabs a pillow from her bed and drops it behind her back, using it as a soft support between her and the bedframe. She crosses her legs and turns to page one. Two chapters in, she hears a knock at the door. "Lake, you're going to strain your eyes. For heaven's sake, turn on the light."

Glancing up at her mom, Lake realizes the day has turned to late afternoon, and on the walls, the sun is casting shadows that weren't there when she'd first started reading the book.

"What time is it?"

"Close to five fifteen," Mom replies. "I'm getting ready to start supper. Do you want to help? I'd love it if you could set the table and make the salad."

What Lake really wants to do is stay in her room reading, but with the time that's passed since her grandparents died, she has mellowed. She tolerates her family in ways she didn't just a year and a half earlier. Now she's ten, double digits. With this new decade of life, she's gained more patience and a broader understanding of people's differences.

"Sure. Just let me finish this chapter first." Quickly turning the pages, she says, "I only have five more pages. I'll be out in a few minutes to help."

Her mom reaches in and flips on the overhead light. "Okay. See you in a few minutes." And then she's gone.

#

It only takes Lake four days to finish the book. When the time comes to turn the final page, she's astonished by the content and has more questions than answers. In short, the book is about a twelve-year-old girl named Mike. She and her mom move to the freethinking community of Berkeley, California, in the early 1970s, live in a communal household, and frequent a women's coffeehouse where there are lesbians. *Lesbians!*

Lake is well aware of the term "gay." She has looked it up in the dictionary at the library before, and she thinks *she* might be gay—because she likes kissing girls. But this is the first book she's ever read that talks about women who like other women. Kiki had never mentioned catching Lake kissing Joey on the TV, but she did see it. Lake wonders if Kiki knew she liked Gretchen and that they made out in the hayloft. To Gretchen, it was just a game, a stepping-stone to learning how to kiss boys the "right way." But to Lake, it was more than that. Their time in the hayloft had initiated a plethora of thought and emotions that Lake clung to and revisited many, many times after the game ended. She had used the same method to test Claire and she'd failed. Claire was not gay, but given her disappointment, Lake knew she must be. Kiki probably knew, it too. And what about Kiki and Veronica? Did they ever kiss?

What the hell, Grandma? How could you give me this book to read and leave me to figure everything out alone?

After dinner, Lake helps her mom clear the table and asks, "Can you take me to the library tomorrow? I want to check out a few books."

"I guess we could swing by there on the way to the store. I swear, Pete drinks more milk than any boy I've ever seen. We'll be out before the week ends unless I buy another gallon tomorrow. I'll drop you off first and then run to the store. Will that give you enough time?"

"I think so. I'm not looking for anything in particular."

"Okay, we'll go after breakfast," says Sylvia.

Lake finishes clearing the table, sets the last of the dishes on the counter, and returns to her room. She can listen to records until it's time for something good to be on TV.

The next morning, Lake's up early and is ready for the drive into town before her mom finishes putting the breakfast dishes in the dishwasher. Tapping her foot on the floor, she sits at the table watching her mom walk back and forth in the kitchen.

"Looks like someone is ready for the library. I'm happy to see you reading again," says her mom.

"It's nice to have time to read the books I want to read," says Lake. Feeling weird about the real reason she's headed to the library, she adds, "I think there's a new book by Judy Blume that I haven't read yet. I'm going to look today."

Lake takes the library steps two at a time, pushes through the heavy doors, and quickly walks to the front desk.

The woman behind the front desk has been working there for years and recognizes her instantly. "Well, hello, Lake. We haven't seen you around here for a while. How are you?"

"I'm good, Mrs. Stone. I was wondering, do you have any books by an author named Helen Chetin? My grandma Kiki mentioned her before she passed, and I was thinking I'd read one of her books this summer."

The expression on Mrs. Stone's face turns to sadness, and she says, "We were very sorry to hear about your grandparents. Let's take a look and see what we can find."

"Thank you." While she's waiting, Lake turns and looks out the front windows. She can see cars passing by, and she realizes how much she's missed being in the public library. She likes the way it smells and how orderly it is, everything tucked away neatly in its place.

"I'm sorry, Lake. We don't have any books by Helen Chetin. Is she a children's author?"

"I think so, but I'm not sure." Disappointed, Lake says, "That's okay, Mrs. Stone. Do you have the most recent book by Judy Blume?"

"I believe so. I think it's called *Just as Long as We're Together*. Let me see if we have any copies here... Just a moment... You're in luck, Lake. We have one copy checked in. It's right over here."

Lake walks behind Mrs. Stone, and the pair make their way to the center of the library.

"Here you go. Is there anything else I can help you with?" asks Mrs. Stone.

"No, thank you. I'll just take this one book and wait for my mom. She'll be back to pick me up soon."

"Well, it was nice seeing you again, Lake. Say hello to your mom for me."

Lake takes a seat on the top stair of the library steps and begins reading the new Judy Blume book. She's frustrated there are no other books by Helen Chetin to check out, but there were no guarantees that Helen Chetin had even written more than one book about lesbians. She'll have to keep an eye out for more books with gay characters. She loves reading and daydreaming about places where other people like her go to drink coffee and spend time together. California sounds like a fun state. One day, Lake will visit and check it out for herself.

Turning the page, Lake hears the familiar honk of her mom's car horn. Looking up, she sees her mom sitting behind the wheel of the station wagon, waiting for her.

"I see you checked out a book. Anything good?"

"It's Judy Blume's latest. If it's anything like all her other books, I'm sure it will be great."

"That's wonderful, Lake. There are only a few weeks left before you start the sixth grade, and I was thinking you and I could have a mother-daughter day of shopping at the mall. We could get lunch and buy some school supplies and a few outfits for you to start the new year fresh. It's your last year at the elementary school," says her mom.

Nervously, Lake says, "I know. I've gone there all my life, and now it's my last year before junior high and a whole new school with kids I've never met before."

"Don't get ahead of yourself, Lake. Sixth grade will be a year for tremendous growth, and you'll be the oldest class in school. Top of the heap! Take the time to enjoy it!"

Lake and her mom plan for a day at the mall the following week, and she takes the better part of a day looking through the Sears and JC Penney catalogs for outfit ideas. She definitely isn't interested in skirts or dresses, but she does like the jeans, button-down shirts, and rib-knit sweaters. Tearing out the pages with pictures of the clothes she wants, Lake places them neatly in a stack on her dresser.

#

"Dad, can you take me to school on the first day so I don't have to ride the bus? I want to get there early and decorate my locker."

"I can drop you off on your first day, but I can't make a habit of it, Lake."

"Okay, thanks, Dad."

Just then, the phone rings, and Jeanne jumps up to answer it. "Hello? Yeah, she's here, hold on." Setting the phone on the counter, Jeanne says in a disappointed voice, "It's for you, Lake."

"Who is it?"

"How am I supposed to know? I think it's Gretchen, but I don't know."

Ugh, Jeanne and Pete are both in high school, and all Jeanne thinks about is cheerleading, boys, clothes, and makeup. Would it kill her to pick up a book?

After Gramps and Grams died, Dad helped Pete fix up the basement so he could move down there, and so Jeanne could move into his old room. He even has his own bathroom in the basement. Lake is going to miss Pete when he leaves for college. He has until the end of November to decide between two different schools that have offered him scholarships, but it's anyone's guess where he'll go.

Jeanne isn't really into school or sports, but she does like being a cheerleader. Her goal this year is to make head cheerleader of her varsity squad. Mom and Dad sent her to an advanced cheer camp this summer, and she's pretty good. Lake hopes she makes head cheerleader and gets to go to college on a cheer scholarship next year. If that happens, Lake will start middle school living alone in the house with her parents for the first time in her life. That's a crazy thought.

"Hello?"

"Hey, Lake, it's Gretchen. What's up?"

"Not much. How's your summer?"

"It's been good. I got a paper route and have been babysitting for kids in the park. I've saved like a hundred and twenty dollars. I opened my own bank account, and I'm saving up for a new bike."

"That's really cool, Gretchen."

"Hey, are you playing soccer this year?"

"Yeah. I signed up for it last week. I haven't been practicing as much as I used to, though. How about you?"

"I signed up, too. I was hoping maybe we could practice at the ranch before school starts. Like we used to before…"

Lake feels a pain in her chest, and she squeezes her eyes shut as she finishes Gretchen's sentence in her head. *Before her grandparents were killed.* It would be nice to hang out with Gretchen and the rest of the gang again, even Jonathon. Well, maybe not Jonathon.

"Do you want to come over tomorrow after breakfast? We can practice kicking against the barn."

"Yeah, okay. See you tomorrow."

#

It feels good to be back in the swing of things, practicing soccer moves with Gretchen and starting a new school year. Although she isn't entirely back to her old self, Lake feels less broken now than she has in a long time. Passing through the double-door entrance of school on her first day of sixth grade, she's filled with determination, intent on earning straight As and playing central midfielder on the soccer team. The position is in step with her goal to be the best—a force to be reckoned with—and make Kiki proud.

Central midfielders are important because the ball always has to pass through them. The decisions they make are crucial to the game, and the position is not for the faint of heart. Lake is up to the challenge and is going to crush it this year.

The first sad, awkward holiday season after her grandparents' deaths is behind them, and the mood is brighter going into fall. For Halloween, Lake dresses up as a soccer player, carries an old pillowcase for collecting candy, and makes out like a bandit trick-or-treating. Her parents let her go out alone with a group of friends, and they have a blast.

The holidays rounding out the year are equally as pleasant. The entire Myers bunch has descended on Uncle Rick and Aunt Joe's house for Thanksgiving. Aunt Joe carries on the tradition of making both a turkey and a duck, and everyone brings a dish. The family eats and drinks to excess, and there is some yelling, but it's mostly directed at the football games. After dinner, Lake makes her way out to the barn with apples for her favorite mares. She misses the smells of the barn and being with the horses. Christy, one her favorites, looks up as she approaches and begins whinnying loudly. "Hey there, Miss Christy. Have you missed me? I've missed you. I have something for you, girl."

Shaking her head up and down, Christy paws at the ground and waits for Lake to feed her the apple. It's gone with just a few bites. Rubbing the horse's head, Lake leans in and smells her neck sticking out over the gate of her stall. It's soft, warm, and comforting.

Without warning, Lake begins to cry. She's been angry for so long since Kiki died, and she's refused to cry or even acknowledge the horrible truth of what happened. Disappearing from herself and everyone around her, Lake has drifted through endless months as a somewhat functioning, deeply depressed girl. There have been occasional tears, but never the ultimate crying session where she emerges with feelings of inner peace and acceptance.

Somehow understanding this is the time and place to grieve the deaths of Grandpa Kevin and Grandma Kiki, Lake allows the tears to stream down her face, absorbed by the soft warmth of Christy's neck. As she sobs, a movie of life on the ranch plays slowly in her mind. Each and every good memory rolls through, making her smile even as the tears continue. The concept of time eludes Lake as she watches each scene play out, and when it's over, she's shattered, but joyful. It's as if a huge weight has been lifted from her shoulders, one she wasn't fully aware she had been carrying until this very moment.

Feeling lighter than she has in months, Lake holds tight to Christy and whispers in her ear, "Thank you, girl. Happy Thanksgiving."

As though she understands the words, Christy lifts her head and whinnies. After giving the mare's muzzle one last stroke, Lake turns and walks out of the barn.

#

On New Year's Eve, Lake is alone with her parents, and they've agreed to let her stay up to watch the ball drop and ring in the new year. Just as she predicted, they fall asleep before midnight, and so she nudges both Jack and Sylvia when the ten-minute countdown begins. Jumping up from her spot, her mom shouts, "Jack, we do this every year! Next time we need to take shifts sleeping before midnight. Before you know it, all three kids will be out of the house, and we won't have the chance to watch the ball drop live together again!"

"You're being a little dramatic, Sylvia, don't you think? If New Year's Eve was always on a weekend, we'd have a better chance of staying up until midnight. But when it falls on a Thursday, it's tough to keep my eyes open until the ball drops."

"Okay, Jack, we're wasting time. Let's go get our champagne ready. Lake can have a glass of sparkling grape juice."

When her parents come back to the living room, Lake hands each a hat and a noisemaker. "I'll trade you," says her dad as he offers a plastic champagne flute filled with bubbly white grape juice. As she takes it from his hand, her dad winks and says, "Take it slow, there, kiddo."

Lake rolls her eyes and takes a seat on the floor directly in front of the TV. She looks up at the ball, and Dick Clark begins the countdown. *Ten, nine, eight, seven, six, five, four, three, two, one...*

Lake blows her paper horn and claps the plastic hands together. They make an obnoxious sound.

Jack and Sylvia kiss and take a sip of the champagne. "Happy New Year, Lake!"

"Happy New Year!"

Chapter 8

It's taken Lake almost two years to regain control of her emotions and feel anything more than anger, despondency, and emptiness. On Monday, she returns to school feeling optimistic and cheery. She tosses her things into her locker and sprints to her classroom. When the bell rings, every seat in the class is taken except the one in front of her. Lake's desk is the second one back, the third row in from the door, and the one open seat is the first desk in her row, directly in front of the teacher, Mr. Bradshaw. When she'd learned which class she had been placed in, it had dawned on Lake it was the first time she'd ever had a man as her teacher. At the class open house, the evening before school started, she and her parents had spoken casually with Mr. Bradshaw. To her surprise, she liked him immediately and was excited for the change. The majority of the kids at the open house had been her classmates throughout the years—same faces, different year.

Claire had been new to her class in the fourth grade, and luckily, they'd had the same teacher in the fifth grade, too. This year Gretchen is in her class, but Claire isn't. Not that it matters—they're all still good friends—and now that she and Gretchen are practicing soccer together, that friendship is stable again. Morning announcements come to a close, and Lake is anxious to get the day started. A faint knock at the door makes everyone turn to see who is there.

Stepping from behind his desk, Mr. Bradshaw motions for whoever it is to come in. Looking back at the class, he says, "Good morning, everyone. I hope you all enjoyed the holiday break. I'd like to introduce you to a new student, Carly Sommerville. She just moved here from Santa Fe, New Mexico, and she will be joining our class for the remainder of the year. Carly, we have an open seat for you right here in front."

Smiling, Carly takes a seat at the desk in front of Lake, and Lake's heart skips a beat. She can feel her face turning red, just from looking at Carly Sommerville from Santa Fe, New Mexico. Carly's clothing is fascinating. Dressed in a pair of faded jeans, a bright yellow crocheted, poncho-style sweater with a scarf; and chunky lace-up combat boots covered in flowers, Carly sticks out like a sore thumb. It's the coolest outfit Lake has ever seen. This girl is definitely not from Ohio.

As far as Lake knows, the new girl is the only one in the sixth grade who has lived anywhere outside of their state. Everyone else had been born and raised right here in town, or at least close by. Lake is in awe of the stylish girl sitting right in front of her, close enough to touch. She stares at the back of Carly's head all morning, wondering how she will muster up the courage to say hello and introduce herself. As luck would have it, Mr. Bradshaw takes care of this for her. At precisely 11 a.m., he stands up from his desk and announces it's time for lunch. As the students begin filing out of the classroom, he motions to Lake and says, "Would you mind taking Carly to the lunchroom and showing her around?"

Swallowing hard, Lake says, "Sure, Mr. Bradshaw. I can show her around."

"Thank you, Lake. Carly, this is Lake Myers. She'll show you where the lunchroom is and help with anything else you might need."

Carly stands and turns so that she's looking directly at Lake. She smiles and says, "Cool. Hey, Lake, I'm Carly, and I'm starving. Let's go."

Lake also stands and smiles, then replies, "Hi, Carly," as they walk out of the classroom together.

"So, what do you like to do for fun, Lake Myers?" asks Carly. "Love your name, by the way."

The question catches her by surprise. Hoping she doesn't sound like a dork, Lake decides to answer honestly and says, "I like to read and play soccer. Oh, and I like hanging out at my family's ranch. We have horses."

"No way! My parents bought the old Landry farm out on Route 307. We have horses, too! What kind of horses do you have on your ranch?" asks Carly.

"We have quarter horses."

Carly's eyes light up, and she says, "I have a quarter horse! My parents have palominos, but I have a quarter horse named Ruby. She's five. I've had her for almost a year and was taking riding lessons before we moved here. We didn't have space for her at our house in Santa Fe. We boarded her on a farm just outside of the city. The guy who owns the farm is a friend of my dad's, and when my dad got the job offer in Mentor, he and my mom looked for a place with a barn for Ruby. The lady who helped us sell our house in Santa Fe found the Landry farm, and Mom and Dad liked it. The house is bigger than what we need, but I like that it has more rooms than our house in Santa Fe, and it's two stories. Our house in Santa Fe was just one story."

As she tells her story, Lake watches Carly's eyes and mouth. She has large brown eyes, long dark eyelashes, and thick eyebrows. Her right eye looks bigger than her left—maybe it's just the way she's looking at Lake, she can't tell for sure—but it makes her more interesting. Carly's mouth is big, too, but not terribly large. Her lips are full and shiny. Lake thinks she must be wearing lip gloss.

Lake says, "My house is only one story, but I like it. Do you have any brothers or sisters?"

"Nope. It's just me, my mom, and my dad. How about you? Any brothers or sisters?"

"Yeah, I have an older brother, Pete. He's a senior in high school. And an older sister, Jeanne. She's a junior."

"Cool."

"Well, here we are. This is the cafeteria and lunchroom. The line starts over here."

Lake is relieved that Carly has showed up on a day when lunch doesn't totally stink.

Today they are serving cheeseburgers, tater tots, corn, and chocolate chip cookies for dessert. The two girls slide their trays down the counter, and each grabs a carton of milk, then they stop at the end, next to the cashier.

Lake says, "Hi, Mrs. Crowne. This is Carly Sommerville. She just moved here."

Without so much as a look at Carly, Mrs. Crowne replies, "I see her name here on the list. Okay. Move along."

As they pick up their trays, the girls look at each other and laugh as they head for a table.

"We can sit back here," says Lake, as she steers Carly toward the back of the cafeteria, away from the tables where most of her friends are eating lunch. She can't explain it, but for some reason, she wants to keep Carly all to herself. She doesn't feel like competing with anyone else for Carly's attention.

After they sit at a table across from each other, Lake asks Carly, "Did your mom and dad move their horses here, too?"

"No, they bought their horses after we moved here. Ruby was used to being around other horses, and we have a big barn, so Mom and Dad decided to buy horses they could ride. We've always ridden together, but they didn't have horses of their own until now."

"I don't have a horse of my own," says Lake. "The horses we have are for breeding and to sell, but I love horses, and I do like to ride."

"You should come over and spend the night at my house one weekend. I'll introduce you to Ruby and my parents," says Carly.

With more enthusiasm than she wants to show, Lake says, "I would love that!"

After lunch, Lake shows Carly the gymnasium, the nurse's office, and the sixth-grade classroom areas. Along the way, she makes sure to point out the girls' bathroom locations and drinking fountains. They arrive back at their classroom right on time.

Lake is happy to be back in class sitting quietly behind Carly. Before today, she wasn't entirely fond of her seat near Mr. Bradshaw. The empty desk in front of her had provided no protection at all when she didn't want to be called on. But now, Carly blocks his view of her, and she's closer to Carly than any other kid in the classroom is. At the end of the day, Carly turns to Lake and says, "I feel a little lost with the subjects we covered today. Do you think you could help me catch up?"

"Yeah, for sure. I have soccer practice tonight and tomorrow night, but we can study after school on Wednesday."

"Cool. Thanks, Lake."

The next morning at school, Carly is already at her desk when Lake walks into class. Sydney Muldoon is standing next to Carly, laughing. Seeing her there talking to Carly makes Lake jealous. But just then, Carly sees Lake, and a big smile lights up her face. "Hey, Lake. Guess what?" she says.

The jealous feeling is gone as soon as Carly smiles at her. Taking her seat, Lake replies, "What?"

When Carly turns to look at Lake, Sydney is all but forgotten. Lake hears her say, "Talk to you later, Carly."

Carly gives Sydney a dismissive wave, says, "Okay, bye," then to Lake says, "I talked to my mom last night about needing to study and get caught up with the class. I told her all about you and your offer to help me. She said you could ride the bus home with me tomorrow if you want, and she'll drive you home before dinner so we can study. Do you think your mom and dad will let you come over?"

"I don't know...maybe," says Lake. "My mom will want to talk to your mom first. I'll give you my phone number so your mom can call my mom."

"Cool, write it down for me now, and I'll have my mom call tonight when I get home," says Carly.

Lake quickly writes her home phone number on a piece of paper, rips it from her notepad, and hands it to Carly just as the morning bell rings.

#

"Mom! Remember the new girl I told you about, Carly? Mr. Bradshaw asked me to show her around the school and help her with things. She needs some help catching up to where our class is with homework and stuff, and she asked if I would tutor her. She wants to know if I can ride the bus home with her after school tomorrow. She said her mom will bring me home before dinner."

Sylvia tilts her head and says, "I don't know, Lake. We don't know her parents. It makes me uncomfortable to send you to her house when we haven't met them at all."

"I knew you'd say that. So, I gave Carly our phone number today. She's going to have her mom call you when she gets home. They live on the old Landry farm. You and Dad know where that is. It's not far from here at all, *and* they have horses. Please, Mom?"

Sylvia looks like she could crack. "I'll speak to Carly's mom when she calls. I'm not promising anything until I've had a chance to talk with her."

Carly's mom, Genevieve, calls before Sylvia starts making dinner. Lake sits at the kitchen table doing her homework and eavesdrops on her mom's side of the conversation. "Santa Fe? That sounds lovely... No, we haven't visited the Southwest, but I'd love to one day. How do you like the Landry farm?... I've always admired the house. It's really quite beautiful and historic... Yes, Lake told me all about the horses... What did you say your husband does?... Oh, an engineer. That's fantastic. Mentor is not too far at all..."

The conversation lasts less than ten minutes. When Sylvia hangs up the phone and turns to look at Lake, she knows the answer is yes.

"Genevieve seems very nice. She's grateful that you're willing to help Carly with her studies, and that's very kind of you, Lake. I suppose it'll be okay for you to go to Carly's house tomorrow and for Mrs. Sommerville to drive you home by dinnertime."

Lake jumps up from the table and throws her arms around her mom's waist. "Thanks, Mom."

#

Lake gives her mom's handwritten permission note to Mr. Bradshaw the moment she walks into class and is fidgety at school all day. She and Carly share a seat during the bus ride to Carly's house, which doesn't take long at all. When Carly told her they'd bought the old Landry farm, Lake had had no idea which farm it was, but now that she's here, she remembers riding past it lots of times.

Walking up to the house, Lake likes that the driveway goes in two different directions. If they walk straight ahead, it takes them behind the house to the barn and fields. But she and Carly veer left, away from the barn, and follow the circular portion of the driveway to the front steps of the old farmhouse. As they climb the stairs, Lake looks to the left and right down the long, covered front porch. Two wooden rocking chairs sit equally spaced on each side of the porch. As they get closer to the landing, she sees an old, metal milk container next to the front door. It's painted red and has a big bow around the top. On the front, painted in white block lettering, it says, WELCOME TO THE SOMMERVILLE HOME. In the center of the massive front door is a large, green wreath. Everything about the outside of the house is warm and welcoming. Once inside the door, Lake stands for a moment taking it all in.

The house is old, but really nice, and Lake instantly feels at ease in Carly's whimsical family home. "I love all of the art and stuff in your house," says Lake.

"Thanks. My mom was really into Santa Fe, and she decided to bring everything from there over here to Ohio. C'mon, I'll show you around the place." Bypassing the stairs directly in front of them, Carly leads Lake to a room on their left. "This is the formal living room. Mom isn't done buying furniture yet, but you get the idea."

On the far wall of the room is a huge, white marble fireplace. Lake thinks it would be perfect for hanging stockings at Christmas. "Over here is the parlor and dining room. We'll probably never use these rooms. We're not that extra."

Lake isn't sure where to look next. The rooms in Carly's house are really big, with high ceilings and all different kinds of light fixtures. Some are mounted on the walls, and some hang down from the ceiling by chains. There's a puffy braided design on the ceiling around the chandelier in the dining room. Sylvia would love this place. It's "tastefully" decorated with Southwestern items and original, framed pieces of art, signed by the artists.

Carly pushes on a door that swings open, and they walk into the kitchen.

"Mom, Lake's here."

Unlike Lake's mom, Carly's mom is not standing in front of the sink or the stove. Carly's mom is standing next to an easel in front of the kitchen windows, painting a picture of the barn. Her long dark hair is loosely braided, and she's wearing a bright pink sweater and oversized denim overalls. Each of her wrists are covered with layers of thin silver bracelets. "Hi, Lake. It's nice to meet you. I'm glad I was able to talk to your mom so you could be here this afternoon."

"Thank you, Mrs. Sommerville, it's nice to meet you."

"Please, call me Genevieve."

"Mom, do we have any snacks?" Carly asks.

"We have some clementine oranges, and I made fresh guacamole today if you want chips and salsa with it."

"Right on, Mom. I'll get the chips and stuff."

Motioning to Lake, Genevieve says, "Lake, come here and sit at the table. I'll slide the paint and brushes down."

Sitting in the chair closest to Carly, Lake says, "You're a good painter. Are you an art teacher?"

With a toss of her braid, Genevieve says, "No. I just enjoy painting."

"Mom painted and made pottery in Santa Fe. She showed some of her stuff at an art gallery and people bought it," says Carly.

"That's so cool. I love your house—it's really neat," says Lake.

"I'm glad you like it. Carly, be careful eating near the painting. I'm going out to the barn while you two study and eat your snacks. See you in a little while, Lake."

After she's gone, Lake says to Carly, "Your mom's so cool."

"Yeah, she's alright. My dad's nice, too. I don't know if he'll be home before you have to leave, but you'll get to meet him when you stay over. Do you want to see the upstairs before we eat?"

"Yeah, totally."

Carly takes Lake up a set of stairs off the kitchen. At the top is a bathroom and a hallway that goes off in both directions. "My parent's room is down that way. My bedroom's down here next to the guest room." The hallway is long, dark, and narrow. Carly pushes a strange little button on the wall, and several lights come on in the hallway. Her bedroom looks out over the barn and the woods behind it. Lake can see Carly's mom walking in the barn.

Like every other room in the house, Carly's bedroom is immense. Her bed is definitely bigger than Lake's, and prettier. The frame is dark metal, and the tall headboard matches the footboard. All the other furniture in the room is made of wood and looks old; none of it matches.

But as Lake looks around, she gets the feeling it is mismatched on purpose. The random furniture is casually flawless and right.

Hanging in the corner by the closet are two large metal stars with holes in them. "A friend of my mom's made those. They're lights." Walking to the corner, Carly flips a switch on a cord Lake hadn't noticed, and the stars light up, tiny beams of light shooting out of each hole. The design cast about from the small shafts of light is beautiful. Lake wonders what it looks like at night and imagines having a similar setup in her own room. She'd use it as a cool night-light every single night.

Above the bedframe is a long strand of yarn with a bunch of fluffy, brightly colored feathers attached, each one pointing down toward the bed. Lake has never seen anything like it before. On the walls, Carly has hung posters and painted pictures of horses. There's a large, green cactus made of metal poking out of a wooden barrel near the foot of Carly's bed. "More Santa Fe artwork. My mom painted most of the pictures. This one's a real photo—it's Ruby."

Lake steps closer to get a better look. Standing alone in a field of flowers, its head turned to look at the camera, is a magnificent chestnut quarter horse, the most beautiful animal Lake has ever seen. "She's so pretty. Did you take that picture?"

"No, my mom took it. She framed it and gave it to me for my birthday."

"I love it," said Lake. "When's your birthday?"

"October seventeen. I'm a Libra. My mom knows everything about astrology. She says Librans are charming, beautiful, and well-balanced. Remind me to ask her about your sign when we take you home. She loves to tell people about their signs."

"Cool. I'll remind you."

Carly shows Lake her parents' room and Genevieve's art studio next to the bedroom. "This is where my mom keeps all her art stuff. Sometimes she paints in here, but she says the lighting in the kitchen is better because of the windows, so she usually paints there."

Just then, Carly's stomach emits a loud grumble, and she laughs. "Let's go eat and get some studying done before you have to go."

On the drive home, Lake reminds Carly to ask about her sign. "Mom, Lake doesn't know her sign. Can you tell her what she is and something about it?"

Genevieve's face lights up, and she says, "Sure. When's your birthday, Lake?"

"January twenty-six. I was born during the Great Blizzard of Nineteen Seventy-Eight."

"You're an Aquarius. The water bearer, a natural-born leader. Aquarians tend to be openminded souls who like to spend time thinking about how things can be better. Does that sound like you, Lake?"

"Maybe, I guess. I like solving problems, and I do think a lot. I really like to read, too."

"Sounds like you're a typical Aquarian. Librans and Aquarians are highly compatible in almost every way. I think you and Carly are destined to be best friends."

Carly looks at Lake and smiles. "I knew it! On the first day of school, when Mr. Bradshaw introduced me to Lake, I knew we were going to be best friends."

Lake's face feels hot, and she turns her head to look out the window. "My street is just up here, on the right."

When Genevieve pulls in the driveway, Lake can see her mom looking out the front window. She's at the open door before they reach the first step. Sylvia invites Carly and her mom inside, and the two women chat while Lake shows Carly around her boring, one-story house. After Carly and her mom leave, Sylvia says, "I just love Genevieve's bohemian style. She's a naturally pretty woman and very unconventional. She reminds me of Kiki." At the mention of Kiki's name, Lake's heart warms, and she smiles.

"I'm glad you like her. Carly invited me to spend the night next Friday."

#

Everything with Carly is easy. Lake's last remaining walls crack and crumble as the two girls form a bond unlike any Lake has experienced before. On the morning after Lake's first night in the Sommerville house, Carly introduces her to Ruby and the other horses. The modest barn is tidy, cold, and drafty, but not one of the three horses seems to mind, tucked away safely in their own private stalls. At the sound of Carly's voice, the spirited animals approach the stall gates and begin to whinny. "I guess they're happy to see us," says Carly.

Lake recognizes Ruby instantly. "You can pet her if you want," Carly says. "She's really sweet." Lake walks over to Ruby and rubs her forehead. Ruby nudges Lake's arm and shoulder. Standing next to Lake, Carly strokes Ruby's thick neck and says, "Okay, Miss Piggy, settle down. We don't have any carrots or apples. We just came to say hello. Ruby, this is Lake."

Still gently rubbing Ruby's forehead, Lake says, "Hi, Ruby."

"And these two are Shirley and Warren."

The two horses both have coats of light gold, but that's where the similarities end. The smaller of the two has a beautiful white mane and tail. The bigger one has a dark brown, almost black mane and tail. Lake asks, "Which one is which?"

"This pretty girl is Shirley, she's my mom's horse. And this guy over here is Warren, my dad's horse. They're named after some famous brother-and-sister movie stars I never heard of."

Lake slowly reaches out and rubs Shirley's head, saying hello. She does the same with Warren, who is noticeably bigger. Standing in front of his stall, Lake says, "He has dark socks to match his mane and tail. That's so cool."

"Yeah. My dad says Warren's a real looker, just like him. My mom laughs every time he says it. They're both so cheesy."

"I think your parents are really awesome. Everything about them is so different and rad."Rolling her eyes, Carly says, "If you say so, Lake. Your mom seems nice, too."

"She's not super hip, but she is nice. So is my dad. Whenever you stay over at my house, you'll get to meet him, and I'll show you the ranch and our horses. It's a fun place to hang out in the summer.

We have a pond and a big field where we used to play kickball and soccer."

"I'm not much of a jock, but the rest sounds neat. I can't wait to see your ranch. It's getting kind of cold. Let's go see if my 'totally rad' parents are up yet. Maybe one of them made breakfast."

#

Lake can sense that she's falling for Carly, but she refuses to use the same old Spin the Bottle trick on her. There's too much as stake with this friendship, and Lake can't risk ruining it or being disappointed. It's not an easy decision, but something tells Lake she's the right one. There has to be a reason Carly showed up at her school and chose Lake to be her best friend. Which is more important? Having a totally awesome best friend or a friend she makes out with once or twice before driving her away?

Sitting at their usual lunch table, Carly says, "I know you probably need to be with your family on your actual birthday, but my mom wanted me to ask if you want to come over the weekend after and spend the night at our house? She wants to make a special dinner to celebrate your birthday and thank you for helping me with school."

"I do usually spend my birthday with the family. It was always a tradition with my grandma Kiki. After she and my grandpa died, we just kept it up," says Lake.

"I get it. That's why we thought you could come over the weekend after. What kind of cupcakes do you like?"

"I always have strawberry cake with chocolate frosting, but I think I might try something different this year."

"Do you like s'mores? My mom makes this s'mores cake with chocolate and marshmallows, and it's so good. She even puts roasted marshmallows on top. I bet she could make s'mores cupcakes if you want."

Lake says, "I love s'mores!"

"Okay. I'll ask her to make s'mores cupcakes for us. Do you like tacos?"

"Yep."

"Awesome. We can have tacos for dinner, with guacamole, and s'mores cupcakes for dessert."

This is the first time Lake will celebrate her birthday twice, but it won't be the last.

At dinner, her dad asks, "Lake, do you want to have a birthday party this year and invite some friends from school? We don't have to have the party here. We could do a movie day at the cinema or have a pizza party in town."

"That sounds like fun, but I don't need to have a party with friends. It's always such yukky weather on my birthday, and it's on a Thursday this year. Mom could make party bags with cookies and glow sticks for me to take to school. That way everyone gets to be there. And we can have dinner as a family on the night of my birthday."

"If that's what you want," he says. "Are you sure?"

"Yeah, I'm sure. Carly asked me to stay over on the Friday night after my birthday. Her mom is making s'mores cupcakes to celebrate my birthday and to thank me for helping Carly get caught up in school."

"That's so nice of her," says her mom. "The Sommervilles are a wonderful family. Your dad and I are so proud of you, Lake."

For her family birthday celebration, Lake's mom doesn't ask what type of cake she wants. Sylvia assumes the answer will be the same as it always has been. Lake still loves spaghetti and meatballs with homemade bread, so when her mom makes it for her birthday celebration, Lake doesn't mind at all. But with her grandma Kiki being gone, Aunt Joe takes over making the cake. She bakes real strawberries into the mix, and it's the most delicious strawberry cake Lake has ever tasted. Jack and Sylvia buy Lake an authentic camera—with film and everything. She had talked about wanting one for her birthday, but they're kind of expensive. She can't believe it when she opens the box.

"Can I take it to Carly's tomorrow? I'll be careful."

"Yes, but you have to be extra careful with it. If dirt gets in the lens, it could damage it." "I promise, I'll be careful."

#

Michael and Genevieve are so cool, and the Sommerville house is funky with room to roam. Because Carly's dad works in an office, her parents are very relaxed with schedules on the weekends.

Weekdays are for work and school, but the weekends are for fun. As the days warm, Carly's parents encourage their daughter and Lake to explore the property and roam freely. Genevieve insists Lake can ride Shirley, and the two girls spend hours trotting along the trails behind Carly's house.

The friends develop a pattern that carries them through the summer. With miles of woods at their feet and no fear of the unknown, Lake and Carly discover new trails, secret clearings, and fern-lined creeks with felled trees where they can sit and eat the sack lunches packed with care by Genevieve. The wide-open space becomes their own private kingdom to talk about their personal thoughts, their budding sexuality—including periods!—things they aspire to become, and places they want to visit.

Lake has developed a real knack for photography, and along the way, she snaps photo after photo. Her favorites are the candid pictures of Carly taken when she doesn't know it's happened. Those, along with some of Lake and Carly together, fill a special album she keeps in a secret spot at the back of her closet. Because the book contains pictures of both girls, it won't raise suspicion with Sylvia or anyone else. Lake is becoming very good at masking her true feelings and intentions.

Late in the summer, the two girls are chilling on a shady log by their favorite creek. Carly asks, "Are you scared about starting seventh grade next month?"

"Not really, why? Are you?"

"I don't know. Kind of. I like having you as my best friend. I trust you, and we watch out for each other. I don't want that to change when we get to junior high. You never talk about boys, but what if you meet a cute boy and he asks you to go steady?"

"Believe me, that's not going to happen. Who has time for boys? I want to keep my grades up, play soccer. And...be your best friend..." As she says this, Lake gives Carly a playful punch in the arm.

Carly turns to have a better look at her friend. "What if *I* meet a cute boy? Would you be mad?"

Lake is instantly filled with jealousy. Boys have always ruined everything for her. She closes her eyes, trying to give the impression that she's pondering the question when all she really wants to do is scream. Then, as the jealous feelings subside, Lake says, "Why would I be mad? Besides, I've lived in this town all my life. There are no cute boys here!"

Laughing, Carly says, "I bet there's at least one. You don't know every boy in town."

To herself, Lake thinks, *Nope, and I don't want to.*

Chapter 9

On the first day of seventh grade, Lake and Carly have home-room together, which is reassuring for both girls because they get to start the school year—and every day of the year—together. They each take a seat, and soon the seats around them are filled one by one with boys and girls neither has ever seen before. There are four local elementary schools that feed into this junior high, and by the time the first bell rings, only a few faces in the room are familiar.

Carly taps Lake's desk. "What do you have first period?"

"Social studies," Lake replies.

"Ugh, I have math. It's probably better I have it in the morning than at the end of the day. It's my worst subject."

"Mine, too," says Lake. "At least we have science, English, and art together, and there's always lunch. We can sit together to eat."

Homeroom is a short period, and when the bell rings, Lake and Carly gather their books and head for the door. Waving, Carly says, "See you in third-period English. Save me a seat if you get there first."

"Okay, same. Bye," says Lake.

Changing classes every period is kind of fun, but Lake misses sitting behind Carly all day. When it's time for lunch, Lake is relieved to see Carly waiting for her in the hall outside the cafeteria. The two walk inside together, go through the line, then pick seats at a table near the windows. Gretchen sees them and heads their way. "Is it okay if I sit with you guys?"

"Sure," says Lake.

Setting her tray down, Gretchen says, "Thanks for letting me sit with you. I hardly recognize anyone here. How's your first day going?"

At the exact same time, Lake and Carly say, "It's good."

Pointing at Lake, Carly says, "Jinx! You owe me a Coke and a candy bar."

"You don't even drink Coke, you weirdo."

"Whatever. *You're* weird," jokes Carly.

Shaking her head, Lake asks Gretchen how her first day is going.

"It's okay. I kind of miss being in the same classroom all day, but I like that the school is bigger and there are new kids here. Are you playing soccer this year?"

"For sure. How about you?"

"Yeah. I talked to my dad about playing on a travel team next year. You should do it, too, Lake."

"Yeah, that'd be cool. It's a big commitment to play at school and on a travel team, but I'll think about it."

As the girls eat lunch, they compare schedules and check out the other kids until the bell rings. All three have eighth-period science together. What a way to end the day—with the periodic table of elements and frog dissection. Yuck.

Lake, Carly, and Gretchen are assigned to the same bus for the ride home, and they find seats next to each other.

Carly's stop is closer to the school, and when she gets up to leave, Gretchen takes her place next to Lake. It's a warm autumn day, and all the windows on the bus are down. As they pull away from Carly's driveway, Lake detects the faint scent of Pert shampoo and is immediately back in the hayloft with Gretchen, playing Spin the Bottle. Feeling as though she's cheating on Carly, Lake gives her head a shake, pushing the thought aside.

The bus is loud, but the familiar faces of her childhood friends and acquaintances is a plus. Approaching the ranch from a different direction, the bus stops at the railroad crossing near the mobile-home park where Gretchen lives. The driver looks both ways and crosses the tracks before slowing and eventually stopping for Gretchen and her group to get off. "See you tomorrow, Lake."

"Bye, Gretch, see you tomorrow."

During homeroom the next morning, Carly kicks Lake's desk with her foot and raises her hand. Mr. Savel is reading a book and doesn't notice Carly's raised hand. She waves frantically, but to no avail, and finally she stands and walks over to his desk. She says something to him, then quickly walks out the door. Lake has no idea what's happening, but she has no choice but to sit tight and wait for Carly to return. Carly walks back into class just as the bell rings. Lake looks at her, shrugging. "What's going on? Are you okay?"

Grabbing her arm, Carly pulls Lake out of the classroom and into the hall. "I just got my period!"

"What? Are you okay? Does it hurt?"

"What? No. Well, yeah, a little. I have cramps, and the nurse gave me this gross pad to wear. Can you see it? Can you tell I'm wearing a pad?"

Carly turns around so Lake can see her backside.

"No. I can't tell. You got your period! I can't believe it!"

"It's not that exciting, Lake. It's gross, and I don't like it. I can't believe this is going to happen every month for the rest of my life."

"I don't think that's how it works. I don't think you have it your whole life," says Lake.

"It still sucks. Just wait and see for yourself."

#

Seventh grade is mediocre at best. The days are longer, and the work is harder, but Lake is adapting. She and Carly know winter is coming, and they devote as many weekends as possible to sleepovers and riding the horses. Carly's twelfth birthday falls on a Saturday, and Lake has a soccer game early that morning, so they make plans for a Saturday night sleepover. Lake's team thrashes the visiting team, and she's feeling pumped up and excited to see Carly. For some strange reason, she wants to impress her. It was Lake who made the plays possible, setting her team up for the win. When her dad drops her off at Carly's house, she can't wait to tell her about it.

"Hey, weirdo. How was the big soccer game?" asks Carly.

"I wish you could have been there. We killed them. I killed it. I'm kind of amazing."

"Of course you are. You're Lake Myers, the force to be reckoned with," says Carly. Lake has shared the story of the day she was born with Carly and her family, and they loved it. Now they all call her "the force to be reckoned with."

"Whatever, weirdo. It was a good game," says Lake. "I *am* a force to be reckoned with, and don't ever forget it."

Giving Lake a friendly push, Carly says, "My mom packed us lunch. You ready to ride?"

"Yeah, let me just say hi to your parents and put my bag in your room."

After saying hello to Mr. and Mrs. Sommerville, Lake and Carly ride along their favorite path by the creek. The days are getting cooler, and the leaves are starting to fall. It's a perfect day to ride and hang out together. Along the way, Lake and Carly talk about school, whether or not they are too old for trick-or-treating, and eventually, boys.

"I thought you might be right about the boy situation, Lake, but then along comes Christopher Thomas."

Damn, Carly. Just punch me in the stomach, why don't you, Lake thinks to herself.

"Christopher sits next to me in math, and he's so smart. I think I might ask him to tutor me," says Carly.

Lake responds a little too fast with, "I can help you with your math. We can stay after school and meet with our math teachers, too. They'll help you if you ask them."

"I know, but it's not the same. Christopher is so cute. I'm not failing or anything, but if it gets too hard, I'll ask him to help me. Don't you think he's cute?"

"I don't really know him. Which one is he again?" asks Lake.

Sighing, Carly responds, "You know who he is, Lake. Tall, dreamy smile, dark hair like mine. He plays soccer, for crying out loud. I know you've seen him before."

Lake knows exactly who Christopher is. He's a good soccer player, and he *is* cute. She just doesn't want to admit that to Carly.

Bored with the conversation, Lake says, "Oh yeah. I do know him. He's okay-looking."

"He's cute, and you know it," says Carly, a little too emphatically.

Trying to play it cool, Lake says, "Okay, he's cute." She has made the promise to Carly that she wouldn't be mad if she liked a boy or went steady. So now she has to act like it doesn't matter. They're still best friends, and she will always love Carly, no matter what. Today's her birthday, and Lake doesn't want to spoil it.

Changing the subject, Lake asks, "So what do you think you're getting for your birthday?"

"I'm not sure. I asked for a new saddle and to start taking riding lessons again. I want to learn how to barrel race."

"That's so cool, Carly. I didn't know you wanted to barrel race. My grandpa Kevin used to barrel race. He was really good at it."

"I know. I saw his ribbons and trophies in your barn. That's kind of what made me think of it."

Lake loves that Carly wants to barrel race and that it is her grandpa Kevin who has made her want to try it. She kind of really wants to kiss Carly right now, but she knows she can't. Not now. Maybe never.

Getting up from her spot, Lake brushes the crumbs off her pants. "We'd better head back. It's your birthdaaaay, Carly Sommerville. Twelve years old! Let's go."

Using a nearby tree branch for leverage, Carly pulls herself up and lets out a loud, "Woooo-hooo, it's my birthdaaaay!" that startles the horses.

"Okay, weirdo. Let's ride," says Lake.

Back at the house, Carly's mom is busy in the kitchen. You can take the family out of the Southwest, but you can't take the Southwest out of the family. The whole house smells deliciously sweet. "Lake, you're in for a special treat tonight," says Genevieve. "I'm making all of Carly's favorites in honor of her twelfth birthday. This is the last birthday before you're both teenagers! You girls grow up too fast. Us moms just wish the time wouldn't pass so quickly." *She sounds just like my mom*, thinks Lake.

Carly's mom has used stencils to make a brightly colored menu, and it rests on a small wooden easel in the middle of the table. On the menu for Carly's birthday dinner are shredded chicken burritos; black beans with *cotija* cheese, whatever that is; *horchata*, another thing she's never heard of; and for dessert, s'mores cake. Mispronouncing the name of the cheese, Lake asked, "What's *cotija* cheese and *horchata*?"

Smiling at Lake, Mr. Sommerville says, "*Cotija* cheese is a salty white cheese that makes everything taste better. It's the Parmesan cheese of Mexico. Do you like Parmesan cheese?"

"Love it! My mom says I smother my spaghetti and meatballs with it."

"Then you'll like *cotija* cheese. *Horchata* is a sweet drink made with milk, rice, cinnamon, vanilla, and ice. Mrs. Sommerville spent all day making it just for Carly."

"It sounds delicious," says Lake.

Genevieve says, "Dinner will be ready at six o'clock, girls. I'll call you when the table is set and we're ready to eat."

#

Lake eats everything on her plate and probably could have eaten seconds if she hadn't been saving room for cake. The *horchata* is her favorite. She loves spending time at Carly's house. Sometimes she wishes she lived here with them.

After the table is cleared, Michael turns out the lights and Genevieve carries in a tall s'mores cake covered in toasted marshmallows and twelve sparkling candles. She sets the cake in front of Carly, and Michael starts singing "Happy Birthday." Lake and Carly's mom join in, and when it's over, Michael adds in a deep voice, "And maaaaany more." Carly looks at each of their faces, squeezes her eyes closed tight, and keeps them closed for a couple seconds before opening them wide. Drawing in a deep breath, she blows at the candles hard. The light on each of the twelve candles is extinguished by her breath. Just as they begin to clap, suddenly all twelve candles magically reignite. Carly blows again, harder this time. The candles go out, then light right back up. In a pissed-off voice, Carly asks, "What is happening right now?"

Michael and Genevieve start laughing, and Michael says, "Surprise. We used trick candles on your cake!"

"Not funny, guys! Now my wish won't come true," says Carly.

Michael says, "Oh, Carly, that's not true. It was just a joke. And besides, you blew every single one of them out on your first try. So technically, you still get your wish."

"I hope that's true, Dad. I really want a new saddle." Realizing she's just revealed her birthday wish, Carly immediately covers her mouth with her hand.

Genevieve winks at Carly and cuts the cake. What a fun birthday! Lake really does love the Sommervilles.

While Carly's mom plates the cake, Lake hands Carly her gift. "I hope you like it."Ripping through the paper, Carly sees a small white jewelry box. She pulls off the lid and finds two purple-beaded bracelets; each has a puzzle piece hanging from it. "I love them, Lake, they're so pretty."

Beaming from ear to ear, Lake says, "The bracelets were my idea. I told your mom what I wanted to do. Then I bought all the stuff at the craft store, and she helped me make them. The puzzle pieces fit together perfectly, like you and me. They're friendship bracelets, and we each get one."

Taking them from the box, Carly hands one of the bracelets to Lake and puts the other one on her wrist. Lake put hers on her wrist, and the two immediately hold the puzzle pieces up, fitting one inside the other.

#

The s'mores cake is delicious! After they finish eating their slices, Michael helps Genevieve clear the table and says, "There *may* be a gift for you in the living room, Carly. Why don't you go check it out?"

Jumping up from her seat at the table, Carly says, "C'mon, bestie. Let's see what it is!" Lake follows Carly to the living room.

Michael had built a fire in the fireplace before dinner, and the glowing room feels warm and homey. In front of the fireplace is a wooden horse with a brand-new saddle draped over it. The saddle is wrapped in an enormous purple bow, Carly's favorite color. Carly squeals with joy. "I got the saddle I wanted! Isn't is awesome? The leather smells so good!"

Michael and Genevieve are standing in the living room doorway, pleased to see Carly happy.

Carly turns and hugs them, one arm around each parent. As she pulls away, Genevieve hands her a card.

Carly opens it, and a small business card falls out. It's from the stables a few miles down the road. Carly flips it over; the back is blank. Unsure what to do with the card, she looks at her parents and shrugs.

"We signed you up for riding lessons at the stables. You start next week, and you can try out your new saddle then."

Carly lets out an enthusiastic, "Yay, me! A new saddle *and* riding lessons. Woop-woop!"

#

With everything they have going on, Carly and Lake decide to skip trick-or-treating and have a movie night at Carly's instead. Lake hates scary movies, but Carly has insisted. Lake is so scared during the movie that she pees a little in her pants. After that, they have just one good riding weekend before the first snow comes.

For Thanksgiving break, the Sommervilles spend the holiday in Santa Fe. Genevieve misses New Mexico, warmer weather, the mountains, friends, and family. It is the longest amount of time the girls have been apart since they met.

Jack and Sylvia are hosting Thanksgiving dinner this year, and Lake is excited to spend the day with her family. Genevieve gave Sylvia her *horchata* recipe, and she promised to make a pitcher of the sweet drink for the kids to have with dinner. It reminds Lake of Carly's birthday and how much she misses her. She's developed a habit of spinning her friendship puzzle bracelet around and around her wrist when she thinks about Carly, and this week has been pure torture. She's counting down the days until the Sommervilles are back. They won't be home until late Sunday afternoon, which means she won't see Carly until school on Monday.

On the morning after Thanksgiving, Lake wakes up feeling weird. Her stomach hurts, and she thinks maybe she has peed in her pants a little again. When she goes to the bathroom, she looks down and sees blood on her panties. She got her period! "Mom! Mom! Are you out there?"

Lake hears shuffling and footsteps approaching the bathroom door.

Concerned, Sylvia says, "What is it, Lake, what's wrong?"

"Can you come in here, please? But don't look at me."

Sylvia opens the door and can see Lake sitting on the toilet. She steps inside the bathroom and turns so that she's facing the door. "Okay, what's going on?"

"I got my period. I need one of those pads you showed me, but I don't want to stand up. There's blood in my underwear and a little in the toilet."

"It's going to be okay, Lake." Sylvia opens the linen closet and pulls out a pad. Backing up, she offers the pad to Lake without looking at her. "Do you need me to show you how to use it?"

"Ew, Mom, *no!*"

"Okay. Do you want me to get you a clean pair of underwear?"

Lake thinks about this for a second. She wants her mom to leave, but she could also use the clean underwear. "Yes, can you grab a pair out of my room and toss them to me?"

Shaking her head, Sylvia leaves the bathroom, muttering, "For Pete's sake, child. I know what a period is all about."

Sylvia opens the bathroom door and walks in, not bothering to avert her eyes from Lake. She hands the panties to Lake, who is still sitting on the toilet. "Are you sure you don't need my help?"

"I'm sure, Mom. Can you please just leave?" begs Lake.

Sighing loudly, Sylvia does as she is asked and walks out of the bathroom. "My baby's getting older," she says quietly. "Oh, how I miss when they were little!"

Lake has so much to tell Carly when she gets back!

#

The first week back at school after Thanksgiving is the longest week ever. Ever since Carly told Lake about her crush on Christopher, she's started acting a little goofy around him in math class. It pains Lake to listen to her friend go on and on about Christopher, a dumb twelve-year-old boy who pays no attention at all to her advances. To him, Carly doesn't even exist. Lake knows better than to look a gift horse in the mouth, though, and she says nothing. There's no need for her to worry about Christopher Thomas. The two best friends remain faithful to their routine weekend sleepovers, and even their menstrual cycles are soon in sync.

A couple weeks before Lake's twelfth birthday, the two are both on their periods and planning a fabulous "period party" to celebrate their pre-womanhood, as well as Lake's Sommerville birthday bash.

Mexican fare is now a birthday tradition at the Sommervilles, and this year, Lake's birthday dessert is homemade *churros* with caramel and chocolate dipping sauces. After dinner and dessert, the foursome cozy up to the fireplace to play board games. Michael and Genevieve let Lake win the final game of the night before announcing they're going to go watch a movie in bed. "Good night, you two. Don't stay up too late. We'll see you at breakfast." Genevieve kisses Carly on the cheek and squeezes Lake's shoulder before following Michael up the stairs.

"Do you want to watch a movie in my bedroom? It's your birthday, Lake, we can watch anything you want."

"I don't feel like watching a movie. Let's just watch whatever show is on."

"'K. Let's get our pajamas on and get in bed," says Carly.

All the floors in Carly's house are hardwood and cool to their feet as they walk to Carly's room. Lake changes into her pajamas and dives under the covers of Carly's bed. "It's kind of chilly in your room tonight," she says, snuggling closer to Carly. The warmth of her body is better than the blankets. The two girls are wired from all the sugar, and neither is that interested in watching TV.

Turning so that she can see Lake's face, Carly says in a hushed voice, "Do you ever make that zingy thing happen when you can't sleep?"

Lake has no idea what she's talking about. "What 'zingy thing'?"

"Seriously, weirdo. Do I have to spell it out for you? Wait. That's it. I can show you by spelling it out."

Confused, Lake looks at Carly.

Without warning, Carly leans closer and kisses Lake on the lips.

"Now that I have your attention, here comes the spelling lesson," whispers Carly as she begins to draw circles on Lake's shoulder. Using just her fingertips, the circles get bigger and smaller as Carly takes her time moving down Lake's arm. On the back of her hand, Carly pauses to spell something that Lake can't quite make out. Carly laughs nervously and resumes the circular motion, moving back up Lake's arm, resting lightly at her shoulder. Lake is certain that Carly is about to kiss her again when she pushes Lake away from her, so that she's lying flat on her back. "Close your eyes, birthday girl." Lake does as she's told and closes her eyes.

Excited and nervous, Lake feels movement on her pajama top. Carly is drawing curlicues down the center of her chest. Lake inhales sharply as Carly moves lightly across each of her breasts. It feels good. No one has ever touched Lake's breasts before. Carly slides her fingertips to Lake's belly and lingers for a moment before going a little farther down. Using the top of Lake's panties as a guide, Carly's fingers draw a line from one side to the other. Returning to the center, just below her navel, Carly's back to drawing circles on her belly. When the circles stop, Carly clearly spells Lake's full name on the outside of her panties going just a little lower with each letter. The sensations are incredible, and even though Lake is unsure of what's happening, she definitely wants Carly to keep going. But then she stops, just like that, and says, "Now you do the same thing to me."

Lake is worried she won't be able to make Carly feel as good, but she does her best to follow the same path Carly took with her. When she gets to Carly's panties, she begins lightly tracing the letters spelling Carly's first and last names. Just as she starts to trace the second *M* in Sommerville, Carly's hand is there next to hers, rubbing the outside of her panties, but lower. She starts to breathe heavy, and then she begins to move her hips and makes strange moaning noises. Lake has no idea what's happening, but she senses that she should keep doing what she's doing and allow Carly to feel this pleasure the two are creating together. Carly rubs faster and faster, and Lake can feel Carly's body tensing up before she lets out a soft moan like whatever has just happened felt really good. Her body twitches a couple of times and begins to relax. Lake takes that as her cue to stop the tracing, her hand resting on Carly's lower belly. The two are quiet until Carly rolls over and kisses Lake again.

She has to know, and so Lake asks, "Carly, what was that? What did you do just now?"

"What do you mean?" asks Carly.

"I feel like something really important just happened. I just don't know what it was."

"Are you kidding me, Lake? I just touched myself until I made that Zingy Thing happen."

"Zingy Thing? I don't know what that is. I've never touched myself and made that happen before."

"You're serious? Okay, we have to make your Zingy Thing happen. Do you want to try?"

"Yeah, I think I do."

And just like that, Carly is kissing Lake again and tracing outlines of something outside of her panties. Lake closes her eyes, concentrating on her *special place* and how Carly's fingers make her feel. When she gets to the point she was at last time, before Carly stopped, she moves her own hand to the general area Carly's hand was and starts rubbing up and down. The sensation is more intense than anything she's ever felt, and Lake naturally applies more pressure and moves a little faster, but not too fast. At some point, she forgets Carly is even there. Lake is alone with this insane new feeling. Her body down there is like a volcano, building an intense jumble of tingles from deep inside her, until the pulsing is so strong it's almost unbearable. The tingly sensation suddenly peaks, and warmth and good sensations flow through every part of her special place. When it's over, Lake feels incredibly relaxed and happy. This Zingy Thing is definitely something she wants to experience again.

#

Lake is drawn to Carly and her family for plenty of reasons. Being in their home makes Lake feel instinctively secure, but at the same time, genuinely unsure of what's acceptable and what isn't. The line is blurred, and Lake is cautious, but not to the point of stopping what she and Carly do now—behavior she adopts and rarely deviates from for all the years to come.

The next time the girls experience the Zingy Thing, Carly takes a slightly different, but equally enjoyable approach. Propped against a mountain of pillows, Carly says, "Give me your hand." Lake places her hand on top of Carly's. Flipping it over, Carly uses her fingers to trace lines all around the inside of Lake's palm, fingers, and wrist, and the inside of her forearm. To Lake's surprise, it feels amazing! And the best part is there's no talk of boys; this is just about making Lake feel good.

Appreciating her handiwork, Carly says, "Here's a tip. You can use your fingertips to spell words or draw figures on any part of the body to make the other person feel good. Doesn't matter what part, and it doesn't matter what you write or draw. If you do it slow and soft, it'll feel good. That's all you have to remember. You can spell out the alphabet or count to ten, it makes no difference at all. My dad always says he's good at his job because he "keeps it simple." Same thing here. Got it?"

Nodding her head, Lake thinks Carly is really smart and worldly. Lake has never felt like this before, and she hopes the two are best friends forever.

#

Lake has never liked that her birthday is in January, one of the coldest months of the year. But now she doesn't mind at all. Succumbing to the confines of the warm indoors isn't half bad because she and Carly have discovered each other and new ways to make that Zingy Thing happen.

The weekend of Lake's twelfth birthday was an awakening, with Carly teaching Lake the most amazing thing ever, and it becomes a regular part of their sleepovers. It isn't uncomfortable or weird for either of them. It feels good, and more importantly, it feels normal and right.

April showers bring May flowers, and life is good for Lake and Carly. Being outdoors is once again an option, and the two return to long weekend rides in the woods. Lake is happier than she's ever been. Her positive outlook transforms her body, mind, and soul, and she radiates confidence and strength. The prior monotony of her day-to-day life is a distant memory. Each morning presents a new opportunity to be great and to see Carly.

On a pinkie swear, the girls promise to maintain their routines during the busy summer months. Lake is committed to playing soccer on two different leagues, and Carly will continue her riding lessons and winning horsemanship. With two barrel-racing ribbons on her wall, Carly is kicking butt in the arena, and Lake has her star soccer moves and excellent grades. If they were a couple, they'd be unstoppable. Their crush is mutual, but their love and the future of what they will be to each other is not.

Sitting at the Sommervilles' kitchen table, Lake and Carly laugh and hold their *horchatas* high as they toast to celebrate the end of seventh grade. Genevieve and Michael drink margaritas from cactus-shaped glasses with salted rims. Following the girls' lead, Genevieve raises her glass high and says, "Your father has an announcement to make."

All eyes move to Carly's dad as he says, "My company is expanding, and I've been offered a position leading a team in a new office. We're moving to San Diego at the end of June. Isn't that terrific? We'll have a place near the ocean, and Lake can visit whenever she wants!"

Well, ain't that a kick in the pants! flashes through Lake's mind. Utterly heartbroken, she is unable to speak. Why is the worst news always delivered at the kitchen table?

"Oh my gosh, Dad. Way to spring the news on us," says Carly.

"I wasn't sure until today, Carly, or I would have said something sooner. But the timing couldn't be better. School's out, and you girls can still have fun together for a few weeks until it's time to move."

Seemingly unfazed, Carly raises her glass again and says, "Congratulations, Dad. I've always wanted to go to California. We have a lot of planning to do, Lake. Maybe you can even visit before school starts again."

Lake has her doubts, but she is determined not to let her feelings of dejection ruin the time they have left together.

#

Carly and Lake are inseparable right up to the day the Sommervilles leave. On their last night together, they kiss and make that Zingy Thing happen one last time. Bodies touching, Lake says, "I can't believe you're leaving tomorrow. I'm going to miss you so much. You're my best friend, Carly Sommerville, and—" What she wants to say is, *"I'm in love with you,"* but adding just two extra words will change the meaning entirely and open Lake up for more heartache and rejection than she can handle right now. So instead she compromises her true feelings and goes with the shorter, more acceptable phrase: "And . . . I love you."

Carly scooches closer and throws her leg over Lake's. "I love you, too, weirdo. We'll always be best friends. My moving to California isn't going to change that."

A tear rolls down the side of Lake's face because she knows that isn't true. *Everything* will change once Carly is gone. Silently crying, Lake falls asleep holding Carly's hand under the covers.

#

Where we come from and whom we interact with shapes and molds our being. It's as much a part of the tapestry of our lives as our DNA. Lake's biggest influences so far have been her grandma Kiki and the Sommerville family.

Sexuality is such an odd thing to decipher, and in her twelve and a half short years, Lake has crushed on more girls than boys. There's no way the first of her many infatuations was random. She was just eight years old when "Joey, the tomboy" came into her life, and she was attracted to her immediately. She never told anyone that she dreamed about kissing Joey and touching her in places that are supposed to be private. Something innate spoke to Lake, willing her to keep her thoughts to herself, burying those feelings deep down inside, locked away for no part of the outside world to see.

Lake is forever grateful for the life lessons imparted to her from her much-loved grandma Kiki and her trendy extended family, the Sommervilles. Both accepted her as she was, considerately curating her individuality and encouraging independent thought.

Family. You take what you get, and you don't throw a fit.

Chapter 10 – Maxen

Losing Carly and her family to California is an unexpected turn. Lake and Carly had established a comfortable routine and had planned their entire future together. But real life got in the way, sending the two girls down alternate paths that will never again intersect, notwithstanding their good intentions.

Lake and Carly write one another regularly and take turns calling every other Sunday. But life in California is sunny, shiny, and new. Carly talks nonstop about living near the beach and how the warm, salty air agrees with her family. Every night after dinner, the Sommervilles walk their new dog, Doug, down to the water's edge, where he chases the tides while the family oohs and aahs over the brilliant Pacific Ocean sunsets. It takes no time at all for Carly to meet new friends and make different plans for her future, plans that no longer include her former best friend in Ohio.

Lake tries to be supportive, but her own reality hasn't changed at all. By the time the holidays roll around, the letters have stopped, and the phone calls have all but dried up. The families exchange Christmas cards and wish one another a happy new year. The year 1990 coming to a close signifies the official end of Lake's life with Carly. She'll be a teenager soon, and it's time to start plotting her own course. One that doesn't revolve around a secret love or circumstances she can't control. She has no idea what she wants to do with the rest of her life, but what Lake knows for certain is that it will be her choice.

\#

On the eve of her thirteenth birthday, Lake puts pen to paper, setting her intentions in permanent ink. What does she like? What is she good at? Sitting on her bed, she ponders the questions and jots down the answers in her private journal. She likes horses, being outside, reading, soccer, and girls. She likes girls!

She thinks about what it would be like to have a real girlfriend, but she has no idea how to find one without revealing the fact that she's not like everyone else. At the end of her last sentence for the night, Lake draws a sad face, closes the journal, and falls back onto her pillows. When they aren't in class or on the soccer field, conversations between Lake and her friends naturally turn to boys. Instead of naming a real, live boy at her school, Lake comments on cute boy actors or singers that all of her friends are familiar with. Her go-to is Uncle Jesse from *Full House*. Lake speaks of him so often, even her friends buy in to the concept that Lake and Jesse are an exclusive, albeit imaginary couple. It's the perfect smokescreen to hide behind, and Lake uses it to her advantage all through her early teen years.

At school, she keeps her head down, works hard, and plays harder. She's a popular girl, and she gets along well with pretty much everyone. With a depressing understanding of what it feels like to be different, Lake lives life on the periphery. It's easier to keep friends and classmates at arm's length and avoid conversations about her true feelings for boys and girls. At a time when everyone is working extra hard to fit in, Lake steers clear of the cliques, careful not to get too chummy with any one circle at school. This approach to life places Lake in a different realm entirely. Her teachers, unaware of her true intentions, deeply admire her focus and maturity. Seizing the opportunity to channel Lake's motivation as a means to help others, two of her teachers ask if she's willing to tutor a couple of her classmates in English and history, Lake's two best subjects. On the promise of racking up extra-credit points, she agrees.

#

Kelsey Juneau moved to Geneva when she was eleven. She has never actually failed a grade, but she did come close a couple of times. She holds her breath until her final grades are posted, but she skims by, barely passing the seventh grade. Unenthusiastic and unwilling to do better, Kelsey is more than satisfied with just getting by. Staring at the big, round clock on the wall in front of the class, she watches the second hand push the minute hand closer to half past the hour. At two thirty, the bell rings, and she's free to sit in study hall and do nothing until it's finally time to go home. Three, two, one...time to exit

Mr. Claus's room and meander down the hall to the last part of this boring-ass day.

"Kelsey, please come to my desk before you leave the classroom," she hears Mr. Claus say.

Throwing her head back, she sighs loudly before getting up. Shuffling her feet, Kelsey slowly makes her way to the front of the class. She's the only student left in the room.

"Have a seat please," says Mr. Claus. When she's settled, he continues. "I've been looking over your homework. You haven't turned in the last three assignments. You promised to get those to me, but I still don't have them. Why is that?"

"I tried, like, for real. I just couldn't get through the chapters. History is so boring, no offense, but it is. It's just a bunch of random dates and, like, things that happened a long time ago."

"You're going to fail my class if you don't complete the assignments. I spoke with Lake Myers, though, and she's willing to tutor you during eighth-period study hall."

Damn! Eighth-period study hall is her coveted naptime/nothingness period. Feeling completely cheated, Kelsey asks, "What if I say no?"

"It's your choice, Kelsey. Work with Lake and turn in the missing assignments, or don't and fail the class."

"Fine. I'll do the tutoring."

"I think that's a wise decision. Starting tomorrow, you'll meet with Lake in the library instead of going to study hall. She'll have the assignments you need to complete. If you're able to finish them by the end of next week, I won't mark them as late."

"Okay. Is that it?" Kelsey asks rudely.

"That's it. See you tomorrow, Kelsey."

#

Lake and Kelsey have had no reason to interact prior to the tutoring sessions. Kelsey is part of the "burnout" bunch at school. Before the morning bell, she and the other stoners can be found lounging in the visitors' dugout section of the varsity baseball field at the far end of campus. The field sits on the edge of the woods and provides a reasonable amount of privacy with the dugout facing the woods. Everyone knows the group hangs out there to smoke weed, but no one really cares. At least not enough to do anything about it. Kelsey Juneau is a classmate whom Lake agrees to tutor because she loves history and enjoys helping other students with the subject. Beyond this, she has no agenda or desire to become friends.

She's been waiting almost ten minutes when Kelsey finally shows up at the library. Lake is kind of miffed that Kelsey is late on her first day of tutoring. Waving her hand in the air, Lake signals to Kelsey from across the room. Trying her best not to be cranky right off the bat, she smiles and introduces herself. "Hi, Kelsey. I'm Lake, your tutor."

In a snarky voice, Kelsey says, "I know who you are. I've seen you playing soccer."

"Yeah, I've played since I was a kid. I'm hoping to get a soccer scholarship and play for a college somewhere out of state."

"Oh yeah? What state?" asks Kelsey.

Lake shrugs her shoulders and says, "One that's not Ohio."

"Well, I've lived in places outside of Ohio. They weren't much better than here."

"Good to know. Do you want to get started with the history assignments?"

"Sure. Whatever," says Kelsey.

Lake pulls the first assignment from the folder labeled *Kelsey Juneau* and starts at the top. As they work through each of the questions, she soon realizes Kelsey knows most of the answers—she just doesn't care enough to do the work.

"Why didn't you do this assignment on your own and turn it in?" asks Lake.

"I don't know. I guess I didn't feel like it," is Kelsey's reply. Lake thinks about this for a few seconds. She understands not wanting to get up in the morning, and not wanting to eat all of her vegetables—especially asparagus, she really doesn't like asparagus—but not completing a homework assignment because she doesn't feel like doing it? This is a totally foreign concept to her.

"Well, I promised Mr. Claus I'd help you get caught up. Are you trying to fail your history class?"

"Not really. But what does it matter, anyway? I don't plan to go to college. Not in Ohio or any other state."

"So, what do you want to do after high school?" asks Lake.

"I haven't really thought about it all that much. Maybe go to cosmetology school. It might be cool to cut people's hair."

"You need to graduate from high school before you go to cosmetology school. You know this history stuff, Kelsey. I'll help you as much as you want, but you have to do the work," says Lake.

Kelsey stiffens and says, "Damn, you sound like Mr. Claus. I'll do the work with you, just get off my back."

Lake can see that Kelsey is trying to act tough, but she doesn't really understand why. Even if Kelsey doesn't want to go to college, she at least has to finish high school. What kind of job could she be possibly be qualified for without a high school diploma?

When the bell rings, Lake and Kelsey have finished two assignments. Not bad for having less than a whole period to work through them.

#

Lake meets with Kelsey three times a week for the next month and a half. Their relationship is all business, and Kelsey runs from the library like her ass is on fire as soon as the final bell rings. Lake wonders what she has going on that's so freaking important.

Lake finally decides to ask one day. "Why are you in such a hurry to get out of here when the bell rings? Where do you go after school?"

With arched eyebrows, Kelsey responds, "What's it to you, soccer girl?"

"It's not. Whatever."

"So why'd you even ask?"

"I just think it's weird that you run out of here so fast when we're done. Seriously. Whatever."

"Well, if you must know, I have to catch the bus home."

"Okay, so you catch the bus. What's the rush? The buses don't leave that quick after school."

"I *can't miss* the bus! If I do, my dad has to come get me, and he gets really mad if he has to leave work early."

Kelsey is clearly agitated by this line of questioning. Lake feels bad for upsetting Kelsey and says, "Look, it's okay. I'm sorry I asked."

"It's fine. Forget it," says Kelsey.

Lake doesn't understand why Kelsey's so upset, but she doesn't want to make it worse, so she doesn't say anything else.

Grabbing her notebook from her bag, Kelsey says, "I got my test back in class today. I got a C-plus, and so that gives me a C in history. I have a C!"

"That's great, Kelsey!"

"Yeah, Mr. Claus was totally stoked when he handed me my paper. Thanks, Lake."

Now it's Lake's turn to arch her eyebrows. "For what?"

"For helping me. It's kind of cool not to be failing history."

Lake smiles and says, "You're welcome. You should be proud. It's very cool you're not failing history."

"I want to cut hair after I graduate and get my own place one day. I don't have to get perfect grades or play soccer to do that. I just need to graduate and go to cosmetology school," says Kelsey.

"True. But soccer's not so bad."

"Do you have a boyfriend, Lake?"

That came out of left field. Caught off-guard, Lake says, "No. I don't have time for a boyfriend. And I don't really want one."

Kelsey looks at Lake and says, "Sure. Whatever, Lake."

"What's that supposed to mean?" asks Lake, with just a bit too much hostility in her voice.

"Like, all the kids in this stupid school are pairing up like it's their fucking job, and you 'don't want a boyfriend'? Get real."

Lake is stunned. How did this tutoring session turn into an interrogation so fast? And why is her face so hot? This conversation isn't about her; it's about Kelsey and her shitty grades.

"Yeah, that's right. I don't want a boyfriend. Relationships are a distraction, and I can't risk getting bad grades or losing my focus in soccer. I don't have time for a boyfriend right now. You just don't get it!"

Lake needs to calm down. If she freaks too hard, Kelsey will just keep hounding her. *Stick to your story and then change the subject.* The last thing she needs is Kelsey, the stoner, thinking she's anything other than normal and blabbing to her stupid friends.

Lake takes a deep breath and says, "Think about what you've done in history. You worked with me and focused on the assignments, and now you're passing the class. I said I was sorry. Can we just get through the assignment for today?" Forcing a smile, Lake adds, "We need to make sure you pass *all* of your classes."

Shoving an assignment across the table, Kelsey says, "I need you to proofread my English paper. It's due tomorrow."

When the bell rings, Kelsey can't leave the library fast enough! Lake rubs her eyes and rests her head in her hands. She's pissed she let Kelsey rile her up like that. *As if!*

There's no way Kelsey really knows anything for sure, but Lake sure as heck doesn't like the direction that conversation was going. Kelsey is smarter than people think. She could easily be pulling Bs in most of her classes if she really wanted to. Tossing her backpack over her shoulder, Lake feels relieved. She doesn't have to meet with Kelsey again until next week.

#

The next time Lake meets with Kelsey, it's like nothing ever happened. The overt inquiry and awkward conversation are all but forgotten. But Lake knows the suspicion and questioning will return if she doesn't do something to prevent it from bubbling up again. This is exactly why she can't let her guard down or allow herself to get close to anyone. The pain she felt when Carly and her family left still tugs at her heart, and she had trusted them one hundred percent. The thought of being exposed deliberately—or by accident—for wanting to be with girls is nearly paralyzing, and Lake knows she has to do whatever it takes to secure her future until she is far away from the present.

Memorial Day weekend marks the official opening of Ohio's oldest resort, known as the Strip. Geneva on the Lake's milelong "main drag" is lined with souvenir shops, arcades, food spots, mini golf courses, the best donut shop in all of Ohio, and a whole bunch of bars. It's a longstanding Myers family tradition to spend the entire Saturday of the holiday weekend at the Strip—along with everyone else in northeast Ohio. Bikers from every part of the state make the pilgrimage to the Strip to raucously usher in the start of the summer party. The roar of hundreds of bikes coming down the strip sets off a tingling in your toes that becomes a rumbling in your belly as the throngs of bikers approach. The first time Lake experienced the passing procession, the intense quiver made every hair on her body stand at attention. Impossible to look away, the feeling started in the pit of her belly and built to a crescendo slowly pulsing outward to each of her extremities. The wondrous event lasted several minutes as hundreds of bikes traveling two by two up one side of the two-lane divided road passed by. The sounds and vibrations of the bikes grabbed hold of Lake and created a lasting memory she would forever associate with summer in her hometown.

The weather is cooperating early that Saturday morning, and the sun shines brightly through the blinds in Lake's bedroom. She blinks a few times as her eyes adjust to the light. The anticipation of a fresh creamstick donut makes her mouth water. Kicking off the covers, she gets out of bed and quickly dresses for a day at the Strip. Home for the summer, even Pete and Jeannie are excited about the day.

Walking past her room, Lake hears her dad ask, "Hey, kiddo, you awake?"

"Yeah, I'll be out in a minute."

"Okay, don't take too long. You know I like to get a good parking spot near the middle of the Strip."

Lake called back through her door, "I know, Dad. We've been doing this every year for my whole life."

"So, humor your old dad and shake a leg. Getting your mom and all you kids in the car is worse than rounding up the horses."

On their third pass down the Strip, Jack spots the glow of a taillight and brakes to allow the car in front of him to pull out. Right blinker on, he eases up alongside the car in front of the open spot, and expertly finagles the family sedan into the waiting space. If asked to list his top three skills, he would for sure say parallel parking was one of them, and today he's proven it. He has snagged a primo spot directly across the street from the donut shop. Never one to overlook her husband's accomplishments, Sylvia's left hand moves to the back of Jack's neck, and her fingers lightly squeeze the area just below his hairline. "Great job with the parking, hon. Let's go get a donut!"

As soon as Jeanne opens the car door, the sweet smell of donuts rushes in. Lake can see the line isn't too long right now. "I'll go get us a spot in line!" she says. The family waits patiently for their turn at the sweet creamy treat. By the time they make it to the front of the line, each one of the Myers has seen and spoken with at least one passing friend or acquaintance. The kids are old enough to branch out alone after the morning donuts, and they all promise to meet back up with the family for lunch. At noon, they will work through the ceremonial burgers, fries, and chili dogs, and afterward all three children will go their separate ways again until it's time for mini golf, a slice of pizza, and maybe even ice cream at the end of the day.

At lunch, Lake and her family grab a booth next to the Longs. Lake and Claire Long were close in grade school, but they haven't spent much time together since then. Both are good students and have plans for college, but Claire's in the marching band and Key Club, while Lake plays soccer for two different teams and tutors kids in history and English.

Getting up from her table, Claire walks over to talk to her childhood friend. "Hey, Lake, long time, no talk. How's it going?"

"It's good. I'm glad it's almost summer." Lake's face feels flushed as she briefly recalls the day she tricked Claire into playing Spin the Bottle. A calamitous memory she'd like to forget. Claire doesn't seem to notice Lake's momentary bout of shame.

"A new arcade opened down near my house. Do you want to check it out?" asks Claire.

"Sure." Turning back to her family, Lake asks her dad for some money. "Claire and I are going to check out a new arcade and maybe ride go-carts. Can I have some money, Dad?"

Jack pulls his wallet from his back pocket, takes an inventory of the remaining bills, and hands Lake a twenty. "Meet us in front of the mini golf course at six o'clock. If you need anything, your mom and I will be at the polka festival down by the old tavern."

"Thanks, Dad. See you later."

It's fun hanging out with Claire again. The arcade is totally retro, filled with old-school bowling, skeeball, pinball, and coin pusher machines. Lake and Claire play everything at least once and still have money left to spend.

"Let's get some lemonade and walk around." Pointing in the same general direction they're headed, Claire says, "My mom said a couple new shops opened down that way. They sell a lot of tie-dye stuff, might be cool."

"Okay," says Lake.

Walking back to where they'd had lunch, each girl buys a frozen lemonade. Lake loves coming to the Strip every year during Memorial Day weekend. The place becomes a veritable melting pot, drawing lots of visitors from different states and backgrounds. It's one of the few times during the year when she can blend in with the crowd and walk almost anonymously down the sidewalks of her hometown summer hangout. She and Claire check out the new shop, then cross the Strip and head back up the other side.

"I have to meet my parents soon. You feel like riding go-karts now?" she asks.

"I don't really like the go-karts, but I'll watch you ride," says Claire.

"Okay, cool."

The go-kart track is at the opposite end of the Strip, overlooking the lake. When they get there, the place is hopping. Claire stands next to Lake in line until it's her turn to ride. When the ride is over, Lake pulls her kart into the spot where the operator is pointing. As she walks back to where Claire is standing, she hears someone calling her name. Scanning the faces around the track, she suddenly spots Kelsey Juneau waving from the opposite side of the fence. *Shit! Shit! Shit!* It's too late to act like she doesn't see her. Lake waves hello, then turns and continues walking toward Claire.

Oh, diddly shit! Kelsey isn't letting her off with just a wave—she's headed straight for Lake and Claire, and she's with a group of kids. As they get closer, Lake recognizes some of the kids from school, but there's a couple she's never seen before. When they all get within a few feet of one another, Lake says, "Hey, Kelsey," and with a nod, asks, "You know Claire?"

"Hey, band girl, I know you! You're in my English class."

Looking uncomfortable, Claire says hello.

A few seconds of awkward silence pass, and a boy Lake doesn't recognize steps up, "Hey, Kelsey, introduce me to your cute friend."

Rolling her eyes, Kelsey says, "Maxen, this is Lake, my tutor from school. Lake, this is Maxen. He works at my dad's shop part-time."

Extending his hand, Maxen looks directly at her and says, "Well, hello there. Interesting name you have, Lake. Nice to meet you."

Shaking his hand, Lake looks Maxen up and down and says, "Hi. I've never met a Maxen before."

"It's a family name, how 'bout yours?"

"It's a long story," replies Lake.

"Maybe you can tell it to me one day?"

Smiling, Lake says, "I wouldn't count on it. Nice meeting you, Maxen. See you later, Kelsey."

As she turns to leave, Maxen steps aside, gesturing with his hands in an overexaggerated way as if clearing a path for Lake and Claire to walk. Lake can't help but smile. Stealing a last sideways glance, she has to admit, he has the shiniest black hair she's ever seen, and he smells super-clean, like a bar of Irish Spring soap. This boy, Maxen, looks a lot like her celebrity crush, Uncle Jesse. Lake is instantly charmed by him, but not in the way most girls are. She isn't daydreaming about running her fingers through his perfect hair or wondering what it would be like to kiss him—she's actually thinking about what it would be like to *be* him. Envious, she admires his confidence, quick wit, and slamming hot look. A trio of qualities that no doubt keep him busy with the girls. *Lucky!*

Glancing at her watch, Lake is jolted from her thoughts. "Oh my gosh. It's almost six. I promised to meet my parents."

#

On the last day of school, Kelsey stops Lake in the hall and says, "Hey, Lake. Thanks for helping me this year. Maybe I'll see you at the Strip again this summer? I live there, in a cottage by the lake."

"You're welcome, Kelsey. Glad I could help." An image of Maxen pops into Lake's head, and she decides it wouldn't be completely terrible to see him again.

Lake writes her phone number on a sheet of paper and rips it from her notebook. "Here's my number. Call me sometime. Maybe we can hang out."

"That'd be rad. Later, Lake."

Kelsey calls Lake a few days later. "Hey, Lake. What's up?"

"Not much. What are you up to?"

"Just hanging out. I'm thinking about getting a summer job. They need help at the fun center."

"You totally should. You could earn some spending money. It's probably an easy summer gig."

"Yeah, that's what I was thinking. Hey, do you remember that guy from the go-kart track? Maxen."

In her mind, Lake sees him clear as day. "Yeah, why?"

"Well, he keeps asking about you. Like he won't shut up about it. He's been bugging me to call you."

Lake thinks about this for a minute. Spending time with Maxen could work to her advantage.

"I have soccer camp almost every day and games on the weekends, but I could probably hang out for a little while Saturday night. Let's all meet at the new arcade at seven."

"Kay. See you Saturday."

Lake isn't sure her parents will let her hang out with Kelsey. She may have mentioned that she tutored her, but they've never met her or her parents. Instead of outright lying, she decides to pretend she's going to the Strip to hang out with Claire. She'll have her dad drop her off near Claire's house, then double back and meet Kelsey at the arcade.

Lake is nervous about seeing Maxen, and she feels bad about bending the truth with her parents, but she feels like she needs to do this. On Saturday, she sticks to the plan, and getting her dad to drive her to Claire's street works like a charm.

"I'll be here at ten o'clock to pick you up. You be careful out there and have fun," says her dad.

Waving good-bye from the curb, Lake feels a momentary pang of guilt as she waits to make sure he's out of sight before she turns to walk to the arcade.

She finds Kelsey inside playing a game of pinball. "Hey, Kelsey," says Lake.

"Hey. Hold on, this is my last ball." Their eyes follow the silver ball as it shoots straight down the center of the machine. The two flippers move at warp speed, but neither is able to send the ball back into play. "Ugh! I totally suck at pinball. What a waste of money!" says Kelsey. "Come on, I'll show you the cottage."

138

The walk to Kelsey's cottage takes less than five minutes. When they get there, the place is dark and quiet. Reaching inside the front door, Kelsey hits a switch. A small overhead lamp flickers, and the ceiling fan starts whirling. The cottage is small, just two bedrooms and one bathroom. Kelsey moves to open the blinds. The modest living room has a nice view of the lake. Outside, the screened front porch is in bad need of repair. Kelsey, an only child, has been living here with her mom and dad for about a year and a half. It feels weird to Lake, being here in Kelsey Juneau's cottage. Neither of them seems to know what to say. It's Kelsey who finally breaks the silence.

"So, I heard your family owns a big horse ranch. What's that like?"

"It's cool, I guess. I used to spend more time there than I do now. It was my grandpa's ranch before my family owned it. My grandparents were killed when I was nine, and it's just not the same now."

Kelsey looks genuinely concerned. "I'm sorry, Lake. I didn't know."

"How could you? Anyway, it's okay, it was a long time ago," says Lake.

Just then, they hear a rumbling. "That's probably my parents," says Kelsey. "Mom helps my dad at the shop on Saturdays, which closes at seven. This is the time they normally get home."

"That's cool. What kind of shop?" asks Lake.

"A bike shop. They build and fix bikes. Motorcycles."

"Oh, very cool," says Lake.

Hearing a loud, stomping noise, Lake turns to see a big, hairy guy with a bandanna on his head climbing the front steps. Before he's in the door, he yells, "Kelsey bug, you home?"

"We're in here, Dad."

Kelsey's dad is nearly six feet tall. He reminds Lake of the stuffed grizzly that used to stand guard in the corner of her grandparents' living room. Wearing a toothy grin, he says, "There she is!" He looks over at Lake. "Who's this one?"

Before she can answer, a woman whom Lake assumes is Kelsey's mom pops her head out from behind her giant husband. The woman is half in, half outside the door, blocked by Kelsey's bear of a dad. "Hey, Kels. Who's your friend?" she asks.

"Mom, Dad, this is Lake. I told you I invited her over tonight so we could hang out."

Kelsey's mom pushes the big man aside and joins them in the small living room. "Oh, right. Nice meeting you, Lake. Thanks for helping Kels pass the eighth grade."

"You're welcome, Mrs. Juneau. Kelsey's pretty smart. She was easy to tutor."

"You can call me Cheryl. And this here's Calvin."

Lake gives Calvin a wave and says hi.

"Nice to meet you, Lake. You girls hungry? Cheryl's going to make some Hamburger Helper for dinner before we head down the road."

"No, thank you. I ate earlier," says Lake.

"I'm good," says Kelsey. "I had a grilled cheese before Lake got here. We're going to ride go-karts."

"Suit yourself," says Calvin. "You know where we'll be if you need us."

#

The short gravel thoroughfare connecting the cottage to the main road has a patch of grass running down the center of it. Lake prefers the soft grass and stays to the middle while Kelsey mindlessly sends small pebbles flying with each step she takes.

"Your parents seem nice," says Lake.

"Yeah. They're okay. They aren't around much, but they're usually close by if I need them."

In Lake's mind, Cheryl and Calvin are way cooler than Lake's mom and dad. In their cottage, there are no curfews or rules. The adult Juneaus are part of the biker crowd and spend every Saturday night partying with friends at the closest bar, which happens to be conveniently located at the end of their street, just two doors down from the donut shop. Their bar of choice is fronted by two garage doors, and when they're open, the place becomes one with the sidewalk. The two girls pass by the place a half dozen times that night, and each time they do, they hear Cheryl or Calvin call out to them. It's kind of reassuring knowing they're right there.

Lake and Kelsey are almost at the go-kart track when Lake hears a weird beep and turns to see Maxen waving at them from his bike. Of course, he rides a motorcycle. He's wearing a bright-white tee, jeans, and biker boots, black hair blowing in the breeze. Seriously, Lake would love to be this guy for just one week. "Where's he headed?" asks Lake.

"He's going to park his bike at the cottage and meet us at the track," Kelsey replies.

"Cool."

Lake has a blast with Kelsey and Maxen, and he's a perfect gentleman. He doesn't even try to kiss her, which is a pleasant surprise. Just before she leaves to meet her dad at Claire's house, Kelsey says, "Don't be fooled by Maxen and his sweet ways, Lake. He's a total player. But he likes you. Maybe he could be your summer fling?"

With a shrug, Lake says, "Maybe. Got to bounce now. See ya later, Kels."

#

After a couple weeks of hanging out with Kelsey and seeing Maxen on the regular, he asks Lake to go for a walk on the beach, just the two of them. It's a beautiful summer night, and a nice breeze is coming off the lake. The shoreline isn't far from the Strip's main drag, and as they walk, they see stars over the water and bright neon coming from one of the many shops, bars, or restaurants on the other side. Regardless of where they look, they can't miss the usual Strip's sounds of loud cars, music, and laughter.

At one point during the walk, Maxen casually takes hold of Lake's hand and gives it a squeeze, but then he doesn't let go. They walk along the beach holding hands until the Strip lights and noise fade away. When the shoreline turns dark and the stars are the only sign of light overhead, Maxen stops walking. Still holding her hand, he turns and kisses Lake softly. It's so unexpected that she just goes with it.

Maxen is a good kisser, and having his lips pressed against hers while he explores her mouth with his tongue isn't completely horrible, but it also isn't Lake's ideal version of the players in this scene. This boy isn't who she dreams about when she imagines walking on the beach, fingers interlocked with her person and stopping to make out.

Before she's had a chance to process what's happening, Maxen lightly tugs on her arm, guiding Lake's body to join his on the sand. He's smooth, obviously experienced with women. Lake feels off and seems to be one step behind every move he makes. As he kisses her, Maxen moves his hands over her breasts, then continues going south. Lake gets hold of them and moves them back to her waist. When she lets go, he kisses her harder and slyly moves his hands down again. They play the "hand game" for a while, until finally, Lake grabs hold of Maxen's hands hard and says, "I want to go back to the cottage now."

Maxen mumbles something she can't quite understand before helping her up. They brush the sand from all the places it's creeped into and head back toward the lights. On the ride home, Lake wrestles with a range of conflicting emotions. She's for sure attracted to Maxen, but for different reasons than most girls would be. She feels obligated to keep things going with him even though she feels like she's cheating on herself. It's only for the summer, she tells herself. She can do this.

#

The next weekend, Lake is right back at Kelsey's cottage, even though Kelsey has to work. Sitting by herself on the front porch a little after eight o'clock, she knows her chances of seeing Maxen again are favorable. She hears a bike coming down the path and instinctively turns to see Maxen. He pulls up to the cottage, and they head for the beach.

The walk from the cottage seems shorter than it has in previous weeks, and within minutes, she and Maxen are right back to making out. This time, when she takes hold of his roaming hands, he nuzzles his face in her hair, distracting Lake long enough to wriggle free of her grip. Instead of going back to what he was doing before, Maxen takes hold of her hands and guides them down while pressing them firmly against his flat belly. He lingers along the waistband of his jeans, keeping her hands between his hands and his pants.

Maxen uses his tongue to trace the outline of Lake's lips before entering her mouth and touching her tongue. *Damn, this guy is good!* she thinks. *He's got moves I've never thought of, yet alone used.* Lake makes a mental note to remember his technique, and then she feels it. His hands have lured hers to the sizeable bulge in his jeans. With his right hand, he undoes the button at his waist and pulls his zipper down. Grasping Lake's wrist, Maxen uses his left hand to gently lead her to his thing. *This is new, and his thing is really hard!*

Lake isn't saying stop, and he takes it as a sign to keep going. With all his cards on the table, so to speak, Maxen pulls his jeans, underwear, and all down, and there it is, pointing right at her. The moon is full, and Lake can see Maxen's entire package quite clearly. This phase of the lunar cycle leaves nothing to the imagination.

Lake is fascinated by the sight of Maxen in all his glory, but she has no idea what he expects her to do with it. Clearly he's more aroused by their make-out session than she is. Framing the situation as a learning experience, she allows him to show her the way. Cupping her hand in his, he uses her hand to take hold of his thing, rubbing her palm along the tip before moving her hand up and down. Lost in the moment, she feels him nudging her head toward it. Tensing up, Lake almost punches him. She thinks to herself, *Is he out of his flipping mind?* There's no way her mouth is going anywhere near that thing.

He seems to have picked up on the vibe she's throwing out because he immediately stops. Switching tactics, Maxen practically begs her to keep stroking him, so she does. It only takes a few minutes for him to let go of her hand. Maxen twitches, moans, then kisses Lake slowly. She knows this is supposed to be some sort of "moment" for them, but honestly, she's kind of grossed out by the texture and smell of his stuff. She can't quite describe the odor, but it's sticky and sort of sweet smelling.

Maxen picks up the windbreaker that was tied around his waist and uses it to clean himself up. Thinking that's the end of it, literally, Lake turns to leave. Grabbing her hand once again, Maxen says to her in a low, sexy voice, "Where do you think you're going? Now it's my turn to make you feel good."

Without warning, Maxen kisses Lake again, doing that tracing thing with his tongue on her lips, tongue, and along the inside of her mouth. Easing her body down to the sand, he gently cradles her head in his hand. He pushes her T-shirt up, and his mouth moves over bra and breasts while his fingers trace an invisible line down the center of her belly.

Lake is wearing thin cotton shorts and can easily feel each of Maxen's fingertips as they slide farther down. He's on the outside of her shorts rubbing her down there, and it feels good. Arching her back, Lake presses herself into him. Maxen moves his hand, sliding his warm fingers inside her panties, and continues to rub. His fingertips move up and down, applying just the right amount of pressure—not too fast and not too slow—and she lets it happen. It feels amazing.

Lake closes her eyes, relaxes, and pictures a cute girl she passed earlier on the Strip, allowing herself to imagine she's the one rubbing her down there. That crazy volcano feeling begins to build, and when she lets go, her entire body shudders with pleasure.

Maxen kisses her and lies next to her on the sand. Looking up at the stars in the sky, he takes hold of her hand. Lake stares at the moon while trying to process the evening's events. *What does all this mean?* Lake thought she knew who she was and the path she was on, but what happened tonight doesn't exactly mesh with the plan.

Maxen squeezes her hand, bringing her back to the moment. Rolling onto his side, he kisses Lake and asks, "Are you ready to go back?"

It's an interesting question. Is she ready to go back to the time before she met Maxen? Or is she ready to own this night and make it work for her? She's here now, and ultimately, she decides to press on.

Lake spends two more Saturday nights with Maxen. Each time they go for a walk on the beach and the evening unfolds the same way. Lake's physical interaction with Maxen satisfies her need for basic human touch. It's a short-lived union formed for mutual benefit. Maxen shares just enough detail with Kelsey and his guy friends to make himself look good, and Lake earns enough "straight" street cred to pass as normal going into high school.

Eventually, there's a clean break with no hard feelings that allows her to hide in plain sight.

Operating under this cloak of invisibility, Lake becomes a master at compartmentalizing her true feelings and keeping her deepest secrets.

#

According to the experts, productive high school freshman–year goals include effectively managing the workload, participating in extracurricular activities, cultivating relationships with teachers, and making new friends. Dude! It's like the gods have finally heard Lake's prayers!

Everything she's already been doing is now expected from her entire grade. She's so far ahead of the curve, she basically coasts through her freshman year. But not all of her classmates possess the same level of maturity, insight, and ambition. Childhood friends come and go. Some of them she just naturally grows apart from; others are lost to a boy. A few of them slip quietly away without a second thought.

With her eye on the prize of attending college out of state, Lake knows that with each passing month, she's at least thirty days closer to becoming who she's meant to be. With her "legit" lesbian life on layaway, she pays what's needed now to one day collect the life that's rightfully hers.

Chapter 11

"Hey, kiddo. You're in my chair. Can we trade? It's almost time for the news."

Lake looks at her dad's face, but it takes her a few seconds to fully wake and realize who's talking to her. Swinging her legs around, she sits up in the chair and says, "Sorry, Dad. I was reading and fell asleep."

"Nothing to be sorry about, Lake. You're burning both ends of the candle with school, soccer, and yearbook."

Lake stands and says, "Here, sit in your chair. I need to finish my homework and take a shower."

She stretches a few times while her dad settles into his recliner. "Thanks for keeping it warm for me. How's everything going at school, anyway?"

Lake replies, "It's good. I like working with the yearbook committee. But geometry is hard. I may need a tutor myself."

"You're a bright girl. You'll figure it out. What was it that Kiki used to say? You're a…"

"Force to be reckoned with," says Lake, finishing the sentence for him. She still thinks about her grandma Kiki almost every day, and she misses her even more often. Lake's sweet sixteenth birthday was last month. Birthdays are supposed to be momentous, joyous occasions, but for Lake, the day was both a blessing and a curse. It was on her ninth birthday that they had last gathered with both Grandpa Kevin and Grandma Kiki. The evening itself was nearly perfect, from the dinner with her family to her favorite cake, and of course, Grams telling the absolute best version of the story about the day she was born. Hands down, it was one of the most favorite nights of Lake's entire life. The blessing.

The following morning she'd waved good-bye and watched as her grandparents drove away, headed for a well-deserved vacation in the

Keys. They never came back. No more hugs, kisses, or stories from them—ever again. The curse.

Lake's family did their best to make her sixteenth birthday special and sweet, but after the happy, the sad sets in. Then, there is the weather. January is always the coldest, snowiest month of the year. Like it or not, the month just isn't conducive to celebration. But it's great for hibernation, which is what Lake tends to do. From mid-January through about the end of April, Lake wholeheartedly promotes minimal, indoor-only activities. In other words, she mostly reads and sleeps.

All her friends talk about is the freedom that will come once they have their driver's licenses, but Lake is content to play soccer, walk in the woods, and read. Familiar activities that allow her to operate on autopilot and forget about her reality. Lake's personal, real-life drama is heavy stuff. It's easier to just push it down or get lost in a good book.

Her sixteenth birthday fell on a Wednesday this year, and her family had decided to celebrate on the weekend after so Pete and Jeanne could be there. On Saturday morning, Lake woke to the smell of bacon cooking and the reassuring sound of her parents talking in the kitchen. Footsteps in the hallway moved past her door, and she heard her brother, Pete, say, "Good morning."

Jeanne, the social butterfly of the family, would be the last one out of bed that morning. When Pete moved down to the basement and Jeanne took his room down the hall, their dad put a twenty-foot cord on the hall phone so Jeanne could take it into her room. On the weekends, Lake would hear her sister talking and laughing until all hours of the morning. Jeanne rarely emerges from her bedroom before noon, and Lake's birthday was no different. Lake had missed having her brother and sister in the house every day, and she was glad to have them home for a long weekend.

Caught up in the moment, Lake didn't hear the light tapping on her door. "Lake, are you awake?" Her brother, Pete, was calling to her from the other side.

"You can come in, Pete. I'm awake."

"Good morning, little sister. Happy birthday."

"Thanks, Pete."

"Mom asked me to check and see if you were up. Breakfast is almost ready."

"Okay, be there in five."

Padding down the hallway, Lake heard her mom's hushed voice. "Quiet, guys, she's coming." Anticipating what was about to happen, Lake rounded the corner and was greeted by her mom, dad, and brother's goofy grins. In unison they exclaimed, "Happy birthday, Lake!"

Her usual chair at the table has several helium-filled balloons tied to it and a banner above the windows reinforces the message: Happy Birthday!

"Come sit in your chair, birthday girl. I made all your favorite breakfast foods, and your dad insisted on fresh strawberries with whipped cream."

Lake takes her seat, and the four of them eat, talk, and laugh. When her mom gets up to make a fresh pot of coffee, Lake thanks her parents for breakfast and is about to get up when her dad says, "You sure you don't want to go out to eat tonight? We can go anywhere you want. A girl only turns sixteen once."

"Daaaaad, we already talked about this, and for the hundredth time, I just want to have dinner at home, with you guys."

"Suit yourself, it's your celebration. Uncle Rick and Aunt Joe are coming over for cake and ice cream later, but it'll just be us for dinner."

"That's perfect, Dad. It's exactly what I want, really."

In her bare feet, impervious to the cold, Jeanne ambles by the table without a word. "Well, look who's up before noon," says Dad.

"I made a fresh pot of coffee and saved you some bacon and biscuits. They're on a plate in the microwave."

Reaching into the cupboard, Jeanne pulls out a mug and pours herself a cup of coffee. Without bothering to heat it up, she takes the plate from the microwave and carries it and her coffee to the table. She sits and yawns before reaching for the sugar. Two heaping teaspoons go in. She stirs and reaches for the milk as she looks up. Seeing the balloons tied to the chair, she finally speaks. "Oh, shit. Sorry, Lake. Happy birthday."

They all bust up laughing.

#

After dinner, Lake's dad built a fire in the fireplace, and the family moved to the living room so Lake could open presents before her aunt

148

and uncle stopped by for cake and ice cream. The scene reminded her of her ninth birthday. This year, in place of an actual book, Pete and Jeanne pooled their money and presented Lake with a gift card to the biggest bookstore in the mall. It was enough for at least three books! She hugged her brother and sister and sat back down, waiting for her parents to reveal their big, secret gift to her. They'd been acting weird all week, whispering and cutting conversations short whenever she entered the room. Her dad pulled a card out from behind the throw pillow next to him, handed it to her, and said nothing. Confused, she took the card and opened it. As she pulled the card from the envelope, a gift card dropped to the floor. She picked it up and turned it over. It was a $50 gift card to her favorite athletic store at the mall. Lake loved shopping at this store and could easily spend fifty dollars there, but she was expecting something different and bigger. After all it was her sweet sixteenth.

Sensing her disappointment, Sylvia said, "Read the card, Lake."

She set the gift card aside, read the front of the card, then opened it. There was a photo taped to the inside. A picture of a sporty, dark red pickup truck. Was that their horse barn in the background?

"Well, what do you think?" asked her mom.

"I don't understand. Why is there a picture of a truck inside my card?"

"It's your birthday gift. We bought it for you, so you'd have your own truck to drive to school, soccer practice, and anyplace else you need to go."

"But I don't even have a license yet," said Lake.

Shaking his head, Jack said, "We know that. We thought you could practice driving and parking on the ranch for now, and when spring comes, you can schedule an appointment for the driving portion of your license test, you know, when the weather is better."

Lake had never imagined she'd get a car of her own, but now that she had *a truck*, it was exciting to think about what this meant. No more asking for rides or standing outside in the freezing cold waiting for her parents to pick her up. She could come and go as she pleased. This gift is a gem!

#

March turns out to be relatively warm and free of snow. Uncle Rick and her dad set up a makeshift parking lot at the ranch, and Lake practices pulling into spots, backing up, and parallel parking. She loves that her truck sits up high and she can easily see everything around her. It doesn't take long to discover she and her dad share the excellent parallel parker gene, and they joke about including this unique talent in their top-three skills. It helps that her truck isn't a full-sized pickup—and it isn't brand new. Admittedly, she backs over the cones and hits a few of the plastic rods before she becomes a capable driver.

Once she gets the parking part down, Lake enrolls in a driver's education course. By mid-April, she's completed both parts of her driver's license exam and has passed with flying colors. To celebrate this rite of passage, Lake and her parents have dinner at her favorite downtown pizza parlor.

When they arrive home, Sylvia hangs her jacket on a hook in the mudroom and realizes she forgot to have Jack stop at the store on their way home. They are completely out of coffee. She turns to Lake and says, "I need you to run to the store for coffee before it gets too late. Ask your dad for some money—and drive safe."

Totally surprised, Lake says, "Wait, what? You're sending me to the store by myself?"

"Lake, you're sixteen, and you have a license now. The store is only a few miles from the house. But if you don't think you can do it, I'll ask your dad to go."

She knows her mom is just messing with her, but she accepts the challenge. "Mom, please. I can drive to the store and back."

Lake's dad gives her enough money for the coffee, and she says, "I'll be back soon. Love you."

"We love you, too. Drive safe. No speeding!" says Sylvia.

From over her shoulder, Lake yells, "Mom, I got this!" And she does. She's totally got this. Driving by herself to the store, Lake feels like a million bucks. She turns the volume knob on the radio to high and sings along loud and proud: "Whoomph! There it is. Whoomph! There it is..." Bobbing her head to the beat, Lake signals and turns into the lot. She parks like a champ and jumps out of the truck, convinced all eyes are on her. She does a pirouette and says to no one in particular, "Yeah, that's right. I just drove here alone." The freedom of having her own means of getting around town is a total rush. Oh, the places she will go!

#

Lake decides she needs to branch out and push herself to compete on a whole new level. Right now, she's a big fish in a little pond, but if she wants to get noticed by the out-of-state schools, she needs better exposure. At dinner, she says, "Coach told me about a new girls' travel soccer league with players from all over northern Ohio. He thinks it would be good for me to try out for a team now while it's just getting off the ground. If I make it, I can switch to the new league."

Lake's mom is always supportive, but she refrains from saying whether Lake should or should not do something when it comes to soccer. Jack is more direct since he's the one paying for the travel teams. In his roundabout way, he asks, "What are we looking at in terms of commitment? Did your coach say how much this new league costs? What about practice and games? If it includes girls from the northern part of the state, where do you practice and compete? I know you want to get into an out-of-state school, but you need to make sure your grades don't suffer if you decide to do this."

"Dad, I won't let this affect my grades. I don't know how much it costs or where they practice. It's teams of girls from different cities, but practice is probably local. I'll see if Coach has a brochure or something I can bring home for you to look at, okay?"

"Okay. See what you can get. I'll take a look and we'll make a decision then," says her dad.

Practice and tryouts are in a neighboring city, and dues for the new league are pretty much in line with what they're paying now. It's the cost of the new uniform and the travel expenses that sends Lake's dad into a tizzy.

"I can help out on the ranch more if that's what you want," says Lake.

"You fall asleep in my chair before dinner now because you're so worn out when you get home. How do you expect to help out on the ranch? You don't have time for that."

Lake knew she was just blowing smoke with that statement. She doesn't have time to help with the ranch, and her dad doesn't really need her help. The thing about her dad is, he tends to view certain material goods through a thirty-year-old lens and expects to pay the same price today as he did back then. He has sticker shock right now, but he'll come around. He always does.

"You're right. I can't help with the ranch, but I would if I could."

"I know that, Lake. We'll make the new league work. Just work hard and get into a good school. You kids are going to have to take care of your mom and me one day—remember that," he says with a wink.

Her dad is a goofy guy, but she loves him a bunch. "Thanks, Dad. You and mom will be well taken care of. Don't you worry."

#

The new league has her running ragged, and her team is a challenge, no kidding. Lake isn't one to brag, but she knows she's a good soccer player—like, a really good soccer player—but she's no longer the best on her travel team. It's a humbling smack in the face, and there are days she wants to quit, but her dad would totally wig and she's no quitter. Besides, she's still better than anyone on her high school team, so at least there's that. Lake basks in the glory of her high school wins and propels her team to an undefeated season.

Coach had said there could have been college scouts in the stands today. It's doubtful any would come to see a sophomore play, but it is possible.

Patting her on the back, Gretchen says, "That was an amazing game, Lake! We totally killed it."

"Heck, yeah, we did. Good job out there, Gretch." Walking a few feet in front of her, Lake stares at the number on the back of her friend's jersey. Number 6 belongs to Lake's first real girl kiss. Gretchen and Lake are both midfielders and have practiced and played soccer together since they were little kids. "Hey, Gretch, let's get some pizza after we get cleaned up. See if any of the other girls want to come."

"Yeah, okay. I'll ask."

Lake looks up to the stands and sees her parents making their way down the stairs. Her parents, the ranch, her school, her town. One day she'll leave this place to learn and grow in a new city, and she'll miss all of it, but for her, there is no other choice.

For all intents and purposes, Lake is an insider in her town, school, family, and community, but every minute of every day, she feels like a fraud. A girl possessed by an innate need to be in with the out crowd. Pun intended.

"Lake. Lake Myers. Do you have a minute?" Lake turns to see a woman she's never seen before. "Do I know you?"

Holding her lanyard out so Lake can see it, she says, "My name's Alice Winger. I'm a reporter with the *Plain Dealer*."

OMG! The *Plain Dealer* is a Cleveland newspaper. A big city news reporter is asking Lake if she has a minute. This is a huge, freaking deal! Lake wills herself to calm down.

"Nice to meet you, Miss Winger. How can I help you?"

"You must be really proud coming off a win like that. Your team is undefeated for the season, ten and oh. What do you think of that?"

"I think it's awesome. The team is great. Everyone gave it their all this season, and it paid off."

"It sure did. How long have you been playing?"

"I started kicking a ball around when I was eight. Then I joined the school soccer team, and the rest is history. I've always loved the game."

"That's a long time. Watching you play today, it's obvious you have a passion for it. Do you hope to play in college one day?"

"That's my plan. I also play for the new northern Ohio travel league. Hopefully, we get some scouts out to see us play next season."

"I'm sure you will, Lake. Good luck. Thanks for your time today."

"You're welcome, Miss Winger. Thank you."

Lake is on cloud nine when she opens the door to the locker room. Two steps in, and the team starts chanting, "Lake, Lake, Lake, Lake!"

She lets the chanting go for a few seconds before raising her hands and gesturing for them to stop. "Thanks, guys. What we did was a team effort. And we kick ass as a team!" she shouts.

That gets the girls going again. There's barking and clapping and pointing at the ceiling. "We're number one, we're number one!"

Lake holds her hand up and joins the team in this chant as she heads for the showers. She's tired and hungry, but she's super fired up and ready to celebrate with her friends.

#

The last to finish in the locker room, Lake joins some of the girls milling about in the hall and yells out, "Who's ready for pizza?"

Too many hands to count fly up, and Lake's overcome with emotion. She really does care for these girls, her teammates, classmates, and friends. She's amped up and doesn't feel like sitting for the short ride to town.

"I'm super pumped by our win," Lake calls out. The girls cheer in agreement. "It's a freaking awesome night, and I feel like walking. It's just a few blocks to the pizza shop. Anyone else up for burning off some winning energy?"

The response to this is more cheering and whistling.

With arms draped over each other's shoulders, the girls spill out onto the sidewalk and make their way toward town as one collective group.

A memory of crossing the street to visit Grandma Kiki pops into Lake's mind as she looks at the girls on her left, then to her right and back to her left again. She may not be close with all of them, but she would say most are her best friends. She's known all of them for years, helped them with homework, held their hair back when they drank too much, and acted as their sounding board when they needed to vent. Always a good listener, rarely a talker, holding back for fear of giving too much away.

"I'm so happy to have you guys as my friends... I just love you," declares Lake.

The level of trust and confidence in the group is beyond high, and this affirmation starts the ball rolling. She can't recall who spills the beans first, but once it starts, it can't be stopped.

Each girl falls in line with Lake and agrees they, too, feel love for everyone present. Then someone makes it weird and takes it to the next level. Serene admits to cheating on her lab final to avoid a low grade and the possibility of not getting accepted to her top college pick one day. Connie tells everyone she's seeing a shrink because she's a kleptomaniac, which explains a lot, and the bomb drops hard when Harper, the quiet one of the bunch, admits to getting pregnant and having an abortion over Christmas break.

It's the walk of the Kumbaya girls, and Lake feels extreme pressure to share something, too. But not just anything. These girls, her friends, have fully exposed themselves, opening up to the group and showing their most vulnerable sides.

Lake only has one big secret. Her heart is racing, sweat begins to bead on her upper lip, and her mouth is dry, like she's got a mouth full of cotton.

She can't find her voice. Lake has never said the words out loud. To anyone.

Be brave, Lake. Just do it.

"I'm gay."

The unified procession of besties comes to an abrupt halt. All eyes to the left and right are fixated on Lake. No one says a word. Slack-jawed, the girls just stare at her, boring an even bigger hole into her already pierced heart.

How could she let herself get caught up in the moment like that?

Even though it's a warm and sunny day, it's like a silent breeze has blown in, bringing with it a sudden drop in temperature. The air is immediately cool, almost cold, all the sunshiny happiness sucked right out of it. She wants to take it back, has to take it back. She quickly decides to play it off like a joke.

Lake erupts in forced laughter and shakes her head. "You should see your faces. I totally got you guys!"

A couple of the girls smile, and others join in the laughter.

Still laughing, Lake says, "Things were getting super serious. We just came off an incredible win, and it was all I could think of. I was just trying to lighten the mood."

Connie, the klepto, says, "Geez, Lake. Way to freak us all out! But it *was* pretty funny. You kill me."

With a smile on her face, Lake thinks, *I kill myself. Pretty funny, confessing my deepest, darkest secret to my so-called best friends, only to find out they can't handle it. They can't even fathom that I might actually be gay. This day flipping sucks!*

What was she supposed to do? Would it have made a difference if she took baby steps? Maybe plant the seeds over a few weeks or months before just blurting it out like that? She'll never know for sure.

It was her best, most truthful attempt to come out to her friends, and she was immediately forced to recant, play it off as if it were some stupid joke she'd made to lighten the mood.

Connie and her ignorant comments set the tone, helping to diffuse a bad situation. The other lemmings quickly followed suit. The group's snickers create a swirling energy strong enough to sweep Lake's bitter-cold confession firmly under the rug. With the unthinkable quickly minimized, she makes nice and eats pizza with the girls, but on the inside, she feels completely empty and totally betrayed. Forced to take a defensive stance, Lake digs in, and the walls go up. On the walk back to school, she makes a vow to permanently detach from this group of girls emotionally. She will address them only as acquaintances and teammates, taking time to sterilize each and every future word before speaking.

#

The feeling of never being settled, being too guarded to join the in crowd, or allowing herself to feel the joy of acceptance by a group, comfortable in her own skin, is something Lake hasn't felt for most of her life. It will shape the way that she lives and how she will love for most of her adult life.

Chapter 12 – Hope

The reporter from the *Plain Dealer* writes a flattering piece on female high school athletes that is featured in the Sunday edition. The picture she uses is an action shot of Lake scoring a goal and includes her quote: "Everyone gave it their all this season, and it paid off." The Sunday edition of the paper is seen by hundreds, probably thousands of people, and the notoriety that comes with it lights a fire under Lake's soccer career. Her travel league coach decides to give her more field time, and Lake eagerly uses it to step up her game and show off what she's got.

Tweeeet! Lake hears the whistle and turns her head. *Why is Coach blowing the whistle and motioning us back to the touchline?* Confused, Lake and the other girls make their way back up the field.

"Hey, Coach. What's up?"

Coach Donnelly turns and looks around to make sure he has all the girls within earshot. "Listen up, ladies, we have a new player joining us today. She's been playing soccer a long time, was an all-star on her school team, and just moved here from the other side of the state. Their loss is our gain! Hope, do you want to say a few words to the team?"

Lake steps closer to see who's speaking.

"Hi, everyone. My name's Hope McCallister. I'm way excited to be on the team and look forward to getting to know everyone. Thanks."

Hope McCallister is about the same size as Lake, and from where Lake's standing, Hope looks cute. Her strawberry blond hair is up in a loose braid, but large hanks of it have fallen free, gently framing a face full of freckles with a tiny button nose.

Coach turns to the team and says, "Girls, say hi to Hope, and do your best to make her feel welcome."

In unison, the team says, "Hi, Hope," then the girls look to Coach for further instructions.

"If you need anything, Hope, just ask," Coach says. "Okay, girls, Hope is a goalie, and she's going to jump right in. Back to the field now. Let's see what you got."

The new girl is definitely an all-star. Lake and the team work her just as hard as anyone else, but Hope is shutting them out, refusing to give up any points at all. Coach calls for a time-out and motions everyone back to the sideline.

"That's what I'm talking about, girls! I can see you're all working hard out there, doing your best to score against the new girl, but she's not about to let that happen. Lake, you and the girls have been a team for a while now. You all get back in there and see if you can score against Hope. Let's see one point before we call it a day."

Coach is big on encouraging them to play, win, and lose as a team. Every girl on the team is a good player. Some are better than others, but in Coach's mind, it takes more than a few star players to make a winning team. Under his leadership, the stars put their egos aside and play their best for the team.

Lake and the other girls return to the field and wait for the single whistle blow.

Tweeeet!

The sound indicates the game is back on, and the girls start running. Fueled by Coach's words and the desire to score at least one goal before practice ends, Lake and her teammates move swiftly and gracefully toward Hope. The only thing standing between them and a point is her. Lake remembers reading somewhere that when they are under pressure, goalies tend to dive right. Using that same logic, she does her best to keep the ball moving down the center of the field, then lining up the shot before passing it off to her right for a kick that sends the ball sailing solidly over Hope's left shoulder just as she dives right.

Goal!

What a way to end the practice! The team is stoked to have scored a goal against Hope. Picking up the ball, she smiles and throws it back on the field. Coach blows his whistle twice, and the girls head back. "Nice job, everyone. That was some terrific teamwork, and Hope, you were great out there. I couldn't be prouder of you girls! Let's line up for stretches and a cooldown before you all go home."

The girls fall into place, forming three lines on the field. Hope takes the spot on Lake's right and follows along as Coach shouts stretching orders from the front of their formations. As the commands wind down, Hope says, "You were awesome today. It's Lake, right?"

"Yeah. Thanks. You were great, too. Where'd you move here from?" asks Lake.

"Bowling Green. We moved here for my dad's job, but most of our family is still there. I'll probably go back there for college."

"That's cool. Do you want to play soccer in college?"

"Yeah. A soccer scholarship would be unbelievable, for sure. I want to go to nursing school."

"Wow. I don't know what I want to do yet. I just know I want to play soccer!"

Coach is walking the line behind them. "Alright, girls, on your backs. Get your legs up, and get 'em moving. Shake those legs and get the blood moving down. Light legs are fast legs. Keep it going now, thirty more seconds."

Hope giggles and looks over at Lake, who smiles and continues to shake her legs.

"Three, two, one. Stellar practice, everyone. Have a good weekend. See you back here Monday afternoon," says Coach.

Walking off the field, Lake says good-bye to Hope and heads for her truck. Hope is parked on the other side of the lot, and Lake watches in the rearview mirror as she gets into a late-model Honda. The car starts, and Hope pulls forward out of her spot, drives past Lake, and turns right out of the parking lot. Lake turns the ignition key, backs out of her space, and takes a left out of the parking lot. From the rearview mirror, Lake watches Hope drive away in the opposite direction and wonders where she's headed.

#

Lake's attention span is seriously depleted most of the day on Sunday, but she forces herself to spend a few hours at the library finishing a reading assignment and the last of her homework. Pulling a dictionary from the shelf, she flips through the pages and stops in the section of words that begin with *H*. She turns the pages one at a time until she finds the word she's searching for: *hope*.

Hope—(noun) a feeling of expectation; (verb) desiring a certain thing to happen.

Two different ways to define a similar feeling or action. Interchangeable cravings synonymous with Lake's attraction to girls and her vision for a future love life that will blossom the way she sees it unfolding. Is she crushing on Hope, or is this something else? When practice ended on Saturday, Lake had walked away with a certain level of respect and admiration for Hope. She's a kick-butt soccer player with what it takes to help the team win the championship, but Lake didn't get that indisputable feeling in her lady parts when they talked. Was the lack thereof to be trusted?

Lake isn't totally sold on the concept of "gaydar" because there've been times when she was so far off, she couldn't have been more wrong. Midwest girls come from hearty stock and can be hard to decipher. In Lake's opinion, girls from the region could present tough or uncompromising, indicators that could lead others to falsely believe in the intuitive "queer connection." But she mustn't be fooled. One wrong read could get a girl like her beat up—or worse.

Lake, and girls like her, can become very guarded, especially in new situations, social settings with new faces, cute faces, female faces. Still, Lake is curious.

The next day, Lake makes it a priority to arrive at soccer practice early. She parks in the far corner of the lot so she can sneak a peek at Hope undetected. Hope pulls in a few minutes after Lake is settled. When she steps out of her car, Lake can see that she's not dressed for practice. Instead, she's wearing a plaid skirt, a white polo top, and black Doc Martins with white knee-high socks. She must have come straight from school. Hope tosses her backpack over her shoulder and heads for the locker room.

Lake jumps out of her truck and fast-walks to catch up to Hope, deliberately kicking up gravel to bring attention to herself. The ruse works, and Hope turns to see who's making such a racket. The quizzical look on her face is quickly replaced by a warm smile as she says, "Hey, Lake."

"Hi, Hope. How was your weekend?"

"Too short. How about you?"

"Same. I spent most of yesterday at the library."

"Ugh, I *should* have been at the library. I slept until noon and then hung out with my boyfriend. We had a pop quiz in Latin today, and I'm pretty sure I didn't do so hot. I told my parents I didn't want to take Latin, but my dad says it will help with the reading parts of the SAT. Whatever. It's totally hard."

"I think it's cool you take Latin, maybe your dad's right? What school do you go to?"

"I go to a Catholic school just west of here." With a slight nod in the direction of her school, she adds, "It's okay."

"Well, I bet you did better than you think on your quiz."

Shrugging, Hope says, "I like your optimism, Lake. Let's go play some soccer."

Her curiosity crushed, Lake mulls over the fact that Hope has a boyfriend and sleeps until noon on Sundays. The sleeping-until-noon part is harder to wrap her brain around than Hope having a boyfriend. Lake's gut and lack of a special sense about which side of the fence Hope leans to is spot-on, and that's okay. But due to the recent loss of nearly all her friends, Lake is now in the market for a new one. No more spying or pining for Hope. No time like the present to start fresh and see where things land. What a clever approach to friendship.

Without bias or preconceived emotion, Lake and Hope's friendship flourishes, developing organically over time. With a shared passion for soccer and a strong competitive drive, the two dominate on the field and off. Lake and her travel teammates lack personal history and prior knowledge of past regrets. The group forms a fierce familial bond, a welcome surrogate for Lake's former trusted circle of friends. On the field, the team supports Lake at every turn and would never leave her high and dry. Their practices and games present the perfect outlet for the pent-up frustration she feels when she plays on her home turf.

Hope and Lake have an undeniable chemistry on the field that translates effortlessly off the field. The mall is halfway between their houses, and being teenage girls, it seems the logical place to meet up, shop for clothes and makeup, get food, and go to the movies. The peculiar thing is, Lake is fully aware of the boundaries in this friendship, and she would never dream of crossing the line or even hinting at anything inappropriate in Hope's presence. But when left to her own devices and thoughts, she does tend to drift to the homoerotic dream starring none other than Hope McCallister. It's human nature to desire the things we see most often, especially things we genuinely like and appreciate. Having a dream girl as the object of her deepest affection might not be the healthiest thing, but for Lake, it's the safest option.

#

In a way, Hope is Lake's first real lover. Not in the physical sense, of course, but in her mind, they do it all. With Hope, she takes her time, savors every moment. The one-sided affair begins on a random Saturday night after a big win against a rival team. Hope's boyfriend and her parents are there to support her, and Lake's mom and dad are also in the stands. Grabbing her by the hand, Hope says, "Lake, I want you to meet my boyfriend, Stuart, and my mom and dad. They're in the bleachers, right up front."

"Okay, cool. My mom and dad are here, too. I want you to meet them."

Still holding her hand, Hope leads Lake to a handsome older couple near midfield. "Mom, Dad, this is my friend Lake. I told you about her."

Hope's mom extends her hand, and Lake shakes it. "It's nice to meet you, Mrs. McCallister."

"Likewise, Lake. And this is my husband, Paul."

Lake's hand automatically gives a small wave, and she says, "Nice to meet you, Mr. McCallister."

"Hello, Lake. Hope's told us a lot about you. She says you live on a horse ranch."

"My dad and uncle own the family horse ranch. We live across the street from it."

"That must be fun. We love horses. Are your parents here today?"

"Yes, they're sitting right over there," says Lake, pointing in the general direction of where Jack and Sylvia are seated. "They usually go to the concession stand and walk around a little during halftime."

"We'd love to meet them," says Mrs. McCallister.

"Okay. If you don't see them at halftime, I'll introduce you after the game.""Great. Good luck today," says Mr. McCallister.

"Thank you," says Lake, turning to go.

Hope grabs her hand and says, "Wait, I want you to meet Stuart."

On the other side of Hope's dad, Stuart stands and shakes Lake's hand. He's tall, probably close to six feet, with an athletic build and sandy-blond hair cut in a trendy style, intentionally messy and perfect.

Lake is the first to speak. "Hi, Stuart."

Shoving his hands into the pockets of his jeans, Stuart gives his hair a toss and says, "Hey, Lake. It's good to meet you. Hope says you're almost as good a soccer player as she is."

"Not true," says Hope. "I said she's a better player than I am."

Playfully, Stuart says, "Oh, is that what you said? I could have sworn you said something different."

Hope gives Stuart a soft shove on the shoulder and says, "Whatever, Stuart. You know what I said. Anyway, we have to go. We'll see you after the game."

Waving, Lake says good-bye, and the girls run to join the team. As two of the more seasoned and focused players, Lake and Hope are an awesome pair, equally devoted to the attack and the defense. The rivalry between the two teams has been a thing since the league began, and neither team is willing to give up a point. The game is intense, providing plenty of suspense and drama. After multiple close calls, the score is 0-0 at halftime, and emotions run high on both sides. Coach has the girls huddle up and encourages them to fight the good fight as they enter the second half of the game. It's a line he's delivered to them more than once: "Don't give up at half time. Concentrate on winning the second half. I have faith in you girls. Now get out there and show 'em what you've got!"

Feeling recharged, Lake returns to the field ready to score. The opposing coach must have delivered a similar speech. At kickoff, the other team is on them like nobody's business, ready to rumble. Lake is in position to steal the ball, and she does so with grace and control. As she makes her way down the field, she's challenged and deliberately charged by the other team's midfield anchor, causing her to go down hard.

The team rushes to her defense, and a heated shoving match ensues. The referees blow their whistles long and hard, rushing in to break up the squabble, as spectators on both sides of the field rise to their feet. The sasquatch who clocked Lake gets a yellow-card warning for starting the brawl, which leads to cheers and boos from both sides of the stands.

Tension across the entire field is thick. Just as Lake is walking away from the situation, the girl who charged her yells, "I'm going to thrash you!"

Carolyn, one of Lake's teammates, hears the threat and says, "This is bullshit. That crazy bitch needs to go!"

A free kick is awarded but comes up short. The game gets more heated with each passing minute and ends in a tie score of 0-0. A penalty shootout is called, and Carolyn is the one who tips the scales in favor of the win. She flashes a big grin directly at the angry sasquatch. *Take that, you dumb muckety-muck.* The stands erupt simultaneously in applause and protest as Lake and her team surround Carolyn. The win feels just and good.

Lake and Hope leave the field together, each girl scanning the crowd in search of their families. Lake spots her mom and dad first and says, "My parents are over there by the gate. I think your mom and dad are there, too."

Waving, Hope says, "Let's go introduce them to each other."

Stuart spots Hope and starts clapping. Beaming, he heads for Hope, hugging and kissing her before her parents even realize she's there. "Babe, you were a freaking rockstar today! I'm so glad I got to see you play."

Lake's mom and dad remain standing until Lake reaches them, each wrapping an arm around her when she arrives. Her mom and dad both start talking at the same time. "What a terrific game! It was intense right up to the very end. Congratulations on the win!"

"Thanks, guys," says Lake.

"It wasn't very sportsmanlike of that girl to knock you down like she did. I'm glad she got that card against her," said her mom. "Are you alright?"

"I'm fine, Mom. Come over here, I want to introduce you to Hope and her parents."

Hope's group is just a few feet away. The crowd has thinned some and isn't as loud.

Lake says, "Mr. and Mrs. McCallister, these are my parents, Jack and Sylvia." The two men shake hands as the ladies smile and acknowledge one another. Turning to Hope, Lake then says, "This is Hope and her boyfriend, Stuart."

Jack and Sylvia say hello and congratulate Hope on the win.

The adults ask the obligatory questions about work and home and make other small talk as Hope says to Lake, "Stuart and I are going to grab a bite. You want to come?"

"Yeah, sure," says Lake.

They exchange parting pleasantries with their parents and agree to meet at a nearby restaurant. The conversation flows easily, and Lake is surprised at how much she and Stuart have in common. He plays the guitar, has an appreciation for music, and likes to read. The two realize they are fans of a lot of the same musical groups and rattle off the ones they've seen live in concert. Stuart is a year older and has seen four times the number of concerts Lake has, but it's fun to listen to him and watch how he and Hope interact. Stuart has an arm around her most of the time, and she kisses his cheek and feeds him fries until her plate is empty. When they're done eating, Hope gives Lake a hug and invites her to the mall the following weekend. "We can see a movie and hang out. My parents are renting a house at the lake this summer, and I need to start looking for a new bathing suit."

"Great, I'll meet you there."

#

Lake genuinely likes Hope, in a "real friend" kind of way, and she realizes what they have is a healthy girlfriend relationship. The one thing lacking is Lake's willingness to share honest pillow talk. Hope and Stuart have "done it," and sometimes Hope talks about their sex life. Lake is inexperienced in this department, but she uses her moments with Maxen to beef up the conversation the best she can.

"He sounds hot. Why'd you two break up?" asks Hope.

"He's a little bit older and kind of a player. I liked him a lot, but it just wasn't meant to be. Not like you and Stuart." Lake adds this last part to deflect and move the conversation back to Hope. It's another talent she's perfected in order to hide who she really is. Hope takes the bait and shares another story about the sweet and amazing Stuart.

Minus the pressure of a doomed crush, Lake and Hope fall into a comfortable friendship that benefits both girls in different ways. Lake is a good listener, and Hope rewards her with endless chitchat and "Stuartisms." In return, Hope helps Lake shop for cute clothes, makeup, and accessories. She also teaches Lake how to flirt, which turns out to be a priceless life lesson that can be applied to either gender, really.

"See that boy over there? I caught him looking at us a few times. Next time he does it, smile at him…slowly. Like, let a slow smile spread over your face instead of busting into an instant grin, and keep looking at him. Don't break eye contact. I guarantee he'll smile back." The food court is packed with teenagers, and Lake does what Hope says. The boy in question is kind of dorky, not the sort of guy Lake would ever think twice about. He reacts exactly as predicted.

"No way! I told you what would happen. Go talk to him."

Oh, no. Lake's flirting is too good. Looking at Hope, she takes a long sip of her soda and swallows hard.

"What are you waiting for, Lake?"

It's like she's glued to her seat and her legs won't work. She doesn't want to do this. Stalling, she wipes her mouth with a napkin and asks, "Do I have anything in my teeth?"

"No, you're good."

"My lips are dry. Hold on." Rummaging around in her bag, Lake digs for her Chapstick. She has ahold of it but acts like she's still looking when Hope says, "Here, use my lip gloss."

Reluctantly, she takes the lip gloss from Hope and applies a thin layer to her lips. "Do you have any gum?"

"I think so," says Hope. While she looks for gum in her purse, Lake glances over at the boy and sees him walking away. He flashes her a toothy grin and waves.

She gives him an unenthusiastic wave and watches him as he goes.

"Found it," says Hope. Handing her a stick of gum, she tells Lake, "Now go!"

Lake starts to get up when Hope says, "Where'd he go?" She stands up to look around the food court. From her tippy toes, she adds, "I can't believe he left. Maybe he has a girlfriend?"

Lake says, "I don't know, maybe."

#

Lake is lucky at the mall that day, but she knows that Hope desperately wishes she had a boyfriend. "Is there anyone at your school you like?" Racking her brain to come up with a name, Lake says, "There is this one guy, Simon. He plays football."

At the mention of football, Hope becomes super cheery, almost giddy. "Oh my gosh, Stuart plays football! We could double date!"

Whoa, slow down, sister.

"I don't know, Hope. I don't really talk to him."

"Why not? Is he dumb?"

"No, he's not dumb. He's cute. But he's shy. I tutored him in the ninth grade," says Lake.

"Cool, so you know him at least. Just say hi. Or do the smile thing. You're super cute, Lake. He'll smile back. I promise."

"Maybe. I'll let you know how it goes," says Lake.

This seems to pacify Hope, and she moves on to another topic. Lake zooms in on her lips as she talks, and her mind begins to drift. She smiles and nods, dropping the occasional "yeah" and "totally" when it seems right. She's zoned out completely when she hears, "You're so easy to talk to. I love Stuart, but I swear, sometimes I think he's somewhere else."

Lake gives Hope a slow smile and nods.

Lying in her bed that night, Lake closes her eyes and allows an image of Hope in her school uniform to fill her mind. She's wearing the lace-up boots, and her hair is pulled back in a loose ponytail. She has just a little bit of makeup on her face, and her long eyelashes are curled upward. Her lips are full and shiny, covered in a thin layer of pink lip gloss. They complement her strawberry blond hair and emerald eyes.

Lake licks her lips. *Shit!*

Kicking the covers off, she quietly gets out of bed and checks to make sure her door is shut tight. It's never happened before, but if

Jack or Sylvia ever walked in on her, she knows it would scar her for life. Of course, her door wasn't shut tight. Thank goodness she checked!

She climbs back into bed careful not to make too much noise. She's warm and decides to pull just the sheet over her body. It feels cool against her skin.

Lake closes her eyes, and the picture of Hope is back, cute as ever. Lake runs a hand over her breasts, drawing circles around each nipple until both are hard and standing at attention.

Slowly, her hand moves down her belly, fingers lightly grazing the outside of her panties. It's been a couple weeks since she last indulged in some "me time," and she's ready. She smiles as her hand makes its way inside her panties.

When Lake fantasizes about Hope, she likes to change it up, each time adding a new, exciting element to the scene. Why not? It's her show. For sure, there's always a lot of foreplay. Sometimes it's sweet and romantic; sometimes it's hungry and more aggressive.

Under the cover of darkness, Lake and the make-believe Hope are in no rush. Time stands still while they act out every possible sexual scenario, from their first kiss to touching and tasting their "everythings," and of course, all the magical stuff that happens in between.

Once they're spent, relaxed and happy as clams, that feeling of intense satisfaction and validation for how they please each other settles in and doesn't leave. Their warm, slick bodies are wedged in tight against each other, and that's where they stay, holding one another until both eventually fall fast asleep. Make-believe Hope is always gone before Lake wakes up. But one day, her real-life replacement will be there, waiting for Lake to open her eyes and kiss her good morning. It's a pleasing, anticipatory thought. Add to her list of growing skills, patience and the ability to readily manifest her ideal future.

#

In the actual world, however, things are moving in a very different direction. In the blink of an eye, Lake's final year of high school has arrived, and she isn't about to escape the experience completely unharmed. Her senior year Thanksgiving is truly a holiday to give thanks. Lake and her travel team sweep the fall season, ending her high school career on a high note. She's applied to multiple colleges, in and out of state, and has been accepted by all but two that she's still waiting to hear from. Her family is healthy, and everyone is doing well. Pete's in a master's program, working part-time, and he has a steady girlfriend. Jeanne has completed her undergraduate degree and is working full-time as an event planner. As busy as they are, they both make it a priority to be home for the holidays, and Lake loves having them here.

The week before Christmas, two thick packets are in her mailbox. It's the news she's been waiting for. Acceptance letters from her last two college picks. One is in state; the other is a few states away. Lake is in the mood to celebrate.

Bouncing from one foot to another, she can hardly contain her excitement. *Pick up, pick up, pick up.* She hears the *click*, and Hope says, "Hello?"

"Hope, guess what!" shouts Lake.

"What? Is everything okay?"

"Yes, everything is more than okay. I got in! Both schools I was waiting to hear from, I got in!"

"That's awesome, Lake. Which one are you going to choose?"

"I'm not sure yet. I have to lay everything out and make a pros-and-cons list. I have plenty of time to make my final decision."

"True story," says Hope. "We should celebrate!"

"That's why I called! What are you doing this weekend? Do you want to go to the mall?"

"Me and Stuart have a date night planned for Saturday, but I can go on Sunday."

"Sweet! Let's meet for lunch. We can see a movie or shop after."

She hangs up the phone, feeling euphoric and untouchable.

#

Lake flips through the pages of a new book waiting for Hope to join her. Hope spots her immediately and walks over to their usual table in the food court. "Hey, bookworm. What's up?"

"Hey, Hope. You know, there's nothing wrong with reading. You should try it sometime," replies Lake jokingly.

"I do read, and I already committed to Bowling Green. I'm all set," says Hope in a similar joking manner.

Lake gives Hope an exaggerated eye roll and says, "What are we eating today?"

"Ummm, pizza. Same thing we always eat," says Hope.

The food court is busy with holiday shoppers, and Lake doesn't want to lose their seats. "Here's some money. Will you get me a slice and a soda?"

"Sure. Be back in a jiff," says Hope.

It's been a few weeks since the two girls have hung out, and they have a lot of catching up to do. Hope is well into a story about a secret overnight ski trip she took with Stuart when Lake notices Hope's eyes shift and she's looking up over her head. Lake's eyes automatically track the shift, but before she can turn to see what Hope is looking at, she hears it.

"Hey, Lake. What's up?"

Please, please, please, don't let it be true.

Turning around in her seat, Lake's eyes confirm it. It's Connie the klepto. And her pushy mom is with her.

"Hi, Connie."

"I can't believe how long it's been since we've talked or hung out. The team misses you this year," says Connie.

Lake blinks to make sure it's really her. Yep, it's her, alright. "I know. It has been a long time. I had to focus on the travel team this year. I couldn't really play on both teams, so I had to drop one."

"Well, no one's *really* pissed that you dropped us," says Connie with a fake laugh. "We heard you won the championship." More sarcasm with a bit of condescending inflection for added color.

Making a big show of it, Connie turns her attention to Hope and says, "Who's this?"

Lake reluctantly introduces Connie to Hope and immediately regrets the interaction. She doesn't trust the hometown mother-daughter duo, and the hair on the back of her neck stands up. Lake feels a shiver run through her body, an unwelcome reminder of the unspeakable, most terrible, traumatic summer event of her small-town life.

Unaware of the past 'incident,' Hope is cheerful and pleasant to Connie and her mom.

"You must be the same girl Harper and her boyfriend saw with Lake when they were here shopping a few weeks ago." Looking at Lake, she adds, "She mentioned seeing you with a cute strawberry blond."

Hope replies, "Lake and I have been coming here for a while. We love it."

Looking back and forth between Lake and Hope, Connie says, "Cool. Well, we should probably get going. See you, Lake." "Bye, Connie." As though she's seeing herself from outside of her body, Lake is filled with a sense of dread as she watches Connie slither away.

#

The feeling of impending doom is no joke. Sure enough, it's Connie the klepto who stirs up shit, rehashing that particular part of the 'incident' when Lake blurted, "I'm gay."

"So, me and my mom saw Lake and some girl named Hope at the mall over break. They were all chummy and giggly. Like, none of us have ever even heard of this Hope person before, but I guess they hang out all the time."

"So what, Connie? Hope is on Lake's travel team. They're friends," says Gretchen.

But Connie won't let it go. "What if they're *more than* friends? I mean, Lake doesn't date. Have you ever even seen her with a boy?"

"I know she fooled around with that guy from the lake. I don't remember his name, he was older. But they hung out most of the summer," says Gretchen.

Harper says, "That was, like, two summers ago."

Gretchen gets defensive and says, "I've gone to a few of Lake's games, and I know who Hope is. She has a boyfriend. I saw them kissing after one of the games."

"That doesn't mean anything. I'm telling you; Lake was acting weird. I think she might be gay for real."

Now Gretchen's really pissed. "Just shut up, Connie. Lake isn't gay. She's way smarter than you and a helluva lot more serious about her future, so just zip it."

Connie is surprised by Gretchen's reaction and backs off. "Whatever. You don't have to get all huffy."

#

Lake closes her locker and turns to see Harper walking by. She waves, but Harper acts like she doesn't see her and just keeps walking. Lake gets a sick, uneasy feeling. Something is off, but she's not sure what it is. She hurries to class and goes straight home afterward.

It's Gretchen who calls Lake and tells her what Connie is saying behind her back. Lake feels completely unmasked and super angry. She has a strong urge to throat-punch Connie the klepto and bring her to her knees. *Get real, you dumb fart knocker. Why do you even exist?*

"I just thought you should know," says Gretchen. "Connie's a big asshole. No one really even likes her anymore."

"Thanks for standing up for me, Gretchen. Connie's always been a loudmouthed jerk." No time like the present to lay her defensive groundwork. Pausing, Lake adds, "I was sort of bummed I couldn't go to Homecoming this year because of soccer. Now that it's over, I can take a deep breath and focus on senior prom. How about you, Gretch?"

"Dale and I have dated since junior high. I'm sure we'll go to prom. I mean, it's our senior year. We have to go."

"I know. It's like a tortuous high school ritual that if missed, will haunt us for the rest of our lives," jokes Lake.

"So who are you going with?" asks Gretchen?

"I'm not sure. I've always thought Simon was cute."

"He's totally cute—and single. You should talk to him, Lake."

"I will. I just don't want to come off as desperate or anything," says Lake.

"You won't. Dale knows Simon—I could have him drop a hint. Maybe say you're interested in going to prom?"

"Okay. Just be discreet. Tell Dale not to overdo it."

"I got you, Lake. I'll make sure he's subtle," says Gretchen with a laugh.

Lake laughs and says, "Dale, subtle? If you say so."

"Bye, Lake."

"See you later, Gretch."

No one says a word to Lake's face, but she can feel the eyes on her when she walks the halls. It only takes a few days for the rumors to begin bubbling up, and Lake is terrified of what will happen if she doesn't redirect and fast. In a school and town of this size, she can't afford to be labeled as a lezzi, dyke, lesbo, homo, carpet muncher, or queer. If just one of those words becomes synonymous with her name, it'll follow her through high school and beyond. It will ruin her reputation and pilfer her opportunities, instantly removing any chance she has to escape the horrors of Connie the klepto and this microscopic part of the world. There's no way she can let that happen.

Lake decides to double down and use her new flirting skills on Simon during AP Chemistry. She's known him practically her whole life and is fairly confident she can finagle a prom invite out of him. Simon sits behind Lake, two seats over to her left. This will take some planning on her part, but she can handle it. The teacher calls on her twice during class, which helps to draw attention to her. Out of the corner of her eye, she can see that Simon is looking at her. Moving her book to the side, Lake lets her pencil fall to the floor. She bends down, reaches for the pencil, and makes eye contact with Simon as she comes up. He smiles at her and looks down at his desk. Is he blushing?

Simon. He's not entirely tragic-looking, and he's not dumb or obnoxious. When the bell rings, Lake takes her time gathering her books and bag. She stands just as Simon is walking past her aisle. He smiles again, and this time she smiles back. Progress in just one period. Lake is all about using time efficiently.

That night, Gretchen calls and tells her Dale brought up her name at lunch and Simon said he thinks Lake is cute and really smart. He likes smart girls.

Sweet! She's basically got the prom invite from Simon all buttoned up, and it's still four months away! Preparation is the key to success. A sense of relief washes over her and she says, "I think the same about Simon. I've had a crush on him ever since I tutored him."

Gretchen says, "I feel like a real-life matchmaker. I can already imagine us double dating! Wouldn't that be fun, Lake?"

"For sure. We haven't hung out in months, Gretchen. A double date would be awesome."

"I think so, too. I'll see what I can to do to help make that happen!"

Gretchen is so excited about the idea of a double date, Lake doesn't have it in her to object. "Alright, Gretchen. Work your magic. I'll see you tomorrow."

The flirtatious banter with Simon escalates, and the next thing Lake knows, he's asking her out. By March, the two are exclusive, but taking things slow. Like, moving-at-a-snail's-pace slow. The timing is ripe for exposure, and Lake is sure to make their relationship very public. She and Simon watch every hometown girls' soccer game from the first row, center field. Lake cheers loud and proud, hugging and kissing Simon after every goal. This stage of their relationship is all about open displays of affection.

Lake keeps things light with Simon. She laughs at his jokes and asks a lot of questions about his family, school, and plans for the future. Simon is very comfortable talking about himself. So much so, that he literally jabbers nonstop about accepting an offer from his number-one college pick. He's committed to his dad's alma mater and a baseball scholarship. A full ride to college, and he leaves in August.

Four months. She can keep this charade going for four months. That's how long a soccer season is—four months for each of the fall and spring seasons. That's nothing!

In April, Lake lets Simon on second base just to keep him interested. It's the same things she did with Maxen. Unfortunately, Simon's completely incompetent when it comes to manual stimulation of the opposite sex, and Lake has to jump in and assist. Who knew guys were totally into this? Simon can hardly hold back and totally blows his spooge without any help from her. Oh dear, boys are incredibly low maintenance, and Lake has picked a winner! Getting to August will be a breeze.

The first weekend of May, Simon pops the question. It's not the most extravagant invite, but she does give him an A for effort. He suggests a pizza and movie date, which Lake is totally into because she's off the hook for planning. When they walk into the pizza place, Simon asks Lake to grab a table, and he makes a beeline for the counter, all secretive and whispery. When the waiter sets the pizza down, Lake notices the word *PROM* with a question mark is spelled out in pepperoni.

Simon turns to her and says, "Lake Myers, will you go to prom with me"? Aw, this is actually very sweet. Even though he's a boy, Simon is super thoughtful and kind.

"Yes, Simon. I will go to prom with you."

The employees behind the counter applaud, and Simon turns bright red. Lake is hammered by a fleeting twinge of guilt but hastily pushes it aside.

#

The prom theme is Carnival Extravaganza. It's Lake's first dabble into the world of school dances, and she's actually having a lot of fun. She and Simon are on a double date with Gretchen and Dale, and she's happy to have a friend to gravitate to when the hometown girls parade by their table. Around ten, things start to wind down.

She and Simon are slow dancing when he says, "We can leave anytime. Everyone's headed to the afterparty. Do you want to go?"

Lake looks at him and says, "Sure, let's finish dancing to this song. Then we can leave."

A short while later in the car, Lake soon recognizes the neighborhood they've entered, even though it's pitch dark outside. "What are we doing here?" asks Lake.

Simon looks at her, puzzled. "Going to the afterparty? You said you wanted to go."

"Right. Who's having the afterparty?" asks Lake. Inside she's pleading, *Please don't let it be Connie.*

Simon finds an empty space on the street and parks. A couple of guys pass the car and bang on Simon's window as they pass. "Woooo, let's party!"

Laughing, Simon says, "It's at Connie's house. Her parents are totally cool with it."

Lake replies with a halfhearted, "Awesome."

Simon reaches for her hand. "C'mon, it'll be fun."

"Okay. I'm just going to change really quick." Gretchen, her friend, buffer, and beacon of loyalty, had told Lake to bring a change of clothes for after the dance and she did. Thank goodness! She climbs over the front seat and does a quick change. She can see Simon sneaking a peek in the rearview mirror.

As she climbs out of the backseat, Simon takes her hand, and they walk toward the house. The music is super loud, and the front door is wide open. Sylvia would not be good for this. She's kind of particular about the house and bugs getting in. Lake wishes she was home with her parents right now, but she knows she has to see this night through.

The scene inside is out of control. This is definitely an "anything goes" kind of gathering with plenty of alcohol and couples sneaking off to do whatever.

"I'm going to get a beer. Do you want one?" asks Simon.

"Okay, yeah. I'll take a beer."

"Okay. Be right back."

Lake looks around and catches Connie and Harper watching her from the other side of the room. She smiles and gives them a big wave. Harper returns the smile and waves, while Connie glares at her and does nothing. Lake feels cornered and totally out of place.

Just then, a red Solo cup appears before her eyes. "Here you go, my lady," says Simon. Lake takes the cup from Simon, says "cheers," and drinks half of it before setting the cup down. Simon empties his cup, wraps his hands around Lake's waist, and gives her a big, wet kiss. Connie hasn't moved from her spot, and Lake gives her a show, kissing Simon back with tongue. He takes this as some sort of cue, pushing his body against hers while keeping the sloppy kiss going.

Pulling away, Simon takes her hand and leads her down a brightly lit hall. She can feel Connie's eyes on her.

Turning the knob to a door at the end of the hall, Simon says, "I wonder what's behind door number four?"

Pushing the door open, Simon hits the light switch, revealing Connie's parents' room. It's empty.

He fast-walks across the room and flips the switch on the night-stand lamp. Walking back to Lake, he turns off the overhead light and leads her to the bed. Sidestepping the foreplay, Simon just goes for it, but he is tender and respectful, asking Lake if she wants to keep going each time he advances. Lake doesn't want to keep going, but she knows there is no other option here. She's reached a crucial point in her relationship with Simon. If she doesn't do something drastic, Connie and her mean-girl eyes will haunt Lake's every move, silently judging and endangering Lake's carefully constructed bubble of well-being.

Simon pushes Lake's shirt up; he's clumsy, but not aggressive. Sitting up on his knees, he pulls a condom from his back pocket. The bedside lamp light goes off, and Lake silently thanks Simon for coming prepared. A glow from the streetlamp produces a silhouette of her high school prom date but reveals no embarrassing details. Lake is on automatic pilot and does nothing to stop Simon when he unzips her pants and pulls them off, panties and all. Squeezing her eyes shut, Lake tries to imagine a girl on top of her—literally any girl—but it's useless. She's stuck in this moment with the one and only Simon.

She could be an active participant, but she just can't bring herself to reciprocate. It's like the moves she makes when she's with her imaginary lovers are private and reserved for her true, female desires. It's inconceivable to think of replicating those feelings and acts with a boy. So she just lies there like a wet noodle, and he doesn't even seem to notice.

Simon lands a kiss on her lips. Through tightly sealed eyes, Lake feels a slight stab of pain, followed by a few minutes of uncomfortable movement, and then it's over.

She opens her eyes when she feels him getting up. Simon makes his way to the bathroom, and she listens as he pees, flushes, and washes his hands. When he opens the door, the bright lights of the bathroom are harsh. Lake feels vastly visible, lying there with no pants on, breasts poking out from under her bra. He picks up her pants and places them next to her on the bed, then leans over to kiss her. Neither of them realizes her panties have fallen out of her pants and are lying on the floor.

"I'll go out first so you can get dressed and use the bathroom," says Simon. When he turns to leave, Simon's toe catches her undies, and he unknowingly kicks Lake's panties just out of sight.

She waits for him to leave, then fixes her bra and shirt and pulls on her pants. Lake stands, takes a deep breath, exhales, and does her best to straighten up the bed. All she wants to do is go home and take a long, hot shower.

She slips out of the bedroom and finds Simon in the kitchen talking to Dale. He smiles when he sees her and kisses her softly. Connie walks by with a smirk on her face and heads down the hall toward her parents' room. She's got a whole lot of swagger for someone who could be president of the itty-bitty-titty club.

Lake turns to Simon and says, "Do you mind taking me home? I'm ready to go now."

"Sure, okay." He chugs what's left of his beer and says, "Let's go."

With a sigh of relief, Lake and Simon turn to go. They're just two short steps from the door when they're stopped dead in their tracks by Connie and her idiot boyfriend, Kyle.

In a voice loud enough for everyone to hear, she says, "Don't forget these, Lake." Confused, Lake starts to say something, then stops. Kyle is twirling Lake's undies on his finger. "I think these belong to you," he says while laughing.

Lake reaches for her panties, and Kyle pulls them away.

"That's enough, Kyle, just give them to her," says Simon. Kyle looks at Connie, gets a nod, then flings Lake's underwear over her head. They hit the door without making a sound and fall silently to the floor.

Connie looks at Lake and says, "Slut."

A few of the guys are whistling, and some of the girls are hooting and clapping. It's the best possible outcome to one of the worst, and best, self-deprecating nights of her life so far.

In one fell swoop, Simon collects Lake's panties and shoves them in his pocket. Moving his hand to her lower back, he leads Lake out of Connie's house and straight to his car.

Prom night is the one and only time Lake and Simon have sex. He and Lake date until graduation but never round fourth base again.

#

The small-town pressure got to Lake, and she succumbed to being penetrated by a boy, losing her virginity during her senior year of high school. It was not one of her finer moments, and it certainly wasn't all that special or memorable. She was just relieved to get it over with after the "I'm Gay" debacle. How sad that when she'd tried to come out to her so-called friends, she was shamed and made to feel like she had to run back into the closet before someone actually believed her. Lake's losing her virginity was a direct consequence of her ill attempt to come out, and so she did what she had to in order to keep the hetero hounds at bay.

It is utter anguish to feel so tied to the dirt and land she calls home, but at the same time, to be so uncoupled from most of its occupants. This town, defined not only by physical boundaries, but also the glaringly invisible boundaries of connected thought and action. There's no easy way for Lake to stay and live up to the expectations heaped upon her. Her kind and generous family are not the fundamental concern; it's her so-called friends and the greater societal norms. She wishes it was possible to find true love and acceptance here, surrounded by a few close friends and family, but she knows it isn't meant to be. For girls like her, small towns like this are just a pitstop, a place to refuel and make minor adjustments before getting back in the race and crossing the finish line farther down life's topsy-turvy road.

Chapter 13 — Sara

*E*ven though she has officially lost her virginity at the afterparty, in her mind, and in every cell of her being, Lake loses her virginity to Sara the summer before college.

Lake knows she will be leaving for college in the fall, so she makes the plan to dedicate her entire summer to work. A new travel center, complete with twenty-four gas pumps, sparkling-clean restrooms, and a large convenience store, fully stocked for summer beachgoers, has recently opened near the interstate. The place is nonstop action, a constant crawl of people coming and going at all hours. Like most northern towns, the bodies that pass through Geneva are here to harness every minute of the too-short summer season. Both the natives and the seasonal inhabitants are intent on transforming every bit of time awake into the most pleasurable and unforgettable moments. Those who have been here their whole lives focus on the ritualistic firsts that must be re-created every year. Long-standing traditions passed down to generations. Some could argue they're more sacred than football or secret family recipes. Others are here to create new memories.

While it was being built, Lake drove by the site almost every day, waiting for the HELP WANTED sign to go up. Just days before school is out, there it is in the window. She pulls a hard right into the lot and applies. Even though she's overdressed for the part, the manager is impressed by her maturity and willingness to learn, and he offers her a position on the spot. Lake begins her new, full-time cashier job the Monday after graduation, and she almost cries real tears the day she receives her first paycheck. After taxes, she clears more than one hundred and fifty dollars for just one week of work, and it wasn't even hard. This is way more money than she ever made babysitting!

#

"Hey, Lake, how was work today?" Sylvia is sitting in the living room watching one of her daytime programs, drinking a smoothie.

"It was great. I got paid!"

"Your first paycheck! Let me see," says her mom.

Lake hands Sylvia the check and asks, "What kind of smoothie is that?"

"Strawberry, banana, and peanut butter with yogurt and fresh mint from the garden. There's some of it left over in the blender—help yourself." Sylvia refuses to acknowledge any signs of aging, even though she has to hold the check out as far as her arm will reach just to make out the print. Squinting, she says, "Woo-hoo. That's a righteous amount of money for a young lady your age. What do you plan to do with all this cash?"

Lake pours herself a smoothie and sits in her dad's chair across from Sylvia. "I think I'm going to open a checking account and put some in savings."

"That's a smart idea. Sock away some cash every week so you have your own money when you go away to college."

"Yeah, I have ten weeks when I can work before I leave for school. My goal is to save, like, a thousand dollars."

Nodding, Sylvia finishes her smoothie and goes back to watching her program.

"Good talk, Mom," says Lake. "I'll be in my room if you need me."

"Okay, honey. Dinner's at six. We're having meat loaf and mashed potatoes."

The next day, Lake opens a checking account and puts a hundred dollars of her hard-earned cash into her savings. At the end of the transaction, the teller hands her a piece of paper detailing her deposit and the current balance in the account. Looking at the slip of paper, she feels a sense of accomplishment, and she's motivated to make that number grow. She imagines how having a four-figure balance will make her move that less stressful. Financial security and independence is a liberating thought. She can't wait to arrive at the tree-lined streets of her new school with all that money in the bank.

\#

Not long after she starts her job, Lake notices that some of the same customers come in almost every morning for coffee, a newspaper, cigarettes, or snacks. Others stop by just once a week to fill up, and a few of the road-construction workers pop in on weekdays for a sandwich and a clean place to pee. After a month, she's on a first-name basis with most of her regular customers, anticipating their purchases and moods without saying a word. One of her favorites is Owen. He manages a furniture store in town and stops by nearly every morning for a large soda and the local newspaper. An avid sports fan, Owen usually has the paper open and is shaking his head in despair before even reaching the counter.

"Morning, Owen. What's going on in the world of sports today?" asks Lake.

Shaking his head, Owen says, "Coach needs to get his head out of his ass if he expects to make it to the playoffs. How are you today, Lake?"

"I'm good. That'll be…" Before she has a chance to give him the total, Owen lays down a dollar and the exact amount of change to cover his purchase.

Looking at Lake, he smiles and pushes the money toward her. Owen takes great pride in paying with exact change most days.

"What are you going to do when the cost of a soda or the paper goes up?" asks Lake jokingly.

Owen shrugs and says, "Hey, Lake, do you know any reliable babysitters around here? Me and my wife, Sara, have a date night planned for this weekend, and our regular babysitter canceled on us."

"For what night?" asks Lake.

"Saturday. It's just dinner and a movie. We won't be out late."

Lake shrugs. "I don't have any plans for Saturday night. I could babysit for you. How many kids do you have?"

Owen looks surprised. "Really? That'd be killer, Lake. We just have one girl, Jess, she's three."

"Three-year-olds are easy. Give me your address, and I'll be there."

"You're a lifesaver, Lake. Sara's home with Jess most of the time and could use a night out. Thanks!"

Lake pulls off the top sheet of a Post-it Note, and hands it to Owen. He grabs a pen from the jar on the counter, jots down an address and phone number, and hands it back to Lake.

"Here's the address and phone number in case you have any trouble finding the place. We're not that far from here."

Shoving the piece of paper in her pocket, Lake says, "No problem, Owen. See you."

#

Owen and Sara live in a charming, but simple Cape Cod–style house about two miles east of the travel center. Lake arrives ten minutes early and is unclear whether she should wait in the car or knock on the door. If she has to guess, she'd say Owen is around twenty-four or twenty-five, but she's terrible at guessing people's ages, so she's really not sure. He seems young to have a three-year-old, but what does she know?

Glancing up at the house, she can see movement behind the curtains. She doesn't want to come across like a creeper, so Lake decides to just go up to the door. She did kill three minutes in the car trying to guess how old Owen should be to have a three-year-old, but that was pointless. What does she know about parenting? He must be old enough, because here she is, about to babysit his daughter.

Lake rings the doorbell, steps back, and runs her hands down her legs. Why is she so nervous? She's just here to do a job.

Owen opens the door and smiles. "Hey, Lake. You made it. Come on in."

She climbs the three steps to the door, then enters the living room. The house is small and tidy. "Cute house, Owen. It's so welcoming."

"Thanks, Lake. My grandma left it to me. I wasn't sure I'd want to live here, but Sara loves it, so we moved in. We've been here for about a year."

"Sorry about your grandma, but that's cool she left you a house," says Lake.

"Yeah, Sara and I are really blessed. Speaking of Sara, I'm just going to go check on her. She was giving Jess her bath before you got here, but I don't want to be late. Be right back."

Owen takes the stairs two at a time, and Lake can hear him calling for Sara. The fireplace mantle is covered in photos, and Lake moves closer to get a better look. There's a photo of a little girl wearing a bright yellow sundress, blond curls blowing in the breeze. Lake assumes this is Jess. The photo next to it is one of Owen holding the little blond girl. A beautiful blond woman is standing next to him. This must be Sara. The woman in the photo has curly blond hair, similar to the little girl's. She's perfectly petite with full, pouty lips and expansive green eyes. Lake reaches for the woman in the picture, placing the tip of her finger on her lips.

"Hi. You must be Lake. I'm Sara."

Lake's head jerks to attention. As she turns to address the lovely Sara, she knocks the photo over.

"Oh my gosh, I'm so sorry."

Was that a soft giggle? "It's fine, don't worry about it."

Sara is standing directly behind Lake, and the heat from her body permeates the space between them. Instead of stepping to the side, Sara reaches around Lake, setting the photo upright. When she pulls her arm back, Sara's hand lightly brushes Lake's shoulder. She smells delicious, like fresh strawberries, Lake's favorite summer snack.

She turns to face Sara and seems to have lost the ability to speak. Her eyes are the color of late-spring grass, intense, viridescent green after a solid month of intermittent rain and sun. She has no words. *Say something, weirdo.* "You have beautiful hair," says Lake. What the hell? Why did she say that? Even if she thinks it, she shouldn't have said it out loud.

Staring directly into Lake's eyes, Sara says, "Thank you."

Lake extends her hand and says, "I'm Lake, by the way." What in the babysitter's nightmare is happening right now? Lake has never felt so focused on the present. Like she is totally here right now, and nothing else matters.

Sara doesn't blink or look away as her soft fingers wrap around Lake's hand.

A thousand tiny tingles pulse through Lake's body simultaneously. Her eyes move directly to Sara's mouth and lips.

Still holding her hand, Sara says, "Nice to meet you, Lake."

Pulling her hand away, Lake's voice cracks, making her sound like a six-year-old. She says, "You have a lovely home." What the heck is wrong with her voice? She's behaving like a socially awkward teen.

Wait, she *is* a teen, but she's not usually this dorky. She wishes she could curl up into a ball and roll away.

"Babe, you ready? I'm starving." It's Owen. Yay, Owen's here to rescue her, and he has Jess in his arms.

Sara is cool and composed. Flashing a beautifully white, toothy smile at Lake, Sara says, "There's a list of contacts on the fridge. Doctors, family members, poison control, that kind of thing. Jess has been fed and bathed, so you two should be all set. She goes down at eight o'clock. Her binky is on the nightstand next to her bed. Any questions?"

Lake's heart is racing. "No. no questions."

Sara grabs a sweater from the coatrack. Looking back at Lake, she says, "We should be home by eleven thirty."

Was that a wink? Did Sara throw in a wink at the end of that sentence? Lake is flustered and can't move.

Owen hands Jess to Lake. Taking the toddler in her arms, she barely gets out the words, "Have fun," before they're out the door.

#

Lake falls asleep on Owen's couch thinking about Sara. Geez, Louise, this is one of her customer's wives. And they have a child together. Stop with the nonsense. Everything that happened earlier was innocent and clearly overexaggerated in her mind. Sara is at least five years older and way too cute to ever be interested in Lake. Oh, and she's married and has a daughter. It's an impossible situation.

Lake wakes up startled by Owen's voice. "Lake. Hi. We're home."

Lake sits up and rubs the sleep from her eyes. "I must have fallen asleep. Sorry, Owen. How was date night?"

"Good. How was Jess? Did she go down okay?"

"Yeah. She was perfect. No problem at all."

Owen hands Lake a twenty-dollar bill and says, "Thanks again for watching her. Are you okay to drive home?"

Lake waves a hand in front of her face. "Oh yeah, I'm good. I don't live far."

When she stands, Lake notices a big drool spot on the pillow. She can hear Sara's footsteps overhead and realizes she would have passed by her on her way upstairs. Did she see Lake passed out on the couch, drooling wet slobber all over her pillow? Great lasting impression.

Lake sighs and makes her way to the door. "Bye, Owen."

#

The common denominator between Lake and Sara is Owen, and she looks forward to his morning visit on Monday.

With a noticeable pep in his step, Owen bounces through the door, waves, and says, "Good morning, Lake!"

"Good morning, Owen. You're in a good mood today."

Smiling, Owen responds, "Date night after we got home was pretty great, and I'm a happy guy. Sara said she felt so comfortable with you watching Jess, she was able to relax and have fun. It was just what we needed, and we'd like to have you over for dinner next weekend. You got any plans?"

Lake glances up at the ceiling and gives Owen an audible "Hmmmm," as she attempts to create the illusion of running through her days and busy social calendar in her mind. "I don't think I have any plans but let me check and get back to you tomorrow."

"Okay. You let me know tomorrow. I've got to run."

Holy Toledo. An evening with Sara sounds exciting and terrifying all at the same time. Lake is scheduled to work Friday and Saturday during the day, and she has no evening plans either day, but she doesn't want to come across as too eager, even though she can't wait to see Sara again.

#

Lake has never been one to obsess about her physical appearance, but she's nervous about this dinner with Owen and Sara. She's convinced she has nothing decent to wear, and so she calls Hope to help her shop for a respectable outfit for the occasion.

"Hope, I need your help. Simon invited me to dinner with his family before he leaves for school," Lake fibs, "and I don't have anything decent to wear. Can you meet me at the mall Thursday afternoon?"

"Yeah, I can meet you. Where are you going to dinner?" asks Hope.

"It's at his house, but I still want to look nice."

"Okay, that helps. I know just where to shop for an outfit for your dinner. It will be casual, summery, and just the right amount of sexy. You might even get lucky," Hope says with a laugh.

"Sounds perfect," says Lake. "I'll meet you at five thirty in our usual spot."

#

Dinner is at seven o'clock, but Owen told Lake she could come by any time after six thirty, so she arrives at six forty-five. The entire outfit Hope had picked was literally plucked off of a mannequin. Lake looks and feels incredible! The blue halter top she's wearing is the same deep blue color of her eyes and really makes them pop. Hope insisted she buy the shorts and sandals, too. "Seriously, Lake. You have amazing leg—they're so tan and shapely. You have to get the whole ensemble, and make sure you wear a little eye makeup, at least mascara and some lip gloss. Show off what you got, 'cause what you got is hot!"

Lake applies a thin coat of lip gloss, smacks her lips, and walks with purpose to the front door. *Deep breath.* She rings the doorbell and waits for Sara to answer.

She hears footsteps, then the knob turns. "Hey, Lake, come on in. Sara's in the kitchen," says Owen.

It's not what she expected, but it is his house.

"Thanks. I brought these." Lake hands Owen a bunch of pink daisies.

"Sara loves daisies. They're her favorite. Thanks, Lake!"

"You're welcome. They were on sale, and I thought they were pretty. Thank you for having me."

"They were on sale?" He doesn't need to know that, Lake. Less is more.

Glancing toward the kitchen, Owen shouts, "Hey, babe, look what Lake brought. They're your favorite!"

Lake hears Sara before she sees her. "Oh, really?"

Lake's breath catches when Sara enters the room.

"Hi, Lake, what do you have for me?" "Hi, Sara. I brought you and Owen a bunch of daisies."

In a playful voice, Sara says, "Thank you, Lake. That's very thoughtful. How could you possibly know pink daisies are my favorite?"

"I…I didn't. I just thought they were pretty."

Sara approaches Lake, her eyes moving slowly up and down the length of her body. Eyes locked on Lake's, Sara takes the flowers from her and says, "Yes, they are pretty. Very. Pretty."

Okay, she is definitely not imagining this. Sara is for sure flirting with her, and it's driving Lake crazy. What's her deal, anyway? Is Sara just some cruel, bored housewife who enjoys playing games with people? What about her husband, Owen? How would he feel if he knew this was happening? This whole thing is weird and wrong on multiple levels. Even though she's insanely attracted to Sara and would like nothing more than to have a slow go at her snack pack, Lake has to be the bigger person here.

"I hope you like chicken," says Owen.

Directing her attention to him, Lake responds, "I love chicken. I mean, who doesn't like chicken?"

"Good. I told Sara chicken would be a safe bet. She made rice, and we have green beans from the garden to go with it. Hope you like those, too."

"I'm easy, Owen. My mom's kind of a health nut. She doesn't let us eat much sugar or junk food, so we grew up eating a lot of fruit and veggies. There's really not much I don't like."

"Your mom sounds a lot like Sara. She makes all of Jess's baby food from scratch, and she refuses to buy soda for me. Says it's poison. Whatever you do, don't tell her about my morning sodas. She'll have a fit."

"What morning soda?" says Lake. "I have no idea what you're talking about."

"Hey, what's going on in here?" says Sara. "Is there something I need to know?"

Owen looks at Lake and says, "You know everything there is to know, my love."

"Ha, nice save, darling," says Sara. "Dinner's about ready, I hope you're hungry, Lake."

Doing her best to avoid eye contact, Lake says, "I'm starving, actually."

#

"So, Lake, what are your plans for the future?" asks Sara.

"Right now, I'm just working at the travel center, trying to save as much money as possible for college. I start in the fall."

"How exciting. Owen and I met in college."

"Really? Tell me the story. Was it love at first sight?" asks Lake.

Owen jumps in and says, "There was a big snowstorm the night before finals week, and we got almost a foot of snow. Sara had an old Jeep, and she made it to campus okay, but when she tried to start it after class, it wouldn't even turn over. It was windy and freezing cold that day, and there she was, head under the hood of her Jeep, trying to figure out what was wrong. She was cussing and looking around, and I just happened to be walking by. I offered to give her a jump, and then I followed her to the auto parts store to make sure she was okay. After the guy there replaced her battery, she wrote her number on the back of my hand and said I should give her a call sometime. I waited two days before I called, and then she acted like she didn't remember me. Can you believe that? I literally saved her butt from perishing alone in a parking lot, and she had the nerve to pretend I didn't exist. I'm not sure about love at first sight, but I was definitely intrigued. I decided to play along, and I asked her to dinner, thinking maybe a warm meal would jog her memory of me. She accepted, and we've been together ever since."

Lake glances from Owen to Sara. Somehow, she imagined a less-practical story of how the two had met.

"So, what happened after college? How did you two end up here?" asks Lake.

Now it was Sara's turn to speak. In a monotone voice, she says, "After graduation, Owen and I got married. The plan was to get jobs in the city, establish our careers, and eventually buy a house. But then Owen's grandma got sick. When she passed, she left this house to him. I fell in love with it the minute I walked in. After we moved here, I got pregnant with Jess. Who's ready for dessert?"

So, she is a bored housewife.

The underlying dryness of Sara's tone and the lack of any romantic embellishments to her story go right over Owen's head. "Sara's an amazing mom and wife. Jess and I are lucky to have her," he says.

Lake feels sorry for Sara and says, "I like the story of how you two met. It's very sweet. Obviously, you were meant to be together. And now here you are. Dinner was really good, Sara. Thank you."

Sara smiles and says, "It was our pleasure. I made a strawberry and cream pie for dessert. Would you like some?"

Lake can't help herself. She looks at Sara with seductive eyes, lips forming an enticing smile, and says, "How could you possibly know strawberries are *my* favorite?"

#

Lake now has a new woman to think about, and Sara occupies nearly all of Lake's waking moments and those really sleepy minutes just before her alarm goes off. It's the early morning times that really get her going, when the moon hasn't quite disappeared, when she wakes consumed by thoughts of Sara. The dreams are so real, that when she closes her eyes, she's right back in them. Lake is drenched in sweat, every part of her body moist and electrified. Knowing she has just a few minutes before her alarm goes off, Lake enjoys the rest of the dream, surrendering her body to Sara, letting her finish what she started. Feeling stupidly happy and satisfied, the abrasive beeping of the alarm clock drives an optimistic Lake out of bed into the welcoming arms of morning glory.

Lake volunteers to pick up extra shifts at work so she can add to her college stash and keep herself from physically seeing Sara. But her logic backfires when Sara starts dropping in on her at work at the most random times. Lake didn't really think that one through. Working as a cashier at a busy travel center literally two miles from Sara's house makes her fully accessible to anyone who might want to see her.

"Have you been hiding from us?"

It's a busy summer day at the center, and Lake doesn't notice Sara until she's standing right in front of her. Lake can feel her face getting red. Geez, this woman has a wild effect on her. Lake ignores the comment and says, "Hi, Sara. How are you?"

"I'm great. I've been going stir-crazy at home, and Owen suggested I get a part-time job. I'm teaching spin class at the gym a few days a week. Do you ride?"

"Actually, I've never taken a spin class before, but it sounds fun."

A line of impatient customers is forming behind Sara, forcing both women to complete the transaction and move on.

"I teach an afternoon class Monday through Thursday. You should stop by—the first class is free, and I promise to make it worth your while."

Lake feels weak in the knees. This tantalizing woman with gloriously perky boobs and a great ass is publicly teasing her in the most discreet and sexy way. She is so turned on at the thought of kissing and touching Sara, but actually being with her is out of the question. The circumstance is maddening! Lake wants to lean over the counter, grab her by the shirt, and scream, "Why don't you just run over me with your car already?" Instead, she says, "I'm working every day this week. Maybe I can come one day next week?"

Picking her change up from the counter, Sara smiles and says, "I would love to see you *come...*"

#

Lake's schedule for the following week was posted days ago, and she knows she has Wednesday afternoon off. She could have mentioned this to Sara before she left, but why spoil the suspense? She has no intention of letting things escalate with Sara, but the back-and-forth is fun. Lake looks forward to the brief interactions with Sara and uses them as the basis for her daydreams and alone-time erotica. It's the only way she's able to maintain her professional relationship with Owen and not feel like a mountainous pile of steaming poo every time she sees him. The threesome develops a dangerous routine that revolves around a lighthearted husband and his fragmented wife.

Lake drops by the gym on Tuesday evening to get a feel for the place. Watching through the window in the door, she imagines Sara leading a group of toned spinners, glistening bodies pumping to the beat and the sultry sound of her voice. She makes a mental note of which bike she'll choose during the class and leaves feeling energized about seeing Sara the next day. On her way home, Lake stops by work to pick up a half gallon of milk for her mom.

"Hey, Lake. Back so soon?" Her manager, Duane, is doing inventory tonight while it's slow.

"You know I can't stand to be away, Duane. This place is like my second home."

"Is that right? Lucky us," jokes Duane.

"My mom called just before my shift ended and asked me to bring home a carton of milk. I forgot, so here I am."

"Well, I guess it is lucky for us. Allan called and said he can't open in the morning. He has a doctor's appointment. Would you be willing to take his shift?"

Lake is really looking forward to seeing Sara tomorrow, but she also hates to say no to the extra cash. Her shoulders slump, and she sighs. "I kind of had plans, but I can change them. I'll take Allan's shift, but you owe me, Duane."

"Name your price, Lake. You're totally saving my ass! My wife was not happy when I told her I'd have to open in the morning after closing tonight. She threatened to leave me. Can you imagine giving all this up?" Duane grabs the spare tire on his waist and gives it a shake.

"You're a lot of man for one woman, Duane."

"You got that right. Thanks a bunch, kid."

"Anytime, boss. G 'night."

Chapter 14

Wednesdays are typically slow at the center. The tourists are nestled into their rentals, and the locals are riding out the day, looking forward to the weekend. The day creeps by without a visit from either Owen or Sara.

On Thursday morning, Owen pops in for his soda and paper. "Hey, Lake, how goes it?"

"Hey, Owen, things have been kind of slow. We missed you yesterday. Everything okay?"

"Yeah, all's good. Jess had a bad dream the night before last and snuck into bed with Sara and me. She tossed and turned and kicked me in the back, kept me up most of the night. I overslept, was late to work, and tired all day yesterday. It's fun having a three-year-old."

"I bet. You look well rested today, though."

"Yeah, much better. I've got to run. Have a good day, Lake."

"You, too, Owen." As soon as he's out the door, Lake finds herself thinking about Sara and hopes she follows Owen's lead and stops in for a little something before spin class. Lake keeps one eye on the pumps while the other eye scans the store, looking for a petite blonde with curls. At half past three, Lake spots Sara's SUV pulling in, and her heart skips a beat.

The parking space directly in front of the cashier's counter is open, and Sara takes it. Her eyes lock on Lake's before she's even out of the vehicle. Lake has a flashback to the ranch and recalls a Kiki moment: *"It's the eyes that tell the story, Lake."*

Oh, Kiki, I wish you were here. I know it isn't right, but I can't stop thinking about this woman.

Lake's grandma had been the kindest, least judgmental person she'd ever known. If she were still alive, Lake feels confident she could have had an honest conversation with her about Sara. It might not change the outcome, but having someone to talk to would make things easier.

There's only one other customer in the store when Sara walks in. She's dressed for class and looks good enough to eat.

Sara glances around, seizing her moment of near anonymity. Without saying a word, she approaches the counter and leans in close, bouncy boobs resting on the space between them. Lake has a clear line of sight to her cleavage, and both of her nipples, which happen to be hard, appear to be standing at attention just for her. Lake is torn between the thought of kissing Sara's luscious lips and lightly biting on her nipples.

Lake and Sara are thunderstruck, each completely consumed by naughty thoughts of the other, when a booming female voice jars them back to the present. "I'll take ten dollars on pump six, please."

Looking past Sara, Lake says, "Yes, ma'am, thank you."

Sara stands up straight and moves to the side as Lake takes the woman's money.

"Have a nice day," says Lake as the woman turns and walks out.

With wide eyes, Lake looks at Sara, and they both bust up laughing. "Today's my last class for the week. I take it I'm not going to have the opportunity to take you for a ride?"

Lake's body is burning up. She'd like nothing more than to let Sara give her a ride, but it's not meant to be.

"I don't get off until six," says Lake.

"Wouldn't it be nice if you could get off sooner," says Sara while batting her eyes at Lake.

A shock wave runs through Lake and rocks her to her core. Heavens to Betsy, woman!

Sara is well aware of her effect on Lake and is loving every minute of it.

The bell above the door rings as a customer walks in, jolting Lake back to reality. She smiles at the man as he passes by the counter.

Her eyes settle on Sara's. "I'm off next Tuesday. What time is your class?"

"It's at four. Owen's aunt has Jess while I teach. Maybe we could go somewhere after?"

Lake inhales deeply and responds with a breathy "Okay. Yes."

Sara tilts her head slightly, licks her lips, and says, "Great. I can't wait."

The next four days are the longest of Lake's life. The only way to get through them quickly is to keep her hands and body busy and her mind off Sara.

Lake spends Sunday, her only day off, preparing for Tuesday. She tries sleeping in, but she has always been a morning person, so that doesn't work. Sunday mornings are reserved for family breakfast time, and now that she's about to leave for college, Lake's mom insists they don't miss a single one. The morning meal is served at 9 a.m. sharp, and Lake relishes the regularity of the routine.

Joining her parents at the dining room table, Lake greets them with the standard, "Good morning."

Without looking up from the paper, her dad says. "Good morning, Lake."

Popping her head out from behind the open fridge door, Sylvia responds with, "Good morning, honey. Do you want some juice?"

"Sure, but just a small glass."

Sylvia pours the juice and sets it on the table. "We only have you here for a few more weeks. I know you've been picking up extra shifts at work and saving most of your money, but your dad and I want to make sure you have everything you need. How do you feel about a trip to the mall today?"

A trip to the mall with her mom would kill at least five or six hours. "That'd be great, Mom. I could use a couple new pairs of jeans and maybe a sweater or two. Oh, and a new pair of shoes. And maybe a few school supplies."

Taking a sip of his coffee, Jack says, "Sounds like a full day. Rick and I have some work at the ranch, but you two ladies have fun. Breakfast was delicious, Syl." Dad gives Mom a kiss on the cheek and pats her butt on the way out of the kitchen.

"You're a scoundrel, Jack Myers. Go on now..."

Lake laughs at her goofy parents as she takes a big bite of bacon. Sylvia looks at Lake's hand and says, "Your cuticles are a mess. Working the register and handling all that dirty money, you need a manicure."

"Mom, I'm fine. I don't need a manicure."

"You most certainly do. If you don't want to go today, I can try to make you an appointment for tomorrow."

Lake thinks about Tuesday—and Sara. It would be nice to look good for the class. "Can I get a pedicure, too?"

"Yes, of course. What time do you get off work tomorrow?"

"Three o'clock," responds Lake.

"I'll call the salon after I finish my coffee. We can go together. I'm about due for a mani-pedi myself. It'll be fun."

Lake is going to miss Sylvia. "Okay, Mom. I'm going to get ready for the mall. Give me an hour and we can go."

Lake has a really nice day at the mall with her mom and enjoys their mother-daughter time at the salon the following day. Her hands do look a lot better now. She picks a shade of pink for her toes that reminds her of the daisies she gave Sara and Owen at dinner. Sara had said they were her favorite.

#

On Tuesday, Lake gets to spin class early so she can claim the bike she'd picked when she came to check out the gym. She has decided on a monochromatic look and is wearing black leggings, a black sports bra, and black tennis shoes. Too keep her hair out of her face, and to add a splash of color, she has brought a bright orange headband. Lake throws her towel over the handlebars of the bike she's claimed, but she isn't sure what to do next. People are coming into the room, and most have a water bottle with them. The bike has a built-in drink holder. She panics, grabs her wallet from her bag, and runs out into the hall. The front desk sells water. She'll buy a bottle and get back to her bike before Sara gets here, hopefully. Standing at the counter waiting to buy the water, Lake feels a hand on her shoulder, followed by a whisper in her ear. "I'm happy to see you." It's Sara.

Before Lake can turn around, Sara is gone. "Hi, can I get a water please?"

Lake walks back into the room and sets her water in the drink holder. She's chosen a bike in the second row. From this vantage point, she has a clear view of Sara without being directly in front of her. The class is tougher than Lake expected, and Sara is all business. When it ends, everyone in the room is drenched in sweat. Lake is glad she brought the headband.

Lake dawdles while people exit the room. Sara thanks each of them as they leave. Finally, they are the last two in the room, and Sara walks toward Lake. "Are you sure this was your first spin class? You looked pretty good from where I was sitting."

Lake blushes and says, "I've played soccer most of my life and have a love for pretty much all sports. You're a really good teacher. It was easy to follow you."

"So, where do you want to go now?" asks Sara.

"I haven't really thought about it. Where do you want to go?"

"There's a new café not far from here. They make really good smoothies."

"Okay. I'll follow you there," says Lake.

Once inside the café, Sara says, "I can't stay long. I have to pick up Jess and be home by six."

Lake is disappointed and tries not to show it. "Oh, okay."

Sara reaches across the table, placing her hand over Lake's. "We have twenty-five minutes to spend together. Tell me everything about you."

"That's not much time—what if I want to know about you?" asks Lake."

I asked you first. I'll tell you all about me some other time," says Sara.

Without hesitation, Lake starts with her grandma Kiki and the ranch and tells Sara the G-rated version of her life story, up to the point they are at right now. Sara listens quietly, never once interrupting or appearing to be bored.

"What a remarkable life you've had, Lake Myers. You're going to do amazing things."

Lake is embarrassed to have talked so long. "Thanks, Sara. I can't wait to hear about you."

"Well, that's for another day. I have to get going now."

Lake looks at her, pleading, "Just one thing. Tell me one thing about you that I don't already know."

Sara's pupils are huge, but she doesn't look away when she says, "I think you're the most beautiful thing I've ever laid eyes on."

Lake's heart is pounding, and the low hum between her legs is getting more intense.

Sara is gathering her things, rooting around in her purse for her keys. When she looks up, she says, "Owen's going to be out of town this weekend, and he knows I hate being alone in the house. I want you to come for dinner Saturday and spend the night."

Lake's head is spinning. If she says yes, there's a very high probability things are going to happen. Things she told herself would never and should never happen.

Sara stands, waiting for a response from Lake.

Lake's gaze falls on Sara's lips before moving to her eyes. "What do you want me to bring?"

"Just you. All I want is you, Lake."

#

There's no pressure to dress up or be anything more than Lake. When she arrives, Sara answers the door wearing cutoff shorts and a plain white tee. Her hair is loose around her face, and she's not wearing any makeup. Lake is moved by her natural beauty, and it takes every ounce of self-control she has not to push Sara up against the wall, rip off her clothes, and ravage her right there. Lake wonders if she's wearing panties.

"Hi. I know you said I didn't need to bring anything, but I thought you might like this." Lake pulls a small bag from behind her back and hands it to Sara. "I wasn't sure if it was just pink that you liked or what, but I saw these and thought of you."

"What is it?" asks Sara.

"Open the bag and find out."

Sara reaches into the bag and pulls out a box, revealing a twelve-piece crystal refrigerator magnet set.

"Each piece has a different picture of daisies on it. One is a bunch of pink daisies."

Sara looks at Lake and leans in, hugging her tight. "I love it. Thank you."

"You're welcome."

"So I decided to take all of the guesswork out of tonight's meal and made the exact same things as the last time you were here. Jess is kind of a picky eater, but she likes roasted chicken and rice. I hope you don't mind."

"I don't mind at all. Like I told Owen, I'm easy."

Sara laughs softly and says, "Promise?"

She has no idea. There's nothing Lake wouldn't do for this woman right now. Morals be damned.

"Maaaaaama, I'm hungry!" Jess is tugging at the fringe on Sara's shorts. Lifting her up, Sara kisses her on the nose and says, "Okay, little one, let's eat."

During dinner, Jess chatters nonstop, surprising Lake with her rather large vocabulary. "You're a really smart girl, Jess. Who taught you all those words?"

Jess points to Sara and says, "Mama...and *Sesame Street*."

Lake laughs and turns to Sara. "Nice job, Mom. Her vocabulary is really big for a three-year-old."

"I went to school to be a teacher. As soon as Jess is old enough for pre-K, I'll start looking for a teaching job."

"What grade do you want to teach?"

"First. Kids at that age are so innocent and excited to learn. I remember my first-grade teacher, Mrs. Willis. She was my favorite. I can recall the sound of her voice to this day."

Lake loves the way Sara's mouth moves when she speaks. She would be content listening to her talk all day.

"Stop looking at me like that," says Sara.

Lake smirks. "Make me."

Sara gives it right back to Lake. "I will. Later! But first, Jess could use some encouragement with her last couple of bites of dinner." Jess covers her mouth with her hands.

"What a big girl you are! Just two more bites, Jess, and then it's bubbles time."

Jess's hands fly up over her head. "Bubbles!"

After they finish eating, Lake offers to clean up and do dishes while Sara bathes Jess and gets her ready for bed. "You don't have to do that. I won't be long."

Lake takes in the sight of Sara and thinks about having her all to herself. "I don't mind. Go take care of Jess, I'll clean up, and I'll be waiting right here for you when you're finished."

"I like the sound of that. Jess, let's go get you a bath. You can pick out a book for bedtime while the water's running."

"Okay, Mama. I want to pick out two books."

Sara shakes her head, picks up Jess, and heads upstairs. Stopping halfway up, Sara whispers something in Jess's ear. Jess waves and says, "Good night, Lake."

Lake waves back and says, "Good night, Jess."

Forty minutes later, Sara emerges from the second floor and joins Lake on the couch.

"She's finally sleeping. She was thrilled to have a visitor for dinner. I told her we're having a sleepover and that she can talk to you again in the morning. Prepare yourself for a loud and messy breakfast."

"That sounds delightful," says Lake.

Sara leans in close to Lake and says, "Your *lips* are delightful. I'm going to kiss them now."

Memories of the barn, Gretchen, the Sommerville house, and Carly swirl in Lake's mind as she and Sara kiss for the first time. This is what she's wanted for as long as she can remember. For the first time in her life, Lake is kissing a girl who wants to kiss her back, and it feels natural and unspoiled. Lake wraps her fingers around Sara's curls and pulls her closer. She's never been so turned on just by kissing someone before, and she doesn't want to stop. The two kiss slow, soft, hard, and wet, tongues moving over teeth, inside their mouths, and down one another's necks. Lake's panties are soaked, and she's ready to keep going, when she feels a sudden twinge of guilt. Pulling away from Sara, her face in Lake's hands, she asks, "What about Owen?"

Sara kisses each of Lake's hands and says, "He knows you're here, Lake."

That's all she needs to hear. Lake isn't clear on Owen's interpretation of tonight's sleepover, but she's not about to press too hard on the subject. Something inside tells her this will be her only night with Sara, and she's taking this at face value.

Sara stands, takes Lake by the hand, and leads her up the stairs. Lighting a small candle, she says, "I thought you might feel more comfortable in the guest room."

Lake pulls Sara's shirt up over her head and unfastens her bra. Pushing the straps down, she lets it drop to the floor. Lake bends her knees and kisses Sara's chest. She moans and tilts her head back. Sara's nipples are hard, and Lake sucks on one, then the other, before moving back up to Sara's lips. As they kiss, Sara unbuttons her shorts and steps out of them. Lake smiles when she realizes Sara is not wearing panties.

Lake unbuttons her own shorts and wriggles out of them; her panties fall to the floor along with her shorts.

Sara pushes the extra pillows off the guest bed and pulls the covers back. Lake takes off her shirt and falls into bed with Sara.

It takes them hours to work through every conceivable erotic encounter Lake has ever played out in her head. Their time together is sporadic and unpredictable, neither of them willing to waste a single minute talking.

Lake is mesmerized by the sounds Sara makes when she orgasms, and it drives her to make it happen again and again.

Around 2 a.m., an exhausted Lake falls asleep tangled up in Sara's body, the smell of their sex covering her face.

#

In her loudest inside voice, Sara bellows, "I knew you were leaving for school soon, but in ten days? You leave in *ten days!* We just discovered each other, and now you're going away?!"

Worried that Sara will wake her daughter, Lake lies still, quietly tracking the tear as it rolls down the side of Sara's face and disappears in her hair. "C'mon, Sara. This isn't a relationship. You're married. You have a family and a home. Please don't make this harder than it already is," says Lake.

Blinking back the tears, Sara says, "I don't want you to go. Owen won't be home until after lunch. At least stay and have breakfast with us."

"I can't. Tell Jess I said bye."

Lake closes her eyes, and scenes from last night come rushing in. There is no future for her and Sara. She kicks off the covers and moves to sit up, but Sara grabs her by the arm and pulls her down. In an instant, she's on top of Lake, kissing her face, her hair, her neck. They both know this is good-bye, and there's nothing more to say. Words won't change their circumstances. Lake rolls Sara onto her back and kisses her tenderly one last time. When she gets up, Sara turns away from her.

Lake gathers her things and tiptoes downstairs, careful not to wake Jess. Standing near the front door, her eyes go the mantle and the photo of Owen and his family. Sara can never be hers; she has to let her go.

#

Lake is overwhelmed and anxious at the thought of leaving. For one thing, fear of the unknown is often terrifying. Everything she identifies with is here, which is also sort of the problem.

Even so, it's unnerving to imagine living in a completely different state, city, house, and bedroom. She's taking a leap of faith, moving to an unfamiliar place based on promises she's read in a bright, colorful pamphlet. When the big envelope from her chosen school had arrived, Lake went straight to her room and locked the door.

Sitting cross-legged on the bed, she carefully opened the package, slowly removing each piece of paper. With everything arranged in a neat row in front of her, she picked up the cover letter and read every word. *Dear Lake, we are pleased to inform you that you have been admitted to the undergraduate program.* Page two, from the Office of University Financial Aid, listed the estimated cost of attendance and a description of each award, scholarship, grant, and work study offer. An organized and easily digestible list of what would become her new life. A comprehensive offer to earn a degree, play a sport she loves, and experience an entirely new world. Her heart racing, she lay back on the bed and opened the shiny, trifold university pamphlet. Inside is a photo of a majestic, tree lined street. Under the graceful green awning of branches are perfectly spaced, classic black lampposts, and jutting out from each post is a university sign proudly displaying its logo. The photo fades as her gaze is drawn further down the street, but not enough to keep her from seeing the tightly trimmed hedges at the top of the roundabout. Three large letters signal her visual arrival at the university. Just beyond the bright green initials, at the end of the street, is a traditional, Southern brick manor complete with an impressive white-pillared portico.

Lake stares at the photo for a long time as she imagines living there in a different building on campus, walking to classes, studying in the library, and meeting new people. The dream is powerful enough to drown out her fear of the unknown for the time being. Thankful for this new path, she closes her eyes and falls asleep.

#

"Lake, dinner's ready, are you coming down to eat?" Her mom is standing just outside of her room.

She opens her eyes and glances over at the clock radio on her nightstand. She has been asleep for almost two hours! Moving the pamphlet from her chest, she gathers each of the papers and places them back in the envelope.

Dinner is a nonevent, the same as every other night, except for the fact that she has big news. In this house, her mom rarely sits at the table while the family eats. If she's not in the kitchen cooking, or baking, she's outside working in the garden. More often than not, she's in the kitchen. After taking multiple bites of every dish to make sure the consistency or amount of salt is just right, she has no room for a full meal at the table with the family.

Instead, she stands behind the counter, elbows leaning on it, head perched in the palms of her hands. "How was your day, hon?"

Dad turns his head to look at her. "It was good. I think the weather is beginning to turn. It didn't seem quite as hot today."

Nodding in agreement, Mom says, "Are you ready for more beans?" From her place at the counter, Mom's always in position to grab a plate and add more food. Dad's in a good mood, Mom seems to have had a pleasant day, and we're all enjoying the fried chicken.

"I got a package today from the school in Georgia that I applied to," Lake blurts out. Dad glances up from his plate, waiting for her to go on. "They offered me a full scholarship to play soccer. It covers room, board, and tuition. I start in the fall."

Smiling, Dad puts down his fork, lightly hits the table with his fist, and says, "Well, hot damn, Lake!" Turning his head to look at Mom, he says, "Looks like we got us another college girl living here, Sylvia! What do you make of that?"

Mom met Dad when she was just out of high school, they married, and she started having babies right away. Happy as a domestic goddess, she has no idea what it will be like for me to attend college.

"Georgia's, like, four states away. It worries me that Lake will be living there alone, with no family nearby." Content to cook and garden most days, she's not the adventuress type, and that's okay.

Picking up her empty plate, Lake places it on the counter and takes her mom's hand. "I'll be fine, Mom. I promise to call every day, and I'll be home for the holidays and breaks."

Placing her free hand on Lake's shoulder, Mom pulls her close and kisses her on the cheek. "I've never really worried about you, Lake. You're my sweet girl. You do whatever needs to done without being asked. Responsible and strong. Your grandma Kiki would be proud, just like we are."

It's been almost ten years since her grandparents died, but hearing her grandma's name, Lake feels a quick, stabbing pain in her chest. It's not as if she doesn't think of Kiki often, but it's been a while since anyone has said her name out loud. She feels a tear forming in the corner of her eye and absently wipes at it away. "Thanks, Mom. I love you guys."

It's Lake's night to clear the table and wash the dishes. As she goes about this chore, she begins mapping out her move in her head. Having something to plan and look forward to can be almost as exciting as actually doing it. She holds the power to control each step and the eventual outcome. When she isn't thinking about Sara, the move occupies all her other waking thoughts.

On the day before Lake sets out for Georgia, Jack insists she fill up her tank with gas to eliminate having to worry about this on her way out of town. She's almost packed and will load the car that evening after dinner. It's about a twelve-hour drive to the university. She originally planned to leave before the sun came up and drive straight through, but Sylvia wasn't having it. "Absolutely not. It's not safe for you to be alone on the road that many hours—and after dark. I'll call my cousin Abigail in Charleston and ask if you can spend the night at her house on your way through."

Lake had met Abigail once, when she was eight. Abigail is actually a cousin on her mother's side. She and her husband live in Charleston,

West Virginia, with their two kids, Clara and Bo Junior. With ten years having passed since she's seen Abigail, Lake has no idea what she'll be walking into, but Mom assures her, "They're good people." Fine. She'll have dinner with them and spend the night.

#

Lake turns into the travel center and takes the first available pump on her left. She turns off the engine and reaches down to pull the gas cover lever. As she looks up, she sees Sara pumping gas two stalls over. It stings to see her there, hair blowing in the breeze. Standing at an angle, facing the front of her car, she doesn't see Lake.

Lake takes a deep breath, opens the door, and walks around to the pump. With her back to Sara, Lake takes her time filling the tank, hoping she isn't spotted. Finally, the gas pump clicks loudly, the signal that her tank is full. Lake removes the nozzle and places it back in its holder just as Sara drives past the rear of her car. They look directly at each other as she passes. Lake's heart feels like it's being twisted and torn from her chest. She swallows hard as Sara raises her left hand from the wheel in a sad attempt at a wave. Lake watches her car until it's a tiny silver speck in the distance, and then it's gone. She doesn't know it now, but it's the last time she'll ever see Sara.

Lake drives back to her childhood home, tears streaming down her face. Her breathing becomes shallow, and she wonders if she's making a huge mistake. Doubting her decision to leave the safest space she's ever known, she finds herself sitting at the end of the driveway, staring at the house she's lived in for so many years. A figure is moving in the kitchen, going from the counter to the cupboards; it's her mom, putting away the dishes. Breathing in deeply, Lake savors this moment of safe familiarity. She loves this place where she's grown up and lived, but it's time for her to move on. Life has given her a beautiful gift, and at the tender age of eighteen, she's ready to move forward, shed her confining skin, and develop a new, more comfortable one.

Lake makes a final pass through the house, and when she opens the door to her bedroom, it seems smaller than it did the day before. She walks across the room and opens the closet to check one more time that she's left nothing behind. She takes a couple steps back. Standing on her tiptoes, she can see up to the shelf above the clothes rack and notices her Magic Eight Ball in a far back corner. She's taken to consulting the toy on numerous occasions. It's not an item she'll need in college, but what's the harm in asking it one more question?

A comforting detail of the Magic Eight Ball lies in the fact that while the questions might change, the answers never do. There are eight chances to make you believe, tell you to come back later, or destroy all your hope.

Lake uses a hanger to maneuver the eight ball in a way that she can reach it. When it's within reach, she picks it up, gives it a thorough shake, and asks, "Magic Eight Ball, will I ever be happy, in love with a woman?" Lake slowly opens her eyes and looks down. The blue triangle behind the window says, "Cannot predict now." Stupid Magic Eight Ball. It's never been reliable or accurate.

Placing it back on the top shelf, Lake looks around her room one last time before closing the door to the room—and to this chapter of her life.

Chapter 15 – Margot

Lake has been at her school in Georgia for seven months and hasn't met a single lesbian. Obviously, she can't be the only one here, but for some reason, she just can't seem to connect with any. Maybe it's because she doesn't socialize outside of her roommate/soccer/study group bubble. Lake's always on the lookout for opportunities to find females of the same persuasion, but as long as she's sleeping under the watchful eye of her roomies, a homebase meet-and-greet is out of the question. Her full-ride athletic scholarship at the smallish, private university in the South includes room, board, tuition, and books, and she's grateful. Still, it would be nice to have a room that isn't bursting at the seams. Lake completed the roommate questionnaire honestly to avoid any issues, but the limited questions were basic at best. It's a mystery to her how the answers she provided landed her in a cramped quad with three very distinct coeds. Amanda was the first to arrive and greet Lake at the start of the fall semester. In a strong Southern accent, she said, "Hi, I'm Amanda, but you can call me Mandy."

"Hi, Mandy, I'm Lake."

"Oooooh, you're the Yankee in our group. How'd you end up here? Have you ever been to Georgia before?"

"It's my first time in this state. I'm here on a soccer scholarship. But how am I a Yankee? I'm from Ohio."

"Ohio's not a Southern state, so therefore, you're a Yankee. But don't mind me. I'm from an itty-bitty little spot no one's heard of, and I've never been anywhere but Georgia, unless you count that one time when Daddy fell asleep in the car. We were going to a family reunion over in Columbus, and Momma took a wrong turn so we ended up in Alabama. We spent over an hour backtracking, and Daddy was all spun up."

"Wow. That's some story. So, what made you pick this school?" asked Lake.

Mandy gives her mousy brown hair a flip and says, "I've wanted to be a schoolteacher for as long as I can remember. I worked hard in school, and my guidance counselor showed me a picture of this place and said I could probably get in, so I applied."

"Cool. You got a boyfriend, Mandy?"

Shaking her head, Mandy says, "Used to. But we split up when I said I was coming here. He accused me of choosing my education over him, and I said, 'Hell yeah, I am.'"

"Good for you! Mind if I choose this bed near the window?" asks Lake.

"Suit yourself. I'll take this one here. It's closer to the ladies' room. I pee a lot."

Jaime walks in just after Mandy and Lake claim their beds. Tossing her duffel bag on the bed near Lake's, she says, "Hey. I'm Jamie. What's up?"

In her polite, Southern drawl, Mandy says, "Pleasure to meet you, Jamie. I'm Mandy, and this is Lake." Then, in a hushed tone, Mandy adds, "She's from Ohio."

Lake gives Mandy a look as if to say, *What was that all about?* then replies, "Hi."

Jamie gives them a nod and leaves without saying another word. Mandy looks genuinely hurt. "Well, that was rude."

"What? She introduced herself and asked what's up. Maybe she has someplace to be?" says Lake.

"Or maybe she just thinks she's better than us. She's from the big city," says Mandy.

"Give her a chance, Mandy. I doubt she thinks she's better than us," says Lake. And she's right. Jamie isn't a snob, but she *is* moody and elusive. She's a whiz at science, particularly chemistry, and when it comes to circadian rhythms, she and Lake are polar opposites. Seems Jamie's a night owl who likes to sleep late. Coincidentally, she gravitates to a like-minded group of science phenoms who spend their late-evening hours at the library debating methods and theories. Jamie's boyfriend, Julian, is a drummer in a grunge band, and she goes home almost every weekend to be with him.

Nicole is from North Carolina, and she misses all their first-day activities due to car trouble. She is a wannabe debutante with a hometown sweetheart, and Lake can hear her talking to Ryan at all hours of the night. Mandy keeps a slipper nearby so she can chuck it at her head. "We're trying to sleep, Nic!" she says. Unfortunately for Nicole, she and Ryan are off more than they're on. To ease the pain, Nicole likes to frequent the local watering holes, and she drags Lake and Mandy along for moral support. The girl can put a hurting on some beer when she puts her mind to it. Well into her second semester, Nicole's major is still Undecided.

#

It's a long holiday weekend, and all of Lake's roommates have gone home to visit boyfriends, family, and friends. Lake is excited to have the room all to herself, but soon she finds herself lonely and bored. With literally no gay options in town, she decides to make the easy drive to Savannah to check out the one gay bar she knows of. Mandy and Nicole love to party, and Lake's no stranger to the historic city's beauty and charm. Rumor has it, their St. Patrick's Day celebration is top rated. The river is dyed green, and residents throw a massive party that fills the cobblestone streets and squares with rabblerousers from all around. Marked by a poorly drawn green shamrock, the shared calendar in their dorm room promises an evening of drunken madness fueled by green beer. Nicole has booked an inexpensive room easily accessible to the festivities by a short cab ride, and the girls have been looking forward to the trip for months. Also, they occasionally visit the beach and hit up the shops at Savannah to purchase things they don't have access to in their town.

Lake has heard there are gay clubs in Savannah, and once, during a shopping trip, the girls throw caution to the wind and decide to go wherever the sidewalk takes them. "Let's just walk down Bay Street away from the hustle and bustle and find a quiet place to sit and grab a coffee," says Nicole. Mandy and Lake agree to take a breather from their holiday shopping and fall in with Nicole. Lake has never experienced a holiday season in a place that doesn't get snow, and she is in awe of the cheerful décor and Christmas merriment here. Bright bows, wreaths, and garland frame windows, homes, and fountains.

With so many dazzling sights to take in, Lake says, "I bet this place is even prettier at night. There must be thousands of lights strung up in the trees alone."

It's one of those times when Nicole and Ryan are on the outs, and she's feeling less appreciative of the picturesque scenes that surround them. In a cranky voice, she says, "We can plan a night visit for another time. Right now, our goal is to find a less crowded place where we can fill up on sugar and caffeine." Mandy looks at Lake and pretends to strangle Nicole, who's walking fast in front of them.

"Actually, I wouldn't say no to a piece of pecan pie and a latte right about now," says Mandy as she picks up the pace.

With the roommates so focused on finding the perfect café, no one but Lake notices the unassuming blue awning announcing the entrance to what looks to be a club. A small rainbow sticker in the lower left window sends a silent signal to Lake of what might be a safe haven on a later trip to Savannah.

For months, she obsesses over the blue awning and what could possibly lie behind it.

#

Lake waits patiently for the right moment to present itself, and this weekend is it. She has a regular study group that meets at the library, and she has a part-time job on campus, but neither take her out on a Friday or Saturday night or keep her out past midnight. But this weekend is different. Since she's so far from home, it's sweet that Mandy and Nicole care enough to be worried when she's not back in the room at a time when she should be, but it's also kind of annoying.

Feeling freer, with room to breathe and wander now that they are out of town, Lake has no one to answer to and no one to ask where she's going. She is the absolute worst liar. She simply cannot look someone in the eye and lie. It's just not in her. Instead of just blurting out something halfway plausible, she has a tendency to start looking around, and eventually up, as if there's something very interesting overhead that's suddenly caught her eye. When she does decide to speak, she usually begins with a "Well...,"and from there, it's any-one's guess. The words that fall out of her mouth are so half-baked and unbelievable, anyone with a pulse immediately knows that she's lying. That then forces her to backtrack and come at it from another direction, which only makes things worse. She's been known to known to stop midsentence, turn, and run out of the room without saying another word, thereby proving the fact that she lied. Then things become all weird and uncomfortable with whomever she's lied to, and they probably won't trust her after that. It bothers Lake to her core to think she's broken trust with anyone, so after any ill attempts at spinning a lie, she customarily hangs her head in shame and admits that she lied. Then she tells the truth. It's like being presented with two equally terrible options. How could anyone choose anything other than the truth if they know that the outcome of any version of a lie will leave them in much worse position? So, Lake welcomes the impulse to always be truthful. And to make things easier, she tells herself it's a noble trait.

#

Lake is giddy at the thought of spending an evening in Savannah at an actual gay nightclub. She might possibly meet someone worthwhile, or at the very least, take pleasure in an interesting conversation.

Thanks to the calamitous escapades of her youth, and the one exquisite night she spent with Sara, Lake is familiar and quite comfortable with the concept, but she's never stepped inside a gay bar, or been surrounded by a crowd of queers. It's intoxicating to imagine the inside of a club filled with gay men and women of all shapes and sizes.

Anxious to get the show on the road, she quickly showers, but she takes her time getting ready. Her intent is to look good but not come across as desperate or inexperienced. It's mid-February in coastal Georgia, and the weather is splendid. Lake stands in front of her closet for what seems like hours before choosing a pair of jeans that fit her just right; a new white peasant blouse that she's been saving for a special occasion; and a pair of black, wedge-heel platform shoes. Simple, stylish, and not overstated. She applies her makeup with the same philosophy. With the humidity levels low, it's a good hair night. She feels well put together and confident.

Lake steps off the elevator in her building and stops to make sure she hasn't forgotten anything. Dorm room door locked—check! Sticky note with the address of the bar—check! Fully charged cell phone—check! Driver's license, fake ID, credit card, and cash—check! This is her night, and she's ready to go forth and conquer!

A night this special calls for the perfect tunes. Lake pushes PLAY on her favorite mix tape and heads for the interstate. Traffic is light on this random Saturday evening, and she's able to grab a parking space just a few spots away from the club. Alone in her car, she takes a deep breath as her eyes hit upon the visible blue awning. She can't believe she's here, about to walk into a gay bar alone for the very first time. Tilting the rearview mirror down, she does a quick check of her hair and makeup. Studying her face in the mirror, she finds her appearance pleasing to the eye and hopes someone behind the blue awning will, too.

With a handful of change, Lake walks to the parking meter and discovers her spot is free until 8:00 a.m. Monday morning, *cha-ching!* She drops the coins into her pocket and walks toward the club. She's stopped at the door and forced to show her fake ID. A cursory glance at the photo and birthdate is all the man needs to give her the nod. "Enjoy your night," he says. There is no charge to get in before 10 p.m., so she's literally free to enter. With a dopey grin on her face, Lake takes a few more steps into the main level of the building. The club is sparsely populated at this hour, and she finds herself wandering around, checking out the space. She discovers a basement bar with multiple TVs, each playing a different music video. She's not really feeling the basement scene at the moment. She climbs the stairs back up to the main level, does a quick scan of the room, and picks out a spot at the bar. Oh my gosh, she loves this song! Walking to the beat of a steamy song by Madonna, Lake claims her stool, a soft and plush form that fits her body like a glove. Happy to be in a place where she can enjoy a drink and people-watch, she has absolutely no expectations for how the night will go.

One advantage to showing up before practically everyone else is the ability to choose a premium seat at what will soon become a very busy bar. She has a line of sight to the restroom sign, and she's a comfortable distance from the dance floor, within just feet of the baby grand piano tucked away in the corner. Always a farm girl at heart, Lake automatically rises early and seldom stays up late. It was just past 9:30 when she arrived, so it's still early by nightclub standards, and the place is nowhere near capacity. An attractive older woman floats across the dance floor and sits down at the piano. There's just enough light on the woman for Lake to see she's dressed in a shiny, full-flowing cocktail gown. It looks to be black satin, form-fitting, exquisitely simplistic, very Holly Go-Lightly, right down to the woman's pearls.

Lake orders a beer, sits back, and relaxes. She's obsessed with the piano woman and watches her attentively. The woman takes a sip of her drink, smooths her dress, and nods at the bartender. He gives her a thumbs-up and the Madonna song fades away. Leaning into the microphone, the piano lady has a quick look around the room, then, in a seductive voice, she introduces herself as Helene. Happy to see the crowd, Helene announces this will be her final set of the night and then begins playing. She's quite talented, this one, playing songs from various decades. She concludes with a smoldering version of a Peggy Lee classic that has everyone in the room on their feet clapping. A lady 'til the end, Helene stands, takes a bow, collects her tips from the enormous fishbowl on top of the piano, and walks toward Lake's end of the bar.

Dillon, the bartender, has a bubbly concoction ready for Helene, and he places it on a waiting napkin just as she surrenders her curvy form to the stool next to Lake's. By the time Lake summons up the courage to pay Helene a compliment, the pianist is surrounded by fans, and the club music is back, pumping at high volume. Lake can feel the beat all the way down in her bones.

#

While Lake was tuned in to Helene at the piano, the club has gained about a hundred bodies without her even noticing. The dance floor seems to fill up almost instantaneously, and Lake tucks a couple dollars under her empty beer bottle for Dillon, then smiles at Helene as she gets up and heads back downstairs.

The feel of the basement has changed; it now seems cozier and more inviting. The screens play eighties videos one after the other, and Lake sings along as she waits in line at the bar. A seat opens up just before she has a chance to order, and she grabs it. The bartender at this end of the bar is a woman, and she's in front of Lake in a flash. Wiping her hands on the towel at her waist, she says, "What can I get you, hon?"

"I'll take a beer please."

The woman grabs a bottle from the ice-filled sink behind the bar and pops the cap off. "That'll be three dollars."

Lake hands her a five and tells her to keep it. The bartender winks, nods, and is off to the next person in line for a refreshing beverage. Her stool at the basement bar isn't as comfortable as the swanky stool upstairs, but it does offer a decent view. Lake nurses her second beer as she soaks in the sights and sounds of this all-inclusive watering hole filled with gay, lesbian, and transgender people. For the first time in her life, she feels free, like they're all in on a secret that nobody else knows about. She can be herself here; she doesn't have to worry about what other people will think if she kisses a girl. There's an underlying feeling of respect and solidarity in this space, and she's totally digging it.

When she orders her third beer, it's after eleven. She asks for a glass of water with the beer, then drinks the entire glass before taking a sip of the last beer. She's not yet ready to leave, but she's tired and doesn't want to risk getting tipsy.

It's been a terrific evening, far exceeding any preconceived notions she may have had. Ready to call it a night, Lake sets her half-full bottle of beer on the bar and makes her way to the bathroom. On her way out the door, she runs into someone. Like, she actually runs into her—hitting her with her body. Boobs squash together uncomfortably as they narrowly miss butting heads. Lake jumps backs. "Oh my gosh, I'm so sorry!"

The girl looks like she's about to go off on Lake. With a hand on her left bosom, she says, "It's not your fault. I really have to pee, and I wasn't paying attention." Dancing from one foot to the other, she adds, "My name's Margot."

Lake smiles and says, "I'm Lake. Maybe you should go pee."

"Hi, Lake. Don't go anywhere. I'll be right back."

Lake steps away from the door, props herself against the wall, and watches the bodies in the basement move to the music. She curses her mind for falling prey to her body's biological clock. Every other person in the place seems to be just getting started, and she's ready to crawl into bed and go to sleep. Next time she plans a gay bar outing, she'll take a long afternoon nap first.

A tap on her shoulder is followed by Margot's voice in her ear. "Whew! All better now. Thanks for waiting. Can I get you a beer?"

Lake turns to look at Margot and thinks, *Damn, she's cute.* "No thanks. I'm good."

"Well, do you want to dance?"

"I do, but—"

Margot interrupts Lake midsentence. "This is a 'no but' zone. It's a yes-or-no answer." "I wish it was that simple, Margot. My mouth will say yes, but my body screams no. My people are not rhythmic. We're the opposite of rhythmic. When I dance, I look like Pinocchio— wooden and stiff."

"So, the answer is yes. Great!" With that, Margot grabs Lake by the hand and leads her to a small dance floor at the other end of the basement. The bright dance floor is made up of several large tiles that light up intermittently. The crowd from earlier has thinned a little, making the area feel open and airy. Margot squeezes Lake's hand and says, "Just go with the beat. No one here cares what you look like when you dance."

Lake is nervous and feels self-conscious. She closes her eyes and listens for the beat…it's slow and sensual. The lyrics reinforce the fact that no one is paying attention to them: *"Any time and any place. I don't care who's around…"* Lake moves her head, and her shoulders begin to sway.

When she opens her eyes, Margot is smiling, her sinuous body moving before her provocatively. She's close enough to touch, but Lake holds back. The corners of Margot's mouth rise as her smile widens. She blinks and turns so that her back is facing Lake. A teasing glance over her shoulder confirms she has Lake's full attention. Margot then raises her arms above her head and begins moving her upper body in a deeply sensuous way.

Lake is captivated by her sultry moves and wants so badly to reach out and run her fingertips down Margot's back. With her arms still raised, Margot turns back to face Lake. She moves her hands slowly to Lake's waist, coaxing her body to sway in unison with hers. Margot's grip is light but firm. The touch of her fingers is searing and sumptuous. When the song ends, Lake feels energized and extremely turned on.

Margot leans in close, her lips lightly brushing Lake's ear. "I have no idea what you were talking about. You're a great dancer. Want to go again?"

Lake nods her head and follows Margot's lead. The next song is classic club, upbeat and loud. Bodies flood the floor, forming a protective bubble around Lake and Margot. The pretty boy next to Lake grabs her hand, encouraging her to jump to the beat. Joining in the fun, Margot takes Lake's free hand and begins bouncing with the collective group. Floor tiles flash, briefly illuminating each and every spirited face on the floor.

Reveling in this shroud of unconditional acceptance, Lake's eyes flit from face to face, until one in particular holds her gaze. The woman across from her could pass for Kiki's twin. Neither woman looks away. As the song comes to a close, her grandmother's doppelganger smiles and waves. Closing the gap between them, the older woman's hands envelop Lake's. Seizing her moment, she capitalizes on the quiet interlude between songs and says, "It warms my heart to see new faces here enjoying themselves. Please do come back again."

Caught off-guard, Lake's hesitation to respond causes her to lose the last still moment. As she opens her mouth to speak, the music erupts forcing her to swallow the words as she watches the woman disappear into the crowd.

Turning her attention back to Margot, Lake is touched by the positivity and lack of pretense in the room. Margot, the woman before her, is uncharacteristically adorable because she isn't trying to be anything but Margot. Her dark hair is cut in a blunt bob and barely hits her shoulders. Arrow-straight and shiny, it curls up at the ends when she tilts her head and says, "Do you know that woman?"

Lake shakes her head and says, "I've never seen her before, but she seems nice."

"Well, look at you, making friends left and right. I could use some hydration. How about you?" Lake nods again and allows Margot to lead her to the bar. "What'll you have?" asks Margot.

"Just water for me," replies Lake.

Margot turns slightly to face the bar, and Lake studies the form next to her. Dark eyes, beautiful skin, just a hint of mascara on her long eyelashes. No other makeup that she can see on her face. Her desirable new companion is dressed simply in a pair of Levi's button-fly jeans, a white T-shirt, and a pair of dark slides.

Not yet finished, Margot catches Lake staring at her and says, "A water for you and a vodka tonic for me. Cheers!"

Lake touches her cup to Margot's and says, "Cheers!"

Margot takes a sip of her drink and says playfully, "You're trouble, I can feel it."

Lake smiles and says, "Is that so?"

Margot shrugs, takes Lake's hand, and leads her upstairs. The main floor is bopping, leaving plenty of open seats near the bar. Taking the two open spaces closest to them, Lake and Margot sit facing the dance floor. The music is impossibly loud, and conversation is out of the question, so they sit quietly watching the people before them.

When their cups are empty, the music fades, the lights grow a little brighter, and a voice comes over the speakers. "Last call for alcohol, bitches. Get it now or wait another day."

Margot moves her hand to Lake's arm and says, "You want to get out of here?" "Okay." Lake hadn't planned to stay this long, and now she was dreading the hourlong drive back to her place.

Outside, the air is cool, and there's a light breeze coming off the river. "Hey, are you hungry? There's a Waffle House not far from here. I mean, if you're hungry."

Lake is in no hurry to hit the road. "Sounds good to me, let's go."

Margot stops walking and says, "I had a friend drop me off tonight. Do you mind if I ride with you?"

"Okay. I'm not too familiar with the area, so I'll need you to navigate for me."

"Deal," says Margot.

Chapter 16

*C*onveniently located just off the freeway, the Waffle House is packed with weary travelers and party people. By the time they order, Lake is starving. They both start with coffee and decide on a two-egg breakfast with all the fixings. Between bites, Lake is able to ask Margot a few of the usual questions.

"Do you live here in Savannah?"

"I do, but I'm originally from Columbia, South Carolina. I moved here to go to school. I'm in a nursing program at a local university."

"That's awesome. A friend of mine from high school is going to college to be a nurse. Do you like it? What year are you?"

Margot finishes chewing and says, "I'm a junior, but I'm taking summer classes so I can finish early. It's been harder than I thought it would be, but yeah, it's good. I like it."

"So, what do you do when you're not at school or partying at the club?"

"I spend most of my free time studying, but I also like to bike and explore the city. There's a lot of history here. And I like the beach."

"It would be nice to be closer to a beach. I grew up close to Lake Erie. I know it's not the beach, but it's kind of like it."

"What state is that?"

"Ohio."

"Wow, you're far from home. How'd you end up here?"

"I'm here for school too. I got an athletic scholarship to a university about an hour away from here."

"Now it's my turn to be impressed. A scholarship? You must be pretty good. What sport do you play?"

"Soccer."

With a completely straight face, Margot says, "You're a pickup-driving jock and a lesbian. Way to live the stereotype, Lake!"

It takes Lake a few seconds to realize Margot is just messing with her. Still, she can't help but defend herself. "I grew up in the Midwest, and my dad runs a horse ranch. My pickup is practical, and I happen to love it. And trust me, not every girl soccer player is gay. I know this from experience!"

Margot laughs and says, "You're cute when you're riled up. You know I'm just teasing you, right?"

Lake doesn't respond.

From out of nowhere, their waitress appears. "Can I get you ladies anything else?"

"Just the check," says Margot.

Pulling her pad from her apron, the waitress lays their check on the table and says, "I can take that at the register whenever you're ready. Thanks for coming in."

Margot reaches across the table, laying her hand on Lake's. "You okay? I'm sorry."

"I'm okay. That's the first time I've ever heard anyone refer to me as a lesbian. It sounds weird to hear it out loud."

"Wait, you're not gay?"

"No. I mean, yes. I'm definitely gay. I just haven't told anyone."

Margot sits back in the booth and says, "What do you mean you haven't told anyone? No one at your school knows? What about your parents?"

"I haven't told *anyone.* I tried to tell some friends once, and it blew up in my face. I spent the last two years of high school trying to prove to everyone I *wasn't* gay. I just wanted to leave and start fresh in a place where no one knows anything about me."

"I get wanting to start over, I do. And don't worry about it. You don't have to say or do anything until you're ready. Okay? I'll be right back."

Margot walks over to the register, pays the bill, and comes back to the table.

Lake yawns and stretches. "Thanks."

"Hey, are you going to be okay to drive?" asks Margot.

Lake finishes the last of her coffee and says, "I honestly don't know. It's way past my bedtime."

"You can stay at my place if you want. I'll take the couch."

"I can't ask you to do that. You've already been so nice, buying me breakfast and all."

"You're not asking me to do anything. I offered. I'll be worried if you drive home now. The sun will be up soon. Just come to my place and get a few hours' sleep before driving back."

Lake is too tired to argue, and besides, what could possibly happen? Margot hasn't even tried to kiss her. Lake pulls her keys from her pocket. "Since I have no idea where you live, do you mind driving?"

"Not at all. C'mon."

#

Margot's apartment is nice—a stylish one-bedroom with all the latest gadgets and technology. Lake wonders how Margot can afford all this.

"The bedroom is straight down that hallway. There's an en suite bathroom, so please make yourself at home. I just need to grab a few things before you go to sleep."

"Of course."

As Margot heads toward the bedroom, she says, "There's glasses in the cupboard next to the sink. Help yourself to a glass of water. There's milk, soda, and juice in the fridge, too."

"I'm good, thanks."

Lake takes a seat on the couch while she waits for Margot to return. There are photos of Margot with various people spread throughout the living area. Lake assumes the other people in the pictures are friends and family. If she wasn't so tired, she'd take a closer look. Maybe later.

"Okay, the bedroom's all yours. Sweet dreams, Lake."

Lake wants to kiss Margot but decides against it. She needs to brush her teeth and get some sleep. "Good night, Margot."

#

As if on cue, Lake is wide awake at 7 a.m. She lies in Margot's bed and allows her eyes to adjust to the light and the new surroundings. The bed, a queen, is luxurious and ultra-comfy, not a bad place to land after her first gay club experience. Lake burrows deeper into the sheets and pulls the comforter up high.

The apartment is still, quiet. She's curious about her host—is she awake? As much as she'd like to go back to sleep, she knows she can't, the downside to being a natural morning person. Lake sighs and pushes back the covers; she has to pee.

Margot's bathroom is sexy and sleek, and the tile feels cool on her feet. When she's done, Lake flushes, washes her hands, and admires the glass block shower. For a college student, Margot is living large.

Lake is feeling weary after her night out on the town. She wonders if Margot would mind if she took a quick shower before she heads out. She did tell Lake to make herself at home. Going with that notion, Lake steps out of her panties and into the shower. The water feels amazing, soft and warm against her body. She closes her eyes and tilts her head back while the water revives her tired muscles. With her roommates gone for the weekend, there's no need to rush. As she reaches up to run her hands through her hair, Lake hears a *click*. Then hands caress her shoulders and move slowly to Lake's hands.

"Good morning. I hope you don't mind me joining you," says Margot as she presses her body against Lake's backside.

With her eyes still closed, Lake responds, "No, I don't mind." She recognizes the sound of shampoo being squeezed from a bottle. Anticipating what's about to happen, Lake relaxes her shoulders as her head tilts farther back. Then Margot's hands are in her hair, thumbs pressed firmly against the back of her neck, fingertips moving in a swirling motion.

The nerve endings in Lake's scalp erupt in a sensory fireworks show as she leans farther back, and a quiet gasp escapes her mouth. Margot's nipples are pressed against Lake's back.

The gentle pressure of warm water and the firm touch of Margot's capable fingers running around her head in a froth of shampoo lather is almost too much to bear.

Lake's head is tilted forward for her while the water washes away the soap. Margot's hands move to Lake's neck and trail down her backside, landing in the small of her back. The feeling is sensual and electric. Every part of Lake's body is dripping wet.

She turns to face Margot and kisses her hungrily. She wants this woman right here, right now.

What starts in the shower spills over to the bedroom, and it lasts until late morning. Margot's boudoir skills are beyond anything Lake could have imagined, let alone experienced. By the time their antics end, both are drenched in sweat.

Lake kisses the inside of Margot's thigh and licks the wetness there; it's creamy, salty, and sweet. She can feel the heat radiating from Margot's body, especially the delicious space between her legs.

When she looks up, Margot is smiling at her, her head propped up by multiple soft pillows.

"Are you really a nursing student?" asks Lake.

Tilting her head, Margot responds, "Yes. I'm a nursing student. Why would you ask that question?"

"Because your apartment is so beautiful. It's way nicer than any student housing I've ever been in and…you're freaking incredible in bed. Don't get me wrong. I totally enjoyed all your moves, but I feel a little inadequate."

Margot laughs softly and says, "Trust me, nothing you did to me was inadequate. Just talking about it makes me want to go again."

Lake smiles and moves up Margot's body, kissing her stomach lightly before resting her chin between Margot's boobs. "You haven't answered my question about your place."

"I didn't hear a question. You said my apartment is beautiful. Thank you. My parents wanted me to be comfortable during my last two years of school. I was in college housing before getting my own place."

She studies Margot's face for a moment. Her explanation sounds plausible enough. Lake lets the issue drop.

Inching up Margot's body once again, Lake gives her a sensual kiss before saying, "I have a paper to write, and I'm starving. I'm going to rinse off really quick before I take off."

Margot runs her fingers down Lake's back, tracing the outline of her butt cheeks. "You have a great ass. I want to bite it. It's so round and perky!"

Lake rolls over, gets out of bed, and bends over, giving Margo a long last look at her round and perky backside. "Next time," she says with a wink.

Lake rinses off and wraps her head in a towel. As she's getting dressed, she hears a loud pounding on the door that rattles the whole apartment. It's followed by a reverberating female voice shouting. "Bitch, you better open this door and let me in. I know you're in there!"

What the flip? Who the hell is that, and who is she calling a bitch?

The pounding gets louder. Lake's first instinct is to hide, but she has nowhere to go. She's trapped in Margot's bathroom. *Margot…where is she? Is she still in bed?* Lake cracks the bathroom door expecting to find Margot hiding under the covers, but the bed's empty and the bedroom door is closed. She hears voices, but she can't make out the words. Whoever's in the apartment, Margot must know them. Otherwise, why would she let them in?

Creeping quietly to the bedroom door, Lake presses her ear against it. It's no use, she still can't make out the words. She left the fan on in the bathroom, making it hard to hear. Worried that the voices will hear the fan shutting off, Lake turns the knob and barely cracks the door. The booming voice is clear now. "Where's your girl, Margot?"

In response, Margot says, "I have no idea what you're talking about. There's no one else here."

"Do I look like I just fell off the turnip truck? Oh, honey, I know you done picked you up a sweet little dish and took her out to eat last night. My people are everywhere, and Tasty knows everything. While you was enjoying hash browns, smothered, covered, and chunked, you shoulda been out there spending time with Therese."

"That's total bullshit. It was my night off, and I spent it how I wanted."

"Gurl, I own your ass! If you have any hope of finishing what you done started at that fancy-shmancy school, you do as I say. You understand?"

What? Seriously! Who is this person, and what is she talking about?

Lake is a bit scared, but her curiosity and the need to get home gets the better of her. Slowly inching the door back, she tiptoes down the hallway, her body glued to the wall, just out of sight. Trying not to move, she waits for one of them to speak again, but the room is quiet.

Not sure what's happening, Lake shifts her body, and her stomach lets out a loud growl. The woman takes a few steps toward where she's standing. Lake presses her eyes closed, willing her body to stay silent. She can feel the woman's presence. She's close.

#

"Oooooh, gurl. She every bit as cute as they said. Diddly-dang! Gurl, step out here where Tasty can see you."

Lake does as she's told, sidestepping Tasty and walking over to join Margot near the couch. Margot closes her eyes and looks away, avoiding eye contact with Lake.

"You one compact little something, aren't you?"

Umm, thank you? Lake remains quiet, unclear as to what the dynamic is here. She looks at Margot again. Nothing.

She looks back at the woman. *Is* she a woman? Is that an Adam's apple sticking out of her long, dark-skinned neck? She's a lot to take in, this tall drink of water with the bleach-blonde beehive, lime-green stilettos, and earrings to match.

"How'd you get all toned and tan like that?" Hypnotized by her ensemble, Lake's eyes stall at the deep cleavage created by the plunging neckline of the woman's sheer black jumpsuit. Her eyes follow Lake's gaze down to her bulging bosom. The woman snaps her long fingers, causing Lake to jump. "Hey, half pint, eyes right here. I asked how you got all toned and tan." "I'm outside a lot. I play soccer at school."

"Well, look at you. Two schoolgirl peas in a pod. Isn't that just something?"

Margot has yet to speak.

"I can see how you got sidetracked by this one, but don't let it happen again, Miss Thang. I'll make things right with Therese tomorrow. Right now, I gots to meet my girls at church. And by church, I mean brunch—with mimosas! You take care now, little one."

With all the fanfare of a runway model, Tasty sashays out of the apartment, leaving the door wide open.

Margot's trance is broken by Tasty's dramatic departure. She walks to the door, closes it softly, and rests her forehead against it.

"Who was that? And why did she keep saying she 'owns' you?" asks Lake.

Without turning around, Margot says, "I sort of work for her."

"What does that mean, exactly? Who's Therese?"

"Therese is a client. One of my regulars."

"One of your 'regulars'?" asks Lake. "What is it that you do for her? Like, what kind of 'services' are you providing?"

Margot turns to face Lake, sighs, and says, "Sexual. My services are sexual."

Oh, my God! No wonder Margot is so good in bed. Lake's "date" is a student by day, a swanky-ass hooker by night. Looking at Margot, Lake says, "I have to go."

"Lake, wait. Let me explain."

Lake shakes her head. "There's nothing to say. I made a mistake, and now I have to go."

"Lake, please. Just hear me out. If you still want to go after that, I won't stop you."

Crossing her arms, Lake takes a defensive stance. "Fine."

"My family was so proud when I got accepted to nursing school. It's a good career for me, and I like it. Both of my parents are hard workers and they're really supportive, but they can't afford to pay the full cost of my tuition and living expenses. I was out at the club one night and met Tasty. We got to talking, and she offered to help. Tasty's a legend in this town and has a lot of connections. She set me up in this apartment and takes care of everything. My parents think I got a grant. They don't really question the how—they just appreciate the fact that the burden of my school bills is lighter than it used to be. I'm sorry, Lake. I shouldn't have gotten you involved in all of this."

Lake doesn't know what to say. She believes Margot's story, and she did have a great time with her. But dating an escort? Really? What if she gives Lake an STD? Like, for real, that could happen.

It's like Margot can read her mind. "If it makes you feel any better, I only sleep with women. No men—ever. Believe it or not, there are plenty of wealthy women in this town who will gladly pay for the discreet services of another woman. And just to be safe, I get tested once a month. I'm clean, Lake. I promise. It's not as if my dance card is full every night of the week. I have a respectable list of regular clients that I work with. No strings attached. It's an easy gig that pays well while I go to school. I'm not proud of what I do, but I do it because I have to. I've come too far to quit. That's why I'm staying here and going to summer classes. I want to finish as soon as I can, so I can leave and start my nursing career somewhere else away from here."

Lake totally gets wanting to leave a place to start fresh somewhere else. And who is she to judge? After all, she slept with a married woman while her husband was out of town.

Lake gathers her things and is just feet from the door when she stops. Margot is sitting on the couch watching her but doesn't say anything. Lake walks to the couch, kisses Margot, and says, "Give me some time to process this, okay?"

Margot nods, takes Lake's face in her hands, and kisses her back.

Lake is conflicted. Margot was a terrific lay. She even did a few things to her that she's never experienced before. At one part, when Lake was just about to come, Margot did this thing with her tongue, like she was drawing circle eights with it. Just thinking about it makes her feel the familiar, tingly sensation down there. Lake has never orgasmed like that before.

Margot takes Lake's hand, presses a piece of paper into her palm, and closes it. With the paper firmly in her hand, Lake leaves.

She doesn't even realize she's still holding the paper in her hand until she reaches for the steering wheel and it falls to her lap. She picks it up and unfolds it. Written there in neat handwriting is Margot's full name and her phone number.

#

Two weeks pass, and Lake can't deny wanting to be with Margot again, but with school, work, and her roommates, getting together again is no easy feat. It's been over a month since Lake has seen Margot. She's tried to think of reasons why she would need to go to Savannah alone and spend the night, but she can't seem to come up with a credible story. Lying to her roommate's faces is not an option, so she waits.

Then the most amazing thing happens. Lake's favorite professor asks her to stay after class and offers her a job housesitting while he's out of town.

"My dad isn't doing well, and my mom has her hands full with him and the house. I'm going back home to help out and will be gone for at least a couple of weeks. I have two dogs that hate going to the kennel. I don't want to stress them out and send them there for two weeks.

I know they'd be more comfortable at home. How do you feel about dogs? Do you like them? You're not allergic, are you?"

Lake responds, "I love dogs! And I don't have any allergies that I know of."

"Great. My place isn't far from campus, and the boys are very well behaved," says Professor Johns.

"Okay, no problem. When do you need me to stay?"

"I booked a flight for this Thursday. I've got a ride to the airport, so I'm good there. Can you stop by Wednesday after class so I can show you the house and introduce you to the dogs?"

"Sure, I can do that," says Lake.

"Thanks so much, Lake, you're really helping me out. You do great work in my class, and I feel like I can trust you."

"You can, sir. I'll take good care of your dogs and the house. You can count on me."

"I had a good feeling about you, Lake. Here's my address and phone number. I'll see you Wednesday."

Lake takes her professor's address and phone number. His house is old but well maintained. It has character, charm, and a cozy fireplace. The dogs are sweet fluffballs, full of energy.

"So, here's the address of my parents' place. Emergency contacts are on the fridge. I watered all of the plants today, but they'll need watering again in a few days. Try not to overwater them. The mail comes through this slot on the door. You can just stack it here on the hall table. I'll go through it when I get home.

"The fridge is full of food and drinks, and there's plenty of stuff in the pantry. The dogs sleep in their kennels at night." Pointing to a writing pad on the dining table, he adds, "Everything you need to know about their schedules is on that sheet there. Do you have any questions?"

Lake looks around the house and says, "Where should I sleep?"

"It's up to you. I washed the sheets in the primary bedroom, so everything there is clean. If you feel more comfortable in the guest room, you can use it. I'm fine either way."

"Okay, thanks."

"Alright. So, here's the spare key. Please lock up the house whenever you leave. My car is parked in the garage."

"I will. I have my truck. I'll just park in the driveway."

"Great. Call if you have any questions. Oh, and you can have one guest over at a time, but no ragers, okay? This is nonnegotiable."

"Sure, no problem. I have a study group, but we meet at the library or the common area of our dorm. I do have one friend that I like to hang out with, but she's very responsible."

"That should be fine. My flight is at ten a.m. tomorrow. You can come over any time after lunch to let the dogs out and settle in."

"Sounds good. Safe travels," says Lake.

Professor Johns's dad has a lingering illness that forces him to make many trips back home over the course of several months. A comfortable and private place to hook up has literally fallen into Lake's lap, and she and Margot become semi-steady lovers.

It's Lake's first real female relationship, and she embraces everything that comes with it. This is how she envisions her future. It's how she's always wanted to live: in a secure and comfortable home, with a dog or two of her own, and a beautiful woman to wake up to every day.

On the rare occasion when she can sneak away, Lake goes to Margot's place.

Tasty always gives her shit and asks Lake if she can touch her arms and legs. Why is this woman obsessed with her limbs?

At the end of the fall semester, Margot graduates with honors from nursing school. Lake is there to watch her receive her diploma, sitting two rows behind Margot's family, flanked by Tasty and two of her fellow "churchgoers."

Lake has accepted Margot for who she is and has never asked for more than she can give. After Margot graduates, Lake goes home for the holidays, and Margot accepts a nursing job in South Carolina just a few hours away from her parents. She is gone when Lake returns to school.

#

Attending school out of state presents both positive and negative points. It's great to experience a whole new culture and climate, but being at a small, private college in the South on a full scholarship means having to live in the dorms. Years of tight quarters with little to no privacy.

In her senior year, Lake's luck takes a turn for the better when she's placed in a double with a new roommate. Tracy, also a senior, is from the capital city, Atlanta. A serious student, she enjoys sports and is always up for a good time. Tracy has a plan for after graduation and is never one to pry. She has a steady boyfriend and is as straight as they come. She's also totally cool and is open to going to gay bars in the city.

"Jasper's birthday is next weekend. You should come home with me. My parents don't like that I drive home alone, and they would love it if I had company in the car. And I know they've been wanting you to meet you. If we leave early enough, we can check out one of the clubs in town. They have drag shows on Friday nights. I've wanted to go for a long time but didn't have anyone to go with. I hear they're a lot of fun."

Lake has never been to Atlanta before. "Sure. I don't have any plans this weekend. Count me in."

"Cool. I'll let my parents know you're coming. You're going to love Atlanta. Maybe we can go thrifting on Saturday morning? I know a bunch of places in the city."

Lake misses Margot, but she's happy to hear she loves her job and is doing great. The trip to Atlanta is a much needed getaway, and the drag show is the most fun Lake has had in months. Even though it isn't her first time in a gay bar, the club she and Tracy goes to is on a whole new level. And it isn't the only gay bar in town. Lake is like a kid in a candy store. There are literally so many tantalizing queer distractions, she has a hard time focusing on just one. The place is running on endless amounts of high current that flows well into the wee hours of the morning. In this space, Lake doesn't have a care in the world.

On the drive back to school, Lake says to Tracy, "You were totally right. I love Atlanta, and I'm going to apply for every job available there when we graduate."

Tracy smiles and says, "The Big Peach claims another. Yes!"

Chapter 17 – Maribel

*L*ake graduates in the prescribed four-year time frame and receives multiple job offers, the majority of which are from firms and offices in Georgia. Earning a political science degree from a university with an exceptional reputation makes Lake a desirable candidate for several analyst and specialist positions. In the end, she accepts a position as a legislative assistant to the incumbent democratic senator of Georgia.

"I just can't believe our little girl is in politics, working for a senator, no less!"

"I know, Mom. It's crazy, right? I had to pinch myself on my first day at work, I couldn't believe it, either," says Lake. "Now that I'm settled and have my own place, you and Dad should visit sometime. I can take the pullout couch, and you guys can have my room."

"That's really sweet of you, Lake. I'll talk to your dad. We're smack-dab in the middle of foaling season, and you know how he and your uncle Rick are this time of year."

Lake thinks of the ranch and smiles.

"Well, see what he says. Even if he can't come, you and Aunt Joe could visit. Atlanta has a great restaurant scene and lots of places to shop. I miss you guys!"

"We miss you, too. Your brother and sister say hello. We don't see too much of them these days. You kids are just so busy, off living your own lives with your own families."

Lake's brother, Pete, is married and has a son. Jeannie, the career woman, is thriving as a big-city event coordinator for a well-known company. She and her boyfriend have bought a condo with a lake view and have been together for four years. He wants marriage and kids, but Jeannie isn't ready to be tied down. Good for her—if she's not ready for family life, she shouldn't be forced to decide. Jeannie has always been stubborn, and Lake doesn't see things going Tim's way if he gives her sister an ultimatum. It will be interesting to see how that one plays out.

"So, how are things at the new job? What's the senator like?" asks her mom.

"I haven't actually spent much time with him, Mom. He's kind of a busy guy. But I really like my job. It keeps me on my toes."

"I'm glad to hear that, Lake. I've got to run soon. The ladies are coming over for bridge tonight, and I want to make some light hor d'oeuvres before they get here."

"Okay, Mom, tell Dad I love him, and say hi to Pete and Jeannie for me."

"I will, honey. You be safe there. I don't like to think about you being out alone late at night. Do you keep your Mace in your purse?"

"I carry it with me at all times, Mom, don't worry. Have fun tonight. Love you!"

"Love you, too. Bye."

#

In the summer of 1999, before Lake is offered the position at the capitol, President Bill Clinton declares the first-ever Gay & Lesbian Pride month in June. It's the biggest step forward for "her people" that Lake has ever witnessed. Proclamation 7203 leverages America's greatest strength:—its diversity—and instills a confidence and a hope within Lake that she carries with her to Atlanta.

The Capitol Building is a bustling hub of activity with people rushing here, there, and everywhere on the daily. Lake learns early on that the parking situation for her new job is iffy at best. If she happens to be lucky enough to snag a spot anywhere within walking distance, it will cost a pretty penny, and on her salary, every penny counts. The easiest and most economical mode of transportation is MARTA, Atlanta's rapid transit system, and Lake adapts to it quickly. Her stint on the train provides just enough time to drink a coffee and catch the morning headlines.

An accomplished multitasker, Lake rarely looks up from the paper, instead choosing to listen for the automated train announcer's declaration of each stop as they approach the destination. But on this day, the barely discernable brush of a body against her arm is followed by the dreamy scent of freshly laundered white tees as it wafts and settles on the laps and arms of those in her aisle. The combination of the two compels her to look up.

The woman responsible for the enticing fragrance takes an open seat near the doors and acknowledges Lake as she does. The two exchange a smile before Lake turns her attention back to the paper. The woman's sunshiny-clean scent evokes a range of emotions in Lake that instantly transport her to Sunday mornings at the ranch: warm air, jasmine, newly cut grass, and Grandma Kiki hanging a fresh load of cottons on the clothesline.

Filled with warm, fuzzy feelings and a slight buzz from her double espresso, Lake prepares to exit the train. The automated proclamation comes across loud and clear: *Georgia State Station*. Lake is up, and so is the woman who reeks of nostalgia. Unintentionally, Lake follows her all the way to the door of the Capitol Building. Once inside, the woman turns and confronts Lake. "Are you following me?"

"Yes, but I didn't mean to. I work here, as a legislative assistant."

"Oh, cool. I work here, too. My dad is an attorney, and I'm his assistant, for the time being. My name's Maribel. I'm on the third floor."

"Nice to meet you. I'm Lake, and I'm on the second floor. I don't mean to be rude, but I have to run."

"No worries. Catch you later, Lake."

Lake goes about her day without giving Maribel another thought. But then, a few days later, there she is, in the second-floor breakroom.

"Hey! Lake, right?"

"Yep, that's me. What are you doing down here, consorting with us lower-floor folk?"

"I heard your coffee doesn't suck, so I made the trip down," says Maribel.

"I don't know who started that rumor, but I'm pretty sure it's not true. But don't listen to me, the coffee here's probably okay if you're desperate."

Maribel pours herself a cup and asks, "So, where are you from, Lake? If I had to guess, I'd say you're not native to Georgia."

"That's a good guess, Maribel. What gave it away? My unconventional name or my accent?" asks Lake.

"Both, actually. But I like your name—it's original. We can work on the accent."

Lake laughs.

Maribel hasn't yet reached her twenty questions and keeps going. "How long have you been in Atlanta?"

"I moved here in August, for the job. But I've been in Georgia for a few years. I went to college closer to Savannah."

Maribel's eyes light up at the mention of Savannah. "Our hostess city of the South! , and America's first planned city. At least you're not like *new*, new to Georgia. But seriously, do you know anyone here in Atlanta?"

"I've met a few people. My job is pretty demanding, so I work a lot of hours, you know?"

Maribel yawns and says, "Boring!"

"I'm not boring, I'm fun! I just don't have an abundance of free time at the moment," says Lake.

"Only boring people *say* they're fun! You're coming out with me and my friends on Saturday. No excuses!"

"Okay, but when I drink you under the table, don't say I didn't warn you. I'm *super* fun!"

Maribel laughs and grabs Lake's cell phone. "What's your passcode?"

"I catch you loitering in our breakroom and drinking our coffee that doesn't suck. You're kind of sketch, I'm not giving you that information," says Lake as she takes the phone back.

Lake punches in the code and says, "What's your last name, Maribel?"

"Nelson. And my number is 404-555-2212. Text me with your name, and I'll let you know where to meet us. We don't usually get our shit together before ten."

Lake makes a face, which doesn't escape Maribel.

"Is that a problem, Miss 'Fun'?"

Lake shakes her head and says, "Nope. Just texted you my info. Don't drink all our coffee."

"Unlikely. See you Saturday," says Maribel before leaving the breakroom.

Lake sighs as she mentally rearranges her plans for the weekend, building in time for a late-afternoon nap on Saturday before meeting Maribel and her friends that night.

#

With multiple pending deadlines, it's a late night at the office on Friday. Around nine thirty, Lake receives a text from Maribel: *Hey, you. We thought you might appreciate all the ATL has to offer. Meet us at the Clermont Lounge at 10. It's just the first of many stops we'll make, so rest up, Miss Fun.* Smiley face with tongue, eggplant, beer mugs, flamenco dancer, and two more eggplants. Before this, Lake isn't sure about Maribel, but there's no mistaking the D references in the text. *It's one night, just go with it,* she tells herself. *It might be fun, minus the D.*

Lake does a quick search of the Clermont Lounge and is surprised to learn it's a bona-fide old-school strip club. What the hell has she gotten herself into, and how does one dress for a place like this? Unclear of what's happening after the Clermont Lounge, she decides to play it safe and wear jeans, a white blouse, and wedge sandals. Her go to, comfortable, classic, stylish.

Lake is surprised at how long she naps. When her alarm goes off at 8 p.m., it's already dark outside. She rolls over, stretches, and gets out of bed. She pads to the kitchen and drinks a full, twenty-ounce glass of water, then jumps in the shower. Her goal tonight is to stay hydrated and keep up with Maribel.

At ten minutes after ten, Lake pulls into the parking lot of the Clermont. She parks and texts Maribel to let her know she's here. A couple minutes go by before her phone buzzes. *On our way, be there in five,* the text reads. Rather than go in alone, she decides to wait. A few minutes later, a white Range Rover pulls into the lot, and several people pile out of the vehicle. When the driver's door opens, Maribel climbs out. Lake gets out of her truck and walks over to where the group is standing. A cloud of smoke hangs over them, and they smell like weed. When Maribel spots her, she claps and shouts, "Everyone, this is Lake!"

Each waves and says hi. Maribel laughs and points to each of her friends. "Lake, this is Jules, Keenan, and Xavier, but we call him Xav."

Lake waves and says, "Nice to meet you."

Throwing an arm around Lake, Maribel says, "This place is going to blow your mind."

Lake studies the bright red sign on their way to the door, reading the last line as she passes it: "Alive Since '65." The place does not disappoint. They grab a table close to the bar and watch as women of all shapes and sizes dance on the bar. When an older black woman appears, the place goes crazy. Blondie is legendary here, and she's amazing. At one point, between songs, she pauses to read a poem she's written. When she's finished with the reading, everyone snaps their fingers, beatnik style. Blondie takes a deep bow and gracefully steps down from the bar.

The first stop of the night ranks high on the list, but the evening is just getting started. Walking out the door, Maribel takes hold of Lake's hand and says, "It's going to be a bitch finding parking at the other places. Just leave your truck here and ride with us. I'll bring you back later."

Lake shrugs and says, "Okay," as she climbs in next to Maribel.

The next stop is a nondescript warehouse off Cheshire Bridge Road, with girls in cages and guys on leashes. After an hour watching various bondage and submission acts play out, Lake and the others make their way to the front of the club. Next to the front door, a good-looking guy wearing a cock ring and combat boots is chained to the wall. Another guy wearing a similar outfit is dripping hot candle wax on the chest of the guy chained to the wall. He cries out in pain just as they step outside.

"Well, that was interesting," says Lake.

Xav turns to Lake and says, "This place is one of our favorite spots, but it gets so crowded!" Looking at Maribel, he adds, "I'm ready to dance. Let's hit Backstreet."

At just after 1 a.m., the Range Rover parks on Peachtree, and the group walks into the legendary Backstreet, a three-story gay club open 24/7. The cavernous dancefloor speakers reverberate a celebrated tune as hundreds of glistening bodies gyrate to the beat beneath a giant, shimmering disco ball. Standing on the balcony, overlooking the electric show landscape, Lake is hypnotized by the scene. The place is like the beautiful fairy godmother of all gay clubs, and she's fallen under its spell.

Catching a second wind, Lake and the others party 'til dawn. On the dance floor, a high Maribel is flirty and attentive, and Lake is having a great time. The fivesome meshes well together, feeding off each other's energy. Eventually they are dog-tired and drenched in sweat, and the sun is just peeking out as they push open the door and clamber into the car. No one's ready to call it a night yet, though, so Maribel drives them to a landmark diner for breakfast. The place is popping. Lake recognizes a few faces from the club they've just left. Their waitress, a woman in her fifties, barks out, "What are you having?"

One by one, they give their orders. After ordering, Lake says, "Can we get separate checks?"

Their waitress, Irene, glares at Lake and says, "No," as she turns and walks away.

"Was she kidding?" asks Lake. Together, they all respond, "*No!*"

Jules looks at Lake and says, "Did you see the button under her nametag? It said, 'I love my job'!"

Lake laughs and says, "How ironic! Oh, Irene…"

It's just past 6 a.m. when Lake finally climbs into bed.

#

Fall in the city is colorful and eventful. It's Lake's first Thanksgiving away from home and her family.

On the train to work, Maribel asks, "Are you going home for the holidays?"

"No, work is going to be crazy busy the next few months, so I'll probably just stay here. Why?"

"My parents do a big Thanksgiving dinner. You're welcome to come home with me if you want."

"That's so nice, thank you! I'd love to come. Thanksgiving is my favorite holiday."

"Mine, too," says Maribel. "I'll text you the address. We dress up for Thanksgiving dinner at my house. No jeans. My mom's kind of strict about it… And don't worry about bringing anything. It's all catered."

Lake looks at Maribel but doesn't say anything. A formal, catered Thanksgiving dinner? She doesn't do dresses, but she does have several pairs of dress slacks. Maybe she'll go shopping and buy something new for the occasion.

Thanksgiving Day is cool and blustery. Lake wears a light pair of wool slacks and a sweater she bought for when the weather turned colder. As she studies her reflection in the mirror, she thinks her outfit could use a splash of color. Opening the lid of her jewelry box, she lifts the inside drawer and pulls out one of Kiki's headbands. The fabric is a floral print—brown, green, pink, and white—the perfect accessory for her winter-white ensemble. Placing it on her head, she thinks about her grandmother and how much she loved this holiday. It's heartwarming to know she's bringing a little piece of Grams to dinner with her today.

Lake maps the drive to Maribel's parents' house. It's just outside the city and will take at least thirty minutes for her to get there. She allows extra time in case she gets lost and marvels at the grandeur of the homes as she draws closer to her destination. Slowing down to read the house numbers painted on the curb, she does a double take at the address on her phone and the number on the curb. This is the place.

The property is gated, and the house behind the gates is massive. She pushes the buzzer and provides her name to the voice in the box. The gates open, and she drives through.

A man approaches her truck. Opening her door, he says, "Welcome to the Nelson residence. Happy Thanksgiving."

"Thank you," says Lake as she steps out. The man hands her a ticket and smiles. She watches as her truck disappears behind the house.

Lake drops the ticket into her purse and rings the doorbell. A good-looking kid answers and says, "Hi. Come on in. Everyone's in the back." Lake looks at him and wonders which way to go. There's a stairway beyond the foyer and hallways to her left and right. Pointing to her right, he says, "It's that way."

She nods, says, "Thanks," then walks in the direction the kid pointed. She can hear voices, which assures her she's headed in the right direction.

Entering the massive great room, she glances around the space, hoping to spot Maribel, but she's not there. Not recognizing a single face, Lake walks farther into the room. Beyond the large, open fireplace is the dining room and kitchen, where more people have gathered. She finally sees Maribel in the dining room, standing next to a handsome older man.

"You made it! I was worried you might have gotten lost," says Maribel. "Lake, this is my dad, Grant. Dad, this is Lake. She works at the Capitol Building, too."

"It's a pleasure to meet you, Lake. Welcome to our home," says Mr. Nelson.

"Thank you, sir. It's nice to meet you."

Maribel takes Lake by the hand and says, "C'mon, I want you to meet my mom."

Maribel's mom is a stunning older woman. Dressed to the nines, she's definitely the belle of this Thanksgiving ball. Lake's always had a hankering for attractive, older women, and this one's exceptional. "Mom, this is my friend, Lake. She's new to Atlanta, and it's her first Thanksgiving away from her family."

Mrs. Nelson smiles at Lake, a hint of recognition behind her deep blue eyes. Taking both of Lake's hands in hers, she says, "We're happy to have you, Lake. Please make yourself at home. Have a glass of wine."

Mrs. Nelson's hands are soft and warm, and Lake doesn't pull away. "Thank you, Mrs. Nelson."

What is she doing? This is her friend's mom, for Christ's sake.

Just then, a woman appears with a tray full of wineglasses. "Glass of wine?" she asks.

Withdrawing her hands, Mrs. Nelson says, "White or red, Lake?"

"White, please." The woman hands her a glass of white wine and moves on.

When Lake turns to address the lovely Mrs. Nelson again, she's gone.

At exactly 2 p.m., a dinner bell rings, and the guests begin taking their seats. The dining table seats twenty, and everyone has an assigned seat. Lake is seated next to Maribel at her dad's end of the table. Her mom is at the other end, unfortunately, but at least Lake has a clear line of sight to her.

Dinner lasts almost an hour. When the coffee is finally served and dessert is brought out, Maribel excuses the two of them and motions for Lake to follow her out to the pool house.

Shutting the door, Maribel asks, "I thought you might want a break from all the excitement. I couldn't help but notice that little exchange between you and my mom."

Lake is embarrassed and decides to play dumb. "What are you talking about?"

"C'mon, Lake. I know you're gay. It's cool. My mom's a total MILF, and you're not the first of my friends to crush on her."

Lake doesn't respond. Maribel's mom is gorgeous and confident, an appealing combination for any woman. Lake's attraction to her was instant, only because strong women tend to recognize and understand her desires, even if they don't possess the same physical attraction.

Pulling a small pipe from a shelf on the wall, Maribel smiles and says, "You want to smoke with me?"

"I'm good, thanks."

"Okay. Let me know if you change your mind." Lake watches Maribel inhale deeply. Holding her breath, she coughs, then exhales slowly.

"So, did you grow up here?" asks Lake.

"I did," says Maribel.

Lake looks around at the pool house, which is bigger than her apartment. When she looks back at Maribel, she realizes she's just inches from her face. Without saying a word, Maribel pulls Lake in and kisses her. Lake thinks of Maribel's mom and kisses her back. Maribel presses into Lake, and the kissing goes on for several minutes. When Lake moves beyond Maribel's mouth, she abruptly pulls away and leaves Lake standing in the pool house alone.

Confused, Lake follows her back to the house.

Maribel takes her seat at the table, fills her mouth with a fork full of pumpkin cheesecake, and joins the conversation. Her father is talking sports, and Maribel begins sparring with her brother, the good-looking boy who had opened the front door for Lake.

The rest of the afternoon is strange and slightly uncomfortable. Lake's always been careful not to cross the line with her friends, and she didn't initiate what happened in the pool house. Maribel has been flirty with her since the first night they went out, but what is this all about? Is Maribel bored, does she have mommy issues, or is she just a heartless soul seizing the occasion to exploit Lake's sexuality?

Lake never expected Maribel to kiss her like that, and it wasn't completely dreadful. Maribel is a younger, prettier version of her mother; however, Lake had not planned on making out with either of them at any point during the dinner. But who's she kidding? If the opportunity were to present itself again, she wouldn't turn it down. She hasn't had sex since her time with Margot, and she misses being kissed and touched by a woman.

Lake excuses herself and goes to use the ladies' room. When she returns, Maribel is nowhere to be found. Unsure of what to do, Lake thanks Mrs. Nelson for dinner and leaves. She texts Maribel from the car and thanks her for dinner, explaining she had to leave, playing it off like it was no big deal that Maribel dropped out of sight without even saying good-bye.

On Monday, she hopes to see Maribel on the train, but she doesn't. Several days go by before she runs into her outside the breakroom.

"Hey, Lake. Where you been?" asks Maribel with a smile.

Incredulous, Lake looks at her and says, "Around, I guess. How about you?"

"Same," says Maribel. "Hey, a few of us are going out for happy hour on Friday after work. You want to come?"

Lake looks at Maribel, searching out her face for any indication or recollection of what happened between them in the pool house. Maribel gives nothing away, her face void of any emotion.

"Yeah, sounds fun," says Lake.

"Cool. We'll meet here in the breakroom at four thirty and take the train. Bye, Lake."

Lake watches Maribel walk away and realizes she wants nothing more than to kiss her full, luscious lips again. That night, she touches herself, thinking about Maribel and all the things she'd like to do to her. Lake moans as she orgasms, then falls asleep content.

On Friday, she spends the better part of her day fantasizing about Maribel and watching the clock. At four thirty, Lake practically sprints to the breakroom. Standing near the windows is a girl she's never seen before, along with a handful of guys, one of whom looks vaguely familiar. Maribel walks in as Lake is assessing the group.

Circling her collection of followers, Maribel says, "I think this is everyone. Let's go."

Lake falls into step next to Maribel. "How was your day?" she asks.

240

"Good," says Maribel. The polite response would have been for Maribel to then ask Lake about her day, but instead, she quickens her pace to join one of the guys, leaving Lake to walk alone. The other female takes a seat next to Lake on the train and tries at small talk. Slightly pissed off, Lake's not in the mood. Thankful for the short ride, Lake smiles politely as they exit the train and make their way to the lounge.

At the bar, Maribel turns to Lake. "What are you drinking? My treat."

"You don't have to do that," says Lake.

"I know I don't have to. I want to." Taking Lake's hand, Maribel adds, "What do you want?"

Lake is so easily led astray. "I'll have a whiskey sour."

Maribel orders two whiskey sours. Handing Lake her drink, she says, "To us—and to a fun night."

Forgiving her completely for acting like a bitch, Lake clinks her glass to Maribel's and says, "I'll drink to that."

The bar they're at is only two train stops from work, but it's Lake's first visit to this spot. It's just the right amount of dark and plush. The music is low enough to allow for conversation, and Lake is starting to have fun.

Lake steals a quick look in Maribel's direction. Maribel catches her glance and winks. She motions with her head toward the door and says to the group, "Excuse me, I'll be right back." Looking at Lake, she shifts her eyes, willing her to follow. Lake takes a sip of her drink and waits a few seconds before excusing herself, as well.

Walking past the door, Lake sees a hallway leading to the restrooms and continues. Slowly, she opens the door of the ladies' room and steps inside. There are three floor-to-ceiling stall doors, with a small circle on each indicating if they are vacant or occupied. She's just about to call out for Maribel when the "occupied" door opens and Maribel pulls her into the stall. Lips connect, and this time, the intensity of the kiss is mutual. Lake is immediately wet. They explore each other's mouths for a couple of minutes before Lake takes the initiative and moves her lips downward.

Maribel tilts her head back, giving Lake full access to the silky soft skin on her neck. She's wearing the same perfume she had on the first time Lake noticed her on the train. The fresh, clean scent drives Lake insane. She unbuttons Maribel's shirt enough to gain access to a breast, then flicks the nipple with her tongue and gently bites it. Pushing her bra up to free the other breast, Lake kisses the skin of Maribel's cleavage. But just as she reaches the other nipple, Maribel pulls away, standing still to listen for any movement in the room. Satisfied they're alone, she fixes her bra and buttons her shirt. Again, without saying a word, she unlocks the door, steps out, washes her hands, and leaves.

Lake has no words for the way she's been duped twice by Maribel. This woman has demeaned and pissed her off for the last time. Standing there, she realizes she actually does have to pee, so she locks the door and uses the toilet.

When she comes out of the stall, the other woman in their group is walking in. She smiles at Lake and enters the stall to her left.

Lake washes her hands, composes herself, and walks out of the restroom.

When she returns to the table, Maribel is at the bar. Lake takes aim and shoots multiple daggers at her back. *Take that, you stupid douche canoe.*

Maribel turns and walks back toward the table with two drinks in her hands. Lake assumes one is for her and some of the anger she feels subsides. But then, Maribel stops short of Lake and hands one of the drinks to the guy she'd been chatting up on the walk to the train station. Instead of coming back to where she had been standing next to Lake, Maribel remains there with the dude.

Lake is fuming. *What the hell?* This is the second time in less than two weeks that she's allowed Maribel to manipulate and humiliate her. Lake attempts to make eye contact with Maribel, but she's avoiding her like the plague. Maribel laughs pretentiously, flips her hair, and touches the guy's shoulder. She's totally flirting with him and screwing with Lake.

Her overstated *F U* sets Lake off. She didn't come here to further Maribel's personal experiment in the time-honored traditions of sapphist love. Lake finishes the last of her drink and takes a deep breath, conjuring up the spirit of her grandma Kiki.

Remember your namesake, Lake. You're a strong woman, a force to be reckoned with. Don't allow that wretched little woman to get away with using you to sidestep her predetermined hetero-path just to try on some-thing new and shiny. This isn't a game. It's downright malicious to mess with someone's psyche that way.

"You're absolutely right, Kiki!" Lake says aloud.

Lake walks over to Maribel and gives her an earful. Maribel stands there speechless, looking shocked and ashamed. The entire exchange lasts just seconds and ends with Lake leaving the bar.

#

In a city with more than enough lesbians to go around, Lake had let herself fall for a straight girl. Shaking her head in disbelief, she wonders whether Maribel planned the whole thing. It doesn't matter; she's glad it happened. Lake should have trusted her instincts. That day at work after Thanksgiving, Maribel's eyes had told her everything she needed to know, and accepting that now stings.

I don't like you that way, Lake. I'm not gay, and we'll never be a thing. Please stop pining after me.

Lake cannot believe she allowed herself to be sucked into Maribel's fanciful game of gay hokey-pokey. "You put your right foot in, you take your right foot out..." Hurtful as it was, she chocks it up as another unpleasant learning experience and gleans whatever morsel of wisdom she can before cautiously dipping her foot back in.

Maribel was a danger because unhappiness sits at the root of her current-day circumstance along with entitlement and immaturity. Sara's discontent stemmed from being stuck in a life she didn't imagine. Margo was the least threatening because her anguish was short-lived. She had sex with women for money because it was an end to a means. Still, however brief the interludes were, the time Lake spent with each of these women affected her in ways she hadn't anticipated.

So far, Lake's life as a semi-assured young lesbian has been a series of disappointment, depravity, near-misses, and short-lived joys. Getting so close to her desired end state and just missing it. Or worse yet, reaching it, but never being permitted to bask in the glory of the moment, because the timing is off or the other person just isn't her person. But Lake is young and she's yet to meet the person who "makes her heart beat so fast it feels like it's about to explode," so she presses on.

Chapter 18 — Amy

Maribel Nelson had been a disaster. Lake hasn't felt so vulnerable and rejected since, like, forever. She knew this would happen if she allowed herself to be strung along by a straight woman, and that's exactly why she has stayed in her lane up to now. She was fortunate to be spared the humiliation with Sara, but not the heartbreak. Being made to feel gullible and weak is not in her nature, and there is no way in hell she'll allow it to happen again. She totally gets that some people might dabble as they try to figure things out, but it won't be with her.

With her armor firmly back in place, Lake leaves Maribel in the past. She won't go so far as to say the city caters to gays, but it does have a predilection toward them. In simpler terms, she doesn't have to travel far to find a new focus for her affection. The Indigo Girls are playing in town in a few weeks, and she intends to be there. She decides to give her college roommate Tracy a call. It's been almost a year since they'd graduated, and Lake's been meaning to reconnect.

"Hey, Tracy, it's Lake. How are things?"

From the other end of the line: "No way, man! I was just thinking about you. Heard you took a job here in town, working for our esteemed senator. Nice."

"I sure did, and it's going great. I totally owe you for introducing me to this great city."

"I'm glad things are working out for you. Where you living?"

"I found the perfect apartment in Little Five Points. I can walk to the bars and shops, and the train station is close, too. What about you? Are you working now?"

"For sure. I'm at a firm a few miles outside of town. You're talking to a certified public accountant, my friend."

"Wow, Tracy, you're my hero. I don't do math and numbers, but that's cool that you dig 'em."

"It's not the Capitol Building, but I like it. We should get together for brunch or something."

"I have a better idea. You want to go see the Indigo Girls with me?"

"Yeah, totally. I love them."

"Cool, I'll text you the details. If you want, I can buy the tickets, and you can just pay me back when we see each other. We can do brunch or something beforehand."

"That sounds awesome, Lake. Can't wait!" "Cool, I'll see you soon, Trace."

#

Lake is excited to hang out with Tracy and catch up. Waving from her seat at the bar, Lake spots Tracy as soon as she walks in. "You haven't changed at all. You look amazing, Tracy!"

"Thanks. And same, girl. Look at you!"

"Right? We're just a couple of fit college grads making our way in the world," says Lake. "Seriously, I'm so happy to see you!"

"Me too. I'm really glad you suggested this. It's been too long," replies Tracy.

Lake nods and asks, "Are you and Jasper still together?"

"No. He took a job in DC after graduation. We tried the long-distance thing for a while, but it was too hard to maintain. We split up a couple months ago, but we're still good friends."

"Man, that's a bummer, but it's cool you're still friends."

Tracy orders a drink, raises her glass in the air and says, "Here's to friends. What about you, Lake? Are you seeing anyone?"

Lake studies Tracy's face. The topic has never come up before, but she trusts this friend. She has no reason to feel guarded or weird about who she is, so she just answers truthfully. "No. I spend a lot of time at work, and I just haven't really connected with anyone here. But I'm open to meeting someone."

Tracy gives Lake a knowing smile and says, "Maybe you'll meet someone at the concert? You know there's going to be all kinds of happy girls up in there, right?"

Lake laughs and says, "If 'happy' is code for 'gay,' the thought has crossed my mind. You're cool with going with me, right?"

"I told you I was. You're seriously adorable, Lake. I'm sure you'll meet someone soon."

"That's so sweet. Thanks, Tracy. I'm sure you'll meet someone soon, too. Maybe not at the concert, but one never knows. When you least expect it, right?"

"That's what they say. Let's grab a table, I'm starving!"

#

The concert park is a medium-sized, outdoor venue, and the intimate setting provides for a thoroughly entertaining evening. There's not bad seat in the place, but there's no need to test that theory as Lake has purchased the best seats available, and they are spectacular. She and Tracy are super close to the stage, and they have a clear view of the Indigo Girls while they're performing. Attending the event with a local is advantageous for Lake, as they run into several women whom Tracy knows.

On a quick trip to the restroom, the two stop to purchase beverages and are standing in line behind a small group of self-assured, hip-chic rockers who appear to have it all together. One looks back at them and says, "Tracy? It's me, Carla. We went to high school together..."

Tracy embraces Carla and says, "Holy fuck-knuckles, Carla! I can't believe it's you. You look terrific!"

"You, too, sister. Who's your friend?"

"Shit, so sorry. Carla, this is Lake. We went to college together."

Lake automatically extends her hand. "Hey, Carla, nice to meet you."

"Hi, Lake. Nice to meet you, too. Tracy, these are my friends, Chris and Amy."

They all exchange hellos while Tracy and Carla catch up. Lake's eyes lock with Amy's and stay there.

There's no mistaking the sexual orientation of this one. Amy is fit, and she has an amazing head of short, dark hair, olive skin, and fetching brown eyes Lake could easily get lost in.

When it's her turn to order, Amy is forced to look away as she asks the man behind the counter for a beer. Lake uses the time to get a look at Amy's backside. Nice ass, toned back, and a long neck. There's a small tribal tattoo at the base of it. She's not the type of woman Lake is usually attracted to, but the question of her sexuality is an open-and-shut case. She's definitely more butch than fem.

With a handful of beers, Carla, Chris, and Amy bid the two farewell, but Tracy promises to stay in touch. As she punches her friend's number into her cell, Lake gets another peek at Amy.

Very little makeup. Effortless beauty.

Back at their seats, Tracy is trying to get settled and says to Lake, "Could you hold my beer for a sec? Someone's blowing up my phone."

Lake sits, takes Tracy's beer, and looks a few aisles ahead. Carla's waving at them. Her group is right in front of the stage. The lights flicker, and the crowd goes crazy as the musicians appear from the darkened sidelines. The anticipatory first chord is struck, and whoever's blowing up Tracy's phone is all but forgotten.

After the show, the estrogen-enriched crowd disperses, and Lake loses sight of the handsome woman named Amy. On their walk back to the car, Tracy's phone buzzes loudly again. She pulls it from her pocket, then using the back of her hand to lightly hit Lake's arm, she says, "Dude! That chick Amy is totally asking about you."

Scrolling through her text messages, Tracy can see that Carla was the one who'd been blowing up her phone before the concert started, asking all kinds of questions about Lake. "She wants to know if you're seeing anyone, and are you gay? I was totally sidetracked when everyone started clapping and whistling. Anyways, she just said her friend Amy wants to ask you out. What do you want me to say?"

Lake thinks about it for a second and says, "She's totally tempting. Give her my number, and we'll see where it goes."

Tracy replies to Carla's text, and the next morning, Lake wakes up to a text from Amy. All it says is, *Are you free for a drink sometime? Amy.*

Lake studies the text. Eight simple words, and she's not sure how she should respond. Should she play it cool and wait a couple of days? Or should she go with an immediate witty reply, a flirty response, or a simple, straightforward one?

Amy's humble question begs an unpretentious, uncomplicated reply. Lake waits an hour before responding to the text, then types, *Hi! I am free to get a drink sometime. Lake.*

A few minutes later, another text from Amy: *How about this Saturday?*

Lake fires back: *Saturday would be great. What time are you thinking?*

Amy texts Lake a time and suggests a place nearby, taking the guess-work out of the first date agenda. Lake is a fan of the place, and she responds with a smiley-face emoji and *See you Saturday.*

With the plan in play, Lake does what she always does: overthinks the situation. She's been skittish with women her whole life, and this one's no different, except…she is. Lake characteristically admires the ladies from afar, rarely putting herself out there, because when she does, it almost never goes as planned. So, she waits and lets them come to her, but even then, they aren't always the real deal gay mobile. This time it was Tracy who substantiated Lake's gayness via text, which led to Amy making the first move. Her follow-through in asking Lake for a drink should be enough to soothe her weary nerves, but there's something else there she just can't put a finger on. Lake finally pushes any hesitation to the far reaches of her mind and moves dutifully through her workweek.

When Saturday evening arrives, Lake is suddenly hit with the realization that this is her first proper, real date with a woman. Any previous female contact or encounter was a byproduct of luck or circumstance that came suddenly or unexpectedly, but tonight's aus-picious occasion is ripe for meticulous thought and preparation. Still, Lake's not feeling it in the "preparation" realm. When she met Amy, she was dressed for a fun night out with a friend, and she'd like to think it was that casual, down-to-earth impression that drew Amy to her in the first place, so why go in a different direction now?

Pleased with this logic, Lake replicates her unadorned approach to an unassuming evening with a friend and walks to the pub to meet Amy. No muss, no fuss.

When she arrives, Amy's sitting at the bar waiting for her. The place is almost full, and as Lake makes her way over, Amy immediately stands and offers her seat to Lake.

Lake dismisses the offer, saying, "Oh no, you sit. I'm fine."

"I put my name in for a table, so it shouldn't be too long. You look great, by the way," says Amy as she leans in and gives Lake a lingering, full-body hug.

Feeling immediately self-conscious, Lake pulls away and says, "Thanks, so do you."

The weird, can't-put-her-finger-on-it feeling is back. Amy is the most obviously gay woman she's ever been with, and she appears to have no hang-ups about who she is. But in this very public setting, it's a little much for Lake. Amy doesn't appear to be phased by Lake's response to her warm welcome. If she's picked up on Lake's apprehension to remain in the embrace, she reveals nothing.

Returning to her seat, Amy smiles at Lake and says, "Can I get you a drink while we wait?"

Lake grins and replies, "I would love a beer—anything local on tap is fine."

Amy motions to the bartender and orders Lake a beer. Lake's been here enough to know most of the staff by sight. When the bartender returns and places her beer on the counter, Amy lays several bills on the bar and says, "Thanks so much."

Scooping up the bills, the bartender thanks Amy, then looks over at Lake and back at Amy. Pegging them as a couple, she flashes Lake a knowing smile and a wink. It's a quick exchange that leaves Lake wondering if everyone they encounter will assume the same. *Ashamed* would be too harsh a word to use, but it's close. Her heartbeat quickens as she secretly yearns for the power to become invisible.

From the corner of her eye, a hand reaches past her, tapping Amy's shoulder. "Your table is ready."

Turning to the hostess, Lake is more than ready to leave the bar and shrink into a seat far, far away. The situation improves as they are led to a table near the back of the restaurant. Lake takes a seat facing the wall, and Amy sits across from her. The arrangement puts Lake in a position of attentive interest as she has nothing else to focus on besides Amy.

Before either of them has a chance to speak, their waiter is at the table greeting them warmly. He inquires if both are familiar with the menu, to which they both reply, "Yes."

"Terrific, my name's Chad. I'll be your server this evening." Chad walks them through the specials, makes note of their current drink situation, and promises to return shortly to take their orders.

"I probably don't have to tell you, but this place has the best beer-battered fish and chips in the city. They even make their own homemade tartar sauce," says Amy.

Looking intently at Amy, Lake replies, "What, are you psychic or something? The fish and chips happen to be my favorite thing on the menu!"

Amy takes a sip of her beer and puts on her best poker face before saying, "Why, yes, Lake, I do have the ability to read your mind. It's why I picked this place actually."

For a split second, Lake recalls her thoughts from the bar and shifts uncomfortably in her seat. She would die if Amy knew she felt even an inkling of embarrassment to be on this date with her. Filled with dread, she's genuinely worried for a moment.

"Wow, you must be having some interesting thoughts right now. I just watched the blood literally drain from your face." Amy laughs and keeps going. "I'm seriously just messing with you, but what I would give right this minute to actually be able to read your mind. There's only one thing that can make a girl that uneasy with her thoughts—sex!"

Relieved, Lake quickly replies, "Guilty! Can we please move on to something else now?"

With a coy look, Amy says, "Are you kidding? This date just got a whole lot more interesting. Dare to share?"

Tilting her head, Lake fires back, "Maybe later…if you play your cards right."

Amy leans back and looks at Lake in amazement.

Chad is back, soaking up the vibe. "What'd I miss?" he asks.

Amy diverts her attention to Chad and says, "My friend here just told me she's been coming here for months and has never tried your fish and chips before. Can you believe that?"

Looking slightly offended, Chad turns to Lake and says, "The fish and chips are probably the most popular item on the menu. You have to try them!"

Throwing her hands up in a voluntary act of surrender, Lake looks Chad square in the eye and says, "It's settled then. Tonight, I will try the fish and chips. I hope they live up to the hype!"

"You won't be disappointed—they're delicious. Can I bring you another beer?"

Crossing her legs, Lake replies, "Absolutely. Thank you, Chad. Oh, and a glass of water, too, please."

"You got it. I'll bring two waters." To Amy, he says, "And for you?"

"I think I'm going to go with the fish and chips, as well. And another beer, please."

Chad nods and says, "Do you ladies want to start with an appetizer?"

Lake shrugs, and Amy asks, "Do you like artichokes?" Lake nods and says, "Yeah."

"We'll start with the steamed artichoke."

"Excellent choice," says Chad. "I'll have those beers out in a jiff."

Feeling more relaxed and in control, Lake deflects and says, "I want to hear about you. What's your story, Amy? Are you from Atlanta? What do you do? What are you passionate about? Tell me everything."

Amy cocks her head to the side and asks, "How much time do I have?"

"As much as you need. I'm in no rush this evening…the floor is yours," responds Lake.

"I want to be sure to leave time for your story, too, so I'll give you the semi-abbreviated version of mine. How's that sound?"

Lake gives Amy a warm smile and says, "That sounds wonderful. But by 'abbreviated,' I hope you don't mean 'clean.' Don't spare me any nuggets that would prevent me from knowing the real Amy. I have a feeling she's a pretty cool chick."

Amy's face flashes a quick red glow, but she doesn't look away.

Chad is back with drinks and lets them know the appetizer will be out in a few minutes. He apologizes and adds that the kitchen is a little backed up due to a large party, but it shouldn't be too long.

Amy seems relieved to know she has time to share her story without feeling rushed and begins by telling Lake she's originally from Utah. She's the middle child of three, and her parents and younger sister still live in her childhood home. Her older brother, Dale, is married with two kids and lives less than a block from her parents.

Lake stops Amy there. "You're a long way from home and your family. What brought you to Atlanta?"

"It's more like what didn't keep me in Utah. The suburb I grew up in is just outside of Salt Lake. It's far enough to feel like its own community and town, but close enough to take advantage of the big-city activities. My hometown caters to families, and that's not my life, at least not for now. The Western United States is beyond gorgeous, and I think Utah is the most exquisite state I've ever been to. I grew up loving to ski, and I have a huge appreciation for nature and the outdoors. Sometimes I miss home and my family, but I know it's not the place for me, at least not long-term. I did stay long enough to finish college, and it was my job that brought me to Atlanta. I'm a graphic designer, and I work for a firm here in the city. I enjoy the work, and the company I work for is footing the bill for graduate school. I have about a year before I get my master's in marketing."

"Wow. A master's in marketing. That's impressive—good for you. I can relate to wanting to leave your hometown, but it's so hard to be away from family and friends. Are you close to your parents?"

"I talk to my mom a couple times a week. I check in and let her know I'm okay. My dad owns his own business, so he's always at work. My mom takes care of his books, and sometimes she helps at the store during the busy seasons. I usually go back at least once during the holidays to see the family and to ski."

"What about your friends?" asks Lake.

"There's a few friends I reach out to when I visit, but none that I'm really close with. I was kind of a geek in school. I was really into art and design, never that social or outgoing, so I guess it's on me that I don't have any close friends from my childhood. But enough about me—what's your story? I like your name, by the way. It's different."

Lake's breath catches as she thinks of Kiki. The story of her name is more of a second- or third-date narrative. It's intimate and calls for a warm, cozy setting, not a loud and crowded restaurant.

"Actually, our stories are strangely similar. I'm originally from a small town in Ohio. I'm one of three kids, not the middle, but the youngest. My dad also owns his own business, and I miss my family a lot. I haven't been home in almost a year, but I plan to go back this year for Thanksgiving. It's been my favorite holiday since I was a kid, and I missed it last year. I stayed here and went to a friend's house for

Thanksgiving, which turned out to be a calamitous occasion. I mean, the dinner was fine, but the friend is no longer my friend. We had a big blowout, the relationship ended, and I threw myself into work. Then I met you."

Amy's hand goes up, and she says, "I see what you're doing there. You throw in a tidbit about a disastrous relationship that ends abruptly, and you close all casual-like with, 'Then I met you.'" Jokingly, Amy adds, "I'm onto you, Lake."

"There's not much of a story there. The woman's name is Maribel, and I met her on the train. She works in my building. She's a confirmed native of Atlanta and offered to show me the city. Her friends are truly magnetic, and we had a few fun nights out on the town, and…she's straight. She led me to believe otherwise, though, but my advances fell flat, and when I finally grew wise to her tomfoolery, I let her have it and that was that."

"Not much of a story, huh? I'm sorry that happened to you, but I'm glad you stopped it before you were in too deep. And if it makes you feel better, I've been there, and I know what it feels like to be rejected and have your heart stomped on by a basic straight chick. I fell for a married woman back home. A friend of the family, and it was terrible and hurtful. The wound is still gaping, and it's a big reason why I don't go home more often."

Now it is Lake's turn to offer comfort. She can see by her misty eyes that Amy is still upset at what happened. "Thank you for telling me that. It does help to know I'm not alone here, but it makes me sad to see you sad. Do you want to talk about it?"

"No, but thanks for asking."

"You're welcome. And I'm here if you change your mind."

The appetizer arrives, and just as they start to eat it, the meal also arrives. The timing isn't ideal, but the artichoke pairs well with the fish and chips, and they go with it. The conversation is flowing, and neither one of them wants to dampen the mood with a negative comment. Chad had warned them about the backup in the kitchen, which appears to no longer be an issue.

Amy takes a bite of her fish and makes a throaty sound of pleasure, almost like a happy humming.

"I take it you like the fish?" asks Lake.

"Like it? I *love* it! This fish makes me happy. Take a bite—I bet it makes you happy too. I bet you can't help but smile or make a weird sound of your own when you do."

"Well, you know what they say. The moment you stop accepting challenges is the moment you stop moving forward!" is Lake's reply.

Lake spritzes her fish with malt vinegar and takes a big, dripping bite. The vinegar is tangy, and the fish is a buttery blend of flaky, crunchy yumminess. Lake closes her eyes and emits a barely audible, "Mmm."

When she opens her eyes, Amy is leaning back in her seat, arms crossed. "Do you realize you were smiling when you said, 'Mmm'?" asks Amy.

"No. Are you sure that's what you heard? It's pretty loud in here, maybe you're mistaken..."

"Nope, no mistaking what I heard. And you were smiling," says Amy.

"Fine, the fish does make my mouth happy, and you win. Satisfied?" asks Lake.

"More than you know. I'm a sore loser, and it's okay that your taste buds betrayed you. The fish is heavenly. So, tell me, what kind of business does your dad own?"

Lake wipes her mouth and says, "He and my uncle Rick took over the family business when my grandfather passed. It's a horse ranch. They raise quarter horses."

"Did you have a pony when you were little?"

"No, I never had a pony, but I did ride occasionally. I was really into sports when I was little—I still am. The ranch was a magical place for me as a kid, and all the neighborhood kids just naturally gravitated to it. We spent our summers playing kickball in the field, swimming in the pond, and exploring the woods. I used to read for hours in the hayloft."

"That sounds amazing, a real Norman Rockwell childhood, and you're an outdoorsy type, too, like me. Do you like to hike?" asks Amy.

Lake is caught up in the moment, remembering her childhood at the ranch and losing her grandparents far too soon.

Amy asks again, "How do you feel about hiking?"

Lake realizes Amy's asked a question and is waiting for an answer.

"I haven't really spent a lot of time hiking, but I like being outside. I'm sure I'd love it if I gave it a try."

"Well, I know we just met, but one of my friends has a cabin up in Blue Ridge. Sometimes I go up there just to escape all the craziness. If you ever feel like you need to get away from the city one weekend, you should come with. It's a little rustic, but it's cute. There's two bedrooms, so you'd have your own space and bed, but we would be sharing a bathroom."

"I've heard great things about Blue Ridge. Isn't that where the Appalachian Trail starts?" asks Lake.

"Look at you, flexing your knowledge of the North Georgia mountains. The trail starts very close to Blue Ridge, but technically it's not in the town itself. I've hiked that portion of the Appalachian Trail a few times. It's beautiful all year round, but especially in the fall."

"Fall is right around the corner, so count me in. If you're up for company next time you go, let me know. It'd be fun to check out a new town and hike in some real mountains."

"Cool beans. We'll plan a trip," says Amy.

When Chad brings the check, Lake looks around and notices the crowd has thinned out considerably. It's almost eleven o'clock, but neither of them is ready to call it a night yet.

Amy picks up the check, looks it over, then places her credit card in the clip at the top of the holder.

Reaching for the holder, Lake says, "I can't let you pay for dinner. Please, let me pay my share."

Amy has catlike reflexes, snatching the check up before Lake can get to it. "It's no problem. I want to pay. I asked you out, and I'd like to pay for dinner."

"At least let me split it with you," says Lake.

"It's okay. I want to do this. We can split it next time," replies Amy.

Reluctantly, Lake agrees. "Okay. Thank you for dinner, then. It was great, and the conversation and company were even better."

With an intent look on her face, Amy says, "Hundred percent agree. If you want to stay and have another drink, we can move to the bar. Or we can have a nightcap at my place. I live just a few blocks from here."

Lake is curious about Amy's place and is totally open to having another drink with her in a quieter space. Jokingly, she says, "Just as long as you don't think I owe you because I let you pay for dinner!"

Amy's eyebrows shoot up, and she says, "I would never! I genuinely enjoy your company, and I have some really tasty beers at my place."

Getting up from her seat, Lake says, "Alright. Show me the way to your place." Amy follows Lake to the front of the restaurant, then hastens her pace so she can hold the door open for her. "After you, lovely lady," says Amy.

Lake is caught off guard by this chivalrous act and doesn't know what else to say other than, "Thank you."

"You're quite welcome. My place is this way," says Amy as she points in the opposite direction from Lake's place.

They make the short walk to Ponce and wait for the signal to let them know it's safe to cross. Amy reaches for Lake's hand, and when the little man appears lit up, Amy and Lake step off the curb together. The situation makes Lake feel uncomfortable, like every driver is watching and judging the pair as they make their way across the busy street. She wriggles her hand free of Amy's grasp and quickly walks to the other side of the street. It's a sweet gesture, but it's one Lake isn't used to. She's never held hands with another woman in public before. Amy takes it in stride and keeps the pace, chatting all the way to her place.

It's early for this part of town, and the sidewalk is packed with people on both sides of the street. As they pass by several restaurants and bars, Amy draws her fair share of looks from women of all types, and she doesn't seem to care that people assume she's into women, because she is. Her level of comfort with being queer far surpasses Lake's, even on her best day.

Amy's physical beauty is every bit as attractive as her inner beauty, and when you throw in the fact that she seems to have a successful career and confidence exudes from every pore, it's a hard package to pass up. So, why is Lake all bunched up and self-conscious about being with her?

She shrugs off the feeling and continues walking alongside Amy. Just before they reach the center of the Highlands, they veer right, then walk a block or so before Amy says, "My place is right up here on the left."

Lake looks up to see a beautiful gray bungalow with a massive front porch. "Your house is amazing!"

"Thanks, but that's not my house."

Puzzled, Lake looks at Amy. "My place is around back. I rent a detached garden apartment from the owners of the house."

Lake nods and follows Amy to her apartment. When they walk in, the scent of vanilla is heavy in the air. Amy immediately says, "I'm kind of obsessed with candles. I like anything vanilla."

Lake smiles and says, "Who doesn't?"

"Ready for another beer?" asks Amy.

"Sure," replies Lake. With Amy off in the kitchen, Lake walks the few steps into the center of the living room and looks around. Amy's place reminds her more of a carriage house than an apartment. The place is small, but charming, with rich, dark-wood floors. The focal point of the living room is a white brick fireplace flanked by deep-set built-in shelves. The shelves on the left are filled top to bottom with a mixture of hard- and softbound books. The shelves on the right are packed with a thoughtful assortment of framed photos and tchotchkes, a carefully constructed display of mementos. The furniture is mid-century modern, and each piece is a different shade of earth tone, a sharp contrast to the prints on the walls, which are all black and white.

Returning with a beer in each hand, Amy sees Lake looking at her prints and asks, "Do you like those?"

"They're beautiful. I was just admiring them."

"There are five national parks in Utah, and I spent a summer a couple of years ago visiting each of them. I was going through a rough patch, and I guess I was kind of on some sort of vision quest, searching for answers about being gay. Anyway, I took those pictures during that time of isolation, and it's comforting to have them here on my wall as a reminder."

Lake is looking at Amy through a new lens, admiring the layers that lie just beneath the surface of her provocative exterior. "So, which one is your favorite?"

Studying her photos, Amy asks, "It's hard to pick just one of these pictures. They all represent a distinctive moment of time to me."

"Sorry. I was talking about the parks. Which park is your favorite?"

"Got it. If I had to choose, I'd say my favorite was Zion, but they're all pretty spectacular."

"I never would have guessed you took these—they're really good. You've got some mad photography skills," says Lake.

"Just one of my many talents," says Amy as she hands Lake her beer.

Lake clinks her bottle top to Amy's and says, "Cheers!"

Chapter 19

It turns out Amy's super easy to talk to. The more time they spend together, the more Lake likes her. On the night of their first date, Amy and Lake spent four hours sharing their life stories and fooling around. Toward the end of the evening, there was more kissing than talking, but it was fun and filled with passion and first-date excitement. Amy's place is delightful and safe. Lake would have been perfectly content to stay there indefinitely, swimming in the dark pools of Amy's eyes, exchanging kisses and scintillating touches. This feeling of belonging reminds Lake of the gay bars. It's not that straight people aren't welcome in a gay bar, but there are spaces where their bias doesn't belong, and Amy's house is one of them.

When queer people get defensive of their spaces and feel threatened by the grand opening of yet another hetero-centric brewpub, it's because their spaces are overwhelmingly outnumbered by the other spaces, and it sucks. Everyone deserves a space to freely be who they are, and for Lake, Amy's couch seems like home base for her woman-loving demographic, and Amy offers it on the notion of not wanting her to walk home at that hour of the morning.

"It's not safe," she says. "Just stay here and get a few hours of sleep. You're welcome to head out anytime you want, but I'd prefer it be during daylight hours."

"I appreciate that, I do. But I'm so close, I'd rather fall asleep and wake up in my own bed, you know?"

"I get that. But if you won't stay, at least let me drive you to your place. I'll feel much better knowing you got home safe. Fair?" asks Amy.

"Fair," says Lake.

Amy grabs her keys from a dish next to the door and motions for Lake to follow her. Of course, she drives a super-cute black Jeep Wrangler. This very kissable, kind, and talented hip chick drives an equally cool vehicle and lives in a highly desirable place.

As far as first dates go, Lake is living the lesbian version of the Cinderella story, minus the wicked stepmother and ugly-ass stepsisters. Even though Lake isn't kept enslaved or in rags, she did enchant Amy at a happy girl concert, and they did spend a magical first night together. Amy's a real-life Prince Charming—a stud, if you will—who could have anyone she wants, and she's chosen Lake. Amy's house is the equivalent of the glass slipper in the story, and it fits Lake perfectly.

Occasionally, the pair spend an evening at Lake's apartment, but usually they end up at Amy's house. At her own place, Lake cooks out of necessity, to keep from starving, but Amy enjoys cooking and is good at it. So, when she offers a tasty, three-course meal complete with alcoholic drinks and her drop-dead gorgeous body as dessert, Lake would be an idiot to decline. Because they're both busy career girls, the two fall into a habit of Saturday night dinners at Amy's, followed by cuddly movie time and sleepy sex.

Lake appreciates the regularity of the relationship and sees no reason to change or switch things up. Amy, on the other hand, is ready to get out and be at one with nature. One evening, the two are standing at the sink close enough to touch shoulders, Lake is washing and rinsing their dinner dishes, and Amy is drying and putting them away.

"Hey, remember our first date—when I mentioned my friend's cabin up north?" asks Amy.

Lake stops washing and says, "Yeah, we talked about going up together sometime. You said fall is the best time to go and that we could hike."

"Wow, that was basically exactly what I said," jokes Amy as she bumps Lake's shoulder playfully. "Anyway, the leaves are starting to change now, and Trish asked if we want to come up next weekend. It's the only weekend this month she won't be there. I know it's kind of late notice, but do you want to go?"

Incredulous, Lake replies, "That's amazing. Yeah, I want to go."

Amy sets down the plate she's drying and pulls Lake close to her. "I'm really glad I met you. I can't wait to show you Blue Ridge. You're going to love it."

Lake reaches behind Amy's back, grabbing her ass with both hands. Pushing her pelvis into Amy's, she kisses her lips softly before exploring the soft, salty skin of her chin and eventually her neck. She's never met a woman who gets so turned on by having her neck kissed. When her lips connect with an earlobe, Amy shudders, takes Lake's hand, and leads her to the bedroom.

#

After work on Friday, Lake takes the train to her stop and makes the short walk to her apartment to finish packing before Amy picks her up. She's packed and ready to go when she hears the familiar beep of the Jeep's horn. She makes a quick pass through her place to make sure the stove is off and that she's not left anything behind. Tossing the duffel bag over her shoulder, she flips the switch of her end table lamp to on and pauses to conduct a mental inventory of what's in her bag.

Beeeep, beeeep.

Okay, I'm coming already. Satisfied she's remembered everything, Lake walks out the door, locking it behind her.

Amy spots Lake as she emerges from her building and jumps out of the Jeep. "Hey, you. Let me have your bag, I'll toss it in the back for you."

Lake gives Amy the duffel and climbs into the Jeep. She buckles the seat belt and is settling in when Amy joins her up front.

"Our weekend mountain getaway officially begins now," says Amy as she leans in for a kiss.

Just then, Lake looks up to see a woman and a young boy walking past the Jeep. She and the woman make eye contact, and without realizing what she's doing, Lake physically pulls away from Amy to avoid kissing her in front of the woman and the little boy.

For a second, Amy looks hurt, and it's in that instant that Lake recognizes what she's just done. Feeling around the space between the seat and the passenger door, she acts as though she's looking for something there. By this point, the woman and boy are safely past the Jeep. With no one else in sight, Lake gives Amy a quick peck on the cheek and says, "I'm so happy to be here with you. Let's get this adventure started!"

Amy gives Lake a halfhearted grin and starts the car. She's about to say something to Lake, but she stops herself, instead turning on the radio. They listen to the late-afternoon drive-time show on a local radio station as they make their way out of the city.

As the traffic begins to thin, Amy is the first to speak. "I loaded the CD changer with all your favorites." She hands a piece of paper to

Lake with the artists and titles listed in order. "I wrote them all down for you. You can play them in whatever order you want."

Lake feels like crap for the way she behaved earlier. Amy's been nothing but sweet, kind, and respectful of Lake ever since their first date. She doesn't deserve Lake being hot and cold to her for no reason.

Impulsively, she reaches for Amy's hand, squeezing it and bringing it to her lips. She kisses the palm of Amy's hand before cradling it between her own two. Looking out the front window, she says, "I'm sorry if I hurt your feelings before. I know it shouldn't matter to me what other people think, but I'm just not used to being openly affectionate in public."

Out of the corner of her eye, Lake can see Amy looking at her. When she turns to meet Amy's gaze, Amy looks away, choosing to focus on the road instead. Lake has apologized—what more can she possibly do? She decides to let the matter drop but vows to be extra sweet to Amy later.

Lake picks up the list of CDs and studies it for a moment before shuffling to number four on the changer, *Rapture* by Anita Baker. The first song on the CD, "Sweet Love," is her favorite, and when it begins to play, Lake closes her eyes, and rests her head against the back of the seat. Listening to the words, she thinks it's ironic that she has picked this song to listen to first. How does this relate to her situation with Amy? For sure, Lake cares about Amy, but she wouldn't go so far to say she's in love with her, and the line about "feeling no shame" is certainly not true. Maybe she chose this song because she can feel Amy pulling away from her. It's not glaringly obvious, but each time Lake is standoffish, she knows it creates a small wedge between them, and it's getting bigger with every stunt she pulls.

The sun's starting to set, and the constant, uneven ride of the Jeep lulls Lake to sleep. She wakes to find Amy gently shaking her arm.

"We're here, sleepyhead."

"Sorry I fell asleep. I was just listening to the music, and then I was out," says Lake.

"It's fine. I just let the music play, and honestly, the drive wasn't that bad. Are you hungry? I know a cute little Italian place in town."

"I love Italian food," replies Lake.

"Okay. We can drop our stuff inside and unpack when we get back."

"Sounds great," says Lake.

Amy grabs both bags from the back of the Jeep and heads for the front door. The cabin is exactly as she described: small and rustic, but intimate. On the table just inside the door is a bottle of wine with a note: *Have fun this weekend. We love you guys, Trish.* Amy's friends are as kind and caring as she is.

Amy drops the bags next to the couch and says, "I have to pee, and then we'll go."Before Lake can respond, Amy walks into the bathroom. She can hear her peeing. She wasn't kidding when she said she had to go—that's a strong stream. It reminds Lake of the ranch and the sound of horses peeing in the stalls. The toilet flushes, followed by the sound of running water, Amy washing her hands.

When she comes out, she says, "I'm starving! Let's go carb load and drink some wine."

"I'm right behind you," says Lake.

#

The downtown area is artsy and quaint. The restaurant, a freestanding older Victorian house, is set back from the square, and a row of trees with amber leaves beautifully lines the walkway. Stepping up to the hostess stand, Amy gives her name and is told it will be fifteen to twenty minutes before their table is ready. Placing her hand on the small of Lake's back, she leads her in the direction of the bar. It's only a few steps away, but Lake is immediately tense and feels self-conscious. Amy doesn't seem to notice.

"What are you feeling tonight? Red or white?" asks Amy.

"White. I'll take a pinot grigio if they have one," says Lake.

Amy orders two glasses of pinot grigio, pays the bartender, and hands Lake her glass of wine. "Do you want to look at a menu? I can grab one from the hostess desk," asks Amy.

"That'd be great, thanks," Lake answers. The place smells absolutely ambrosial, and Lake can feel her shoulders relax as Amy makes her way over to the hostess stand. As she's weaving in and around people, Lake notices a few of the patrons tracking Amy's every move. A short, bald man near the door whispers something to his wife. She looks at Amy, looks back at her husband, says something, and they snicker. The place is busy and overflowing with people. It's mostly families and couples. Heterosexual couples.

Lake looks at Amy, and her eyes light up when she sees Lake looking back at her. The pang of guilt she felt on the night of their first date is back. Lake has wanted a girlfriend to love and kiss whenever she felt like it since she was eight years old. Now she has one who's ready to reciprocate on the fly, and she's suddenly embarrassed to be a lesbian.

Her date, however, is not. Wearing her standard attire of ripped jeans, fitted white tee, black leather biker jacket, and boots, Amy is handsome and draws the attention of most everyone in the room. Lake loves being the woman on Amy's arm, but she just is not completely on board with all that implies.

Amy hands Lake the menu, and suddenly it's the most interesting read of the day. Having the menu as a common focal point moves their conversation in a different direction. Lake is genuinely interested in learning about the items available and doesn't notice the hostess standing next to her until she announces their table is ready. Amy motions for Lake to walk ahead of her, then falls in behind, her hand naturally finding its way to Lake's backside. She knows the gesture is rooted in caring and kindness, but it makes her feel as though they stick out like a sore thumb. *Look at that butch dyke parading her girlfriend through the dining room as if they belong here. Who do they think they are?*

The hostess stops in the middle of the dining room indicating the table at which they will sit. Amy and Lake are literally the centerpiece of the massive main room. Amy pulls a chair out for Lake, and then, by the grace of all that is good, she walks to the other side of the table to her own seat without first pushing Lake's seat in.

Dinner is a blur as Lake makes it a priority to get through the meal as quickly as possible so she and Amy can hightail it back to the safety of the cabin. Lake's motivation to rush through dinner is not completely lost on Amy, and midway through the entrée, she calls Lake out on it. In between bites, she calmly says, "You're doing it again."

Lake knows exactly what it is that she's doing, but she plays dumb anyway. Innocently she asks, "Doing what?"

"Don't play me like that, Lake. You know exactly what I'm talking about. We're two women having dinner together, and you can't deal with whatever the fuck you think that means."

Lake's never seen Amy this pissed before, and she's not sure how to respond. Before she has a chance to say anything, though, Amy stands, forcefully pushing her seat back from the table, and says, "I need some air. I'll be back in a few minutes."

Lake watches Amy leave through the front door and knows she should go after her, but she can't bring herself to do it. Five minutes later, Amy's back at the table. She looks at Lake apologetically, as if she's the one who was out of line, and says, "The tiramisu here is phenomenal. If it will make you feel better, we can order dessert to go and take our leftovers to eat later."

Lake feels like a sleazeball and blinks repeatedly to keep from crying. Knowing how much she's hurt her partner makes her sad, but there's no denying she's ready to leave the restaurant. Mustering up a smile, she says, "Okay, sure."

When the waiter passes by, Amy places an order for dessert to go and asks for containers for the leftovers. "We'll take the check, too, please." The waiter nods and walks away.

A light rain is falling when they walk outside, and Amy immediately offers her coat to Lake. "Here, babe, take my jacket. I'll run and get the Jeep while you wait here under the awning. Be right back."

As they begin the short drive back to the cabin, Lake gently sets the food containers on the floor. With the seat belt restricting her mobility, she turns to face Amy as best she can. Reaching out, the back of her hand lightly brushes Amy's face before moving to her neck and finally settling in the space between her breasts. While her fingertips slowly graze Amy's soft skin, she says, "I'm sorry for the way I acted at the restaurant, I was wrong to treat you like that. I wish I could say it won't happen again, but I'm having a hard time coming to grips with the anxiety I feel when people clock us as lesbians. I wish I was more like you, confident and comfortable in your skin. You don't give a rat's ass what anyone thinks. You're the most beautiful woman I know, inside and out, and I mean that."

Amy kisses Lake's hand and places it back on her chest. "It took me years to reach this level of acceptance and ease with who I am. Everyone's journey is different, so I'm trying to accept where you are and do what I can to motivate and support you without being too pushy."

Lake doesn't deserve this woman. "I wish we had just one solid lesbian role model. We have nothing—not one single TV show with openly gay actors in a healthy relationship. I mean, look what happened when Ellen finally came out as a gay character on a TV show. She took that leap of faith, revealing her true self to the world, and faced a mountain of criticism from all sorts of hateful people. They even cancelled her show, for crying out loud. I mean, what do we have to hold on to? A few books, and maybe a story or two, passed down like urban legends, and we cling to them because it's all we have. What about the everyday heroes of the LGBTQ+ community? Surely there are other people like you—brave, proud people making a real difference. But we don't hear about them, ever, and it makes me sad. We literally have no support but each other, and not everyone can commit to that. The only place I feel one hundred percent comfortable is in a gay bar or at home within the four walls with the shades tightly drawn to hide behind and keep the judgmental nosy Parkers of the world away."

They're at the cabin now. Amy turns the Jeep's motor off, unbuckles her seat belt, and kisses Lake passionately. "One day, our time will come. It could be a long, painful process, but I promise, things will change. If you can believe that, you can begin to accept yourself and live outside of your head."

Lake unbuckles her seat belt and makes a run for the cabin. It's still raining, and all she can think about is a warm bath and the taste of Amy's velvety skin. She puts the leftovers and the dessert in the refrigerator and shuts the door.

When she turns to look for Amy, she's standing right behind her. Lake smiles and pulls her wet shirt off, dropping it on the kitchen floor. Amy reaches for her, and she squirms to the side, just out of reach. Leaning down, she pushes her shoes off her feet and leaves them near the door as she makes her way down the hall. With her feet free, she unbuttons her pants and peels them off, leaving them in a pile just outside the bathroom door. Amy's there behind her when Lake turns and motions with one finger for her to follow.

Lake has planned for a romantic night with Amy, packing candles and bubble bath in her duffel. She turns on the water faucet in the bathtub and says, "I'll be right back."

Wearing just her panties, Lake retrieves the necessary items from her bag. When she walks back in the bathroom, Amy is standing next to the tub, naked. Anticipating Lake's next move, she's already placed the stopper securely in its hole. Lake dumps a generous amount of bubble bath into the tub and then lights the candles, setting one on the small vanity and carefully placing the other on the windowsill. Turning to face Amy, she removes her panties in a teasingly seductive manner. Then, acting as though she's going to kiss her, Lake smiles and stops just short of Amy's lips, instead taking her hand and guiding it between her legs. Amy takes over from there, and Lake yields to the pleasure of Amy's long, nimble fingers. It takes only a few minutes for her to climax.

The tub is half full when Amy eases Lake to the edge of it, directing her to sit as she kneels in front of her. Placing her hands on Lake's thighs, Amy spreads her legs wide. Without hesitation, her tongue is on Lake's throbbing vulva, gently lapping at her juices and sucking on her engorged clit. The entire area is sensitive and enjoying the ripple effect of an intense orgasm. Lake shudders, involuntarily drawing her legs closed. Amy playfully pushes her legs open wider, pressing her mouth against the vibrating folds of Lake's inner labia.

The sensation is more than she can stand. Pulling away from Amy's thick, penetrating tongue, Lake slips into the tub. Before climbing in, Amy bends and kisses Lake, her mouth covered in a film of sweet milkiness. When their lips connect, Lake gets a small taste herself. The situation has them both running hot, and Lake begs for Amy to get in the tub. She climbs in behind Lake, and they both lie back, allowing the warm water and bubbles to wash over them.

Ultra-relaxed, Lake allows the post-orgasm moments of pure erotic pleasure to seep into every muscle of her body. Through closed eyes, she feels a large, soft sponge moving back and forth from her belly to her breasts. Comfortable in Amy's arms, Lake murmurs, "That was amazing."

Squeezing the water from the sponge onto Lake's neck and shoulders, Amy says, "Making you come is one of my favorite pastimes. Tasting your come is also enjoyable."

"Well...since I benefit from both, I totally agree," replies Lake. "And now, I'd like to return the favor."

Amy kisses the back of Lake's wet neck and says, "I say we enjoy the bath while it's warm. My turn can wait."

Lake folds her arms across her breasts, and Amy pulls her body in closer, their two bodies become one. When the water begins to turn cool, Amy uses her toe to flip the stopper from the drain. The draining water exposes their skin to the cool air, forcing Lake to stand and quickly cover herself with a towel.

Amy stands, casually drapes a towel over her shoulders, and leads Lake to the bedroom. In a gentle, but forceful manner, Amy pushes Lake onto the bed. Then, lying on top of her, she pins Lake's hands above her head and kisses her hard. Lake is immediately turned on and kisses her back hungrily. Letting go of Lake's hands, Amy whispers, "Roll over."

Lake does as she's told, rolling over and arching slightly so that Amy can take her from behind. Lake can feel the swell of her lover's clitoris as she rides her backside. Lake matches Amy's rhythm, pushing against her hardness until she feels the pace quicken. Amy's wet and slippery body tenses, and she barely gets out the words "I'm coming," before her movements slow and her body jerks several times involuntarily.

Lake relaxes as Amy collapses, burying her face in her hair. The two lie like this for several minutes, a lusciously hot, sticky mess. Amy's breathing evens out, and her body begins to twitch again; she's falling asleep. Lake smiles and reaches behind her, then touching Amy's damp hair, she says, "Babe, I have to pee."

Amy yawns, peels herself off Lake, and rolls to the side of the bed.

While sitting on the toilet, Lake recalls their first date, when Amy asked her about her name. She's never told Amy the story behind her name, and she isn't sure she ever will. Grandma Kiki always told her how strong she was and that she was a force to be reckoned with, but she doesn't feel strong right now. Lake is doubting who she is because of pressures from the outside world. She's lived her entire life as a square peg trying to fit into a round hole, and she can't seem to make it work. She just had incredible sex with an amazing woman who cares about her, but she still can't bring herself to treat her with the same respect when they're in public. Amy has zero reservations about who she is. Lake can't ask her to downplay that for fear of drawing unwanted attention to them as a couple.

When she returns to the bedroom, Amy is snuggled under the covers, fast asleep. Lake wishes she could stop time and stay in this densely wooded cocoon with Amy forever. Letting out a heavy sigh, she climbs into bed behind Amy, cradles her body, and falls fast asleep.

#

The next morning, Lake feels like she's been hit by a bus, and her throat is on fire. She has to go to the bathroom, but she can't stand the thought of moving from the bed. While she lies there dreaming about ways to teleport her body without getting up, Amy opens her eyes.

Reaching for her, Amy says, "Hey, are you okay? You're burning up."

The light streaming in from the window hurts Lake's head, and she struggles to keep her eyes open. "No, I'm not okay. I feel like shit. My throat is killing me, and my whole-body aches."

"There's a twenty-four-hour clinic not far from here. Let's see if we can get you in. Are you hungry? Do you want something to eat first?"

"No, I'm not hungry, but I could use a cup of iced coffee. Something cold might feel good on my throat."

"Okay. I'll get dressed and bring the Jeep around. Can you be ready in fifteen minutes?" asks Amy.

"I can be ready in ten," says Lake.

Amy takes Lake to a local coffee shop and gets them each a coffee. When they get to the clinic, there's only one other person in the waiting room. They're in and out in less than thirty minutes.

"Ugh. I feel like such a goof. I haven't had strep throat in years. Sorry if I'm putting a damper on the weekend. I really wanted to go hiking today," says Lake.

"It's not like you got sick on purpose. I'll grab some things for us at the grocery store while you wait for your antibiotics. There's a ton of movies at the cabin. We can relax and watch movies, and I'll take care of you."

A feeling of relief washes over Lake, and she wants nothing more than to kiss Amy's sweet lips right now. Standing in the grocery store in front of the pharmacy counter, surrounded by at least a dozen other people, though, Lake can't even bring herself to hug Amy, let alone kiss her. Standing a safe distance away, she simply says, "You're the best."

Back at the cabin, Amy insists that Lake drink a huge glass of water and eat an entire bowl of chicken soup to stay hydrated and strong. Lake does as she's told, chasing a healthy dose of the antibiotic with the last of her water. With her feet resting in Amy's lap, she struggles to keep her eyes open long enough to make it through twenty minutes of a movie.

The next twenty-four hours is measured in bowls of soup consumed, three in all before it's time to head back to the city. In between bowls of soup, Lake stays awake long enough to take her medicine and drink more water before giving in to the intense need for sleep. Like the ride up, the ride back is quiet. Amy plays the music low while Lake sleeps. In the blink of an eye, they are parked outside of her apartment. Amy carries her duffel in, sets it on the floor, and kisses her head.

"I'll call to check on you before bedtime. Feel better." Amy squeezes Lake's shoulders, then leaves.

There's a finality in her tone that Lake can't readily assess. On impulse, she walks to the window and watches Amy drive away.

#

A kind and classy soul to the end, Amy phones to check on Lake as promised, but the call seems compulsory and scripted. Amy says all the right things, but once the call ends, neither follows through with a next step. Lake refuses to reach out and validate the fact that it's her actions that are causing Amy to pull back. It's her shame that's making her feel "less than," unworthy of Amy's passion and truth. If she can't bring herself to step up, she doesn't deserve to be with Amy. It's like she's asking Amy to step away from herself until she catches up, and that's not fair to anyone, least of all Amy.

With the walls closing in, it's Amy who makes the first of their final moves. When she calls and asks Lake to dinner, Lake already knows how this will play out.

Bringing it all full circle, Lake agrees to meet Amy at the same restaurant where they had their first date. Now it's Amy who's polite but detached. She's already moved on and has just this one last item to check off her breakup list.

When the food arrives and the waiter asks if they're all set, Amy replies curtly, "All set," then waves him off with a dismissive hand gesture. Clear that she's had enough, she turns her attention to Lake and speaks the words out loud, "This isn't working."

The events of the past few months move through Lake's mind in a flash. One day the shackles will come off, and she'll be free to love who she wants without fear of homophobic retribution, discrimination, or retaliation, but that's not today. Until she finds a way to escape her self-imposed prison of insecurity, she's trapped, projecting her fear in the form of a heavy black cloud that slowly chokes the life out of her enlightened lovers.

She'll miss the sex and companionship, but the decision has been made. Nodding her head in agreement, Lake says, "I know."

On the way out, Amy pushes through the door without looking back. Her lithe, fantastic body floats away, taking her cool friends and laid-back mountain cabin with her. Lake watches her summer fling bounce along the sidewalk until her figure is lost among the crowd. She'd like to think they could still be friends, but the reality is, they are nothing to each other anymore.

Chapter 20 — Kingston

L ake makes plans to go home for Thanksgiving, and she buys her plane ticket early to reduce any chance of her chosen flight selling out. With work being so busy, she has no other choice but to fly on the day before the holiday, the busiest travel day of the year. Traffic in the city is horrendous on a normal day, and Lake's worried about finding a parking spot at the airport, long checkin lines, and the possibility of missing her flight. Maybe it would be better for her to take a cab to the airport? She can call for the car early and not have to worry about parking.

On Wednesday morning, Lake is sleeping soundly in her warm and comfy bed when the sound of a lawn mower pierces the quiet of her dreams, jarring her awake and making her sit straight up. Rubbing the sleep from her eyes, she squints to see the time on the nightstand clock. It's 7:15 a.m., the sun is just now rising, and more importantly, her alarm hasn't yet gone off. She has thirty more minutes to sleep, but now some fool has robbed her of the last half hour of early morning bliss. Everyone knows the final moments of sleep before starting the day are most intense and restful. This unwelcome interruption will affect her mental well-being and leave her feeling unrested on this important travel day.

Pissed off, Lake throws back the covers, exposing her body to the cold air in her apartment. Immediately regretting the decision, she pulls the covers back over her body and lies there quietly. Ever since the breakup with Amy, she's tried to focus more on her mental health and inner happiness. As the sound of the mower moves farther away from the space below her window, Lake feels her body relax. She's read somewhere that starting the day with a positive mantra can set the stage for a better experience and outcome to the day. Waking up earlier than expected gives her more time to relax and enjoy her morning coffee. No need to rush and worry about things she cannot change. As her body calms and her breathing becomes more even, she prepares for a slow departure from bed, intent on beginning her day in a healthier frame of mind.

Just then, the mower heads back toward her space. It seems louder than before, and within seconds, the machine being used to cut the grass in her courtyard sounds like a helicopter hovering just outside her window. The earsplitting beast is in some sort of holding pattern directly below her bed, and she wants nothing more than to shoot it down, taking the pilot out with it.

She has no choice but to confront the thoughtless, evil landscaper. Pushing the bedcovers back once again, she's on her feet, opening the window in no time. Screaming at the top of her lungs, Lake berates the idiot in charge of the mower. It's a senseless act of fury because the nincompoop riding the hideously loud piece of machinery obviously can't hear her. The mower makes its way out to the sidewalk, quickly spins around, and comes back at her.

Still screaming, Lake begins waving her hands, her fists clenched into tight little balls. This seems to do the trick. Suddenly, the face behind the mower looks up, smiles, and waves cheerfully at her. Oh my God, the person is a total boob.

Barefoot and cold, Lake takes the stairs two at a time. Forcefully, she pushes the door open and stands on the stoop with her hands on her hips, shooting eye daggers at the happy horticulturist. The mower stops abruptly as the engine is cut. Relief floods through Lake. Finally, the morning quiet she seeks is here.

"Hey there, you alright? Where are your shoes? It's cold out here—you should be wearing shoes. But it sure is a beautiful morning, I'll give you that…"

Lake stares at the woman, incredulous. Her dumbass landscaper is a woman, and she's questioning her choice to go shoeless for this confrontational moment.

"It *was* a beautiful morning—until you woke me up with your stupid, obnoxiously loud lawn mower."

Still wearing a wide grin, the woman removes her large straw hat, then shakes her wavy, coffee-colored locks free to cascade over her shoulders and down her back. Her freckled cheeks and bright eyes smile along with the rest of her face, and Lake feels her fuming façade fading away.

"I'm so sorry I woke you from your beauty sleep, which clearly you do not need. I'm just doing my job. My name's Kingston."

Lake forms a slow smile and says, "I'm Lake. I'm sorry I came at you like that. I have a big day of travel planned, my first time back home to see my family in more than a year. I guess I'm just a little anxious."

"First time home in more than a year? That *is* a big deal, but it's a good thing, right?"

"Yeah. It's totally a good thing. I mean, I'm excited to go home. I'm just freaked out about traffic and long lines at the airport, you know?"

"Perfectly understandable, but I'm sure everything will be fine. What time's your flight?" asks Kingston.

"Eleven fifty," replies Lake.

Fanning her chest with the hat, Kingston says, "Goodness me, sugar. You've got almost four hours until take off. I think you're going to be fine."

This sends Lake into a tailspin. "I know it seems like a long time, but I still have to shower, eat breakfast, run through my various checklists one last time, and then call a cab to take me to the airport. What if the cab is late or never shows up? Then I'm screwed, and I spend another shitty Thanksgiving here, without my family. I can't. I just can't do that."

"Alright now, that's not going to happen. Let just be positive. Maybe there's another way for you to get to the airport?"

"There isn't—not unless I drive myself, and I don't want to do that. The thought of it is even more terrifying than waiting on a stranger to take me in a damn yellow cab," says Lake.

"Okay, I have an idea," says the woman. "I realize we just met, and you're not really happy with me right now, but I live east of town, and I could easily drop you at the airport this morning on my way back home." Pulling a card from the pocket of her jacket, she holds it out for Lake. "This is my business card, and that's my truck over there. My full name, phone number, and the name of my company is on the card. It matches the sign on my truck. I'm not some wingnut out to get you, I'm just offering you a ride because it's the holiday season, and

I feel compelled to relieve you of some stress and help get you to the airport."

Lake studies the woman's face, trying to gauge her age; she guesses her mid-thirties. She's adorable, pocket-sized, and fit. Something about the woman reminds her of Kiki. Flipping the card over, Lake takes her time reading it.

KINGSTON KENNEDY, LANDSCAPE ARCHITECT.
LEAVES OF GRASS LAWN & GARDEN SERVICE.

"What made you choose this name for your company?" asks Lake.

Kingston replies, "'A blade of grass is the journeywork of the stars'."

"So, you're a Walt Whitman fan. That doesn't make you a safe bet for my trip to the airport," says Lake.

Arching her eyebrows, Kingston fires back, "True, but unless I'm mistaken, you have no other offers. I need to finish up here. It's going to take me about an hour to edge and clean up the flower beds. I can have you on the road to the airport by nine thirty, giving you plenty of time to make your flight. It's up to you."

"That doesn't give me a whole lot of time, but it is a nice offer. Maybe I'll see you back here later this morning," says Lake.

"A girl can only dream," says Kingston as she turns and walks back to her mower.

#

At nine twenty-five, Lake descends the stairs leading to her apartment. When she opens the door and steps out onto the stoop of her building, the landscaper's truck is parked at the end of the sidewalk. Using her truck as a prop, Kingston is leaning against the side of it, grinning from ear to ear.

Rolling her oversized suitcase down the cracked and bumpy sidewalk, Lake feels a sense of calm wash over her. She has plenty of time to make her flight, and she is confident this woman gardener whom she's just met will transport her safely to the airport as promised.

Standing before Kingston, Lake isn't sure where her suitcase will go. The truck is specially made to haul landscaping equipment, and there doesn't appear to be room in the front. "I hadn't planned for a passenger with luggage riding shotgun today, but I can make room for your suitcase in the back if you're okay with that," says Kingston.

Smiling, Lake replies, "I'm grateful for the ride to the airport. My bag can go anywhere it will fit."

"Alright. Give me a sec to stow it securely in the back, and then we'll be on our way," says Kingston. "The passenger door is unlocked, so you can go ahead and get in."

Lake presses the handle of her suitcase down and pushes it toward Kingston before walking around the truck and climbing in. The passenger seat is cluttered with empty to-go cups, plastic fruit containers, and paper bags. Grabbing a bag, Lake places the cups, containers, and other trash into the biggest bag she can find. She's holding the bag full of garbage when Kingston climbs in.

"Sorry about the mess, it's usually just me in here." Taking the bag from Lake, Kingston shoves it under the driver's seat. "Buckle up for safety, please."

Setting her backpack on the floor in front of her, Lake leans back in her seat, reaches for the seat belt, and snaps it firmly into place.

With a turn of the key, the truck's heavy-duty diesel engine roars to life. The familiar sound instantly transports Lake back to life on the ranch. It's been years since she's heard the distinct *rumble rumble rumble* of a diesel engine, and it's somehow reassuring. She's been looking forward to this trip home to be with family, and she finds it to be odd, but perfect timing that her happenstance chauffeur seems inexplicably familiar.

Consumed by thoughts of childhood and past holidays surrounded by family, Lake is surprised when Kingston pulls up to her terminal and puts the truck into park. "We're here, and we made it in record time." Glancing past Lake, Kingston exclaims, "Looks like you picked the exact right flight to take home. Traffic was light, but it looks busy in there. I'll grab your bag and meet at the curb."

While standing on the curb, Lake watches the fine woman greenskeeper effortlessly hoist her supersized baggage from the truck and place it before her. Home. Kingston Kennedy reminds her of home.

Reminiscent of a Midwest woman, she's strong, confident, and attractive, but she doesn't fit the mold of a classically feminine woman.

Releasing the handle and raising it for her, Kingston says, "Here you go, young lady. I hope you and your family have a very happy Thanksgiving."

"I don't know how to thank you, Kingston," replies Lake as she reaches for the handle of her bag.

"It was my pleasure—now go," says Kingston.

Suddenly aware of the throngs of people moving all around them, Lake says, "Happy Thanksgiving," then heads for the terminal. She can feel the woman's eyes tracking her journey forward. Stopping just shy of the automatic doors, Lake glances back to see Kingston watching her. Throwing an arm up, the woman waves and points to the sign on her door before shouting, "Hey, Lake, call me if you need a ride home!"

Lake waves back before turning and walking into the terminal.

#

Four days in her childhood home is the perfect amount of time. Jack and Sylvia are excited to have her back in the house, and at times it feels like she never left. Her mom is up early, and breakfast is waiting each morning when Lake rolls out of bed. Because her dad works with live animals, he's required to be at work every morning to make sure the horses are fed and the stalls are clean, but he's always back at the kitchen table, cup of coffee in hand, when Lake makes her way to her usual seat. It's funny how they automatically sit in the same seats they've always sat in. Pete and Jeanne's chairs are empty this morning, but later today, they, too, will be occupied by their rightful owners.

"Morning, kiddo, Happy Thanksgiving," says her dad. "Your mom and I are so grateful to have you here with us this year. Being empty nesters isn't all it's cracked up to be. We miss having you kids in the house."

"I've missed you, too, Dad. What time are Pete and Jeanne coming over?"

"They should be here shortly after noon. Your mom promised your uncle Rick and aunt Joe we'd be at their house by one. Dinner is at two."

Lake is excited to see her brother and his family. He and his wife, Deanna, have had a baby, Lucas, while she was still in college, and Lake hasn't spent much time with her only nephew. Jeanne and her guy, Tim, are recently engaged, but Mom says Jeanne has no intention of getting married. She only agreed to the engagement to appease Tim and his family. Lake wonders how long the engagement will last.

Hidden behind the morning paper, her dad asks, "So how's work going for you? Do you like working for the senator?"

"Yeah, I like it, alright. It's been a great experience, but I think I've learned I don't want to work in politics forever."

Jack lowers the paper so he can see Lake and asks, "What does that mean, exactly? Are you looking for a new job?"

"No, I'm not looking for a new job, but I am thinking about going back to school. I may be eligible for a grant. If I can get it, that would help pay for my master's degree. There's a very good public university steps from the Capitol Building. I can work during the day and take classes in the evening." "What do you want to study?" asks her dad.

"I haven't decided. I've also been tossing around the idea of law school, but I'm not sure of anything right now, Dad. It's just an idea."

"That's a lofty idea, kiddo. Have you talked to your mom about this? She still thinks you're going to move back here one day."

"I'm not moving back to Ohio, Dad. I like where I'm at now, and no, I haven't talked to Mom about this. But when I do come to a decision, you two will be the first to know."

#

It's her first full day back home, and the weather is unseasonably temperate and dry for this time of year, begging Lake to take a walk. She pushes through the front door and lets it slam shut without meaning to, and Sylvia is on her immediately. "For crying out loud, child. You're home one day and already back to your old ways. You don't need to slam the door like that!"

"Sorry, Mom. I didn't mean to," calls Lake.

Without missing a beat, her mom yells back, "Look both ways before you cross the road!"

Her response makes Lake smile. When she makes her way to the end of the driveway, she has two options: to cross the street and wander the endless acres of the ranch, or veer right and head over to see if Aunt Joe needs help with anything. As if on autopilot, she stops, looks both directions, and just before crossing the road, looks left again. With the all-clear, Lake makes a beeline for her grandparents' house, stopping short of the back door. The home is no longer occupied by anyone in her family, and she has no business walking in unannounced.

Unable to move, she stands there just outside the door and looks to the windows. The house is quiet and appears to be empty. Maybe the tenants are away for the holiday? A home reflects the personality and lifestyle of its inhabitants, a collective snapshot of the people who move about the floors and take up space in the rooms. Often, the first impression a home gives is its scent.

Closing her eyes, Lake can easily bring forth the scents that filled the house when she was young, and like the Indian summer that surrounds her, the memory fills her with warmth and joy. She wonders what the place smells like now with the scents of Grandpa Kevin and Grandma Kiki long gone. She's also curious to know how the house is decorated these days. Has anything changed in the last few years?

With a shrug, Lake turns and begins walking toward the main barn. The place still smells the same, and as she moves through the building, she inhales deeply, holding in the timeless aroma of leather, saddle oil, and horse manure. It's a familiar scent, one she will love forever.

Climbing the ladder to the hayloft, she steps onto the floor, covered in bits of hay that have broken free of the tightly wound bales. The loft is full this time of year, and there's barely enough room for her to walk. As she leans comfortably against a towering stack of haybales, Lake's mind is overtaken by a series of childhood memories. Her eyes go in and out of focus as they track the images that bounce through her mind, one after the other, like a wiggly, jiggly Slinkie. With nowhere to be, she enjoys the celebrations of her youth and the hayloft happenings that helped her to better understand who she is and whom she's meant to love.

The last image that comes to her is of the woman who drove her to the airport, Kingston Kennedy. Saying the name out loud, she likes the way it rolls off her tongue. *Kingston Kennedy*—it's a rhythmic, lyrical name as beautiful as the woman to which it was assigned. In this moment, wrapped in nostalgia, Lake decides she will call Kingston and arrange for that ride home.

Lake typically takes a backseat approach to romance, but in this case, she is actively grasping at every opportunity to hear Kingston's voice. Lake has left her phone at the house, but she will call her before they leave for dinner.

She climbs down from the hayloft to nuzzle the horses and wander the ranch. Looking down at the ground, Lake follows the well-worn path from the fields and fence-lined pasture out to the pond. Each step connects her form to the nutrient-rich soil of her youth, and she greedily sops up the energy of her homeland, recharging each and every cell along the way.

Over the course of the past year or so, Lake's personal life has taken a beating, but the spirit of her beloved Kiki guides her now, course-correcting her as it replenishes her mislaid strength and courage. Gazing up to the sky, arms stretched out wide, Lake twirls freely in the sunshine, feeling lighter than she has in months.

Anxious to spend time with her family, Lake practically sprints back to the house. Pulling Kingston's card from her backpack, she dials the number, expecting to get her voice mail. "Hello, this is Kingston, how can I help you?" She has answered!

Stumbling, she manages to get out, "Hi, it's Lake. You gave me a ride to the airport yesterday."

"Hey there, Lake. Happy Thanksgiving. How's it feel to be back home?"

"It's great, actually. Happy Thanksgiving to you, too."

"So, to what do I owe this honor?"

Lake is taken aback by the woman's spunk. Her mind draws a blank, she has no witty comeback, so she decides to answer her question with a question. "Uh, I wanted to see if your offer still stands?"

"What offer was that?" asks Kingston playfully.

"Your offer to drive me home from the airport when I get back."

"Oh right, *that* offer. Yeah, that was the real deal. I can pick you up, no problem. When do you get back?"

"I have an early flight back on Sunday morning. It gets into Atlanta at eleven fifteen," says Lake.

"Sunday, fun day! What are you doing after you get home?" asks Kingston.

"Nothing, really. Just getting ready for work on Monday, why?"

"I usually do brunch with my girls on Sunday and thought you might like to join us. Unless you're opposed to bottomless mimosas and a good time?" says Kingston.

"I'm not opposed to either of those things," replies Lake.

"Good. Text me your flight info, and I'll be waiting for you when you get in."

"Okay. Thanks, Kingston."

"You're very welcome, Lake. See you Sunday," says Kingston before disconnecting.

Lake stares at the ceiling of her childhood bedroom and wonders what Kingston meant when she referred to "her girls." She wishes now that she had asked while they were on the phone. Surely, she wasn't referring to *literal* girls when she followed up with a remark about endless mimosas. That would make no sense at all. Guess she'll have to wait and see, come Sunday. Girl reference aside, she has a good feeling about Kingston and their brunch plans.

Meanwhile, at the dinner table, true to form, Jeanne seizes upon a lull in the conversation to blurt out, "Hey, little sister, you seeing anyone special down there in the big city?"

Lake gives Jeanne the stink-eye before responding, "Not really. Work's been crazy busy, and I'm thinking about going back to school. But enough about me—when are *you* going to commit to a wedding date and stop living in sin?"

Pete clears his throat loudly, then coughs to keep from laughing. All eyes are on Jeanne as she squirms in her seat. Everyone at the table knows her fiancé would like nothing more than to be married and working on a family, but Jeanne's not of the same mindset. Her eyes dart around the table in a mad attempt to focus on anything other than the man seated next to her. Reluctantly, Jeanne finally says, "We've kicked around a few dates, but haven't been able to settle on one yet. Work has us running in all sorts of different directions."

Tim turns to look at Jeanne, but she refuses to meet his gaze. An awkward silence settles over the table until Aunt Joe finally says, "So,

Lake, it must be really exciting working at the Capitol. Do you have any fun stories you can share with us?"

"I wish," says Lake. "Unfortunately, I don't hear much in my position. Every once in a while, the usual office rumors bubble up, but I don't know any of the people involved, so it's not really all that juicy. Sometimes I see homeless people arguing over bench space in the train stations, but that's just sad."

Aunt Joe's hand goes to her heart, and she says, "I don't know how you function down there, Lake. I can't imagine living in a city that size with all those people and the noise."

"It's not all that bad," says Lake. "I'm used to it now. I really like the city… I don't think I could live in a small town again."

The adults stare at her, incredulous, but no one says a word. She's glad that cat's out of the bag. Now it won't come as a surprise when she doesn't move back.

"We have three different kinds of pie for dessert," says her mom. "Who's ready for some?"

#

With the leftovers neatly packed and stacked on the dining room table, Lake and the immediate members of the Myers family grab a Tupperware dish or two and hit the timeworn path that leads them home. Like Grand Canyon mules, each follows the leader, mindlessly placing one foot in front of the other until they reach their destination. Along the way, Lake comes to the realization that being home has her in a pickle. One the one hand, she's delighted to be here and is savoring her time with the family, but on the other, the pull of her new home and life as she left it is hard to ignore. The old saying, "You can't go home again" is true—not because it isn't the same as she remembers it, but because it's exactly the same as she remembers it.

Chapter 21

*P*ulling up to the passenger loading zone at the airport, Sylvia exclaims, "Four days just isn't enough time with you. Please promise your dad and me that you'll stay at least a week next time you're here!"

From the safety of the back seat, Lake rolls her eyes and says, "Okay, Mom. I'll try. You know I had to work the first couple of days this week, and I am due back in the office tomorrow. You guys got all the days I had free. I may try to come back next summer, though. If I do, I'll plan for at least a week."

"Your dad and I would love that. We could all pile in the family sedan and go for donuts at the strip, like we did when you were little. You and Jeanne can argue in the back seat just like when you were kids."

"How can I possibly say no to that?" asks Lake.

Smiling at her in the rearview mirror, her dad winks, reaches over to squeeze his wife's knee, and says, "Safe travels, kiddo. Let us know when you make it home safe, okay?"

"Will do, Dad. Love you guys."

Turning so she can face Lake, her mom's eyes are misty when she says, "We love you, too."

#

To Lake's surprise, Kingston is there waiting for her at baggage claim, and the two lock eyes when she rounds the corner. Goofily, Lake waves and walks over to where Kingston is standing. All smiles, she asks, "What are you doing here?"

Flashing a wide, white smile, Kingston responds, "I got a text from a cute girl asking if I could pick her up from the airport today."

"Someone else texted and asked you to pick them up at the airport today? That's crazy."

Rolling her eyes, Kingston says, "The cute girl was *you*, Lake. How was your flight?"

"It was good, quick. You didn't have to come in to the airport. I could have met you outside," says Lake.

"I know that. Truth is, there's no place like the airport for people-watching. It's been nonstop entertainment since I got here, and I had to use the ladies' room."

"Ah, now we get to it. The real reason behind the why. I totally feel you. I have a bladder the size of a chickpea, so no judgment here."

With her back to the baggage claim area, Lake is startled when the buzzer sounds loudly, indicating the start of the baggage carousel. Checking the signage above them, Lake confirms it's this carousel that will deliver her bag. Normally, she'd move closer to the opening to collect her baggage as soon as it appears, but today she's in no rush.

Keeping one eye on the belt as it pushes luggage from her flight past them, she sneaks a quick peek at the woman standing next to her. It's the first time she's seen her dressed in street clothes, and she looks amazing. The woman standing next to her is dressed for the season in jeans, a collared shirt, a delightfully comfy-looking burnt-orange cardigan, a loosely draped plaid scarf, and cowboy boots.

"So, where'd you say you're from again?" asks Lake.

"I didn't," responds Kingston. "But if you're asking, I moved here from Texas. I took the long way around, checking out a few states I'd never been to before settling here. It's a good place for my business, and I've developed a great friend group. Why do you ask?"

"I was just trying to place the accent. It's not local, but you do have a slight drawl when you speak. What brought you to Georgia?"

"Research. My ex and I had a landscaping business in Texas. When we split, I decided to look for a new place to call home. Georgia has four seasons, doesn't get unbearably hot or cold, and the city has something for everyone. I've been here almost six years, and I love it."

Lake spots her bag and steps closer to the carousel. In her mind, she's trying to do the math, but she isn't sure where to start the clock for an added six years. She desperately wants to ask Kingston how old she is, but she knows it would be inappropriate.

Shaking the thought from her mind, she pulls her bag off the carousel, releases the handle, and asks, "Where are you parked?"

"I found a spot pretty close—follow me," says Kingston as she motions to Lake. For some reason, Lake was expecting the truck, and she is surprised to realize the *beep, beep* of the car being unlocked is coming from a sleek, silver sports car.

Pressing the key fob to release the trunk lid, Kingston says, "I'll put your bag in the back, hop in."

Lake gets in the passenger seat, breathing in the wonderful scent of new car smells. Joining her up front, Kingston starts the engine, carefully checks the rearview mirrors, then slowly begins backing out of the parking spot. As they begin to move forward, Kingston asks, "How was your time back home? What did you do—besides eat?"

"Not too much, really, I kind of stayed close to home. My brother and sister came over, and we had dinner at my aunt and uncle's place. They live next to my parents, and my uncle works at the ranch with my dad. My brother, Pete, and his wife have a little boy, Lucas. He's so cute and sweet, and this was my first time spending any real time with him."

Kingston seemed to perk up at the mention of her nephew. "It's fun to have kids around, especially during the holidays. How old is Lucas?"

"He just turned three a few months ago. He was a baby when I first met him, and now he's a toddler running around the house and getting into all kinds of stuff. He keeps my sister-in-law, Deanna, on her toes. I can't imagine chasing after a little one all day long. I was exhausted after just a couple hours."

"He sounds like a typical boy, curious and full of energy," says Kingston.

The city skyline is coming into view, and Lake relaxes, sinking further into the passenger seat. "He's an adorable bundle of energy, for sure. Pete said there's been some talk about baby number two. My parents seemed excited about that, but I'm not sure Deanna's ready. And then there's my sister, Jeanne. She's recently engaged, but she's in no hurry for marriage or kids. It was kind of a shitshow when I mentioned it at dinner. I'm sure she would have slugged me good if she'd have been sitting any closer."

"Your family sounds fun. I come from a huge family. It's been years since we all had a holiday meal together, though. I try to get back home every couple of years or so, but it's tough getting the whole family together."

Lake looks at Kingston and smiles, admiring her cute profile. An image of her having dinner with Kingston and her family pops into her head, and she realizes she's never invited an adult home to the ranch before. What a strange thought.

"This is the place," says Kingston as she pulls up to the curb. Lake naturally glances up and to her right. They're parked in front of a house on a small hill with multiple porches, patios, and terraces jutting off the front and sides. She's driven by this place before, but it's never occurred to her to stop or check it out. There are people lulling about, waiting for a table, perhaps, or still catching up after a meal. It's hard to say which.

Careful not to scrape the car door on the curb, Lake slowly opens it and steps out to join Kingston near the front of her vehicle. Together they make the short walk to the restaurant's entrance. The host, a handsome guy about Lake's age, screams like a little girl when he sees Kingston. "Hey, boo, look at you, all fabulously fall-like! You... look...gorge!"

Kingston hugs him and says, "Thank you, sweetheart, so do you. I'm loving that haircut on you. I bet the boys do, too!"

"You know they do, girl," replies the cute boy. "We got your table right over here. Let's get a cocktail in your hand!"

Walking behind him, Kingston chimes in, "That's what he said!"

Laughing at Kingston's reply, the host winks as he pulls out the chair at the head of the table for her. "Here you go, naughty girl, enjoy."

Kingston blows him a kiss and pulls out the chair next to hers for Lake. The two sit, and Lake looks up to see three women she's never seen before completely fixated on her, curiously sizing her up. These are Kingston's "girls."

Anyone passing the table of smartly dressed women would peg them as a group of friends who went to school together and are now catching up during a weekend brunch. The telltale signs of gayness are there, but it's not strikingly obvious, which sets Lake's mind at ease.

"Hello, lovely ladies," exclaims Kingston in a booming voice. "Before we begin, thanks for sharing your Sunday fun day with me. Our golf outings and brunches are the best part of my week!"

As Kingston addresses the women, Lake notices a change in their demeanor. They appear to be relaxing, as though the sound of Kingston's voice is physically calming them. Placing a hand on the arm of Lake's chair, she continues, "This is my new friend, Lake. She just came back from a few days in Ohio visiting family for Thanksgiving. We all know how trying family can be." The girls laugh and nod in agreement. "She's got to be back at work first thing tomorrow morning, and I thought inviting her to join our brunch might help take the edge off."

These ladies clearly arrived well ahead of Lake and Kingston. Holding their half-empty mimosa glasses high, they welcome Lake to the group. Raising her glass of water in the air, Lake replies with a simple, "Thank you."

Looking past Lake, Kingston introduces the woman seated next to her, then quickly rattles off two more names she won't remember. Scanning each of their faces, Lake is optimistically cautious of their hospitality, as it was intentionally summoned by their leader, Kingston.

Having fulfilled the welcome request, only the woman to Lake's immediate right engages her further during the meal, which lasts for nearly two hours. "Hey, Lake, nice to meet you. I'm Peggy. How do you know Kingston?"

Most of the women at the table are closer to Kingston's age than Lake's, but it's hard to assign an actual numerical figure to any of their ages. All appear to be physically fit and well put together, strong, and attractive in that older, successful woman kind of way. Peggy is a box-blond, with sharp features. A pair of Ray-Ban Wayfarers perched on her head permit access to her warm, brown eyes. Lake is immediately comfortable with her. "We met about a week ago. She was mowing the lawn at my apartment complex, and I wigged out on her for waking me up. She, of course, was nice even though I was a jerk. I felt bad for yelling at her, then she gave me a ride to the airport and invited me to brunch."

"That's our Kingston. Taming angry women is one of her strongest superpowers. She has many, by the way," exclaims Peggy.

"I haven't spent much time with her, but from what I have seen, she definitely has a way with people. She reminds me a lot of someone I once loved very much," says Lake, careful not to say it was her grandmother.

Peggy glances admiringly at Kingston and back at Lake. "So, what kind of work will you return to tomorrow morning?"

Lake is impressed that Peggy picked up on that comment earlier and responds, "I work at the Capitol, as a legislative assistant for the senator." Peggy's eyebrows shoot up, and Lake adds, "It's not as glamorous as it sounds. But it pays the bills. What do you do, Peggy?"

"I'm a psychiatrist."

Now it's Lake's turn to be impressed. She's never met a real, live psychiatrist before. "That's much more impressive than my legislative assistant job. Do you like what you do?"

"I've been at it for a good long while, but yes, I like it," says Peggy.

"Do you get the feeling people think you're psychoanalyzing them when you meet or talk with them, even when it's in a social setting, like now?" asks Lake.

"I do. Your body language changed when I told you what I do for a living. But I get my fill of work when I'm at work, so I'm not leading any covert operations during brunch, I promise. I'm just here to get my drink on and enjoy time with friends," says Peggy.

With that, Lake relaxes a bit. She has the unmistakable feeling of being under a microscope with these women, but she believes Peggy when she says that's not why she's here today. Besides, she hasn't really revealed any big secrets. She has nothing to worry about.

One of the women sitting across from her asks Peggy a question, and the two begin chatting. Lake takes a sip of her mimosa and watches the women around her eat, drink, and carry on.

"How are you doing?" asks Kingston as she rests a hand on Lake's arm.

"I'm having fun. Peggy seems really nice," responds Lake.

"She's a good egg! I met her at a women's business conference a few years ago. I've never seen her professionally before, in case you were wondering," says Kingston.

"The thought hadn't even crossed my mind, but thanks for clarifying," says Lake.

The restaurant is busy and loud, making long-range table conversation difficult. Lake resigns to enjoy the people-watching as she makes her way through the magnificent spread before her. Because her flight was so early, she hadn't had a proper breakfast. This is basically her first, and likely only, big meal for the day, so she may as well enjoy herself.

Between bites and sips, she takes time to study each of the women at the table. Their body language is laid-back and carefree. There's an understood level of trust, as though each would fight to the death for any one of the women seated at the table. Lake is clearly the outsider, tolerated only because Kingston has brought her into the fold.

Even when she isn't speaking, her host holds court at brunch, the center of attention amid a handful of her devotees. The situation has her wondering about all kinds of things, much like the book her grandma Kiki gave her for her ninth birthday. That book opened a whole new world to her, her formal introduction to lesbians and their social lives. Those in the book frequented a coffeehouse in Berkeley, while these ladies enjoy a weekly brunch to unwind and drink mimosas, a slightly more enjoyable beverage, in Lake's opinion. The premises are similar, and she likes that her people have safe spaces to gather and have fun—but how does Kingston fit in with this group? She seems to have a unique tie to each woman, an exclusive history as individual as the women themselves, but Lake has no concrete information to go by, other than what Kingston shared about Peggy. She knows from experience that no matter how deep the lesbian pond appears to be, they do tend to be somewhat incestuous, for lack of a better term. Has Kingston dated any of these women? It's not an appropriate question for this occasion, but she will probe a little more on the ride home, if permitted.

When the check is presented, the women have their wallets out in record time. Apparently, the unwritten rule established eons ago is that it's a cash-only brunch. Each drops a handful of twenties in the center of the table as they drain their glasses of any remaining mimosa nectar. When the wallets are out of sight, Kingston gathers the bundle of bills, counts it, and places several more in the check holder with the others. Lake has her credit card out and hands it to Kingston. "You're my guest today—put your card away," says Kingston.

"Please let me pay for my share. I also owe you for the rides to and from the airport," says Lake.

"I offered to drive you and to bring you to brunch. Besides, we only pay cash here. It's kind of our thing for being treated so well. We're regulars, and we take care of the staff because they take care of us."

Shaking her head, Lake thanks Kingston. Reaching for her bag, she can feel all six of the women's eyes once again on her. As she and Kingston discussed the bill, the table went strangely silent. The women were listening to their conversation. Lake feels like a slug for not participating in the big cash drop, but she's a card kind of girl who hardly ever carries cash.

Picking up on her discomfort, Kingston gives the proverbial nod to the table, and just like that, the chatter is back, and not one of the women is looking in their direction. Her majesty, Kingston, has spoken. A nearly indetectable nod has shielded Lake from any further judgment. Reminiscent of Kiki, Kingston assumes the role of Lake's protector and advocate—even their names are similar.

Lake doesn't know it at the time, but she will later come to understand that this table of women is affectionately referred to as the "lesbian mafia."

#

It's a short ride from the restaurant to Lake's apartment, and Kingston doesn't waste a moment of it. Pulling away from the curb, she instinctively proclaims, "I'm an open book, Lake. Ask me anything."

Sensing this to be true, Lake seizes the opportunity and asks two back-to-back questions. "Okay, so, how old are you? And are you seeing anyone?"

Giving Lake the side-eye, Kingston jokes, "That's all you're curious about?"

Lake looks her square in the eye and replies, "No, but we don't have a lot of time, and I've wanted to ask you these questions since the day I met you."

"So, why didn't you just ask me then?"

"Because they're not appropriate first-meeting kinds of questions. But now you've left the door wide open, so please, answer." says Lake.

Amused, Kingston replies, "I'm thirty-four and a half. I'll be thirty-five in May. And no, I am not currently seeing anyone."

Lake waits for the "but" that doesn't come. There's something about this woman that makes Lake feel untouchable. She wants to be in her presence, and she wants to please her. Oh, my God, she's becoming a Kingston groupie. Staring out the passenger window, Lake knows they're getting close to her place.

"I *was* seeing someone," says Kingston. "We were together for a few years, and it didn't work out. She's not anyone you would know, and she wasn't at brunch today. Those three women who were there are my oldest and dearest friends. I've known Peggy the longest, and I did ask her out. We had one dinner date, but as the evening progressed, we both realized how similar we are, and we decided then and there that we were meant to be best friends—and so that is what we are."

Looking directly at Kingston, Lake wants to ask the obvious follow-up question of whether or not they slept together, but it's not necessary. She assumes they did, but she will never ask.

Soon they are sitting outside of Lake's apartment building. Kingston reaches across the center console and rests her hand on Lake's knee. "Thank you for coming to brunch with me. I hope my girls weren't too much. They can be a little protective and intimidating at times."

"They were fine. I had a nice time, thanks for inviting me," says Lake.

"My pleasure. I'd like to see you again, if that's okay with you," says Kingston.

"Of course. I'd love to see you again."

"Great. I'm having a holiday party at my house next weekend, and I'd like for you to come. Text me your address, and I'll have my assistant send you an invitation tomorrow."

"An invitation?" asks Lake. "Fancy."

"Actually, it kind of is. It's sort of a tradition now, and it's the one time of year I go all-out. It's a formal soiree, so you will need to dress in your best holiday attire."

Why does this not surprise Lake? Her mind jumps to her closet, and she's relieved to remember the new black dress she bought before going to Ohio. Her office also has a big holiday party the week after next, and she'd bought the dress and a cute pair of shimmery gold heels at a great price, knowing she'd be attending. She sends the text with her address to Kingston before she forgets.

"Okay. Just texted you my address. I'll see you next weekend," says Lake as she reaches for the door. She's taking her time getting out of the car in the hope that Kingston will slip in a good-bye kiss, but she doesn't make the move. Instead, she reaches for the trunk latch and says, "I'll get your bag," as she jumps out the door.

Before Lake even has the chance to collect her bag from the sidewalk, Kingston is walking back to her side of the car. Peering at her from over the roof, she flashes Lake the same freckled cheek and bright-eyed smile she gave her the day they met and says, "Enjoy the rest of your day, sweet girl. I'll see you Saturday."

Chapter 22

The invitation to Kingston's party arrives on Wednesday, and Lake tears into it like a child, ripping the embossed envelope to shreds. The classy cardstock invite provides all the details of the evening, including the gate code to Kingston's neighborhood, which she won't need because the guard gate is fully staffed when she arrives.

"Good evening, ma'am. Who are you here to see?" asks the kindly old man behind the window.

"Kingston Kennedy," replies Lake.

The man smiles and says, "Of course." As the arm to the gate lifts, he adds, "Take a left at the second street, you can't miss her place. Enjoy the party."

Lake proceeds through the gate and drives directly to Kingston's house without a problem. There's a valet waiting for her when she pulls up to the front of the house. Opening her door, he says, "Happy holidays. May I see your invitation, please?"

Lake hands the man her invitation, then steps out of the vehicle. He hands it back to her along with a numbered ticket. "Have fun," he says as she tucks the ticket and the invitation into her bag.

Kingston's home is a sprawling midcentury ranch. The exquisite flagstone walkway is cheerfully illuminated by two rows of paper lanterns that lead her to the front door. Lake freshens up her lip gloss before ringing the bell, and she is surprised when a woman who is not Kingston answers. For some reason, she expected Kingston would answer the front door and welcome each of her guests as they arrived, but that's not the case.

The woman motions for Lake to come in and says, "Welcome to Miss Kingston's home. Please come in."

Lake steps into the house and is astounded by the natural beauty of the furnishings. Kingston is a minimalist, just like her mom, Sylvia. Maybe it's a prerequisite to owning a midcentury-style home? Looking around, Lake realizes the bulk of the people are outside. Following the sound of the music, she makes her way out to the garden and back-yard pool area. The back of the house is gorgeously landscaped. The luminaria number in the hundreds as they line the walkways and float effortlessly in the pool. Lake's eyes settle on a giant ice sculpture in the form of a snowflake. The way the light reflects off it is mesmerizing. "I'm glad you could make it."

The sound of Kingston's voice breaks the enchanting spell of the sculpture's sparkle, and Lake turns to see her dressed in a flowing red-sequined suit and matching red sandals. The suit jacket is unbuttoned at the top, revealing the tan cleavage of a bare-chested Kingston. Lake's eyes go directly to the exposed skin and stay there, held by the promise of her luscious left breast. The jacket is keeping Kingston's bosom from being revealed, but still, Lake cannot look away. Without giving anything up, it's the sexiest suit Lake's ever seen on a woman.

Kingston is waving her hand in front of Lake, smiling. Not sure Lake heard her the first time, she repeats, "Hi. I'm glad you could make it."

Lake feels her cheeks heat and at last averts her gaze and blurts out, "You look amazing! That suit is unbelievable! It makes me want to do things to you..." *What in the Merry Christmas was that all about?* Horrified by the words that just came out of her mouth, Lake turns away from Kingston and faces the band on stage. It's a four-woman quartet playing a jazzy version of "Have Yourself a Merry Little Christmas," and they are delightful.

In her left ear, Kingston says seductively to Lake, "I could say the same about your little black dress..."

It's an unexpected zinger that sends a high-amp jolt directly to her lady business. Taking her hand, Kingston asks, "May I have this dance?" The question is phrased more like a statement, and the crowd of women parts as Kingston leads her closer to the stage.

The party is in full swing, and she and Kingston are slow dancing, lost in the moment, as if they are the only two women on the dance floor.

Just as the song comes to an end, an intoxicated woman in a finely tailored black-velvet tuxedo grabs hold of the mic and commences to declare her undying love for Kingston. Zeroing in on the woman to whom she's speaking, the woman smiles at Lake's dance partner and uses her hands to create the shape of a heart. Within seconds, all three women from the Sunday brunch are making their way on stage and looking to Kingston for guidance. Letting go of Lake's hand, she raises it slightly, and the women instantly stop moving. Turning to Lake, she says, "We're not done here," before excusing herself. The band's singer has ahold of the mic and starts to hum as her bandmates begin to play again.

Kingston climbs the stairs to the stage, drapes an arm around the woman who claims to be in love with her, and carefully helps her off the stage. Lake tracks the pair as they move through the house and disappear out of sight. She's still standing in the same spot when Peggy appears next to her with a glass of champagne.

"You look like you could use a drink," says Peggy.

Thankful for the distraction and the drink, Lake takes the glass from Peggy's hand and drains it without saying a word.

"I knew you could use that. Would you like another glass?"

Lake nods yes and follows Peggy to the bar. "Who was that woman? Do you know her?" asks Lake.

"Everyone here knows Sad Sack Shelley. She and her husband, Stan, live next door," says Peggy.

"What?" says Lake. "She's married?"

"Yep. Has been for more than twenty years. She and Stan have lived next door for as long as I've known Kingston. She's tragic, but harmless. Stan travels a lot for business, and being the kindhearted woman she is, Kingston feels bad for Shelley and invites her to all the parties so she doesn't have to be alone. Shelley has mistakenly come to believe that she's a lesbian living a lie with Stan. And she's convinced she is meant to be with Kingston. But she'll sober up, Stan will come home, and tonight's episode of Sad Sack Shelley will never be spoken of again. It's a pitiful pattern."

"That's a really sad story," says Lake.

Standing behind Lake, Kingston asks, "What's a really sad story?"

"Where did you even come from?" asks Lake. "You're like a hot ninja elf."

Peggy laughs and says, "I'll let you two get back to your dance. Lake, it was a pleasure seeing you."

Handing Lake a fresh glass of champagne, Kingston apologizes for the interruption but offers no explanation. As Peggy moves away in the crowd, Lake's initial impression of Kingston's tight circle of brunch friends is spot-on. The three are fiercely loyal to her, defensive line-women who would literally tackle a woeful housewife if instructed to.

There is a hierarchy to the group that takes Lake a while to pick up on. Peggy is Kingston's most trusted friend, the one she's known the longest. The fact that she was safely tucked between the two at brunch was no accident.

As they make their way back to the dance floor, Lake wonders which house belongs to Stan and Shelley. She imagines one of the brunch girls seeing Shelley safely back to her house, helping her lie down. Encouraging sleep and the passing of time to forget the embarrassment of her shenanigans this evening. Lake is sympathetic to Shelley and her lingering fascination with Kingston. Independence in a woman is hugely attractive, especially to a traditional aging homemaker who thinks she missed her lesbian calling in life.

Lake's lamenting for the Shelley Sad Sack scene vanishes quicker than the fast-melting ice sculpture when she feels Kingston's lips nuzzling her neck. "Now, where were we?"

#

Lake and Kingston are inseparable the rest of the night, spending most of their time dancing and holding one another. When the last song of the evening ends, they share a magical first kiss. Lake doesn't want the night to end, but Kingston plays it cool, holding on to Lake's hand as she says good night to all her departing guests. When the last of her visitors pulls away, Kingston kisses Lake passionately and asks, "Are you going home for the holidays?"

Refusing to open her eyes for fear of waking up from this lovely holiday party dream, Lake says, "No. Why?"

"Would you be offended if I arranged for a special Christmas date?" asks Kingston. Intrigued, Lake opens her eyes and replies, "What kind of a special Christmas date?"

"It won't be 'special' if I reveal all the details now. But what I can share is that you'll need to take some time off work and plan for travel. I'll handle all the other details."

"My office is closed from Christmas eve through New Year's Day. If we go during that time, I don't even have to take time off," says Lake.

"That's good to know. I'll arrange for the date to start on Christmas Eve and end before New Year's."

"Will we drive or take a plane on this 'date'?" asks Lake.

"Both," says Kingston.

"Are we leaving the country? I don't have a passport, so we need to stay in the United States," reveals Lake.

"No plans to leave the country. But it will be cold where we go. You're an Ohio girl. Pack for a few days of winter weather," says Kingston. "That's all the hint you get."

"Will I see you again before we leave?" asks Lake.

"Do you like Italian food?" is Kingston's reply.

"It's been my favorite since I was a kid," is Lake's response.

"Really? Then I'll whip up some of my specialties for you here," says Kingston. "I have a busy week coming up, and I know you have your work party next weekend. We'll plan for one night during the week following your holiday party, how does that sound?"

"That works for me. But I'm going to need a long kiss from you right now to get me through the all the days and nights 'til I see you again," says Lake demurely.Kingston draws Lake in and gives her a kiss hot enough to make her toes curl.

#

The parting kiss Kingston laid on Lake gives her plenty of things to think about until the evening of their dinner arrives. Because it was an amazing kiss and nothing more, she can imagine all sorts of scenarios starring her new main squeeze, Kingston. Lake rings the doorbell and glances back at the spot on the walkway where she and Kingston last kissed. She is hit with another intense jolt of sexual current that runs from her head to her toes.

"What are you looking at?" asks Kingston.

"Us," replies Lake.

Crinkling her nose, Kingston gives Lake an odd look and says, "What are you talking about? We're here, not there."

"I know where we are *now*. But we were there, in that very spot, the last time you kissed me, and I've been thinking about that moment a lot since it happened."

The reference to their last kiss makes Kingston smile as her eyes automatically go to the spot where they'd been standing when it happened. Reaching for Lake's hand, Kingston gives her a playful tug and kisses her on the cheek. "Aw, that's so sweet. Cute and romantic. I like it!"

Still holding her hand, Kingston leads Lake toward the kitchen. "It smells amazing in here," says Lake. "Did you really cook for me?"

"I did. I left work early to make my homemade red sauce just for you. It's my grandma's recipe, and it's the best you'll ever taste. I even made her meatballs to go with it, but full transparency—the pasta's straight out of a box. I'm not good at making pasta from scratch, I don't have the right tools." Stepping over to the stove, she lifts the lid from the pot, stirs the sauce, and gives it a taste. "We can eat anytime you're ready."

While they eat, Lake decides to pick up where she left off after brunch, and she starts firing more questions at Kingston. She asks about her childhood, her past loves, where she sees herself in ten years, and perhaps the most important question of the night: Where is she taking Lake for Christmas?

"I'm from a large, loud Irish family, originally from Massachusetts. I have four sisters and five brothers, and all of them stayed in and around New England. My dad passed a few years ago, and my mom still lives in the house where I grew up. She goes to mass twice a week and plays bridge with her friends every Tuesday night like clockwork."

Kingston takes a long drink of her wine, finishing off the glass. She pours herself another and is about to continue her story when Lake stops her.

"Hold up. You have nine brothers and sisters?" asks Lake.

"That's what I said," replies Kingston.

"Wowzers! That's a lot of kids. Where do you fall in all that?" asks Lake.

"I'm third from the youngest. It was me; my brother Jimmie; and then my sister Shannon, the baby. I also have more than twenty nieces and nephews, which is why I rarely go home. It's nonstop chaos, which

I secretly love, but still, it's hard to get away when you have your own business," says Kingston.

"But *we're* going away for Christmas," states Lake.

"You got me there. We are going away for Christmas, but it's just for a few days. I can't unleash my entire crazy family on you this soon. You'd never recover," says Kingston with a wink.

"I'm sure I'd be fine," says Lake. "I'm good with people, especially other people's kids."Kingston eyes her quizzically and presses on. "After college, I spent the summer bumming around the country and ended up moving to Texas. I have a degree in business. I worked as an account manager for a big commercial landscaping firm for about a year. That's where I met my ex, Christopher."

Lake drops her fork and crosses her hands as she practically shouts, "Time out! Your ex, *Christopher*? Your ex as in *ex-boyfriend*, or ex as in ex–business partner?"

Setting her fork down slowly, Kingston takes a breath before responding, "All of the above. Christopher was my boss, and that's all he was for the first couple of years. Working for him was easy. He's very honest, fair, and likeable. My mom is a devout Catholic, and I'm from a small, traditional New England town. I had plenty of boyfriends growing up, Lake. When I went away to college, I experimented some with women, and I had a long-term boyfriend, too. I honestly don't despise sex with men, but once I started being with women, I really liked how different it is from being with a man.

"When I moved to Texas, I dated a woman for about a year. She and I moved in together, but about a month after that, she was driving home from work late at night and was killed in a car accident. Losing her traumatized me. I never told my family that we were together, but I think they suspected. After she died, I couldn't stand being in our place—everything reminded me of her.

"So, I went home for a visit, and it was awkward and terrible. After just a couple of days there, I changed my flight and went back to Texas. The only thing that kept me from losing my mind was work. Christopher was an understanding boss. He never once overstepped, and he was always kind and patient. One day, someone suggested a happy hour, which I almost never went to, but that day I said yes. I spent most of the evening playing darts and pool with my boss.

"Eventually, we started dating, and when it got serious, I started looking for a new job. He was ready to do his own thing, and so we decided to open our own business on the other side of town. New home construction was booming, and our residential landscape business took off. We could barely keep up with demand, and we were happy. He asked me to marry him, and I did."

As Kingston pours out the details of her past, private life, Lake is gripped by her words and movements. It's the first time she's seen this raw, bitterly authentic side of Kingston, and she cannot look away.

"When I agreed to marry Christopher, I saw a future full of happiness and kids—lots of kids. The thought of having a big family, like the one I grew up in, was appealing to me. Christopher, however, did not share the same vision."

This strikes a chord in Lake, and she must blink fast to keep from crying. She takes a sip of her wine and looks past Kingston to her living room full of fine art and furniture. This confident, amazing woman has an abundance of charm and means, but it hasn't always been easy for her. She's experienced the emotional difficulties and growing pains associated with lesbian learning and development, and she has come out on the better side of it. She and her ex-husband shared a love, a marriage, and a successful business together. It's a lot for Lake to take in, but she appreciates Kingston for trusting her enough to share her truth.

"I was angry for a long time with how things worked out between Christopher and me, but the years have helped me understand and accept it. I always wanted a family, but the timing wasn't right for us," says Kingston. "He taught me that I don't need a man to complete me. He was honorable during the split and more than generous with the assets. I took the money and eventually started over here."

Lake reaches for Kingston's hand. "Thank you for opening up to me. I know this sounds cliché, but maybe you needed to go through all that to be here now. From what I know so far, you're an accomplished woman, and I'm pleased to have met you."

Kingston places her free hand over hers and Lake's, then leans in and kisses her on the cheek. Clearing her throat, she feels the need to lighten the mood.

"Having you yell at me because I woke you was a lucky break for me, too," says Kingston. "And it makes for a great 'how we met' story."

"You got me there," jokes Lake. "I'm sorry for being a jerk that day. I was stressed out, and you happened to be there making a bunch of noise. You were an easy target."

"The story of my life," says Kingston as she moves to clear their empty plates.

"Let me help with that," says Lake.

"Don't worry about it, I'll clean up later. Come sit on the couch with me, and I'll tell you a tiny bit about where we're going for vacation."

Lake happily follows Kingston to the couch and sits next to her.

"Everything is set up for the trip. We have a two-and-a-half-hour flight on Christmas Eve that leaves at one o'clock, so you need to be ready to go by ten thirty. I'll pick you up and drive us to the airport. We'll be at our destination for four days. Our flight back is on the twenty-eighth. Pack warm clothes—a coat, boots, if you have them, gloves, a hat, all that kind of stuff. We will go out to dinner, but nothing too fancy. Jeans, boots, and a nice top is fine. And pack a bathing suit. There may be a hot tub," says Kingston.

Lake is intrigued but still not sure where they're going. A two-and-a-half-hour flight could take them west to the Rockies, up north near Canada, or to New England. All those places are cold and picturesque.

Lake is left wondering to the last possible moment. Kingston holds the tickets and they sit at a table near their gate until their flight is called. Standing in line, waiting to board, Lake sees the name of the city spelled out in little red dots: BURLINGTON.

They spend four days skiing, dining, and exploring scenic Burlington, Vermont. It's a town Lake has never been to before and one she will never forget, because everything involving Kingston is larger than life. The unforgettable Vermont adventure, the first of many, will shape and define their existence as a couple.

#

On New Year's Eve, Kingston's home is filled with people. At the stroke of midnight, she toasts Lake and jokes about how easy it is to be with her. "I could get used to having you around. You should move in with me."

Beep, beep, beep. Objects in mirror may be closer than they appear. What in the lightning-fast lesbian U-Haul is happening right now? It's obvious that Kingston adores Lake, but this is an incredibly hasty move, even for her.

But Kingston, kingpin of the lesbian underground, is relentless in her pursuit to cohabitate and will stop at nothing to impress Lake. Lake's twenty-fourth birthday is a blur as she's whisked away to New York for a long weekend. The writing on her cake reads, HAPPY BIRTHDAY, LAKE. SAY YES! Lake politely declines and continues to do so—until it's time for her lease to be up. Three months later, a moving truck filled with Lake's things is parked in Kingston's driveway.

#

Life with Kingston is blissfully easy, which is a little disarming for Lake. This devotion and connection to another woman is what she's wanted for years, but now, standing in the kitchen, she drinks from her glass and places it on the counter. Lake has always been a glass-half-full kind of girl, but tonight she focuses on the empty space above the liquid. There's something unsettling about her flawless living arrangement that she can't quite put her finger on. It's almost like she's being groomed for something—but what?

Kingston is generous and supportive in every way possible. She's not insecure, jealous, or needy. In fact, she's the exact opposite of that: She's mature, mind-fuck and drama free. So why does Lake feel it's only a matter of time before the shoe drops?

Shaking her head, Lake scolds herself for thinking this way. From the bedroom she hears Kingston say, "Babe, are you coming to bed?"

"Yeah, be there in a sec," replies Lake.

She drinks the remainder of the water and places the empty glass in the dishwasher. Lake flips the kitchen light off, then stands perfectly still, hoping the darkness will provide the clarity she needs. Her mate, Kingston, is an undeniably magnetic soul. Her force is strong, the attraction is real, and she is a willing participant. That's all there is to it.

#

Saturday morning time at the breakfast table is Lake's favorite. It's the one day of the week that's totally theirs. No work, brunch plans, or devout followers milling about. She has Kingston all to herself, which is a rarity. Her lover is so popular and well liked, it's hard to get time alone with her anywhere outside of their private domain.

When she was with Amy, she was partial to the times they were alone at home, because Lake was nervous about being clocked as a lesbian even though she clearly was. But Kingston's lesbianism is questionable even when she's straddling a big, commercial-grade lawn mower. Charming and likable, she's everything Lake could ever want her to be: a best friend, sister, girlfriend, shrewd businesswoman, philanthropist, and genuinely good person. Never a hank, dyke, or butch, Kingston has done an exceptional job building her close circle of friends. They're a lot like her.

"So now that you're all settled in, how would you feel about taking a summer vacation somewhere? Maybe go west to San Fran, Seattle, Colorado? Anywhere at all—you pick," says Kingston.

"I've never been to any of those places," says Lake. "I've always wanted to go to San Francisco. The first gay book I ever read was called *How Far Is Berkeley?*"

"I've never heard of it," says Kingston. "What's it about?"

"It's about a girl named Mike. She and her mom move to Berkeley and sometimes go to a coffeehouse where a group of lesbians hang out. My grandma Kiki gave me the book for my ninth birthday, can you imagine? Somehow my small-town grandmother found that book and tucked it away in a basket full of gifts, and she gave it to me at just the right time. Serendipity in its finest form.

"Kingston sets down her mug and asks matter-of-factly, "Is that a true story?"

A little offended, Lake says, "Of course it's true. Why would you ask that?"

"Because it's incredible…and beautiful…and pure. I definitely need to meet your grandma. What did you say her name is again?"

Looking away, Lake says, "Kiki. Her name was Kristina, but everyone called her Kiki. She and my grandpa Kevin were murdered when I was nine."

Kingston looks as though she's been punched in the gut. She stands and kneels next to Lake, hands resting on her knees. "I'm so sorry, Lake. I had no idea."

"I haven't shared a lot about my childhood. You had no way of knowing about Grandma Kiki and Grandpa Kevin. Don't feel bad, it's not your fault," says Lake.

"Do you want to talk about it now?" asks Kingston.

"No," says Lake.

Kingston stands, kisses Lake on the forehead, and sits back down in her chair. She says nothing, waiting for Lake to continue.

Lake looks at Kingston like she's seeing her for the first time. The morning sun on her face makes her freckled cheeks and bright eyes shine. Damn, she's a gorgeous woman, and she's every bit as bighearted as she is fine. Lake stands, kisses Kingston passionately, and says, "I want to share my life with you. I do want to visit San Francisco one day, but right now, I want you to come home with me so I can show you where I grew up. I want you to see the ranch and meet my family."

Reaching for her face, Kingston kisses Lake's lips, nose, and eyes. "I can't wait to meet your family and see where you grew up. Do you want me to help plan the trip, or do you want to take care of it, since it's your hometown and all?"

"I'll call my mom today and let her know we're coming. I promised to stay a week the next time I went home. Can you take that much time off work?" asks Lake.

"I own the company, baby. I can take as much time as I want if I plan for it well in advance. Besides, I have a whole crew of people who can help while we're gone," says Kingston nonchalantly.

"Right," says Lake.

"Remind me to give you my credit card after breakfast. You can use it to book the tickets and rental car. I met a guy from Cleveland at a landscape convention last year. If we swing by his place and make it a business trip, I can write a portion of it off," says Kingston.

Chapter 23

"*Y*our father will be tickled pink to hear you're coming home for a whole week!" exclaims Sylvia excitedly. "We haven't had you kids here together during the summer in forever. Lucas is at such a fun age now, too. Did I tell you Pete and Deanna are pregnant again? We just found out."

"No. I didn't know. That's great—good for them!" says Lake.

"We just can't believe it, grandbaby number two! Your cousins are having babies, too. Holidays will be like they used to be when Kevin and Kiki hosted. Soon we'll have to have a separate table just for the kids," says her mom.

Lake reflects fondly on those days before responding. "Mom, I want to bring a friend when I come home. Would that be okay?"

"Our home is always open to your friends, dear. Pete and Jeanne's old rooms double as guest rooms for when we have visitors. Your friend can choose either one."

The thought of having Kingston sleep in a separate room hadn't occurred to Lake until now. She knows she has to tell her family about Kingston, but she would prefer to do it in person. Laying the foundation for the biggest reveal of her lifetime, Lake says, "Her name is Kingston, Mom."

"What an unusual name. Is she from here? How do you know her?"

"She's originally from Massachusetts, but she lives here in Atlanta now. I met her at my apartment complex last fall. She's the one who drove me to the airport when I came home for Thanksgiving last year."

"That was nice of her. You know, I've always wanted to visit Boston, so much history there."

"She's not from Boston, Mom. She's from a small town in Massachusetts, just outside of Boston. I think it's about the same distance as it is for us to get to Cleveland."

"Oh, well, that's not too far. I'll let your dad know you're bringing a friend. I'm sure Pete and Jeanne will be thrilled to meet someone new."

Shifting the attention away from her and Kingston, Lake asks, "How are Jeanne and Tim doing? Have they set a date yet?"

"You know your sister. She has no intention of marrying that boy, and that just makes him dig in even deeper. They argue nonstop about it. We like Tim, but sometimes he's just so dense. Your dad and I wouldn't be one bit surprised if they broke up tomorrow, what with all the yelling and fighting."

Lake knows what it's like to be in a one-sided relationship, and she feels bad for her sister. They've never been close, but it's not too late to try. Maybe she and Kingston can spend an evening alone with Jeanne. There are a few nice wineries in the area, and now that she's old enough to drink, Lake would like to visit one. She makes a mental note to call up Jeanne and plan for a girls' night out.

#

Lake and Kingston arrive in Cleveland the day before the Fourth of July holiday. The afternoon is sunny and warm, and there's not a cloud in the sky. When she was planning the trip back home, Kingston gave her access to unlimited funds, so Lake rented a new Mustang convertible for unobstructed views of the northeast Ohio countryside. "It warms my heart to see you're spending my money so well," says Kingston. "I can't imagine cruising along the lakefront in anything less fun."

"Are you being facetious?" asks Lake.

"No. I'm serious. I love that you rented a convertible. And you lucked out with this weather," replies Kingston.

"Fourth of July is always a crapshoot, so yeah, we got lucky. I can't wait to show you the lake and the Strip. It's a little kitschy, but I love it, and you will, too. And there's this donut shop—seriously, the best donuts, ever—and they're sweet. So sweet, my teeth hurt just thinking about them, but I'll probably eat a dozen myself," says Lake.

The enthusiasm Lake has for her hometown is wonderful and fascinating. "You know how I feel about donuts, but for you, I will make an exception and try one—but just one," says Kingston.

"Okay, you can have one of my dozen. I'll eat the rest myself, but no judging me. It's a summertime tradition for my family," says Lake.

"It's tradition for your family to put down a dozen donuts apiece? Is your mom a large woman?" asks Kingston playfully.

"No, she's not. But what if she were? Would that matter to you?"

"No way, babe. I'll love your family no matter what, because they're your family, and I love you," says Kingston.

"You're a silver-tongued devil, Kingston Kennedy, and I'm head over heels for you," says Lake. "But I need to tell you something."

Curious, Kingston asks, "What is it?"

"I'm not out to my family, and you have to sleep in my sister's old room," Lake blurts out.

"Okay. I'm glad we're having this conversation now," says Kingston. "Who do they think I am?"

"I told my mom you're a friend and that I met you at my apartment complex—which is true," says Lake.

"Does she know that you moved out of your apartment and in with me?"

"No. But I'm going to tell them. I just didn't want to do it over the phone. I want them to meet you and get to know you first. Are you annoyed that I didn't disclose everything before we got here?"

"Of course not. It's not like I've been totally up front with my family, either. The process of coming out is scary. I get that you want to be honest with your family, but it's hard, and everyone reacts differently. Just know that I'm here for you, no matter what."

Lake gives Kingston's arm a squeeze and says, "Thanks for being here, babe. There's not a day that goes by without you showing me exactly why I love you so much."

#

It's a blessing to be home for the Fourth of July holiday, and it takes less than twenty-four hours for Lake's witty and bubbly lover to charm the pants off her entire family. Even Jeanne seems enamored by Kingston. "There's something about you that's vaguely familiar to me," says Jeanne. "I can't quite put my finger on it, but I feel like I know you somehow."

Silently, Lake says to herself, *She has a way about her that draws people in, naturally, just like Kiki did. Give it time, it'll come to her.*

"I've had the same thought all night," Sylvia chimes in.

"I guess I just have one of those faces," replies Kingston with a smile.

"It's more than that," agrees Jack.

Lake looks at each of the faces sitting around the bonfire and feels warm inside. Her entire family has shown up for the cookout; even Uncle Rick and Aunt Joe are here. It seems the perfect time to share the true details of her life, but she just can't bring herself to say the words. She has no idea where to begin or what to say.

As she struggles for the right words, Lucas appears next to her and tugs violently at her hand. "Come play sparklers with me, Auntie Lake."

Lake looks at his chubby little face and knows she can't deny him this request. Saved by an adorable toddler . "Okay, buddy, let's go play sparklers," says Lake.

"Hey, can I play, too?" asks Kingston.

Grabbing Kingston's hand, as well, Lucas says, "Yes. You play sparklers, too!"

Laughing and dancing around the fire, Kingston, and Lake play sparklers with Lucas until the box is empty. Lake is enjoying this time with her nephew. "Hey, Lucas, look over there!"

Turning his attention to the large, open field, it takes him a moment to focus on the intermittent light from the multitude of fireflies flittering about. "More sparklers!" exclaims Lucas, pointing.

Scooping him up in her arms, Kingston says, "Those are lightning bugs. Let's see if we can catch one."

"Light bugs," says Lucas.

Lake follows closely behind Kingston and her nephew, and soon they're surrounded by hundreds of twinkling fireflies. Swooping the air gently, Lake easily catches one in her hand. Covering her one hand with the other, she creates a small opening so that Lucas can see the bug's light inside her hands. Curious, he leans in for a closer look. Just as his eye touches her hand, the bug shines brightly, bathing the entire space created by her cupped hands in a yellow-green hue.

Lucas gasps and pulls back, his eyes as big as saucers. "Show Mama, show Daddy!" says Lucas excitedly.

"Alright, let's go show them," says Lake.

Kingston sets Lucas down, and he runs to catch up with Lake.

"Light bug, light bug!" yells Lucas.

Standing at the edge of the fire, Pete looks over to see Lucas barreling toward him, "What's going on, Luc?" he asks.

Lucas points at Lake and says loudly, "Light bug!"

"We caught an awesome bug for Lucas," says Lake. "Let's see if Grandma has a jar for it, and you can keep it next to your bed—as a night-light."

Hearing the word "Grandma," Sylvia's head whips up, and she asks, "What is it? What do you need?"

With the firefly still safe in her hands, Lake says to her mom, "We have a lightning bug for Lucas to take home. Do you have a jar we can borrow for the night?"

"I'm sure I can find one for you," says Sylvia. "Let's go in the house."

Deanna, still in her first trimester, is tired and ready to go home. Jeanne and Tim are staying the night, sleeping in Pete's old room in the basement. Most of the family follows Sylvia inside the house. Eager to get the show on the road, Deanna says, "Can I help you look for a jar, Mom?"

"I usually keep a few empty jars in the pantry. I'll grab an old Mason one to use. Deanna, you can help by getting a rubber band from the junk drawer. We'll need a damp paper towel for the bottom of the jar and Saran Wrap for the top. We'll poke a few air holes in the top and wrap the rubber band around it. Pete, can you grab a few twigs and grass?"

"Sure thing, Mom." Turning to Lake, Pete says, "It was great seeing you, little sister. And it was nice meeting you, Kingston. Thanks for keeping Lucas busy tonight. I know Deanna appreciated it. We'll see you guys on Saturday at the Strip."

Lake hugs her brother and gives Lucas a kiss.

"He's fading fast," says Deanna as she mouths *"Thank you"* to Lake and Kingston.

"Who's ready for more wine?" asks Jeanne.

"I'll have a glass with you," says Kingston.

Tim shoots Jeanne a nasty look before saying, "I think I've had enough. I'm going to watch some TV."

Lake's mom, dad, aunt, and uncle take their cues and follow Tim's lead. "We'll leave you girls to it," says Jack. Placing a hand on his eldest daughter's shoulder, he adds, "Do me a favor, Jeanne. Keep an eye on that fire. When you see the flames burn down, throw some water on it, and give it a stir. I want to be sure that the flames are good and out before you come in. Just give me a holler if you need me to help. I'll be awake until the news is over."

"We got you, Dad," says Jeanne. As soon as Jack is out of earshot, Lake's sister turns to her and says, "So when are you going to tell Mom and Dad that you're with Kingston?"

Lake glances over at Kingston before answering, "I don't know. I was going to tell them tonight, but I didn't know how. I can't believe you figured it out. Do you think Pete knows, too?"

"He might, I don't know," says Jeanne. "I've kind of known for a long time, Lake. I wasn't a hundred percent sure, but seeing with you with Kingston made me think you're together. No offense, Kingston, but you're a successful, older woman, and you're here with my kid sister in the Podunk little town we grew up in. I mean, why else would you hang out if you're not together"?

Lake is impressed by her sister's maturity and intuition and suddenly realizes she's been outed. Jeanne picks up on her little sister's alarm and reassures her, "Don't worry, kid. Your story is not mine to tell. I think it's kind of cool to have some diversity in our family for a change. I won't say anything to the parents, but I can be there for you if you want."

Relieved, Lake says, "Thanks, Jeanne. I don't know when I'm going to tell them, but I'll do it before we leave."

"Okay, but don't get too stressed about it," says Jeanne. "Mom and Dad may be from a small town, but they're good people. They probably won't throw you a coming-out party, but I think they'll be okay."

"I hope you're right," says Lake. "I'm tired of keeping this secret from them. It's okay if they're not thrilled. I just want them to know who I am and what Kingston is to me."

#

The next morning, Lake gives Kingston a walking tour of the ranch, sharing childhood stories along the way. As they rest comfortably in the hayloft, Lake tells Kingston the story of how she got her name.

"That's an awesome story, babe. I always wondered how you got your name, and I figured you'd tell me when you were ready." It was a simple statement, but for some reason, it triggered an outpouring of emotion in Lake, and she began to cry—hard.

On her feet in an instant, Kingston wraps her arms around her girlfriend and holds her. Neither knows how much time passes as Kingston comforts Lake, smoothing her hair and kissing her head.

When she's all cried out, she tells Kingston about making out with Joey and the TV and getting caught by her grandma Kiki.

"And she never said anything to you about it?" asks Kingston.

"No. But she gave me that book about lesbians, so she obviously knew. She always knew—and she always did everything she could to love and support me. God, I wish you could have met her. She was the coolest woman I've ever known. It's been almost fifteen years since she died, and I still miss her so much. You know, you remind me of her."

"I do? Why do you say that?" asks Kingston.

"Because you're always the life of the party. Everywhere we go, people are drawn to you, like moths to a flame. They just can't help themselves. My grandma Kiki was like that. Everyone adored her, just like you."

Kingston kisses Lake and says, "Her memory lives on because of you, Lake. And she was right, you know. You *are* a force to be reckoned with. You're strong and smart and kind and beautiful, and you don't take shit from anyone."

Lake laughs. "It feels good to talk about her with you. It's cathartic. The two relationships I had before you were real doosies. Well, only one was actually a relationship, the other was just a hot-mess misadventure with a straight girl—it's not a story worth telling. But I do have other stories to share if you have time to listen."

"I have all the time in the world for you, Lake," answers Kingston honestly

Over the next hour, Lake confides in Kingston, telling her about Gretchen, Carly, Sara, Margot and Amy. Kingston listens quietly, never once interrupting. When the stories end, Lake can't believe she has just divulged the most intimate details of her past loves and sexcapades to her perfectly ideal girlfriend.

Embarrassed, Lake says, "I'm sorry I just dumped all that on you. I don't know why I did that."

"It's been months or years since you were with any of those women. Don't be sorry, I'm not. The time you spent with them made you who you are today, and I love the woman that you are. I want to build a life with you and have a family," says Kingston.

Lake is living in the moment, and everything that Kingston says sounds good to her. Building a life with the woman she loves is exactly what she wants.

#

After spending Saturday afternoon at the Strip with the family, Lake decides to wind down the day and take Kingston to a nearby town for beers and billiards. It's not an area she frequented when she was young, and no one there knows her or Kingston. The two bounce around the harbor before settling on a historic Irish pub that's been around since Lake was born.

Tossing a few bills on the pool table, Kingston asks, "I'll grab us a couple beers. Do you know how to set up an eight-ball rack?"

"I think so," says Lake.

"It's not that hard. The eight-ball goes in the middle, and the back two balls can't be the same set."

"I'll give it a shot. If it's not right, you can fix it. You'll have to break anyway. I'm terrible at that," says Lake.

"Okay. Be right back," says Kingston.

The couple are having a good time, laughing, drinking, and cutting up, when they're approached by a couple of locals. The taller, thicker of the two says, "Me and my friend here have been watching you two ladies. We don't see any rings on those pretty fingers. Can we buy you a couple of beers?"

Lake holds up her beer and says, "We're good, thanks."

The other guy puts his hand on his chest like he's in pain and says, "Damn, girl, that was harsh. My buddy, Dwight here, was just being kindly. You all just started this game. You might need a couple of refills before it's over."

Kingston notices Lake tense up and intervenes. "My friend here is young, she doesn't mean any disrespect. We probably will need some refills before too long, but we're good for now."

Dwight gives Kingston a nod and lays a handful of coins on the table. "We'll just sit here and watch you two play until you're ready for those beers."

Kingston flashes her big, white smile for the men and says, "Alright now, but don't be ruining my concentration. I intend to win this game before letting you two fellas buy the next round."

Kingston's comment puts the men at ease. Each takes a seat on a nearby stool, drinking and watching every move Lake and Kingston make.

Delaying the inevitable, Kingston misses several easy shots on purpose, making a big show of it. "I can't believe I missed that shot. I blame you for that, Dwight!" says Kingston playfully.

Dwight snickers and says, "I can help you with the next shot. I'm real good at sinking my balls in the hole…"

The comment inflates the skinny one's ego, and he reaches out and smacks Lake on the ass. Kingston watches as the blood drains from her girlfriend's face. She steps between Lake and the guy and says, "I do believe my beer is empty. Which one of you boys is the lucky one who gets to buy me another?"

Dwight is off his seat in a flash. "I'll get it. Anyone else need a beer?" he asks.

The gangly, handsy guy nods his head but doesn't take his eyes off Lake. "What about you, young'un? You ready for another?"

Lake looks at him defiantly before answering firmly, " I said I'm good."

Dwight turns and walks toward the bar, but the other guy won't let up.

Still staring at Lake, he says, "Your bottle looks empty to me. I think you need another beer. It might loosen your bitch ass up some."

Lake has a bad feeling about the situation, and she is starting to get scared. The guy refuses to look away, and for the first time, she senses that she and Kingston could be in real danger. Kingston steps closer to him and says, "Hey, man, lighten up. She's cool. She's just not a big drinker."

He looks Kingston up and down and says disgustedly, "You two ain't some sort of lezzies, are you? You been defending this one all night. Do you like her? Is she your girl?"

Feeling boxed in, Lake looks at Kingston, alarmed. Just then, Dwight returns. He hands Kingston her beer and says, "Damn, you ain't won yet?"

Kingston bats her eyes at Dwight, then reaches out and pushes the eight-ball into the corner pocket. "This game is over. I'll rack and you break. Shoot, we might even let you win," she says with a wink.

Lake is frightened and has somehow lost her ability to speak. They had just been having fun, minding their own business, when these two douchebag jackoffs came along and ruined a perfectly good time.

Kingston racks the balls and whispers to Lake, "Follow my lead and stay far away from the guy who's been giving you a hard time."

Lake nods but doesn't say a word. She and Kingston play the game and pretend to drink their beers while the guys hit their bottles hard. The creep who's been after Lake needs a refill and heads toward the bar without so much as a word to anyone. Dwight is pissed at being slighted and follows his friend, huffing and puffing. "Hey, man, you didn't even ask if I wanted another beer."

Kingston turns to Lake and says, "Go to the bathroom. I'll keep the two peckerheads occupied while you sneak out the back and start the car. Be ready to go when I come running. Got it?"

Lake nods and heads for the ladies' room. Luckily, it's at the opposite end of the bar. When the two men return, the skinny dumbass sneers. "Where's your girlfriend?" "She had to pee. Where's my beer?" asks Kingston.

"Neither one of you is empty," snarls the rascally, mean one.

Kingston sees Lake sneak out the door and says, "True, but what we have is warm. I'm going to get a cold one. Be right back."

Taking her sweet time, Kingston walks to the bar and looks at the TV while the bartender takes care of two men at the other end. She looks casually back at the guys and can see them chatting it up. Neither of them is looking at her. When the bartender makes his way over to her, he says, "What can I get for you?"

Loudly, she says, "Do you sell cigarettes?"

"No, but there's a machine in the hallway over there. It takes dollar bills. Do you need some ones?"

"Nah, I have plenty. Thanks."

When Kingston glances over at the pool table, Dwight is looking her way. She smiles and starts walking toward the door.

"Hey, where you going?" yells Dwight.

Ignoring him, Kingston picks up the pace and keeps going.

This time his voice is louder. "Hey, I'm talking to you!" yells Dwight.

"Shit," says Kingston under her breath. Pushing the door open hard, she sprints to where the car is parked. Lake sees her coming, leans over, and opens the door. The car is already running.

Kingston jumps in, shuts the door, and locks it. "Go—and don't stop for anything or anyone."

Lake quickly checks the rearview for the all-clear and pulls away from the curb.

They have no choice but to drive past the pub during their getaway, and as they do, Dwight steps off the curb and smacks the convertible top of the car hard. Both men are yelling, calling them "fucking cunts" and "stupid-dyke dick teasers."

Lake is genuinely terrified at what could have happened. How did those men expect the night to end? There's no good answer as far as Lake is concerned. She and Kingston are quiet the entire car ride home.

Her parents are awake watching the news when they walk in the house, and Lake does her best to stay calm and act as though nothing has happened.

She makes up a story about going to dinner and stopping at a winery on their way back. Jack and Sylvia have no reason to believe she's not telling the truth. The story is plausible, and they're pleased to see Lake and Kingston enjoying their stay.

It's all she can do to keep it together. Lake looks longingly at Kingston and wants desperately to be held until she falls asleep, but that can't happen tonight. Instead, she lies alone in her twin bed, awake for hours reliving the nightmare of the evening, obsessing over how much worse it could have been.

It's a night that will haunt Lake for years.

#

When Lake opens her eyes Sunday morning, the first thing that hits her is the smell of coffee and bacon. Sylvia is hard at work in the kitchen. She can hear her mom talking to someone and realizes it's Kingston. The thought of her mom standing at the stove cooking while her girlfriend sits at the table drinking coffee and spinning a tall tale just for Sylvia melts her heart and pushes the traumatic episode of the prior evening out of her mind. It's their last full day of vacation, and Lake would prefer to stay close to the ranch. Sylvia is making her favorite meal for dinner—spaghetti and meatballs—and after she's fully satiated and unable to move, she decides, she'll come out to her parents.

After dinner, the foursome moves to the back porch to enjoy an after-dinner beverage. Lake searches her parents' faces for any indication of how they may respond to her news, but it's hard to gauge what their reaction might be. Lake thinks back to her conversation with Jeanne and takes a deep breath. It's now or never. Sensing what's about to happen, Kingston winks and gives her an approving nod.

"Mom, Dad, there's something I want to tell you. I've wanted to share this with you for a long time, but I wasn't quite sure how to say it, so I'm just going to say it... I'm gay."

Jack is the first to speak. In an attempt to clear the air and lighten the mood, he turns to Kingston and asks, "Did you know about this?"

Kingston lets out a nervous laugh and says, "Yes, I'm aware."

Sylvia looks at Kingston and then looks back at Lake. "Your dad and I suspected this, but we didn't want to pry. You know we love you no matter what, but..."

There it is, the inevitable "but." Lake has been waiting for it, and her mom can't get her point across without inserting it into her sentence.

"...we think it's best to keep this in the family."

"That's why I'm telling you and Dad this now. You are my family, and I don't want to hide who I am from you anymore."

Jack intervenes. "We understand what you're telling us, Lake, and your mom's right. We're proud of the woman you've become, and we respect your choices. Just be careful of who you tell about this. This isn't the big city, and we don't want to see you get hurt."

Lake loves her parents, but she's having a hard time keeping her cool right now. "This isn't a *choice*, Dad. I've always been gay—it's who I am."

"But what about that boy you dated in high school? Simon, something or other?"

"What about him?" asks Lake. "He was just someone I dated because I couldn't date women in school. I didn't even know any other girls like me."

"That's what I'm trying to say, Lake. It's a small town, and we don't know anyone else here who's gay. I'm sure you're not the only one from here who is gay, but it's not something people here freely disclose or talk about. We just want you to be careful, that's all."

As good as they are, Lake's parents only understand what is real and possible in the here and now. Their reaction to her coming out is "conditional," just like her gay life growing up in this town was, or at least that's what it feels like.

Lake looks at Kingston and smiles, thankful that she's here to act as a buffer—and to be leaving with her tomorrow. "Kingston knows I'm gay, Dad, because we're a couple. She's my girlfriend, and we live together, in her house."

Sylvia and Jack both look at Kingston. Sylvia's eyes are warm, and she's sincere when she says, "Jack and I were just talking about how much we like you, Kingston. We're glad Lake met you."

"Thank you," says Kingston. "I'm glad, too."

"So, Kingston, Lake tells us you're originally from Massachusetts. How did you end up in Georgia?" asks Jack.

Kingston is wise to Jack's need to move the conversation in an entirely new direction, and she launches into her life story. Just like Lake, her parents are flabbergasted when she mentions she has nine brothers and sisters. Thirty minutes later, their glasses are empty, and it's time for the nightly news.

Lake and Kingston watch TV with her parents until it's time to get ready for bed. They've made plans to eat breakfast in the city before their flight, and they need to be up early.

Kingston says good night and makes her way to Jeanne's room. With Kingston out of the room, Jack tells Lake that he and her mom really do like her "friend," and they hope they are happy together.

Jeanne was right about how the night would go. Her coming out wasn't celebrated, but Lake appreciates that her parents accept who she is and that they wish her and Kingston well.

#

When Lake comes home to visit, she appreciates the beauty of the land and the people, but there's a definite shelf life to her time there. One moment she's reminiscing, enjoying a glass of wine with family, and the next she's caught off guard by an old acquaintance and feels immediately exposed. The walls go up, and she shuts down. Her reaction is conflicting and unbalanced. It's unfortunate that home is the only place that has this effect on her. The dirt and soil of where she once lived and labored is not always kind or forgiving. Lake feels fortunate that she's able to extrapolate the best of what she learned and felt growing up in small-town Ohio. And when she closes her eyes, Grams's arms are always open, there to comfort, guide, and assure her that's it's okay to be different.

She can hear her raspy, throaty voice: *"Live your name, Lake. Be fierce and strong. Use your words and look at the world with a truly open lens. It's easy to fall into step with others—don't do that. Lead, don't follow."*

#

The next day, Lake and Kingston return to the sanctity of their shared home. In this place, the neighbors are no real threat, and when they do get out of line, Kingston's lady syndicate is there to restore the peace. The couple is surrounded by a broad, progressive circle of friends with a healthy dash of queers mixed in.

Kingston is standing at the kitchen counter going through the mail that came while they were away.

"Tom and Nadine sent us something," says Kingston.

"You're the only person I know who actually uses a letter opener to open mail," says Lake.

"It's a handy tool that serves a real purpose. Paper cuts are awful, and they hurt like hell. If I can avoid getting one, I will. This little gadget gets the job done," says Kingston as she demonstrates how useful the letter opener truly is.

Kingston pulls the card from the neatly cut envelope and opens it. She smiles and says, "It's an invitation to Nadine's fortieth." Reaching for her glasses, Kingston slides them over her ears and reads, "'Lordy, lordy, Nadine is forty.' Clever. The party is next month, should be fun."

"She deserves a party," says Lake. The woman has three kids under the age of twelve and hardly has any time for herself. "I hope Tom gets her an amazing gift, like a nice spa day or something. She needs to be pampered."

"I agree,", says Kingston. "Nadine is a terrific mom. She should be pampered and appreciated. If that were us, I'd throw you one helluva party and make sure you know just how much I love and care for you."

"Aw, that's sweet, King. But we have a ways to go before I'm forty. You have, like, sixteen years to plan for it," jokes Lake.

"I meant the kid part," says Kingston. "I want a family of my own, and I want to have it with you."

"You're serious," says Lake.

"Yeah, I am. You know I come from a big family, and I love kids. I saw how you were with Lucas, and I think you'd be a great mom."

"He's my only nephew, and I have a lot of fun with him, but I'm not sure I want to be a mom, at least not anytime soon," says Lake.

"I didn't say we need start planning tomorrow, but promise me you'll think about it. We have a good life, Lake. There's nothing I wouldn't do for you. All you have to do is ask."

Kids have never been a part of Lake's life plan, and she's only twenty-four. Her career is just taking off, and she's been kicking around the idea of law school for a while now. There's no way she can both start a family and go to law school.

"What is it?" asks Kingston. "I can see the wheels spinning."

"It's just that, you know I've been thinking about law school. It's hard to get in, and if I do get in, I'll barely have time for us, let alone kids," says Lake.

"Understood, and you know I'm not going anywhere," says Kingston. "You're going to get in to law school. And that's what? Three years? That's just more time for us to plan."

Lake kisses her wonderful girlfriend and says, "I'm going to take a hot bath, with extra bubbles."

"That sounds fabulous. Enjoy yourself, babe." Kingston gives Lake a playful smack on the butt as she walks away, and it triggers a memory of their messed-up night at the pub.

Lake fills the bath with water and bubbles, turns on some Sade, and eases her weary body into the tub.

The feeling of unsettledness is back. When Lake closes her eyes, it's easy to imagine a future with Kingston. Her home is a safe shelter from the worries of the world, and her hand-picked posse is a dedicated group of gangster boos who've taken a silent oath to guard their godmother and her lover, no matter the cost. She doesn't want to disappoint her sweet love, but after the bar episode, she has serious concerns about bringing a child into the fold. Kingston's defenders are real women with jobs; they can't be there to shield her little one from the bullies hell-bent on tormenting the "kid with queer parents." She and Kingston are not legally permitted to get married; Lake has no financial interest in their home—she doesn't even own the car she drives. She did keep the truck her parents gave her when she turned sixteen, but it's old and difficult to maneuver. It sits in the driveway and is rarely driven; Lake opts instead for the sporty sedan.

Lake rubs her temples and sighs. She feels like her head is about to explode.

The legal ramifications of starting a family with Kingston are much too big for her to think about right now. Instead, she hums along to the song that's playing and allows her body to sink farther under the water.

Chapter 24

Talking to Kingston about law school solidifies the idea in Lake's mind, and she begins mentally planning and plotting the best course of action. The application process for law school is extensive, but the mundane day-to-day of work is more reason to note there's no time like the present to start this next chapter in her life with Kingston.

At the breakfast table, Lake says excitedly, "Babe, I've decided to go for it."

Matching Lake's enthusiasm, Kingston says, "That's terrific, babe. What are you going for?"

"Law school," says Lake. "I'm going today to buy the books and start preparing for the LSAT."

"Sweet! I've always wanted to date a lawyer," says Kingston.

"And in just three short years, you will," says Lake.

"Look at you, being all assertive. You're going after your dream of becoming a lawyer! That's really terrific," says Kingston.

"Thanks, babe. Once I start studying, I'll have very little free time. How about we go out tonight to our favorite ladies' lounge?"

"I have a few jobs close to home today. I'll come back here, get a shower, and pick you up at work. We can go out to dinner and then swing by the bar for a drink," says Kingston.

"Perfect. Can you drop me at the train this morning?" asks Lake.

"Sure, baby, happy to," replies Kingston.

Lake had been introduced to the Pink Triangle when she was with Amy. It was a Saturday night, and the place was beyond insane. Until that night, Lake had only experienced gay bars, but this place is a women's bar—designed for women, owned and operated by women, and for the most part, frequented solely by women. Like all

LGBTQ+-friendly spaces, everyone is welcome here, but the intent is to provide a venue that caters specifically to women, because there are so few places like it in the city. The beauty of this very special women's bar can be found in the individual spaces and activities all taking place under the same roof.

At this lounge, ladies who love ladies can dance to the beat of a different drum under the huge disco ball, play a game of pool at one of six tables, or kick back with a cocktail in one of the quieter lounge areas. Here it's all about choices, which is a gloomy scarcity in the lesbian universe.

At one end of the club, there's a sultry piano bar with the sort of crowd that swings like a pendulum, depending on the entertainment slotted for each night of the week. The Martini Room showcases up-and-coming queer comedians and singers of all type. Some pay homage to Barry Manilow and the like while others sing gospel or jazz. Warming the hearts and toes of its female patrons, a massive stone fireplace dominates the center of the room. A downright snazzy joint, the piano bar uses real glassware—no tacky plastic cups here—and in case the ladies need a fond reminder of the place, they can always pocket a pack of beautifully embossed matches on the way out. The piano bar scene is a distant cry from the booming base drama of the weekends. And the happy medium is the billiards room or the patio lounge, where the music is always pumping, but at a more respectable volume.

Lake looks forward to her evening with Kingston, and she is excited for a night on the town with her somewhat-famous lesbian lover. Long before she moved here, Midtown had been the center of the gay community in Atlanta, and like her favorite ladies' lounge, the area offers a plethora of queer possibilities. It's a place where she can let down her guard and just be. A providential byproduct of Kingston's likeability and generosity is that they're treated like royalty everywhere they go. Restaurants, bars, retail establishments, and the like roll out the red carpet for them whenever they stop by, and tonight will be no exception.

#

It's the kind of fall morning one dreams about when they picture the perfect autumn day, and it happens to be a Sunday. Kingston gets up early and kisses Lake tenderly on the forehead, whispering quietly before she tiptoes out of the bedroom, "Have a good day, babe. Love you…"

Lake vaguely remembers the faint smell of Kingston's cologne before rolling over, snuggling down deep under the covers, and falling back to sleep. At eight fifteen, she wakes up and realizes this amazing day belongs to her and her alone. Kingston will spend the entire morning playing an eighteen-hole round of golf with her crew, followed by food and frothy beverages. This gives Lake plenty of time to spend the day doing anything she wants, and she decides to check out the farmers' market.

Lake walks aimlessly along the paved pathways of the park, people-watching and soaking up the few spotty rays of sun that warm her head and shoulders before disappearing behind the tree limbs. Always a pushover for the local artisan, Lake finds it nearly impossible to pass by the wild Georgia honey booth without stopping.

Growing up in northeast Ohio, she suffered from seasonal allergies most of her life. She thought she had escaped the itchy eye, runny nose, sneezy, congested agony of her childhood spring pollen allergies, only to find that those here in Georgia are just as notorious. It wasn't long after she met Margot that Lake fell prey to the ragweed, hay, and grass pollens of the Southeast. Her soccer scholarship forced her to be outside nearly every day, and the airborne pollens released by these plants were harsh.

It was Tasty and her church ladies who taught Lake all about the benefits of local honey. One morning Tasty dropped by Margot's place unannounced, and Lake was in such a bad way she could barely breathe. Worried she might catch something, Tasty took a step back.

"She has allergies, poor thing. It's her first spring down here in Georgia, and she's outside all day kicking a ball around," said Margot.

Satisfied she wasn't going to catch some dreaded illness from her, Tasty said to Lake, "You gots to get you some unfiltered, unblended wildflower honey mixed with the local bee pollen. Start by taking a quarter teaspoon of that for a couple days, then increase it by a quarter teaspoon every two days until you're up to a full tablespoon. Then you repeat the process until you up to two tablespoons. You are just a teensy-weensy little bit, so two tablespoons a day will do ya right, fix you right up."

And she was right. After graduating and moving to the city, Lake sought out the purist form of raw, local honey she could find. She's not outside as much as she used to be, but she still suffers from allergies when the pollen counts are at their peak.

This vendor claims to operate an urban apiary in the area and guarantees her product is the most hyper-local raw honey available in the city. Lake holds the bottle up to the light and admires a beautiful chunk of natural honeycomb suspended within the delicious amber gooiness of the honey. Awestruck by the amount of work that's gone into this one jar, she barely feels the tap on her shoulder.

"Aren't bees amazing?"

Lake turns to see the face behind the voice, but she doesn't recognize the woman. She smiles and extends her hand. "I'm Tara. Is this your first time visiting the farmers' market?" she asks.

There's something vaguely familiar about the woman. "No. I mean, yes," says Lake. "I've driven past this market a bunch of times, but I've never stopped before. This morning, I woke up, and it was the first place I thought of to go."

"As though it was meant to be," says Tara.

Lake sizes up the woman, trying not to be too obvious. She's attractive, stylish, and well-spoken.

"So, what do you think?" asks Tara.

Caught in the act, Lake can feel her face redden. "About what?" she asks, pretending not to know she's been discovered.

"The honey," replies Tara.

"Oh, right," says Lake, relieved.

"If you're in the market for some local honey, you should buy a jar. It's very good. I've used the honeycomb as a spread on warm

English muffins. Add a side of fresh raspberries or blueberries, and it's heaven," says Tara.

"That sounds so good," replies Lake. "My mouth is watering right now. I'm Lake, by the way"

Tara motions to the woman behind the table and says, "Hey, Sue Ellen. How are you?"

Sue Ellen responds with the standard, "I'm good. Things are good, the business is great. How are you?"

Tara shares that all on her end is good, as well. "I talked Lake here into buying a jar of your honey. Told her there's nothing like it. It's amazing."

Sue Ellen smiles, then looking around, she says, "You heard the lady. A genuine customer endorsement for my honey. Get it while it lasts."

"Actually, I'll take two," says Lake.

"Praise *BEE*," says Sue Ellen excitedly. "If only I had a bell to ring. You're my first two bottle customer today. Will that be cash or charge?"

"Cash," says Lake.

Sue Ellen takes the bills from Lake and wraps two bottles in newspaper before placing them in a recycled plastic sack from Kroger. Gauging the weight of the sack, Sue Ellen double-bags the honey before handing it to Lake.

"Thank you," says Lake.

Nodding her head, Sue Ellen says, "Thank you, Miss Lake. See you next week, Tara."

"You come here every week?" asks Lake.

"Not until the weather turns," replies Tara. "It's too hot to be here every weekend during the summer. They shorten the hours and close it down by noon in the summer, but by then it's already blazing hot. I usually start coming out the first week of September. The market gets bigger every season. We have double the number of vendors this year."

"That's great," says Lake. "I'm glad I stopped by today. I'm excited to start using this local honey."

Tara smiles and asks, "Can I buy you a cup of coffee? There's a booth just down on the left, a local roaster. Her coffee is terrific, very smooth. She also has pastries, in case you want to bust into your honey right away."

Lake looks for any sign of flirtatious behavior, but she isn't feeling it. Tara seems to be on the up and up.

"A coffee sounds good. I'm originally from up north, but after a few years down here, I'm kind of a wimp. It's not even that chilly, but it feels cool to me."

"I know that feeling," says Tara. "I'm from a small town in Colorado that gets a lot of snow. I've been here for about eight years now, and I'm a wimp, too. I like the fall weather, but not the snow."

"I still like the snow," exclaims Lake. "But I don't want to live in a place that gets a lot of it ever again."

"I'm with you on that one," says Tara.

Lake orders a cup of the house-blend coffee. "Are you sure I can't talk you into having a pastry, too?" asks Tara. "The honey was such an easy sell, I never imagined you'd say no to a warm, fresh, local pastry."

"Normally, I would not pass that up," boasts Lake. "But I treated myself to a spinach and cheese omelet this morning with a side of turkey sausage, and I'm still full from breakfast."

"Okay. I'm officially jealous. That's the one thing I never could get quite right. Omelets are not a part of my breakfast arsenal, but it's not for lack of trying," says Tara.

"It's my opinion that eggs are the perfect food, and I used to eat breakfast for dinner, like, four nights a week. I don't have the patience for hard-boiled, so when I got tired of scrambled and over-easy, I taught myself how to make an omelet."

"So, what changed?" asks Tara quizzically.

"What do you mean?" says Lake.

Tara looks at her and replies, "You said you *used to* eat breakfast for dinner four nights a week. Why did that change?"

Lake thinks to herself, *This woman is very perceptive*. She hadn't realized she'd said that. "I met someone last year, and we moved in together. I don't have to cook for myself every night anymore, so I don't eat breakfast for dinner as much as I used to."

Lake detects a slight change in Tara's demeanor when she admits to moving in with the person she's met and then it clicks. She remembers seeing Tara at Kingston's holiday party, the one where Shelley Sad Sack professed her undying love for Kingston.

"Have we met before?" asks Lake. "Were you at Kingston Kennedy's holiday party last December?"

In a calm, composed voice, Tara replies, "I was at that party, but I left before it got too late. My date wasn't feeling well, and I was feeling a little overwhelmed. I had recently gotten sober, and Kingston throws one helluva party. It was a lot for us, so we left."

Lake has an uneasy feeling in her stomach. She doesn't really know Tara, but she likes her. She has a calming presence and an old soul. She wishes she could stay and talk to her longer, but she needs to get going. She has more shopping to do, and she and Kingston have plans for dinner.

"It's been really nice talking to you, Tara. I wish I could stay, but I have more shopping to get done, and we have dinner plans." Lake's voice trails off before she adds, "Now that I know you come here almost every weekend, maybe I'll see you again. Kingston's turned me into a mad tea drinker, and we go through a lot of honey. I'm sure it won't be long before we need some more."

"She does love her tea," says Tara before quickly adding, "It was nice meeting you, too, Lake. I hope to run into you again soon."

Lake smiles at Tara and watches as she walks away. With the wind rustling through the trees, a cool breeze blows across her face, and she wonders how Tara knows about Kingston's obsession with tea…

#

At dinner that evening, Kingston says, "I know I've set the bar high for myself, and the only way to go higher is to go bigger."

Shaking her head, Lake asks, "What are you talking about?"

"Christmas is right around the corner, you're taking the LSAT next week, and you're waiting to hear if you've been accepted to law school," says Kingston. "I know how hard you've been studying, and I thought we could celebrate all the good news that's sure to come with another trip. It may be our last for a while, and I'd like to show you San Francisco and wine country. We could even swing by Berkeley."

Lake contemplates another trip with Kingston and is about to politely decline the offer when she realizes her love speaks the truth.

When she's not at work, she's studying for the LSAT, and when she passes the exam and is accepted to her first-choice law school—she must think positive—time for leisure travel will be rarer than a blue moon.

"Eight days. That's all I can give you. Is that enough time to see all the wonders of San Francisco and wine country?" asks Lake.

"It will be tough, but I think I can manage it." With a twinkle in her eye, Kingston keeps going. "We'll have to dedicate two full days for travel time. We'll do two days in wine country, take a drive through Berkeley, check out the redwoods, and that will leave us with three full days in the city. I'll take care of every detail."

Knowing Kingston lives for this shit, Lake says, "Trust me. I haven't got the time or the energy to plan a Kingston-sized Christmas voyage. That's all you, babe."

"I wouldn't have it any other way. Big trips are kind of my thing," says Kingston. Her response sparks a thought, and Lake thinks back to her day at the farmers' market when she met Tara.

The woman has been here, to her home, at least once that she knows of. And she's chummy enough with Kingston to know that she prefers tea to coffee. Kingston drinks a cup in the morning when she wakes up and another, herbal blend every night before going to bed. Lake speculates on how they met. Did they ever date? Has Kingston planned and taken Tara on any big trips? It would be weird to mention the encounter now, like the moment to bring up meeting a nice-looking woman at the market who happens to know her girlfriend has passed.

Lake senses there's more to the relationship than the woman let on, but what does it matter? She and Kingston are happy, rock-solid, comfortable. Sure, there were moments of insecurity in the beginning, but only because Lake found it difficult to acclimate to Kingston's cultlike following. Women she'd never met, and some whom she had, would act as if she didn't exist. They'd be out having dinner or drinks at the club when some woman would lay eyes on Kingston, walk over, and wedge herself in between Lake and Kingston as though she was literally invisible. Fucking queers can be so disrespectful!

"Lake. Babe. Did you hear what I said?" asks Kingston.

"Yes. You said that big trips are kind of your thing," replies Lake as she wills herself back to the present.

Kingston laughs and says, "Yes. I did say that. I also asked if you're good with the itinerary. Is there anything special you want to see in San Francisco?"

"Oh, sorry. Yeah, I'd kind of like to see Alcatraz. Is that dumb?" asks Lake.

"No, that's not dumb. Alcatraz is flipping amazing. You can't spend time in San Francisco and not see the rock. I'll add it to the list of things to do," says Kingston.

Lake looks into her girlfriend's kind brown eyes and knows she'll be stupidly happy never knowing a thing about any woman Kingston was with before her. Knowing makes it real and creates room for doubt and self-comparison. The life they share is too good for that.

#

Lake receives a letter confirming she has passed the LSAT just before Thanksgiving, giving her the ultimate reason to be thankful. After the trip home this summer, she hadn't planned to visit Ohio for the holidays. Instead, she and Kingston volunteer at a local homeless shelter and spend Thanksgiving at home. Kingston has her girls over, and the tight, chosen family spends the day drinking mimosas and eating grilled chicken and vegetables. An invite had been extended to Sad Sack Shelley, but under the watchful eye of Stan just next door, she refrains from partaking too much and leaves after just one glass of the bubbly, keeping the affair low-key and stress-free.

The entire month of December is basically a blur. Together, Kingston and Lake host a large and very merry holiday party at the house. Things get a little raucous at one point, but the girls quickly corral the crazy and send it packing. Shelley Sad Sack is down with the flu and forced to miss for the first time. In hindsight, it may have been for the better, as Stan was out of town and she's been hitting the bottle hard.

The Christmas trip Kingston and Lake take is off-the-hook amazing! Two days into it, they manage to lay claim to a peaceful piece of the vineyard and are kicking back in identical smoky-smelling cedar Adirondack chairs enjoying a glass of pinot noir when Lake's phone beeps several times. "I didn't even hear my phone ring—how is that I have a voice mail?" asks Lake.

"We're in the middle of a vineyard," says Kingston. "I'm surprised your phone has any reception at all."

Kingston's right-hand woman, Peggy, has an all-access pass to their home when they travel. She drops by daily to check on the place, water the plants, and bring in the mail. Like Kingston, Lake trusts her implicitly. Knowing she might receive news regarding her law school applications while she is away, Lake has given Peggy permission to open the mail in her absence. "If I get in, I want you to call and let me know. If I don't, just leave the envelope with the rest of the mail. I'll look at it when I get back. No sense in ruining our trip with bad news."

Lake wonders if the voice mail is from Peggy. With trembling fingers, she fumbles to press the "1" button on the keypad and holds it to connect with the voice-mail system. Clasping the phone to her ear, she listens for the prompt, enters the security code, and waits. It's Peggy. She got in.

"Holy shit on a shingle!" screams Lake. "I got in! I actually got in! I'm going to law school!"

It takes a second for her words to sink in, and then Kingston is on her feet, jumping from foot to foot, waving her arms in the air and acting like a drunken hillbilly. "My girlfriend got accepted to law school! Woo-hoo, hot damn! I got me one smoking hot smartie. Lake Myers, you are the complete package. I love you, babe, and I couldn't be prouder..."

Beaming, Lake joins her girlfriend's happy dance. Once they stop moving, she embraces Kingston, looks her square in the eye, and says, "Thanks, babe. You've been so sweet and supportive. I love you, too."

Staring back at Lake, Kingston replies, "I will always be supportive, love. But I can't make any promises on the 'sweet' part." Lake smiles, but she doesn't respond because she knows Kingston is inherently kind and good. "I can finally request to go part-time at work and prepare for my start date at school. I've dropped enough hints to my boss about applying to law school, it shouldn't be a surprise when I announce I got in, but I'm worried about cutting down on my hours."

"What do you have to be worried about?" asks Kingston. "You're a terrific employee who's trying to do better. I think it'll be fine, just be honest."

"Of course, I'll be honest. But we don't really have any part-timers in my area. What if she fires me?"

"Then you look for a different job, or you don't work at all. I told you that you don't have to work while you're in school. I can take care of us," says Kingston.

"I know," says Lake, "and I appreciate that, but I need to work at least part-time. I'm not going to ask you for spending money when I need it. I'm a grown-ass woman who's about to start law school. I can work enough to make my own play money, at least."

"You're so fierce and independent. I find that to be really hot, a total turn-on," says Kingston. "Makes me want you right now!"

Lake has recently started referring to Kingston as "K" on occasion, and she says, "We're in the middle of a very public vineyard, K. But I think your chances of getting some later are favorable. I have been known to put out—for the right woman." Kingston nearly chokes on her wine.

Realizing she should have been clearer, Lake quickly adds, "You're the right woman, babe. In fact, you're the *only* woman."

"Nice save, love," says Kingston, "but don't for one second think I won't hold you to your earlier comment!"

Lake raises her glass and clinks it gently against Kingston's. "I'm going to rock your world, baby."

Lake looks at her watch and sees it's one forty-five in the afternoon. Considering the time difference, she knows her mom is home prepping for dinner and available to take her call.

"Is there somewhere you need to be?" asks Kingston.

Lake shakes her head and leans in to give Kingston a peck on the cheek. "Just here with you. But I kind of want to call my mom really quick to tell her about getting in to law school."

"I'm not sure you'll have the best reception out here among the vines, but give it a go," says Kingston.

Lake flips her phone open and presses the number assigned to her parents' home phone. The connection is staticky but seems to be working.

Sylvia answers her call after the second ring.

"Hi, Mom. It's Lake."

From the other end of the line, her mom replies, "I know it's you, Lake. You don't have to tell me. I've been your mom for almost twenty-five years. I know you kids' voices as soon as you say hello. Where are you? Is everything okay?"

Lake smiles and pictures her mom standing at the kitchen counter, pressing meat loaf into a pan. "Sorry, Mom, it's just a habit, announcing myself like that. Kingston and I are out of town, and I'm calling from my cell phone. How are you and Dad doing?"

"We're good. We missed you at Thanksgiving."

Lake had called her parents on Thanksgiving Day to say hello and let them know she was thinking of them. During the call, her mom made it a point to tell her how barren the family table was this year. As usual, Uncle Rick and Aunt Joe hosted. Pete and Deanna took Lucas to visit Deanna's family in Michigan, and Jeanne came alone, staying just long enough to eat like a little bird before flittering off.

"She and Tim aren't doing so hot," Sylvia had said flatly. "Your father and I are pretty sure it's only a matter of time before the two of them split. Jeanne's lost a lot of weight, and don't tell her I said this, but she just looks awful."

Lake felt bad for her sister. She and Tim had been trapped on the hamster wheel of a failing relationship for months. It was long past time to jump off and move in a different direction.

"I know, Mom. We would have loved to be with you guys, but Kingston and I were volunteering at a homeless shelter that week." Lake adds that last bit, hoping it will ease the sting of her not being there with her family for the holidays.

"That's very nice of you and Kingston to volunteer your time like that," says her mom.

Bingo! The exact response she is pitching for.

"Thanks, Mom. It was nice to give back, but we did miss not being there with the family. We'll try to do a better job of planning next year."

"That sounds good, dear. How are you?" asks her mom perfunctorily.

Lake has been doing her best to speak in terms of "we" and refer to Kingston as often as possible to remind her parents that they are a couple, but it seems to fall on deaf ears. "We're doing really good, Mom. Better than good. That's why I'm calling."

Sylvia remains quiet, waiting to receive whatever good news is about to come her way.

"When we were home this summer visiting you all, I mentioned to Dad that I was kicking around the idea of going back to school. A couple months ago, I applied to a few law schools, and I got in! I start classes in the spring."

After a brief pause, Lake's mom practically yells, "That's incredible, Lake! I had no idea. Your dad didn't tell me you'd talked about going back to school. Wow! Law school. What made you decide on that?"

Lake detects the hurt in her mom's response. She should have told her she was applying, but she'd held back, in case she didn't get in. "I don't know, Mom. I guess it was the combination of a bunch of things. I like working for the senator, but I want to do more. I've been thinking about law for a while. It's something I can build a career around, maybe business or environmental law."

"Business or environmental law, that sounds interesting and expensive. Can you get grants or scholarships for law school?" asks her mom.

"I applied for a few grants, but I haven't heard back. I'll probably have to take out school loans. The interest rates are low, and I can pay the money back over several years. It'll be fine," Lake says halfheartedly. The matter of money is the one bothersome part of the process. She is looking at tens of thousands of dollars in school loans. She will have to do well and snag an amazing job when she graduates. There is no other option.

Lake subconsciously counts the static clicks as she waits for a response from her mom. She is up to five when Sylvia says, "You have a big birthday coming up. My baby girl's about to turn twenty-five!

What do you think about your dad and me coming out for a visit to celebrate? You've been trying to get us down there ever since you moved to the city. This seems like the perfect time to me."

Lake looks over at Kingston, who appears to be napping in her chair, then excitedly answers for the two of them, "We'd love to have you and Dad visit!"

"We'd love to see you and celebrate your big birthday in person. I'll talk to your dad tonight at dinner and give you a call this weekend to talk more about it," says her mom.

"Okay, Mom. That sounds good. Tell Dad I love him," says Lake.

"I will," says her mom. "Bye-bye, sweetie."

Chapter 25

Lake's parents plan to visit the weekend of her birthday, which also happens to be Super Bowl Sunday. Normally, Kingston would have the girls over for brunch and mimosas, and the group would celebrate loudly, cheering on their favorite team, but this year, the plans are changed to accommodate Lake's parents. Even though the girls aren't exactly masculine, they can be "in your face" and intimidating. So, to play it safe, they've made dinner reservations for four at an iconic hotel with a revolving restaurant and stunning views of the downtown Atlanta cityscape.

Although their home is well equipped for guests, Lake's parents insist on staying in a hotel nearby. "Your father and I appreciate the offer, but we'd feel more comfortable in our own space," says her mom.

"Mom, we have a guest room with its own bath on the opposite side of the house. It has a king-sized bed and is plenty private. You're more than welcome to stay here, and you can drive my truck. You don't have to rent a car," says Lake.

"Really, Lake, we're fine. The hotel is just a few miles from your house, so we may take you up on the offer to use your truck. But let us get comfortable with everything down there in the big city, and maybe next time we'll stay at your place."

Lake dissects her mom's response, getting stuck on the part about "getting comfortable with everything" before choosing to stay at her home. If her parents were to accept the offer to stay with her and Kingston, they'd be forced to watch them go to bed, in their bedroom, together, like a normal couple. That may be the sticking point for them. Her parents accept the fact that she's with a woman, because they love her and want to maintain the parent-child relationship. But to see it firsthand with nowhere to go or escape to, is likely too much, too soon. She'd like to think otherwise, but how can she?

"We get it, Mom. It's your first visit to the city and to our home. We'll give you the grand tour of our house and take you to some really cool places, and next time, you can stay with us," says Lake matter-of-factly.

Glossing over the last part of her response, Lake's mother ends the conversation by saying, "You have our flight information. Your dad and I will wait for you at the baggage claim area. We'll see you soon!"

#

"A quarter of a century!" exclaims Kingston. "That's a historic birthday occasion and one to be celebrated big-time. No trips out of town for this one, but I do have a special night planned. All that I ask of you is that you wear something nice and be ready to leave the house by six p.m. I'll take care of everything else."

Lake can't remember the last Saturday she and Kingston spent a quiet night at home. She'd give anything to spend the night at home, snuggled up to K under a cozy blanket, eating popcorn and watching a rom-com, but it won't be this Saturday. Her near-perfect girlfriend doesn't want to interfere with her family birthday weekend, so she's planned a night out the Saturday before her parents are scheduled to arrive. It's sweet, but damn, what she wouldn't give for that quiet night at home.

"Of course, you will," says Lake. "Can I wear slacks, or would you prefer I wear a dress?"

"That's totally up to you," replies Kingston. "It's supposed to be chilly this weekend, and I don't want you to be cold. We'll be inside, but if you're wearing a dress, your legs might get cold. Don't over-think it. You just need to get from the house to the car and then inside again. You're going to beautiful no matter what you wear."

Lake forces a smile as she mentally walks through her closet and the options she has there. The last thing she wants to do is shop for a new outfit, and she is delighted when she remembers she doesn't have to. Tucked away in the back of her closet is a never-before-worn, navy-blue, wide-legged, sparkly women's suit she bought for the holiday party, but she'd changed her mind at the last minute. The cut is perfectly sexy, like it was tailored just for her small frame. It's perfect for their night out.

Lake rolls her eyes and says, "And you'll be just as beautiful. I have a suit I bought for the party this year, but then I wore the dress instead. I'll be dressed to the nines, and my legs will be toasty warm. Problem solved."

At six p.m. on Saturday, Lake emerges from their room, ready for whatever festivities Kingston has planned. Her date is seated on the couch, waiting patiently, but she stands when she spies Lake. Her right hand goes to her heart as she says, "You take my breath away. You're my one and only, Lake. How lucky am I to spend this Saturday evening with you?"

Lake walks over to where Kingston is standing. She takes her hand from her heart and kisses the inside of her palm. "I could say the exact same thing about you."

Kingston is of average height, but she stands an inch taller than Lake, who's barely five-foot-five. Her skin is perpetually bronzed because of the work she does, and tonight, it looks especially tan under a chic, winter-white pantsuit with a plunging neckline. Draped around her neck is a simple but elegant knotted gold chain. Her girlfriend is a drop-dead gorgeous fox.

Kingston snakes her arm through Lake's and says, "Your chariot awaits, my lady."

Always the thoughtful one, Kingston opens the car door for Lake and makes sure she's fully seated before gently closing it. It's a quick fifteen-minute ride to the restaurant, which is new. The décor is rustic chic, an artful, modern blend of distressed wood combined with the simplicity of clean lines, sleek poured concrete, and a massive stone fireplace.

The pretty hostess smiles when Kingston gives her name, then says, "Right this way, Miss Kennedy."

The food is tapas-style and offers an abundance of interesting appetizers, raw plates, meat and cheese boards, pressed sandwiches, and flatbreads. Kingston orders a bottle of wine and points wildly at the menu, ordering several items from each area. Although the place is packed with people, the dining space is cozy and romantic. As the food begins to arrive, Lake and Kingston *ooh* and *ahh* over each perfectly presented plate, then take time to savor each delicious bite. Dessert consists of two slices of Spanish chocolate lightly drizzled with extra virgin olive oil and a sprinkling of course sea salt. Around the edges of the plate, a tart raspberry filling is used to write HAPPY 25ᵀᴴ, LAKE in cursive script. "This is too amazing to eat," coos Lake.

"I've wanted to bring you here ever since this place opened. People rave about everything from the design, to the service, and of course, the food. It is pretty, but you have to try the chocolate. Rumor has it, it's the flawless ending to every meal."

Lake looks doubtful but decides she must learn for herself if all the hype is true. Using her fork and knife, she manages to get a bite of the chocolate with oil and salt onto her fork. Using the knife, she scoops up a bit of her birthday wish from the plate and scrapes it onto the chocolate. The effort takes a few moments, and just before she places the fork in her mouth, she looks up to see a distinct Tiffany-blue box wrapped in a white bow sitting next to a card on the table in front of her.

"Oh my God, this chocolate is better than sex," says Lake. "You have to try a bite!"

Kingston's eyebrows shoot up, and she gives Lake a playful look. Lake takes another bite of the raspberry sauce and says, "What I meant to say is that this chocolate is *almost* better than sex. When it touches your tongue, it's a euphoric experience, just like when you make me orgasm."

Kingston doesn't appear to be convinced. Laughing, she says, "Happy twenty-fifth, babe."

"I love this night," says Lake. "It's been better than a dream."

Kingston gives a nod and says, "Open your gift and card while I try the chocolate and a better-than-sex moment of bliss."

Lake picks up the box and waits to see Kingston's reaction when she tries the chocolate. As she slowly unties the bow, Kingston goes into full-blown orgasm mode. She throws her head back and moans softly as she clutches the table. The couple next to them looks over at Kingston and then looks directly at Lake.

"She's a really expressive eater. Be sure to try the chocolate, it'll make you whimper like a whore too," Lake says with a smile.

The couple busts out laughing, and Kingston stops her moaning. Looking over at the guy seated next to her, she gives him a wink and a smile.

Lake can't help but laugh, too. "You're out of your damn mind. I'm in love with a crazy person."

"I never claimed to be sane, and you're right about the chocolate. I'm going to have another bite."

Lake responds with an emphatic, "No. No more chocolate for you. This is my night. You just sit there and watch me open my gift and card."

"Yes, ma'am," says Kingston as she sits back in her chair.

Lake removes the lid from the box in front of her to reveal a classic Tiffany link bracelet in silver. It's just the right proportion of industrial-gauge shape and design, neither overly feminine nor masculine. Lifting it from the box, Lake wraps it around her wrist and fastens it.

"I love it," says Lake. "Thank you."

"You're welcome. I was just wandering around the mall window-shopping, and there it was. I didn't hesitate. I'm glad you love it. Now, open your card."

No longer hungry for the chocolate, Lake pushes the plate back and carefully opens the envelope. Expecting just a card, she's surprised to see a piece of paper fall from the card as she pulls it out. Upon closer inspection, she realizes it's a folded check. Puzzled, she looks at Kingston as she unfolds it. It's a blank check from Kingston, but it's signed. No date and no dollar amount.

In a confused voice, Lake asks, "What's this? Why am I holding a signed, blank check from you?"

"I don't want you to stress about the cost of law school. That check can be written for whatever amount you need. I'm offering to pay your way," states Kingston.

Lake swallows hard, unsure of how she should respond. After a few more seconds pass, she carefully refolds the check and places it on the table between them.

"You are the most resplendent person, inside and out, whom I've ever met. Your generosity truly moves me, and I'm so thankful to have you in my life, but I can't accept this." Kingston places her hand on the table and looks Lake squarely in the eyes. "I knew you'd say that, and I respect your decision, but the offer stands indefinitely. It's ever-green, meaning there is no expiration date."

Lake closes her eyes and imagines for a split second how easy life would be if she just allowed Kingston to pay her way through law school. What a tremendous burden would be lifted from her shoulders, only to be replaced by indignity and indebtedness. Kingston's offer is the genuine article—there's no ill intent behind it—but for Lake, the cost is incomparable. It would change the dynamic of the relationship, placing her in a position of weakness, completely dependent on Kingston. The driving force behind her decision to pursue a law degree is so that she can build her own career and wealth. Behind every strong woman is herself.

Lake returns Kingston's powerful gaze and says confidently, "When I look at you, I don't just see a woman whom I admire and adore. You're so much more than that. You've lit a fire in me to broaden my horizons and always be better. That means paying my own way and maintaining my independence. It doesn't mean I love you any less. It means I love you to an even greater extent."

From across the table, Kingston blows Lake a kiss and says, "I love you all the bunches, birthday girl. Let's go home and snuggle."

#

Lake takes the day off work on Friday to meet her parents at baggage claim. The direct flight from Ohio is relatively quick, at just over two hours, and it is right on time. Jack and Sylvia are all smiles when they round the corner. Lake's mom spots her first and hugs her tight. In her mom's ear, she says, "Hey, Mom. How was the flight?"

"It was good. The weather back home was clear, and we had no trouble at all taking off. Your dad read his paper most of the way, and I finished the scarf I was knitting." Reaching down into the far depths of her grossly oversized shoulder bag, Sylvia pulls out a neon-pink scarf. "Do you like it?"

"It's pretty—very bright," replies Lake. "Who's it for?"

"You, silly. I know it doesn't get as cold down here as it does back home, but who doesn't love a knitted scarf?" asks Sylvia.

With all the sincerity she can muster, Lake says, "I can't imagine there's anyone who doesn't love a scarf, especially one as special as this. Thanks, Mom."

Lake's forced enthusiasm isn't lost on her dad. He gives her a quick wink and a hug, then says, "I'll grab the bags."

#

On the way to the truck, Lake says, "Not sure I've mentioned it, but Kingston is an amazing cook. She's making pasta with all the fixings for dinner. We have plenty of beer and wine at the house. Is there anything else you'd like me to pick up?" Sylvia is busy taking in the sights and doesn't respond.

"I can't think of anything," replies her dad.

"Okay. Let me know if you change your mind. I'll drop you guys off at the hotel so you can settle in, and then come back to get you, if that's okay."

"Works for us," replies her dad.

"I thought about making plans for us this afternoon, but traffic here is so unpredictable. I didn't want to risk being late to dinner. Your hotel is within walking distance of a coffee shop and some other places if you and Mom are feeling adventurous or need a pick-me-up. We're excited to catch up with you two."

Lake's truck is old by today's standards and has no clicker to announce their arrival. Tucked between a large SUV and another truck, she's surprised when her dad says, "The truck looks good, Lake. I'm surprised you've kept it in such good shape."

Lake gives the truck a good pat on the hood and says, "I ride the train to work, so it mostly just sits in the driveway. But I filled her with gas and had her washed just for you, Dad."

Jack sets their bags in the bed of the pickup and says, "Appreciate that, but I doubt your mom and I will drive her much. We're only here for a couple days."

Lake jumps in the truck, leans across the front seat, and pops the lock for her dad. Jack opens the passenger door and holds it open while his wife of thirty-five years climbs in butt-first and scootches to the center of the bench seat. Seeing that she's settled, he climbs in after her and closes the door.

With her hands on the steering wheel, Lake looks over at her parents and says, "I wish you could stay for more than just a couple of days, but I know you need to get back to the ranch."

"It's a lot for your Uncle Rick to handle by himself, but it was important for your mom and me to see you this weekend. Twenty-five is a big birthday, and we've never been here to visit you before. Seemed like a good time to make the trip."

"Kingston made a big deal about my birthday this year, too. It's just a number—it doesn't define who I am. I've got three years of law school ahead of me, and I'll have to pass the bar before I can even start my career. I think thirty might be a bigger birthday for me," states Lake.

Sylvia lays her hand on Lake's leg and chimes in, "You make a good point, dear. You may be a hotshot lawyer by the time you turn thirty, but this is the year when your dad and I flew down to watch you blow out your candles and open your extra-special gift."

Lake shoots her mom a curious look. "My 'extra-special gift'? What are you even talking about, Mom?"

Without so much as turning her head, Sylvia says, "It's like your dad said. Twenty-five is a big birthday, and we're just happy to be here with you."

Sylvia can be surprisingly stubborn and tight-lipped when she wants to be. Realizing the door has closed on the subject, Lake keeps her eyes on the road but responds with a snide, "Mmm-hmmmm."

#

Lake's birthday weekend with her parents is more enjoyable than she imagined it would be. Dinner at the house provided the perfect backdrop to showcase the normalcy of her life with Kingston. Their beautiful, sprawling ranch hits home with Sylvia the moment she steps inside. Anxious to share the history of the home and its residents, Kingston is a gracious tour guide. She leads Sylvia back to the foyer and invites Jack to join them. "I'll stay out here with Lake and keep her company while you show Syl the sights," says Jack.

"Tours run every thirty minutes if you change your mind. My only request is that you two make sure nothing boils over or burns while we're off gallivanting," says Kingston playfully. For a minute, Lake thinks she may lean in for a kiss, but she's had the talk with Kingston before her parents arrived.

"I know it's our home," Lake said. "But I've never shown affection toward another woman in front of my parents. It's just for a couple of days, okay?"

"You know the situation with my family," says Kingston. "I'm in no position to judge. If you want to act like we're just roommates all weekend, I can do that."

"Well, when you put it like that, it doesn't sound so good," says Lake.

Kingston rolls her eyes. "I'm trying to work with you here. What is it you want me to do?"

"I want you to play it cool around my parents. I know I'm irresistible, but try to control yourself," teases Lake. "Pretend it's *your* mom who's visiting."

"So, show zero emotion and no physical touching whatsoever, got it," says Kingston.

#

Fifteen minutes later, Kingston and Lake's mom are back in the kitchen. "How was it?" asks Jack.

Sylvia moves closer to her husband and says, "Kingston is quite the decorator and a wonderful storyteller, too. She had a little something to share on each piece of art, and even some of the furniture. She made the tour very personal and special."

Wrapping his arm around Sylvia, Jack gives her a gentle squeeze and says, "Lake's mom takes great pride in our home, too. Thank you, Kingston, for sharing your place with our family and for making us feel so welcome."

"Happy to do it," replies Kingston. "Being able to connect with people is a more valuable test of a great hostess's effectiveness than having a well-prepared house tour narrative. Where the rubber meets the road is how you feel after you've had a bite of her secret, homemade sauce."

Damn, she's smooth, thinks Lake. Looking at Kingston approvingly, she says, "I think it's only fair to warn you. My dad can be critical when it comes to judging red sauce. My mom's had years to perfect her recipe, and it may be too close to call."

Standing between Kingston and his wife, Jack realizes he's just been placed in an impossible position. When the main course is served, all eyes are on him, and he doesn't disappoint.

Using his left hand, Jack carefully unbuttons the cuff of his right sleeve and folds it back twice. Glancing up to be certain he has everyone's attention, he then does the same on the other side. Once his sleeves are rolled up, he adjusts the position of his fully loaded plate of noodles so that it's the perfect distance from his mouth as he leans over it. Comfortable with the setup, he reaches over his plate, stabs three monster-sized meatballs, and plops them one at a time around the edges of his plate, forming a triangle of meat.

The only sound in the dining room is the low, recognizable hum of a traditional forties pop song coming from the stereo on the far wall of the living room. Using the beat of the music, Jack makes a big show of pouring gobs of red sauce over his pasta. Satisfied with his culinary masterpiece, he shakes out his wrists, picks up his fork, and plunges into the center of his spaghetti mountain. He then twirls a generous portion of al dente pasta around and around his fork and raises it to his waiting mouth. It's the moment of truth.

Focusing on a spot just in front of his plate, he chews slowly, swallows, and looks up. Lake shifts her gaze from her dad, to Kingston, and then to her mom. Sylvia's hands are in prayer position, fingertips resting on her lips. The whole scene is hilarious, and Lake wants to laugh, but she knows her timing is off. Without moving her head, her eyes move to connect with her dad's, and she silently wills him to declare Sylvia the winner of this battle. She needs the win more than Kingston.

Jack sets the fork down on his plate, picks up his napkin, and wipes his mouth. He sets the napkin down, clears his throat, and says, "I've had some terrific pasta sauces in my time..." He looks at Kingston and says, "Kingston, this is one helluva red sauce you made. It's the just the right amount of spice, and the consistency is damn near perfect, in my opinion."

Seated at the head of the table, Kingston smiles proudly and gives Jack a nod, her signature Don move.

Mom looks crushed.

Then Jack speaks again. "Lake was right when she said her mom's had years to perfect her spaghetti sauce. This one here's *close to* perfect, but Sylvia's red sauce is still remarkable perfection."

Sylvia's face lights up. She smiles at her husband and says, "Jack and I have been married almost as long as you've been alive, Kingston, and he always knows just what to say."

Jack places his hand on top of Sylvia's and says, "Happy wife, happy life."

It warms Lake's heart to witness the love her parents have for each other after all these years, but it stings a little, too. She loves Kingston deeply and would say yes if the choice to marry was an option for them, but it isn't.

"I'd say you won fair and square, Sylvia. I dreamt about your red sauce after Lake and I got back from Ohio."

Sylvia's eyebrows shoot up, and Kingston presses on, "It's true. I've made my sauce half a dozen times since we've been back, and I just can't get it to taste like yours."

Sylvia clears her throat as though she's about to speak, but stops. She leans in close to Kingston and says, "The secret to my sauce is fresh basil. I add it at the very end, just a minute or two before serving."

Kingston leans back in her chair, nods her head, and says, "Yes, that's it! Thank you, Sylvia, for trusting me with your secret. That stays between you and me."

She's in like Flynn. Lake's parents took a liking to Kingston when she brought her home to Ohio, but after tonight, they seriously revere her. Lake is so sure of it, she'll lay down a triple-dog-dare challenge to anyone who says otherwise.

Chapter 26

The next morning, Kingston gracefully bows out of the Myers family sightseeing excursion so that Lake can spend the day alone with her parents. "Great, my parents are going to feel so let down when I pull up to the hotel alone," Lake says jokingly.

"Oh, come on, babe. I'd kill to spend half a day at Stone Mountain with you all. I just thought you'd appreciate some one-on-one time with the parents."

Lake enjoys seeing Kingston flustered, because it hardly ever happens, so she takes another jab. "I know you have a tee time and brunch plans with the girls. Golf and mimosas, how can you possibly miss that? It's not like you don't do it every week."

Kingston looks like she's just been scolded. "You're right. I'll tell the girls I can't make it and go with you."

Now it's Lake's turn to feel bad. She leans in and plants a big kiss on her girlfriend's lips. "Babe, I can't believe you thought I was serious. I planned the day for Jack and Sylvia based on things I thought they'll like. Go, be with your girls. I got this."

With a serious face and her hands resting on Lake's waist, Kingston says, "It's a good thing you're taking them to Stone Mountain today. It may be the last opportunity you have. I hear they're closing the park this summer for good."

Lake looks alarmed. She hasn't heard anything about the park closing. "What? Why would they close Stone Mountain Park?"

"Because people are taking it for granite. Ba-da-bump," is Kingston's reply.

"Oh my God, you're such a goofball," says Lake.

"And you love me anyway," says Kingston.

"I do. Now go, do your thing. Just promise me you'll be home and ready to go at four fifteen," says Lake.

"I'll be here in this same spot at four fifteen, ready to go," replies Kingston.

#

Lake's excited to show her parents the many landmarks in and around the city. Its rich, deep heritage is progressive and continually evolving, and it will be more than enough to keep her parents occupied.

Her parents are waiting outside the hotel room when she pulls into the lot, and it makes her smile. Prompt and practical, that's her family.

"Good morning, parents. I hope you both had a good sleep, I have a full day planned for you," says Lake.

"We slept fine. It's always a little hard to sleep in a strange bed, but we're here for such a short time, we'll be back to our own bed before we know it," says Sylvia.

"Good attitude, Mom. I like it," says Lake as her mom and dad climb into the truck. Lake chauffeurs her parents up, down, and diagonally across the city, hitting all the sites. For lunch, she wows her mom and dad with a casual bite at the world's largest drive-in fast-food restaurant. Jack loves a good chili dog, and the place they eat at is famous for them. Judging by the smiles on their faces, she'd say the day is a hit.

Pulling up to the hotel, Lake confirms the evening plans. "Our dinner reservation isn't until six, but Kingston and I will be back to get you at four thirty. We thought it would be nice to have a drink and watch the sunset before dinner."

"That gives us just enough time to freshen up," says her mom.

"Okay. Be back soon. I had a lot of fun today with you guys."

"You really know your way around the city," says her dad. "Your mom and I enjoyed it. I especially liked that chili dog."

#

When they arrive at the restaurant, Kingston steps up to the hostess stand and has a short conversation with the woman behind the counter. The woman laughs and smiles at Kingston, and a minute later, she leads them to a table for four that provides the most exquisite vantage point to watch the city skyline inch by. At the rate they're moving, they're in the perfect position to watch the sun slowly drop below the tall buildings until it can no longer be seen.

The conversation and meal are truly enjoyable. Twenty-five is a significantly dignified birthday that mercifully excludes a semicircle of servers clapping joyously and singing "Happy Birthday."

For dessert, Kingston orders the three most popular items. "I thought it would be festive and yummy for everyone to try a bite of each," says Kingston.

Now one of her biggest supporters, Sylvia backs Kingston when she says, "That was genius to order three different desserts. Lake always goes for the chocolate, her dad likes anything with fruit, and my favorite is crème brulee."

Beaming, Kingston says, "It was just dumb luck, but I'm glad everyone's happy."

"We've had such a wonderful time this weekend," says Sylvia. "Thank you both for everything."

The presentation of the dessert dishes is amazing. Every plate is decked out with fresh berries to add color and texture to the already sweet finish.

When the waiter leaves, Sylvia reaches into her purse, pulls out a small wrapped gift box, and sets it on the table in front of Lake. "Happy birthday, sweetheart."

Lake looks at the package. It's the shape and size of a jewelry box, and she wonders what type of jewelry her parents would buy for this occasion.

"Are you going to open it?" asks her dad.

"Yeah," says Lake as she wriggles her wrist. "I was just thinking, Kingston gave me this bracelet for my birthday, and this looks like a jewelry box. Twenty-five must be the year for jewelry."

"You won't know unless you open it," says Jack. "It could be a rock wrapped up all pretty."

"Really, Dad? I'm surprised you didn't say it might be a lump of coal, like when we were kids. Your dad jokes could use some work."

"I'm out of practice, but I'll get to work on them. We have a grand-baby now and another on the way."

Lake rolls her eyes and picks up the box. She gives it a shake. It's definitely not a rock. Setting it down on the table, she pulls the bow off and tears into the paper. When she lifts the top off the box, her breath catches. Looking at her mom, she asks, "Is this Grams's necklace?"

"Yes. She knew how much you loved it. She always said if anything should happen, she wanted you to have it."

Lake carefully pulls the necklace from the box and holds it out for Kingston to see.

"Your grandpa Kevin bought that for her on one of their shopping trips. It's a ruby pendant set in eighteen-carat white gold. We were holding on to it for you until you got older," says her dad.

Lake's favorite photo with Kiki is one where she's sitting in Jack's armchair, holding Lake in her lap. The fireplace built by her father is in the background. Lake can't be much more than a year old. Kiki's face is scrunched up, her brows are furrowed, and her mouth is open, caught in midsentence.

Lake's chubby right hand is reaching up toward her face, fingers outstretched and poised to physically grab and hold on to every word and sentiment her grandma Kiki is bestowing upon her tiny self, huge, shiny blue eyes looking directly into hers. Around her neck is the ruby necklace. Lake can't count the number of times she's held, stared at, and had full-on conversations with the photo. Happy times, sad times, and especially during her moments of self-doubt. At the earliest sign of uncertainty, Lake can look at the photo of her and Grams and instantly feel calm and grounded. The photo is now perched on top of her bureau in the room she shares with her partner.

Kingston immediately recognizes the necklace as the one from Lake's photo with her grandma. Reading the table, she senses the need for family time and says, "If you'll excuse me, I need to use the ladies' room."

As Kingston walks away, Lake blinks back tears and gets out a barely audible, "Thank you."

Seizing the moment, her dad says, "There's more, Lake. Your grandpa Kevin and grandma Kiki were sensible, bighearted people, and they loved you kids very much. There was money set aside for you, your sister, and your brother after they passed. It was placed in a sizeable trust fund that you're eligible for now that you're twenty-five. It's probably not enough to cover the cost of three years of law school, but it will help."

Lake doesn't know what to say. She never expected this.

"We wanted to tell you when we gave you the necklace since it's kind of a package deal, and we were hoping to tell you in in private. We like Kingston, but this is a family matter. The money was intended for you, and we're asking that you keep it separate from anything you have with Kingston, okay? Promise us you'll be responsible with it."

"Yes, I'll be responsible. I think you should know that Kingston offered to pay for my law school, but it just didn't feel right to let her do that. This is something I need to do on my own, and this money will help me do that. You have no idea how much I love and appreciate you guys."

Lake's dad reaches across the table and squeezes her hand. "We love you, too, kiddo. We'll get the money over to you after we get back. Do you have an account set up in your own name?"

Lake squeezes her dad's hands and replies, "I'm twenty-five, Dad. Of course I do."

Kingston is standing behind her now. "Of course you do what?" she asks.

Without hesitation, Lake looks at her partner and says, "Love my parents more than anything."

#

Lying in bed that evening, Lake her reaches up and twists the knob on her bedside lamp to extinguish the bright light shining down on her face and head. Removing the harsh glow allows her to close her eyes and reflect on the events of the day unnoticed. She hasn't fully absorbed the reality of her newfound inheritance, and she is anxious to work through the logistics of how this will change her life for the better.

She no longer has to borrow her life away or stress about money should anything happen to Kingston. They've never broached the topic of assets or estate planning because Lake didn't bring anything of monetary value to the relationship. Kingston owns the house, vehicles, artwork, business, and pretty much everything else of value. Since the day she moved in, she and Kingston have maintained separate finances. Lake contributes what she can, but paying a portion of the utilities and monthly grocery bill hardly constitutes an equitable partnership.

They have an undocumented understanding, built on the promise that Kingston will take care of her, and she does. She trusts her older, experienced, entrepreneurial lover to handle everything.

Kingston's business continues to flourish, and life is wonderfully predictable. With no worldly burdens to bear, Lake welcomes the grueling but secure routine of school, part-time work, and full-time autonomy.

#

"I can't believe I walked willingly into this nightmare called law school. I'd rather poke my eyes out with a rusty fork than read one more book. I'm a sleep deprived bee-otch, and I just want to start the day by saying I'm sorry."

Lake and Kingston are lounging in bed, neither ready to leave the snuggly warmth of the comforter or each other.

Stretching, Kingston says, "You're not a bitch. You're tired twenty-four-seven and sometimes you're cranky, but I wouldn't call you a bitch."

"Oh my God, K. I'm more than cranky," says Lake. In one swift move, she rolls on top of Kingston and kisses her passionately. "I feel good this morning, though. I'm not tired at all, and you know what would be great? Morning sex."

"Whoa! Who are you, and what have you done with my girlfriend?" asks Kingston.

"Very funny," replies Lake. "Sex is a great stress reliever, and I know how you love morning sex. What do you say?"

Kingston smiles, runs her hand slowly up Lake's leg, and expertly pulls her panties down and off. Naked from the waist down, Lake sits up, straddling Kingston, and lifts her shirt over her head while Kingston raises her arms and does the same. Before she has a chance to lower her arms, Lake pins Kingston to the bed and kisses her hard. Lips pressed against lips, breasts to breasts, navel to navel, skin to skin.

It's been a long few weeks since they've last made time for sex, and Lake has missed it. Sensing her lover's need for release, Kingston wraps her legs around Lake and presses against her. She can feel Lake pulsing, and together they move as one. At first it's slow and deliberate, then the rhythm speeds up, but not too fast.

Lake can feel the wetness between her legs seeping into her lover's panties, and she's hyperaware of the single layer of fabric between them. The moisture and bunching of Kingston's underwear creates a crease of pleasure that feels incredible as it rubs against her clit. This is new and different, in a very good and unexpected way.

Lake lifts her chest to press her pelvis harder against Kingston's pelvic bone. She can feel the orgasm building deep inside her. Grasping Kingston's hands tightly, she moves faster, edging closer to climax, coaxing it to come and fully awaken every cell in her body. Kingston knows Lake is there on the periphery of pleasure and does nothing to throw her off course.

When it happens, Lake slows to the point of almost stopping, but doesn't. Her body changes course and begins moving in a semicircular fashion. She moans loudly and lets go, falling hard into a tingling pile of ecstasy.

With her lover's body there to catch her, Lake lets loose of Kingston's hands, laying her mind, body, and soul bare to the mental, sexual, and physical relationship they share.

Kingston revels in the feel of having the entire weight of Lake's fully relaxed and vulnerable body on hers. After a few seconds, she moves her hands to the sensitive area just below the cheeks of Lake's ass. Using just the tips of her fingers, she traces the outline of her perky butt, then rests her fingers in the small of her back. The heat between them is almost unbearable, and the feeling of a deeper connection is too apparent to ignore. The bond these women share is beautifully unbreakable.

Fueled by their intimacy, Kingston's hands creep upward to Lake's shoulders and push gently down. The motion stirs Lake from her love-induced coma and brings a grin to her lips still moist from the beads of sweat that formed above them as she worked hard for her orgasm. Taking the not-so-subtle hint, Lake peels her body off Kingston's and inches her way down, taking time to kiss and lick the salty moisture from her midsection and the flat, sexy area just below her belly button. Lake pauses there to press her nose to the skin and breathe deeply; she can smell and taste the sex on her lover's body, and it's delectable.

Kingston writhes and wriggles beneath her face. Lake enjoys drawing out the act of pleasuring her girlfriend, because once she gets going, things move rather quickly. She admires the speed with which Kingston can get the job done, but she is jealous of her at the same time. Once her tongue lands on Kingston's warm spot, it's game over. She can come multiple times in a matter of minutes, and every time, it amazes her. Lake enjoys the sensation of oral stimuli, but she prefers to be the one in charge of how much pressure is applied to her orgasms. She's forever a top.

#

The super-annoying sound of a very loud bird awakens Lake, and it takes a couple of seconds for her to realize it's still Sunday. After their morning go at it, she nestled into Kingston's backside and fell right back to sleep. Pushing the hair in front of her to the side, she nuzzles Kingston's neck and ear before whispering, "Good morning, hot mama. How does tea in bed sound?"

Sleepily, Kingston says, "Hmmmm? What time is it?"

Lake squints to make out the time on the clock next to their bed. "It's ten after nine."

"Shit! We tee off at ten!" declares Kingston with a sense of urgency. Kicking off the covers, she jumps out of bed and fast-walks to the bathroom buck naked. Lake can hear the steady stream of Kingston's pee over her yelling, "How could we have fallen back to sleep? That never happens!"

"I guess our sex was just so good and deeply satisfying that we had no choice but to listen to our bodies. I feel awesome! Rested and energized."

Her unclothed landscaper emerges from the bathroom and disappears into the walk-in closet. "The sex was mind-blowing, without a doubt," says Kingston carefully, "but it's Sunday, fun day, and I'm looking forward to hitting some balls and kicking it with the girls."

Propped on one elbow, Lake tugs at the comforter to cover her cold boobs. "You don't have to apologize for being bummed about running late for your date with the girls. The course is close, you'll make it in time. I can make you a cup of tea for the road."

Dressed only from the waist down, Kingston walks out of the closet, leans over the bed, and kisses Lake on the head. "I'd love that, babe. Thanks. I need to be out of here in twenty minutes."

"I'm on it," says Lake. "One cup of tea to go coming right up."

Lake is in full-on avoidance mode, looking for any excuse to break away from her usual Sunday ritual of all day studying. Considering how her morning has started, it would be a waste to harsh the high she's on, better to go with the flow.

Still standing next to the bed, Kingston grabs a corner of the comforter and slowly pulls it toward her, exposing Lake's supple skin an inch at a time.

"I thought you were in a hurry to make tee time with the girls," says Lake sweetly.

"I have plenty of time for both," she says.

"'Both'? What are talking about?" asks Lake.

"I have time to watch you get your lovely, naked body out of bed and still make it to the course on time. I have skills, in case you didn't know," says Kingston.

#

Lake is hunched over the kitchen counter watching the birds at the feeders when Kingston walks up behind her. "Did you know there's another big hole in the back of your robe? I just don't get why you won't wear the one I bought you for Christmas last year," says Kingston.

The robe Lake is wearing was at the top of a box her mother had marked for the Goodwill. "You're getting rid of Dad's flannel robe?" asked Lake just before she left for college.

Lifting it from the box, Sylvia held it up and said, "This thing should have been donated years ago. It's a tattered mess. Come to think of it, it's probably too worn to even donate now. It belongs in the garbage."

Lake snatched the robe from her mom's hands. "It most certainly does *not* belong in the garbage. Dad's wearing this robe in every Christmas morning picture we have. I'm taking it to school with me."

Bewildered, Sylvia shook her head and said, "There's probably some old pocket tees and socks in that box, too. Sure you don't want any of those for school?"

Lake looked at Sylvia and decided she wouldn't give her the satisfaction of a response. Instead, she draped the robe over her shoulders cape-style, stretched her arms wide, and pretended to fly off toward her bedroom like a superhero.

Lake turns to Kingston and says, "I like the robe I'm wearing. It reminds me of home."

Kingston smiles and says, "Well, I can see your bum through that hole. And when you reach up to get anything out of the cupboards, I can sometimes see a nipple, depending on the angle."

Lake gives Kingston a kiss and says, "You're the real reason I keep this old robe around. It's all for you, babe. Now, take your tea and go have fun with your girls."

Kingston takes the tea and asks, "What do you have planned for the day? Wait, let me guess. You're going to play classical music, drink coffee, and study for hours?"

"Studies show that playing classical music while studying helps with focus and retention," says Lake defensively. "But I think I'm going to take a break from all that today."

"Good for you," says Kingston. "I've got to run, but you have fun today. Love you."

"Love you, too," says Lake. "Say hi to the girls for me."

Chapter 27

Lake watches Kingston back out of the driveway and zoom away in her sporty sedan. The day is hers to plan, and she decides to start at the farmers' market. It's been months since she was there, and any occasion to meander the tree-lined sidewalks and support local business is a boost to her heart and mind.

Pulling into the parking lot, Lake has her choice of spots. At quarter past ten, it's too early for the churchgoers and lazy Sunday-morning folks to begin rolling in. By the time they start arriving, she'll be long gone.

She picks a spot at the end and backs her truck in. As she walks away from her vehicle, she looks back to be certain her parking job is up to snuff. It's a silly, learned behavior she's never been able to break. She does it in the driveway she and Kingston share, and her girlfriend calls her out on it every time.

"What do you care if I back in or pull in?" asks Lake defensively.

Kingston gives her a light poke in the ribs and says, "It doesn't matter to me one way or the other. I just enjoy getting a rise out of you. Another endearing Midwest quality."

It's true. Lake grew up watching her dad back into parking spots her entire life. Northeast Ohio gets a lot of snow, and during the winter, when Jack has the plow mounted on the front of his pickup, he backs into his parking spots so he's ready to drop plow and drive his way out after a big storm. The rest of the year, it's a habit that just makes sense. When you run a horse ranch, you're always backing the truck up for something. Loading and unloading hay, feed, animals, you name it. Jack taught all his kids to drive, and they started on the farm. The behavior of backing into spaces has been passed down from generation to generation and is deeply engrained in Lake's psyche.

"What can I say? We're practical people."

"Lured back by the tantalizing taste of Sue Ellen's honey, I see."

Lake has looked for Tara on all her previous farmers' markets stops but has somehow missed her every time. Doing a double take, Lake says, "Oh my gosh, Tara! Where have you been? I thought maybe you moved or something."

Tara reaches for Lake's arm and says, "Don't think for one minute I haven't thought about it. Truth is, work got crazy, and I started coming on Sundays, but this is my first time back in months."

"Well, I'm happy you're here today. I think it's my turn to buy coffee if you're up for it," asks Lake.

Tara casts a look of great curiosity Lake's way and says, "I'd love a cup of coffee. And maybe a pastry?"

The look isn't lost on Lake, but she's not sure what to make of it. "I left the house this morning without eating breakfast, and I'm hungry, so I'll get the coffee and pastries," says Lake.

"Terrific. Are you buying one or two bottles of honey today?" asks Tara.

"Definitely two, and some of this fresh lavender. Sue Ellen's growing her own herbs and is selling bundles and sachets of lavender now," says Lake excitedly.

Tara seems amused at Lake's enthusiasm for lavender. "Did you know that in addition to smelling amazing, lavender is an antiseptic, an antifungal, and a probiotic? Sue Ellen's been selling it for a while now. I always buy a bunch when I get my honey."

"I didn't know all that about lavender, but I love the smell of it. My mom grows it in pots in front of the house. When it blooms, she sprinkles it all along the walkways, and when you step on it, the oils get on the cement, and you can smell it for days. Now I can try it at my house."

"What a neat idea," says Tara. "I may have to steal that one from you."

"You're not really stealing it from me," says Lake. "You're just borrowing it from my mom."

Lake and Tara complete their purchases and head over to the coffee and pastry booth. Due to demand, the outdoor dining area has grown in size since they last visited, with more tables and chairs to choose from. They each order a coffee with cream, no sugar, and a chocolate croissant. The pastry is double the size of a normal croissant, with a healthy amount of tiny chocolate bars sprinkled throughout.

Now it's Lake's turn to glance inquiringly at Tara. "How funny that we both ordered the exact same thing when there's so many pastries to pick from," says Lake.

"There's nothing like a warm chocolate croissant fresh from the oven. The first time I had one, I was vacationing in France. The door to the bakery was open, and we could smell the aroma of fresh-baked pastries from three doors down. Paris is a lovely city. I literally ate my way through all twenty districts."

"That sounds like an ideal vacation to me," says Lake. "I've never been to Paris. I just visited Europe for the first time last year. We spent an impromptu five days wandering through Greece, and it was beautiful."

"Greece is on my list," says Tara. "We did Italy and London, but we never made it to Greece."

"You'll love it. The ruins and the beaches are incredible. We went to one beach that had pink sand; it was unreal. When were you in Paris?" asks Lake.

Tara seems surprised at the question. "Gosh, it's been a few years. Maybe 1999? Yeah, it was the fall of '99, so four years ago."

Looking up from her coffee, Lake's head snaps to attention. In the hallway of the house, she shares with Kingston is an oil painting of the Eiffel Tower at night. It's dark, full of dimension and whimsy. Lake has stood in front of the painting and studied it on several occasions, but she has never asked about it. The first time her parents came to visit, she heard Kingston tell her mom that she bought the painting in Paris. She was being nice when she asked Tara about her trip to Paris, but now her neurons are firing, and she has a pit in her stomach. She sets the croissant on her plate slowly and takes a sip of her coffee, willing her body to settle.

Tara's hand is on her arm. "Hey, are you okay?" she asks.

Lake swallows the coffee and says, "Oh, yeah, I'm fine. I was just thinking about a painting that we have at the house. It's a painting of the Eiffel Tower. Kingston said she bought it in Paris."

Tara lets go of Lake's arm, looks directly in her eyes, but says nothing. She doesn't have to. Lake knows what's coming before Tara speaks a word.

"Have you ever mentioned my name to Kingston?" Tara asks.

"No. I meant to tell her that I met a friend of hers at the farmers' market, after I first met you here, but I forgot. Then I looked for you here, and I never saw you again until today," said Lake.

Tara takes a sip of her coffee but doesn't say anything more.

It's too late to turn back now, thinks Lake. "What would Kingston say if I told her that I knew you? And that we had coffee and chocolate croissants and talked about Paris?"

Tara looks directly at Lake once again and says, "I can't speak for Kingston, but I do know she's no liar. With that being said, she probably won't elaborate on our history or how well we know each other, either."

Lake muses on this for a moment. Kingston is a boss, and Lake knows she isn't one to talk just for the sake of talking. If you ask a pointed question, you'll get a truthful, direct answer. But sometimes you have to ask to get anything at all.

Lake shakes her head knowingly and says, "I'm asking you, Tara. What is your history with Kingston? Were you together in Paris when she bought that painting?"

"If I'm going to tell you my side of the story, I'm going to need another cup of coffee. Can I get you one, too?" asks Tara.

"No more coffee, please, but I will take a water," says Lake.

Tara returns with the beverages, pulls her chair closer to Lake's, and sits. Her body language is relaxed and open.

"Kingston and I moved to Atlanta at about the same time. We were both recently divorced and had come here to start fresh. Kingston bought the house, had it renovated, and decided the best way to open herself and her home up to others would be to host a big Christmas party. Her business was becoming well established, and she'd made a lot of connections. I worked with a former neighbor of Kingston's named Kim, who was also a member of the recently divorced club. Kim was invited to Kingston's first annual Christmas bash and didn't want to go alone, so she asked me to be her plus one. I went to the party with Kim, was introduced to Kingston, and the lesbian tendencies I'd been fighting to deny my whole life came rushing back. I spent the entire night watching her work the room. After the party, I couldn't stop thinking about her. I started spending more and more time at Kim's, just on the off chance I'd catch a glimpse of Kingston coming or going. One night, Kim and I drank way more wine than we should have. We got a little toasty, and I started talking nonstop, I really opened up to her. I told her that I thought I might be gay, and that I was basically infatuated with her neighbor, Kingston. The next morning when I woke up, I sat straight up in bed trying to recall what in the purple haze of merlot I'd shared with Kim. It didn't take long to figure it out. I feel like it's common knowledge that it's rude to call someone before seven a.m., unless, of course, there's something terribly wrong. I guess in Kim's mind, the previous night's outpouring of feelings constituted an emergency, and she felt justified to call. In my head, I was already planning my move to a new town because I couldn't afford being outed by Kim. I'm a paralegal in a conservative firm and could very easily lose my job and some of my friends, too.

While I was sitting there trying to guess which friends might be accepting of the news and which would kick me to the curb for being queer, the answering machine picked up. It was Kim, I knew it! When she started to talk, she was kind of excited, but also really sympathetic. I picked up the phone and we talked for over an hour. Kim doesn't have a gay bone in her body, but her favorite uncle is gay, and she's a big supporter of our people.

I never really asked how the subject came up, but behind the scenes, Kim started playing matchmaker, and one night Kingston just happened to stop by the house. She said she noticed Kim had a couple of sprinkler heads that weren't working properly, and she asked if she could take a look at them. When she finished working in the yard, Kim asked Kingston to join us for a glass of wine and then she conveniently disappeared. Kingston and I were left alone to get acquainted, and we had no problem keeping the conversation going. She invited me to dinner, we had a terrific time, and we decided we'd like to see each other again.

Lake wants to be sensitive and respectful of Tara's privacy, but she has questions. Lots of them.

"I know that's a lot to take in, so I'm going to pause and let you process for a minute," says Tara.

"Can I ask you a few questions?" asks Lake.

"Of course. I have nothing to hide, Lake. Kingston and I are done. We're friendly when we see each other, but there's nothing between us anymore."

"I believe you," says Lake. "I'm just curious about a few things. I mean, you're an attractive woman, well spoken, and you seem kind. I'm interested to learn what happened with you two, that is, if you feel comfortable telling me."

Tara can see that Lake needs answers, and she wants to give them. If dredging up her past helps Lake, it's worth it.

Tara says, "Let me preface this once again with the fact that this is my side of the story.""I understand," says Lake. "And depending on what else you tell me, I may or may not ask Kingston for her side of it."

"I get that," says Tara. "But to be fair, it's usually a good practice to get both sides of the story if you want to fully understand the situation."

Lake nods in agreement, and Tara takes her physical gesture as a sign to continue her story.

I was drawn to Kingston like a bee to honey. I never intended to fall so hard or so fast, but with Kingston, it's hard not to. When I was a kid, I loved Winnie the Pooh. I could recite almost every line from the movie. It wasn't long after Kingston and I started dating that a line from that movie popped into my head: 'I wasn't going to eat it; I was just going to taste it.' But it was too late for just a taste of Kingston. My appetite for her was insatiable—she was the center of my universe and we were happy.

Her home became our haven, and we spent most of our evenings and weekends there. It didn't take long for us to decide we should move in together, and since I was the one renting, it made sense for me to move in with Kingston, plus I had Kim right next door. I could pop in for a glass of wine at a moment's notice. We lived a fairy-tale existence for the first couple of years, traveling to Europe and just enjoying our time with each other.

Lake has no words. Tara's story is all too familiar. She takes a long drink of her water and waits for Tara to continue.

It was after we came back from London that Kim was introduced to a guy named Travis at work, and soon they were dating. He started spending a lot of time at Kim's, and one night, she invited Kingston and me over to her place for drinks and appetizers. Kingston and Travis became fast friends, and he asked her to round out his four-some in golf. Once they started playing golf together, it was game over. The four of us became pretty much inseparable. After less than a year of dating, Travis and Kim were engaged. They didn't wait long to tie the knot and start working on their family. Now, you might be asking yourself, why is she talking so much about a couple I've never met? The reason they're important to the story is because we were all about the same age—in our late twenties, early thirties—when we became friends.

My dating experiences were limited before Kingston. I could count the number of people I had gone out with on less than one hand, and the number I had slept with was much smaller. I had my first crush on a girl when I was twelve, and I didn't know what to think of it, so I pretended what I felt wasn't real. I joined the cheer squad in junior high and was pretty good. In high school, I was captain of my cheer team, and I had lots of crushes. But given the size of our town and lack of support for anyone different, I ignored the feelings I had for other girls and pretended to be a normal, well-adjusted teenager. My ticket out of that town was college, and when I was accepted to our state university, three hours from home, I went happily.

Toward the end of my freshman year, I met Brianne, a semi-closeted lesbian with finely honed gaydar. Her sweet sophomore self locked on to my gay virgin behind and wouldn't take no for an answer. She introduced me to the pleasures of being with a woman, and I plodded along behind her like a lovesick little puppy. But sadly, the affair was short-lived. Over summer break, Brianne told her parents about us, they transferred her to a new school, and I went back into the closet.

The threat of being found out at school was real, so I shoved my true feelings back into the box and went about my business. There were no gay bars or clubs in town, and I had no idea how to meet women.

My ex-husband and I met in my junior year, and we were married just after we graduated. We settled in a town not far from the college and were too focused on our careers and buying a house to think about starting a family. The marriage didn't last long, and it was dumb luck that I didn't get pregnant before we ended things. It would have been terrible to be forever connected to that man, but the idea of having a child one day, with the right person, wasn't a completely unappealing thought. Hold on to that last part—it's an integral piece of the puzzle.

Tara shifts in her chair and asks, "How are you doing? Are you okay?"

Lake shakes her head and replies, "I'm okay. It makes me sad to hear about the years you just endured, lying in wait for the time you could be you. I feel like every time I get to know a new gay person, the story of how they discovered a life of value, acceptance, and happiness, if, indeed, they have found it, always includes a bit about lost years."Tara takes a sip of her coffee and looks despondent.

"I'm sorry. I don't mean to sidetrack you or make you recall painful memories. I just hope that one day it will be okay to love freely, without fear of judgment or worse," says Lake.

Tara smiles and says, "That makes two of us. Now, jumping back to our dear friends, Kim and Travis. I know people make fun of lesbians for moving so quickly, but I'm here to tell you, that couple was expeditious. One day I knew Kim as a single woman, and the next, she's married with twins. When Sean and Sam were born, Kim took a leave from work. She and Travis were joyful new parents, but they were also exhausted. Kingston and I were the closest thing they had to family in the city, so we helped with the babies, and Kingston fell in love with the twins.

It was neat to watch the twins grow and develop their own individual little personalities. They had just started crawling and getting into things when Kim found out she was pregnant again. Her house wasn't built to accommodate a family of five, so they started looking for a bigger place closer to Travis's work, on the other side of town. We were crushed when they sold the house and moved. We promised to keep in touch and visit often, but this is a sprawling city with gnarly traffic and getting together in person was tough.

Kingston really missed the kids. She wanted a family of her own, and I felt I had found the right person to share the responsibility and cost of raising a child. We agreed to begin looking for a sperm donor.

It wasn't just the kids that we missed. Kim and Travis were our best friends, and their lives had changed dramatically in a very short time. Kim didn't go back to work, and Travis no longer had the time for leisurely Sunday golf outings followed by lunch and drinks at the club. That's when Kingston started to handpick women from her business dealings to mold her own golf foursome and the secretive tribe was formed.

In my mind, that was the beginning of the end for us. I consider myself to be a healthy, mindful person, but when Kingston and I decided to start a family, I was the one who had to sacrifice and make lifestyle changes. I was committed to getting pregnant because it was what we had decided on, and I didn't want to disappoint Kingston or fail her in any way. But several months and three insemination tries later, I still wasn't pregnant.

Kingston started monitoring my caffeine intake. She forbid me to drink coffee and would count the number of tea bags in the garbage. Alcohol of any type was completely off the table. The tension between us grew so thick you could cut it with a knife. I felt like a hostage in our home, and I began to put up walls.

Kingston started staying out all day on Sundays playing golf and having brunch with her girls. I couldn't handle the bond she has with them, and I resented all of them for going out, having fun, and not including me. I was insecure and angry, and I dealt with that by partying and drinking too much. I even had a favorite bar stool at the Pink Triangle.

Kingston was never nasty or physically abusive. She just told me one day in a very matter-of-fact tone that I was no longer a good candidate for bearing and raising her children. She had already arranged for me to leave and had taken care of my first six months' rent in a new luxury apartment. I guess in her mind, that was severance pay for our time together. Five months later, I saw you with Kingston at her Christmas party.

Lake is dumbfounded by the story she's just heard, and her mind is racing. She has a strong urge to get up and run, but physically her body won't allow it. Feeling wobbly, she rests her head in her hands and takes a deep breath.

Tara knew her story would be hard for Lake to hear and immediately wishes she had held back on some of the details, but it was all true, and Lake had specifically asked what had happened. She wanted to know what had caused Tara and Kingston to split. Placing her hand on Lake's shoulder, she says, "I'm sorry if I upset you, Lake. Can I get you anything? Another bottle of water?"

Without looking up, Lake says, "No. No, thank you. I just need a minute."

"Sure," says Tara. "Take all the time you need."

A full minute passes before Lake looks up. She attempts a smile, but her face isn't cooperating. She's having a difficult time reconciling the woman from Tara's story and her partner, Kingston. It's disturbing to imagine someone you love and share a life with treating anyone with such disregard. When a relationship is new, it's riddled with blind spots. Little dots are there in plain sight, but not always visible.

Lake is grateful to Tara for sharing her version of the story. She decides to mention meeting her at the farmers' market to Kingston, but she will leave out the part where Tara spills the beans about their unraveling.

"You've definitely given me a lot to think about," says Lake. "I'm glad we ran into each other today. I appreciate your openness, and I think it's time for me and Kingston to have an honest discussion about our future. She's mentioned wanting a family, and whenever it comes up, I tend to skirt the issue. I love Kingston, and there's nothing I wouldn't do for her. She's been patient and supportive of my aspirations, but starting a family? I just don't see it."

Tara says, "I shared my experience hoping I could help you in some way. I can't tell you how to feel or what to do, but if you don't see having a family with Kingston, you have every right and the freedom to assert your viewpoint. A respectful relationship has to take into account both people's timelines and what each person wants from the relationship in terms of family planning and when that should happen."

Lake leans in and hugs the woman sitting next to her. "Thanks, Tara. I have to go, but I hope I see you again really soon. Take care."

Tara squeezes Lake and says, "You, too, Lake. See you soon."

Chapter 28 - Kingston

By the time Lake gets home, she's run through numerous scenarios on how the evening will play out once Kingston gets home. She has at least a couple of hours before she's back. Not enough to get any real studying done, and honestly, she's too hyped up to focus or retain anything at this point.

She runs a bath, pours herself a glass of wine, and becomes one with the tub. The house is quiet. Aside from the low blowing of the AC kicking on intermittently, the only sound she's aware of is the muffled, steady *whoosh* of her own heartbeat. With her head partially submerged in the water and bubbles, the sound of her heart becomes overwhelmingly loud. It kind of sounds like a baby's heartbeat when you listen to an ultrasound.

Once, when she was home from college, she went to a doctor's appointment with her sister-in-law, Deanna, because Pete had to work. She was perfectly content in the waiting room, but Deanna insisted she come in and hear the baby's heartbeat. It was cool to hear and see that, but thinking back on it now, it doesn't stir or awaken any maternal feelings in Lake. She's twenty-five, and she likes her life the way it is now. She doesn't know when she'll be ready for kids, but if pressured, she will answer honestly, and what she has to say could be a deal breaker.

"Hey, babe. Didn't expect to find you in the tub," says Kingston cheerfully. "But I'll take it," she adds with a wink.

Lake smiles and says, "I thought you'd be out a couple more hours at least. Everything okay"?

"Yeah, it's all good. We only played nine holes. Peggy has a thing later today. She's met someone, so we cut the game short, grabbed a bite, and here I am."

"Well, I'm glad you're home," says Lake. "How do you feel about ordering Thai food and just hanging out tonight?"

"Sounds perfect. I have to take care of some invoices, so I'm going to work in my office for a little while, and then I'll jump in the shower. I can pick up dinner when I'm done," says Kingston.

"Okay. Thanks, babe," is Lake's response.

At the dinner table, Lake is working up the nerve to casually mention she met Tara at the farmers' market, but at the last minute, she changes her mind. Instead, she blurts out, "Where do you see us in three years?"

Kingston doesn't hesitate. It's like she's been expecting the question. "In three years, you'll be finished with law school, and we can finally focus on our family."

Lake knew Kingston's response would include the *F* word, but hearing it out loud is like a direct punch to her gut. Lake adores the woman beside her, and she wants nothing more than to please her, but the outlook for them long-term isn't comparable. They're not aligned on their future as a couple.

"I've been in this house for a long time," says Kingston. "I thought maybe we could build a new house, one that's completely ours—part of me, part of you—with space for our kids."

"I'm going to school so I can learn about law, pass the bar, and then practice law. It will be grueling, with long hours. I don't see time for picking out fixtures and raising kids in our future."

In a firm voice, Kingston says, "I own a thriving business, and you're on your way to becoming a successful attorney. We can hire people to help with fixtures and the kids."

Kingston's answer every time is a generous redirect.

This isn't going to work, thinks Lake. *We're not on the same page.*

She takes a bite of her food and chews slowly, giving her time to work through her thoughts. She should have listened to her gut and had this conversation sooner, but she's avoided it for fear of upsetting Kingston and facing the "baby elephant" in the room head-on.

Meeting Kingston was unexpected, but also timely. Each of them had a feeling of emptiness in their heart, but together, they filled the void, and hope blossomed. Kingston served as the lover and mentor Lake had desperately needed.

And in return, Lake was the ambitious, athletic young woman who could bear Kingston's children.

When push comes to shove, Lake is a practical, Midwest girl who thrives on hard work and routine. She can't continue down this path, attempting to push this life with Kingston into a mainstream box with a bow and a baby. Same-sex marriage isn't even legal. She would have no avenues for recourse, and she couldn't even come after Kingston for child support if the relationship failed once the kids were born. It's an added layer of complexity that straight couples never have to consider.

Lake sighs. "Babe, I don't want help with the kids."

"Really? You might feel differently once they're here," states Kingston.

"That's not what I meant."

Kingston sets her fork down and asks, "What are you trying to say, Lake?"

This is the defining moment. Answer honestly and blow up her life, or play along with her lover and stay in an easy, comfortable relationship for three or more years? Lake can't afford to give away any more time.

She looks out the window to avoid looking directly at Kingston and says, "I mean, I don't know if I really want kids."

That is it. The statement that seals their fate. Just this morning, Lake had believed with all her heart that she and Kingston's bond was indestructible. Eight hours later, it's being put to the ultimate test.

"Are you serious right now?" asks Kingston. "I've been honest with you since day one about wanting to have a family. I thought we were in agreement on this. You're great with kids, and you'll be an amazing mom. You're just stressed about school, the bar exam, and work. You have a few years before the kids would even come. We'll get a new place, and it will be perfect, you'll see. Trust me."

Lake doesn't know how else to say it, so she repeats what she just said. "I do trust you, but I don't know if I really want kids—ever. I love this place. It's our home. I don't want to move and change everything. I just want to stay here with you."

Kingston doesn't press the issue. She's been easygoing with Lake and a hundred percent supportive of the exams and school, but she's pushing forty. She had been so sure that Lake was the one, but this woman whom she loves infinitely suddenly doesn't know if she wants children, and that's not going to work for her. Kingston's been here before. Not in the exact same circumstance, but the outcome was the same. She can't risk losing her dream to have a family in the hope that Lake will change her mind someday. With a heavy heart, she pushes her plate back and leaves the table.

Lake knows this is the end of their relationship. If either one of them caves and lets go of their own dream just to please the other, resentment and regret will seep into every crack and crevice of their lives, destroying them from the inside out. The process will be ugly, and when it's done, the love they once shared will be unrecognizable.

Both women realize there is no recovering from the words that have been spoken. Across half-eaten plates of takeout, Lake and Kingston's plans for the future have taken a drastic detour.

#

Lying next to the woman who's been her lover and bedmate for more than a thousand nights, Lake thinks about the many wonderful firsts she's shared with Kingston. She is Lake's first long-term, live-in relationship. She's also the first and only woman she's brought home to her family and introduced as her girlfriend. Lake even came out to them with Kingston by her side, and that's a moment she'll never forget.

Their age difference has been a blessing. Kingston is a definitive free spirit, and the life lessons and new places Lake has experienced with her have been invaluable.

Kingston is the first woman whom Lake would love with every ounce of her being, and she's backed her into a corner, forced her hand, and then pushed her away.

Maybe she could be happy living Kingston's dream? A future filled with kids—easy, comfortable, complacent? All she has to do is sell her soul to the fertility devil, and she can live the good life indefinitely.

Lake is seriously contemplating giving in when Kiki's cherubic face pops into her head. In the depths of her mind, she can hear her voice:

"You're a strong woman, Lake. A force to be reckoned with. Don't sell out for anyone. Follow your dream, even when it seems impossible."

#

From that night on, Kingston is distant and unavailable. For a brief moment, Lake's angry that her lover isn't fighting harder to keep her, but what would that argument sound like? How do you talk someone into pregnancy and the responsibilities of a family when they're nowhere close to that mindset and may never be?

Recalling the details of Tara's story, Lake doesn't wait for Kingston to rent a luxury apartment in her name and fork out the money for a half year's rent. Instead, she uses the time that Kingston is away to plan a different future, one without her partner.

With Kingston, Lake has been exposed to the finer things in life, but she isn't living above her means. Her truck, which is so old it's cool again, is paid for, she has a decent balance in her checking account, and the money from her trust will help cover the expense of finishing school.

She rents a small bungalow in an up-and-coming area, and one day when Kingston is at work, Lake packs all that she owns, loads up the truck, and waves good-bye to the fine-looking home and parcel of land over which she never had any rights or control. **

Chapter 29 - Damon

*L*ake couldn't have predicted the immense sadness that set in once the dust settled in her new place. Messy and deep, the last of her first Kingston experiences is the absolute worst. It's like her heart has cracked inside her chest, and there is no easy way to fix it. It does help to talk about it, but the only friend she has, Tracy, is a new mom, and to be honest, Lake hasn't made much of an effort to keep in touch.

Lake calls Tracy to tell her that she and Kingston split, but she's crying so hard, it's not much of a conversation. Tracy and her husband aren't too far from Lake, and she invites her over for coffee the next weekend. Just seeing her old friend is invigorating and healthy. Between them, they drink an entire pot of coffee, laugh, reminisce, and hug one another multiple times.

"Woody is going to be up for days after all the caffeine I had this morning," jokes Tracy.

"Oh no, I'm sorry!" says Lake. "Maybe we should have dusted off the old college trick of one glass of water for every cup of coffee. In our former lives, it was a water between every beer, but it did keep us from getting plastered. Or in this case, it might keep little Woody from bouncing off the walls."

"Don't worry about it. I'll drink nothing but water the rest of the day. Besides, I have plenty of breast milk in the freezer. I'll just give that to him until I've got a few glasses of water in me."

"Resourceful, I like it. So how is it being a mom?" asks Lake.

Tracy's face lights up, and she says, "It's a ton of work, but I love it. Warren's a huge help, and my mom and dad are close. Woody's their only grandchild, so they're here a lot."

"That's great, Trace. It's nice you have a good support system in place." With a slight chuckle, Lake asks, "How'd you come up with the name Woody?"

Tracy rolls her eyes and answers, "Warren hails from a family of three boys, all named after past presidents. His brothers are Franklin and Ulysses. When we found out we were having a boy, Warren's top choice was Woodrow, and I went with it. I mean, the man gave us ratification and the woman's right to vote. The only thing I asked is that we don't call him Woody—for obvious reasons. But Warren was like, his friends are going to tease him and call him Woody anyway, why not just get it out there early?"

"He has a point," says Lake.

"He does. Warren's a good husband and a good father," says Tracy. "I'm sorry it didn't work out with Kingston, but for what it's worth, I think you made the right decision. I know you, Lake. When you set your mind to something, you're all-in. Right now, you're committed to law school and starting your career, and that requires almost all your time and energy. You said you want to make partner in a firm, and even I know you can't work a forty-hour workweek and make partner. Sure, there are some women who juggle a full-time career and motherhood, but if you're not ready to funnel your time and energy into both, you won't be happy, and your relationship would have suffered. I can't say I know how you feel, because I haven't been where you are, and Kingston sounds amazing, but having a family is a permanent decision. You have to both really want it for it to work, and it's okay that you don't. The fact that you recognize that, and you love Kingston and yourself enough to move on, is really brave and mature. I'm proud of you, friend."

Hearing Tracy's words validate Lake's decision to leave the comfortable, loving existence she has shared with Kingston, but it doesn't ease the pain it has caused. Only time, tears, and tea will aid in that department. Her first love and hardest heartbreak has also taught her to appreciate tea with honey, and Lake's new home is stocked to the gills with teas from around the world.

Lake and Tracy have two full hours of uninterrupted time together before little Woody begins to wail. The piercing cries resonate from the baby monitor on the table, causing Lake to visibly flinch. Tracy laughs and says, "Yep, you definitely made the right decision. Babies are predictable—they eat, poop, sleep, and cry. It's a never-ending loop, and it's not for the faint of heart."

When Tracy reaches for the baby monitor, Lake takes that as her cue to leave.

"Thanks for having me over, for listening, and just for being a good friend. I needed it," says Lake.

"I'm glad I could help," says Tracy. "You're easy to be with, and I know your person is out there. I can't tell you when they'll show up, but they will. In the meantime, just call if you need to talk. I can't promise you won't hear a baby screaming in the background, but I'm always here for you."

Lake gives her friend a hug, then returns to her small, quiet bungalow. She spends the rest of the day intermittently studying and crying. She thinks about making tea, but she's already had enough caffeine to carry her through the weekend. She orders a pizza but is too exhausted to get a plate from the cupboard or sit at the table. Wearing sweats and slippers, Lake trudges into the living room, pizza in hand, and gets comfortable on the couch. Still wired from the coffee, she flips through the channels, but she isn't able to find anything interesting. She thinks to herself, *It would be nice to have a DVD player so I can watch a movie whenever I want.* She adds this to the growing list of items she needs for the new place.

She falls asleep sometime after midnight and wakes to find herself lying next to a half-eaten box of pizza. With the smell of cheese still heavy in the air, she pushes the box aside and says out loud, "You need to get your shit together, Lake."

#

It's the beginning of a new semester, and as Tracy would say, she's all-in. Lake survived her first semester of law school with the help and support of Kingston, but now she's on her own, and things are about to get real. She's always been a good student, but law school classes are more demanding than her undergraduate classes were. Her Contracts professor is a fast talker and a complete tool. She's struggling to capture quality notes and is worried it will impact her grade. She barely eked by with a low B her first go-around with him, and she can't afford to continue along this path.

Professor Ward's office hours are right after class, and she needs to get with him to discuss her notes. She's exhausted every other means of trying to figure this out for herself, and nothing is working. He's kind of a creep, but she has no other option.

His office door is cracked open, and Lake can see him seated behind a massive oak desk. A traditional green glass banker's lamp, complete with brass pull chain, provides the only artificial illumination in the room. The dark-wood slats of the window blinds are drawn tight, and the room is dim, cave-like.

Lake knocks lightly on the door frame and announces her presence in a low voice. "Excuse me, Professor Ward?"

He looks up and recognizes her in a moment. With his right hand, he waves and says, "Lake, please, come in."

There are two chairs in front of his desk. Lake chooses the one on his right, closest to the window.

In his annoying, high-pitched, adenoidal tone, he asks, "What can I do for you today?"

Distracted by the sound of his voice, Lake doesn't answer right away. The sound coming out of his mouth doesn't match his old-school yuppy persona. His voice screams nerd, but his blue blazer and Nautica red-striped necktie give off a distinctive douchebag vibe. He clears his throat to indicate his impatience.

Lake shifts in her chair and says, "I'm not sure I'm taking the best notes during your lectures. I was hoping you could give me some pointers."

The professor tilts his head and smiles like a Cheshire cat. "You earned a low B in my class last semester. Is that right?"

Lake nods her head but doesn't respond verbally. *This guy is dodgy.*

"Your work is good, but it could be better. I have an appointment with another student in five minutes, but I'll give you a quick bit of advice. Pay attention to the footnotes. I speak to them during my lectures. I think if you do that, and if we work together, we can get you to an A. Can you come back at three today?" he asks.

Lake doesn't have a good feeling about this, but she replies, "Yes."

"Excellent. I'll see you at three." The way he draws out the word *excellent* makes Lake feel gross. She's decided her new name for him is "Professor Sketch."

Lake leaves his office and walks to the courtyard to study for the hour before she's due back in Sketch's office. She takes a seat on a bench beneath a shining red dogwood tree.

"Hey, you're in my Contracts class. My name's Paulette." Lake looks up to see a thin woman with straight jet-black hair standing in front of her. She's dressed in black from head to toe, very goth. She doesn't look like a typical law school student, but who is Lake to judge?

"Hi, Paulette. I'm Lake."

"Cool name. I've never met a Lake before. Are your parents like hippies or something?" asks Paulette.

"Ah, no. Ranchers, actually. I grew up in a town by Lake Erie. It's a long story," says Lake dismissively.

"I get it, you're busy. I'll leave you to whatever then," replies Paulette.

"No, please sit," says Lake. "I'm sorry if I was rude. I was just looking over my Contracts notes. I have a meeting with Professor Ward at three."

"Dude, that guy is Trevosa for real," says Paulette.

"Trevosa?" asks Lake.

Paulette looks at Lake quizzically. "You know, dark, edgy. He looks and acts all straitlaced and shit, but there's like a spooky undertone, you know?"

Emphatically, Lake says, "I *do* know! In my mind I refer to him as Professor Sketch."

"I love it! That's a perfect name for him," says Paulette.

Proud she came up with it, Lake nods her head in agreement.

"Hey, I'm having a few friends over to my place Saturday night. We'll probably order a pie, listen to some vinyl, and just hang. You can come if you want."

Paulette isn't someone Lake would typically hang out with, but she could use some help in the friend department. Besides, the woman is a law student, not some degenerate she just met on the street.

"Yeah, okay. Let me know if I can bring anything," says Lake.

Paulette tears a piece of paper from her notebook, writes down her address and phone number, and hands it to Lake. "You can bring something to drink if you want. We usually have beer and wine, but if you prefer something else, bring it along."

"Beer and wine sound good, but I'll bring some, too, to make sure you have plenty," says Lake.

"Killer. Later, Lake," says Paulette.

#

On Saturday afternoon, Lake regrets having told Paulette she'd stop by, but she doesn't want to make things weird in class, so she digs the one black T-shirt she owns out of the back of her closet and drives to Paulette's place. Her apartment is a tiny unit in a converted old Victorian home in an area best described as the city's version of Haight-Ashbury.

Lake climbs the squeaky stairs to Paulette's place. She bangs the vintage gargoyle door knocker loud enough for her hostess to hear over the music. When the door opens, she's greeted by a very pretty, obviously very gay black man. "Hey, grrrrl, you must be Lake. I'm Damon. Get your ass in here."

Lake thinks to herself, *Ok, the night's not a total loss. How cute is this guy?*

Reaching for the bag in her hand, Damon asks, "What did you bring me, darlin'?"

"It's just some beer," says Lake.

Opening the bag, Damon lets out a squeal. "Ooooo, Heineken. I loves me some hiney!" he says with a wink. "I'm just gonna throw this in the fridge, and then I'll get you acquainted with the group."

Lake laughs and follows Damon to the living room. The group consists of four other people—two men and two women, including Paulette. What an interesting mix of individuals. One of the men, Cato, is an intellectual type, and Lake recognizes him from her Contracts class. The other is a friend of Damon's, a dancer with the Atlanta Ballet.

When Damon gets to the woman whom Lake's never met, he says, "And this is Cookie. Not her real name, but we call her that because she's a line cook at the voodoo-looking restaurant on the corner. She hooks us up with burgers and booze whenever we go there."

Lake is impressed with the diversity in the room, and she gives Paulette an approving nod after meeting everyone. Over the course of the next few hours, she's introduced to the haunting sounds of post-punk alternative rock and new wave music, and she falls head over heels for Damon and his captivating story.

#

Wedged between the arm of the sofa and Damon, Lake rests her head on the back of the couch and surrenders to the sounds rushing out of the speakers.

"So, I'm guessing you like girls?"

Lake opens her eyes and fixates on the rapid, spinning blades of the overhead fan while trying to figure out if she actually heard the words or if she just imagined them.

"It's okay, sweetie. Me, I like the boys. Always have."

Lake slowly turns her head to meet Damon's penetrating gaze. The arch of his perfectly shaped eyebrows and his dark, almond-shaped eyes make it impossible for Lake to look away. Sweet Jesus, this man is pretty. The tone of his smooth skin reminds her of a creamy milk-chocolate drop.

"Always and forever?" asks Lake.

Damon smiles big, revealing perfect white teeth. "Forever and ever," he says.

Lifting her head off the back of the couch, Lake says, "I'm guessing you're not from here, Damon. What's your story?"

"Which version you want? The sad one or the fun one?" Damon asks.

Lake's not sure if it's the introspective music or the look in his eyes, but her response to his question is, "The sad one."

"Bold choice. Okay, little one, buckle up," warns Damon.

#

Damon's sad tale is the true story of his childhood and early adult years in a small Midwest town.

A now-fledgling artist from Wisconsin, Damon grew up on a dairy farm just outside of Green Bay. A respectable son and student, he worked the farm with his dad and his two jock brothers most week-ends and summers until the day he left for college.

"The parents started in having kids right away, and us boys popped out in quick succession. I think Mom was a little disappointed about never having a girl, but the old man acted like he hit the jackpot with

378

three big, strapping boys. We're all less than a year apart, and up until the time we were all in grade school, we were the best of friends, the three amigos. My oldest brother, Jayden, played football in high school, and my other brother, Izaak, is an amazing baseball player. They both were offered multiple college scholarships to play ball, and our dad nearly burst with pride."

Lake wonders when Damon's narrative will take a turn. So far, his story isn't even a little blue.

"I'm no slouch when it comes to sports or physical activity," says Damon. "I wrestled in junior high because it was a legit way to get all up with the boys, and I was pretty good at it. But my heart wasn't in sports. It was with the arts and self-expression, and girl, did I ever express myself. I been with more straight boys than you can shake a stick at."

Lake doesn't doubt this for one minute. A pretty, athletic boy like Damon will draw out all kinds of self-proclaimed straight men.

"My family knows what I am, but we don't ever talk about it. In fact, we don't talk at all. My daddy was okay with me working hard on the farm all those years, and getting good grades in school, but you can bet your bottom dollar I was scheming to get off that stinky-ass property, far away from those bunched-up brothers and dad of mine, as soon as I could. I graduated from high school with honors, got a decent scholarship to attend an art and design school in Milwaukie, and never once looked back."

Damon rests his hands in his lap, his face expressionless.

Lake has a sinking feeling she knows where this saga is headed and would love to give him a hug, but she isn't sure it would be appropriate.

"You said your family knows what you are. When did you come out to them?"

Damon blinks, and his eyes take on a dejected look. "I never did. I've been tormented and called names my whole life. Jayden and Izaak used to take up for me some when we were little, but once I started screwing around with boys, they stopped. Jayden had this one friend in high school who was a real jerk. He'd slam me up against the lockers and shove me whenever Jayden wasn't around. One night, he was sleeping over at our house and snuck into my room when everyone was asleep. Jayden woke up to find me blowing him and freaked. I don't know if he ever said anything to Izaak or my dad, but after that night, the men in my family didn't talk to me much."

"I'm sorry," is all Lake can say.

Damon shakes his head but doesn't respond.

"Where are your brothers now? Do you ever visit your family during the holidays?" asks Lake.

"I haven't seen anyone in my family since college. My brothers were away at school the day I left, and my dad couldn't be bothered to say good-bye. He was somewhere out on the farm when I drove away."

"What about your mom?"

"My mom's a decent woman, but she'll never go against my father. She calls me on my birthday when he's not in the house. That's the only time we talk."

This is the ridiculousness that gets Lake riled up. Damon is a gorgeous, educated, and talented young man, but because he's gay, the men in his family won't speak to him, and his mom only reaches out once a year on his damn birthday when his dad is nowhere within earshot. What in the actual fuck?

Damon can sense the mood has turned dark. In an upbeat tone he says, "Time to move on, Miss Lake. The sad version of my story that you insisted on hearing is weighing me down. Let's dance!"

Lake doesn't move from her spot on the couch. "Here? To this song?" she asks.

"Yes, right here, right now. This is as good a song as any." Damon stands, does a pirouette, and loudly announces that it's time to dance. "Who's with me?" he calls out.

Lake is surprised to see everyone but Mr. Intellectual stand and begin swaying to the music.

When the song ends, Lake and Damon are facing each other. Resting her hands on his hips, she says, "Yes."

Damon's eyebrows shoot up. "I don't recall proposing. Yes what?"

"I like girls," says Lake.

"Girl, please. I knew you were a friend of Dorothy's as soon as I opened the door." Lake doesn't have a friend named Dorothy, but she decides to let that one go. "Really? How'd you know?"

With a snap, he says, "Some call it divine. I just call it my spot-on, intense queer sense, and it's never wrong."

Lake doesn't question Damon's claim for one second. Her meeting Damon at this precise moment in her life is kismet. They are meant to be.

#

Sunday is the one day Lake forces herself to sleep past seven. She's not always successful, but she tries. This morning her phone is ringing off the hook at seven thirty-five. No one she knows calls her at seven thirty-five in the morning, not even her parents. Pissed off that her Sunday sleep is interrupted, Lake snatches the phone off her night-stand and barks, "Hello," into the receiver.

"What a bitchy way to greet someone."

Lake is stunned that someone would talk to her that way. "Who is this?" she asks.

"Don't play me like that, Mary, it's Damon."

Lake smiles. She vaguely remembers giving him her phone number last night on her way out the door, but she didn't expect him to call so soon.

Clearing her throat, she starts again. In the sweetest voice she can muster, she says, "Good morning, sweet boy. May I inquire as to why you're calling so early on a Sunday morning?"

To which Damon replies, "My boy, Bruno, is up and has to go potty."

Lake is totally confused.

"I usually walk him in the park on Sunday mornings and then grab a bite somewhere that's dog friendly."

This helps clear things up. Bruno is a male dog. Got it.

Damon continues, "You seem like a fit woman. I thought maybe you'd like to go with us, unless, of course, you have other plans."

"It's Sunday morning, Damon, I have no plans."

"So, is that a yes? Bruno can only wait so long," Damon says flatly.

"Yes, I'd love to go for a walk with you and Bruno. I'll meet you at the park in thirty minutes."

"You're a natural beauty, Lake. How about you throw on some clothes and meet me at the park in twenty minutes? We're starving," quips Damon.

"Fiiiiine. I'll meet you at the front entrance to the park in twenty," says Lake in a whiny, annoyed voice.

When she gets to the park, Damon is nowhere to be found. Now she's actually annoyed.

Then, from somewhere behind a row of trees, Lake can hear Damon's booming voice. "Once we made it to the entrance, that's all she wrote. I tried to explain that he needed to wait, but Bruno wasn't having it. He did his business and is ready for breakfast."

"I'd rather take a walk after breakfast, anyway. Let's eat," says Lake.

#

Damon sticks his tummy out like a Buddha, rubs it, and says, "I'm stuffed full of stuffed French toast."

Lake has never tried the stuffed French toast, thinking it would be too sweet for a meal, and she was right. After one delicious bite of Damon's breakfast, she was glad she listened to her gut and went with the omelet.

"You have to come over for a cocktail. Sunday mornings aren't complete without a cocktail. I have all the fixings for bloody Marys and mimosas. Pick your poison."

Damon and Bruno have been such fun company, Lake hasn't thought about Kingston once all morning. But when Damon mentions "mimosas," it reminds her of that first brunch with Kingston and her girls.

"Hey, what's with the sad face, honey bunches of oats?" Damon asks.

"Nothing, I'm fine," says Lake.

"Okay. Not true. When a woman says she's 'fine,' she's anything *but* fine."

It's true. Lake isn't fine, but she's trying. Shaking off the glum, she holds her hand up and says, "One mimosa. I'll have one mimosa with you, and then I need to get home and study."

"Ugh, you sound like Paulette. If she's not at work, she's studying. That's no fun."

"We don't all live the gay cabaret life, Damon. Some of us have to work and go to class," says Lake.

"I work—sometimes. But you have to admit, a theatrical life with music, dance, and cocktails is much more entertaining. We did all three on that magical night when you and I met, and it was lovely."

"You mean last night?" Lake asks.

Damon feigns surprise and says, "We met just last night? How can that be? It seems like I've known you my whole life. You're my little bit o' honey."

This guy's the best kind of trouble. Lake knows she can't deny him a single thing. Lacing her arm through his, she says, "Show me the long way home so Bruno can get his steps in."

Damon's home is a studio apartment two blocks from the park. It's clean and attractive, just like its tenant. As soon as the door closes, Bruno walks over to his bed, spins gracefully two times, lies down, and immediately begins to snore.

Lake is still staring at the wondrously content Bruno when Damon offers her a glass.

"How did you make this so fast?" she asks.

"It's only two ingredients, Mary. The raspberries were already washed and ready to go. I knew when I called you this morning that you'd end up here. You and me go together like peas and carrots."

"Ew, you lost me at peas. I can't stand peas. I like carrots, but peas are gross. They look like little rabbit turds, and then you bite into one and it's sweet. Vegetables aren't supposed to be sweet. Everything about peas is wrong."

"For cryin' out loud. Forget peas and carrots. I was trying to make a point about me and you and this beautiful, bizarre connection we have, but now you've gone and ruined it. What if I said we go together like a fork and a spoon? Is that Midwest enough for you?"

"Why are you throwing the Midwest thing in my face? And why do you keep calling me Mary?" Lake asks.

"Because you're very Midwest at times, and I call you Mary because we're gay. Do you know nothing of our gay heritage? Before it was somewhat okay to be gay, men would sometimes refer to other gay or bi men as Mary."

Lake looks unconvinced. "Is that really true?"

Damon holds up two fingers and says, "Scout's honor. Yes, I was a Boy Scout, and yes, I speak the truth. It's the same as when I said you're a friend of Dorothy's."

"I was going to ask you about that last night, but I didn't want to come across as dense, so I let that one go. But now that you've mentioned it, who's Dorothy?"

Damon throws his hands up and practically yells, "Mary, I swear to God! Answer me this, what movie did you grow up watching at least once every year?"

Lake is worried she'll get this one wrong and really send him into a tizzy. She closes her eyes and thinks hard. She wants to ask for a hint, but she doesn't dare.

She can hear Damon tapping his finger on his glass.

She's running through the Christmas movies her family watched every year. No Dorothy in any of them.

Then Damon starts humming the tune "Somewhere Over the Rainbow," and it clicks.

"*The Wizard of Oz*! You're talking about Dorothy from *The Wizard of Oz* because Judy Garland loves the gays. We're all friends of Dorothy's."

Damon's finger has been replaced with a fork, and he's clinking it loudly against his glass. In the most sarcastic tone, he says, "Winner, winner, vegetarian dinner!"

Opening her eyes, Lake says, "Be gentle with me, Nancy. I don't have a lot of gay friends."

"Touché, Mary. Good one."

Lake smiles, clicks her heels together three times, and says, 'Thank you, there's no place like home."

"I have a splendid idea. Let's watch an old movie and finish off this pitcher of mimosas. Then you can go home and study."

Lake asks, "You made a *pitcher* of mimosas? Was the movie part of your plan, too?"

"Maybe. Just stay. The movie I picked is less than two hours long, and it's all ready to go. It'd be a shame to make me watch it alone."

Lake sighs and gets comfortable on the big, cushy futon.

When the movie begins, Lake is beyond speechless. The opening scene is one she's watched at least a hundred times, and the melancholy notes of the music are undeniable. *Breakfast at Tiffany's* is her all-time favorite movie. How could this man she just met possibly know that?

#

Lake has a standing appointment with Professor Sketch on Monday afternoon, but she's reluctant to go. He insisted on walking her to the door after their last session, which was weird, and just as she was about to turn and thank him, she felt his hand on the small of her back. "I'm happy that you were able to come back and see me, Lake."
She'd have liked nothing better than to smack the disgusting, self-satisfied grin from his smug face. How dare he put a hand on her! "Sure," she said flatly. "Thanks for your time today."

"Until we meet again," he said while ushering her out the door.

Sketch might have been too kind a term for this shitbag. *Professor Putrid* is way more fitting, and she could always adjust as they go.

Today when she arrives for her appointment, he's sitting in one of the two chairs in front of his desk. Legs crossed, pen in his mouth, he's looking down when she knocks. Glancing at his watch, he says, "Lake?"

Taking the seat next to him, she says, "Yes, hi."

"Good afternoon. My chair's a little wobbly. I have a call in to maintenance, and I'm hoping they get to it today. But for now, looks like we're both forced to sit in these hard, uncomfortable old wood chairs."

Lake is uncomfortable just being here, and the chair only adds to it. Her thirty minutes passes without incident. The professor has acted appropriately and given her solid instruction. But just when she thinks she might have misjudged the guy, his hand is on her knee. Lake's mind begins to race. She wants to scream, *"What the hell do you think you're doing?"* but it's too early in the semester to piss this guy off.

"Great work today, Lake. I'd say things are progressing nicely, what do you think?" he asks.

Reading between the lines, Lake feels sick to her stomach. *What's this guy's end game? Is he honestly entertaining thoughts of me and him taking this to some other level?*

"I'm beginning to understand more clearly what it is you're looking for," is her response. She sees right through his little ruse and seriously doubts anything is wrong with his chair. Despite him being such a smart guy, Lake's sarcasm goes right over his head. He tightens his grip on her leg, giving it a squeeze.

"Splendid, same time next week then?" he asks.

For a split second, Lake almost blurts out, *"I'm a lesbian,"* just to keep the guy at bay, but then she decides against it, thinking that would go one of two ways. One, he could be a homophobic bumble-fucker who writes her off entirely and she ends up doing poorly in his class. Or two, he could be a right squirrely fuckstick who's totally into it and her confession makes his hard-on for her even harder. Either way, she loses.

Shifting awkwardly in her seat, she answers, "Yes sir, I will be here."

The steaming pile of poo lets go of her knee, and Lake springs from her seat and bounds for the door. As she passes through it, she hears him say, "Please, call me Chuck."

Wow, Charles goes by Chuck. As in *yuck, you suck, have a great day, shmuck!*

#

Still fuming over what just happened with "Chuck," Lake picks up the phone and dials Damon's number.

He picks up on the fifth ring, and she can hear the smile in his voice. "Hey, love, how was your day?"

She has no time for pleasantries. "It was terrible, Damon. My shit-for-brains Contracts professor made a move on me during office hours, and I'm really mad about that. I mean, where does he get off thinking that's okay?"

"Oh, boy, my little sugar cube is all kinds of displeased with the events of her day," he teases.

"Yeah, you could say I'm displeased—and then some," huffs Lake.

"I hear you loud and clear, shug. What say Bruno and I swing by, and you tell us all about it? Might make you feel better to talk it out."

Lake knows she won't be able to study until she's cleared her head.

"Yeah, you're right. It will help to talk about it, so get your butts over here," she says.

"We'll be there in two shakes of a lamb's tail."

#

Lake feels grungy and is desperate to shed her clothes and take a quick shower before her guests arrive. When she's done and pulling on a clean shirt, she hears the bell ring, followed by a loud bark.

Lake greets her furry friend at the door. "Hey, Bruno, c'mon in, buddy, she says as she pulls the door open wide.

Throwing his hands up, Damon asks, "Hello! What about me? Don't go treating me like Bruno's side dish."

Lake rolls her eyes and says, "Get in here, drama queen. You know I love you more than my luggage."

"Oh, my God, yes, yes! A million times, yes. We have to watch that movie together. Love it!" squeals Damon.

"Only because it's one of the best movies ever," replies Lake, referring to *Steel Magnolias*. "I haven't had an opportunity to buy a DVD player yet, but it's on my list."

"Okay, I know there's a story behind that statement, and trust me, I do want to hear it one day, but today's not that day. Where's your kitchen?" asks Damon as he makes his way through the living room.

"You're headed in the right direction," answers Lake.

"Cute. Small, but cute. Where do you keep the wineglasses?" asks Damon as he pulls a bottle of wine out of his cardigan.

"You brought wine." It's more a statement than a question.

"Of course. I only had one bottle, but I can run to the store if we need more. Judging by the tone of your voice, it feels more like a two-bottle evening," says Damon.

"Wineglasses are in the far-right cupboard, top shelf," says Lake.

Damon pours two glasses of wine and hands one to Lake. Looking out the window over the sink, he says, "You have a nice backyard. Does that fence go all the way around the yard?" Damon asks.

"Yeah, that was part of the reason I picked this place. I like having the outside space. It's fully fenced and private. There's a huge cornflower blue hydrangea in the far back corner—it's amazing. I even have a little firepit." Lake beams with pride.

Damon gives Lake a light touch on the end of her nose and says, *"Boop!* You have the perfect little place to gather. Do you care if I let Bruno loose out back?"

"Not at all. The only thing I ask is that you clean up after him."

"Of course, I will. I'm not that guy, the one who doesn't dispose of his dog's doo. I'd never do that to you, my little sugar plum," declares Damon.

Lake opens the back door, and Bruno is off like a shot, chasing birds and running back and forth along the fence line. She turns to Damon and says, "We can sit outside and talk if you want to keep an eye on him. The sun isn't over the backyard in the late afternoon, and it's actually pretty comfortable."

Damon raises his glass and says, "Sold. Let's move this party outside."

Lake has two chairs and a bench on either side of the firepit. Each of them settles into a chair as Lake shares the details of her run-ins with the colossal creep of Contracts. Damon crosses his legs and becomes one with his chair. He pours the last of the wine into his glass just as Lake wraps up. Bruno, tired from hundreds of laps around the yard, is fast asleep at his feet.

"Thanks for letting me get that off my chest," says Lake as she exhales loudly.

"Are you interested in hearing my thoughts on the situation?" asks Damon.

"Your thoughts are entertaining as hell. I live for the times when you speak them out loud," says Lake.

"Just play the game, darlin', without actually giving the slimeball anything. Smile and nod, flip your hair, and tell him how amazing he is. Shits like him eat that up. Trust me, massaging his ego is like stroking his dick. Give him just enough to make it challenging, and let him think there's a sexy payoff for him somewhere around the corner. And by corner, I mean the end of the semester."

Lake isn't too keen on the idea, but she thinks, *What the hell?* She works hard and deserves an excellent grade.

So, she does as Damon says and keeps the professor at arm's length until her final grade is posted.

Fuck off, asshole.

Chapter 30

"I'll be there to pick you up in ten," says Damon. "I'm taking you out to shop and get drinks. Don't leave me at the curb honking my horn and pissing off your neighbors."

Lake's first year of law school is behind her, and she's open to Damon's plan of shopping and getting drinks. She's been unavailable for weeks, her extracurricular activities shut down completely while she studied and attended class. The crazy, time-consuming course load filled every day and almost every night.

"I'm not sure I'm dressed for all that," is Lake's response. It's only been a day since she turned in her last assignment of the semester. She's missed spending time with her testy new bestie, but one mindless evening to herself would be nice.

"Don't get all uppity with me, Mary. The evening calls for casual dress at best. Just be ready for me," snaps Damon.

"Love you, too," replies Lake as she disconnects.

Lake is near her front window when Damon's car passes by her house, giving her ample time to grab her things and meet him out front when he reappears. Coming from his place, he has to drive past her house, turn around, and then come back to be on her side of the street. She's told him before that she's more than capable of crossing the street for him, but he insists on pulling up to her side. "It stresses me out when you're not ready and I'm holding up traffic. People can be real jerks. I don't want your blood on my hands when that A-hole who's too important to wait hits your sorry ass as you cross the street."

Damon purses his lips and smooches the air as Lake clicks her seat belt into the buckle. "Hey there, sugar snap pea! It's been a minute since your butt was in that seat. I'm happy to see you," says Damon.

Lake rests her hand on his shoulder, and a vision of her mom doing the same thing to her dad pops into her mind. She pushes the thought aside and says, "I'm happy to see you, too! I've missed your sassy ass."

With a snap, Damon says, "That's what he said!"

Lake's amusement turns to confusion when Damon whips the car into a space near the park and announces, "We're here!"

"We're where?" she asks. "I thought we were going shopping?"

"We are," says Damon. Pointing to a high-rise building across the street, he continues, "A friend of a friend is moving out of his too-cool-for-school condo that overlooks the park. He's selling all his stuff and moving to Greece to be with his new beau."

Lake's expression is one of utter bewilderment. "That's way cool and really daring. I still don't understand why we're here."

"I say this in the nicest way I know how," states Damon. "Your place is lacking when it comes to electronic conveniences. I mean, who doesn't have a TV in their bedroom?"

Lake rolls her eyes and says, "I don't need a TV in my boudoir. Bedrooms are for sleeping and sex."

"Bingo! You need a TV—trust me on this one," is Damon's response.

"I'm not following you," says Lake.

"Yes, you are. You're going to follow me right up to the sixteenth floor, and we're going to get you an amazing deal on a TV and anything else we can find."

Lake rests her head on the back of the seat and sighs loudly. She has no interest in buying a TV from this friend of a friend, but she knows Damon means well and he's not about to let the matter drop.

"Fine! Let's go see what this friend of a friend has to offer. If he's not willing to give me an awesome deal, then we're leaving," says Lake.

"We're here to keep this stuff in the family, so to speak," says Damon. "Support gay business and all that. I'll even carry whatever you buy to the car and help with the setup at home." Damon flashes his dazzling smile, and Lake melts. She could just eat him with a spoon.

#

Even with half the furniture gone, the sixteenth-floor condo is gorgeous. The stereotype of gay men being natural domestic experts with an inherent flair for aesthetic home styling could not be truer in this case. Until this moment, Lake had been rather pleased with her home and the way in which she decorated it. Now, she sees there is room for improvement.

Standing in the foyer, Lake channels the spirit of gay man décor while Damon chats up his new friend.

"Hey, Papi, nice place you have here. Your new beau must be one hell of a man to make you want to leave all this behind," he says.

The condo owner's name is James, and he's more attractive than his digs, if that is even possible. Lake is a beginner when it comes to gay men. She still relies on her training wheels, even with five solid months of Damon under her belt. She was captured by his beauty the first night she met him, but she has come to learn the city's cup runneth over when it comes to tantalizing hot-bodied homos. James is one of many.

"Marco is more than just a pretty face. He's sweet, sexy, smart, funny, and the best I've ever had," declares James.

Damon fans himself and replies, "If he's a fraction of what you are, I'd already be in Greece, honey."

Lake is finding it tough to look away from James. His passion-pink lips are incredibly plump. Women paid good money for lips like that. She imagines the many wonderful things he could do with those perfectly pouty puckers and feels her face getting warm. It reminds her of Kingston and the awkward moment at that first holiday party. Kingston was wearing a sexy red-sequined suit, and Lake couldn't stop staring at her sun-kissed chest and inviting cleavage. Unbecoming behavior that took her by surprise.

James is so absorbed in the story of his latest lover that he hardly notices Lake, but judging from the high arch of Damon's brows, the focus of her attention has not escaped him. Like a scolded child, she immediately looks away.

Lake hasn't had time to think about Kingston these past few months, and she'd thought she'd made it through the worst of it, but now, she feels like running out of the condo and taking a long walk in the park, alone with her thoughts. Damon picks up on the change in her demeanor and feels bad, thinking it's due to his reprimanding look.

"You are one lucky man, James. I'm happy for you and Mr. Every thing Bagel. I've never been to Greece, but your plan sounds wonderful."

With her mind back on Kingston, the word *Greece* becomes a trigger for her, and Lake is close to tears. She and her former love spent five glorious days happily romping through Greece, and yes, she still misses her. Lake's pained expression is like a jab to Damon's heart, and he quickly gets to the point.

"So, James, how do we know what's for sale and what's not?" he asks.

"Well, that's easy. Any item for sale has a bright orange sticker on it. Most of the stickers have a price written on them, but if you see something you like and you're not sure of the price, just ask," says James.

"Alrighty then, my dear friend Lake is in the market for a TV," says Damon as he takes her by the hand.

"My ex bought the TV here in the living room last night and is coming back for it tomorrow, so this one's not for sale," says James, pointing to an oversized television on the floor just a few feet away. "But I do have one in the bedroom that's available. It's a TV/DVD combo unit that's about a year old. I think the sticker says seventy-five dollars, but you can have it for fifty if it's something you're interested in."

Damon and Lake follow James to the bedroom. The room is barren except for a bed on the far wall of the room. Against the wall at the foot of the bed is a six-drawer dresser with a television on top of it.

"I was holding on to this one, so I'd have something to watch until it was time to leave, but now it's time to let her go. It's a twenty-inch flatscreen," says James.

Damon walks over to the TV, turns to Lake, and asks, "What do you think?"

Lake takes a step closer. She's never owned a combo unit like this one, but she does need a DVD player to watch movies, and it's the perfect size for her bedroom. For just fifty dollars, she'd be a fool not to buy it.

"I'll take it," she says.

"Done," says Damon. "We'll take it."

Lake turns to James and says, "I don't have cash on me, but I do have my checkbook if you're okay with a personal check."

With just a hint of annoyance in his voice, James says, "I'd prefer cash, but because you're a friend of Damon's, I'll take a check."

While Lake rummages around in her bag looking for her checkbook, James pulls a business card from his wallet and hands it to her.

"My business card. You can make it out to the name there at the top," he says.

Lake isn't about to ask James for a pen. Luckily, she carries several in her purse. Her hand touches what feels like her checkbook, and she pulls it from her bag. There's a pen just below it, and she pulls that out, as well.

Using the top of James's dresser as a table, she writes a check for fifty dollars made out to James and hands it to him along with his business card. "Thank you," she says.

James looks at the check to make sure all is in order and replies offhandedly, "You're welcome."

Damon gives James a hug and also says, "Thank you." The response Damon garners from James is much more enthusiastic. Damon unplugs the unit and easily picks it up. Walking toward the front door, he asks, "Do you mind getting the front door, snookums?"

To Lake's surprise, James replies, "Not at all," as he skips past her to open the front door for Damon.

Lake rolls her eyes as she follows the two men out of the condo.

"Thanks again," says Damon as he carefully makes his way to the elevator. "Enjoy Greece, and more importantly, enjoy Marco," he says with a wink.

"You know I will," James responds as he turns to walk back into his place.

#

"I don't know about you, sugar, but I could use a drink," says Damon as he carefully shuts the trunk lid.

"I'm down," says Lake. "Where are we going?"

"I'm not in the mood for boy drama tonight. How about that place you love?"

"Which place? You mean the Pink Triangle?" asks Lake. "It's basically a girl bar, but if you're okay with that, I'm in. We can kick back in the piano lounge, enjoy a cocktail, and celebrate my new bedroom TV."

"Sounds good to me, girl."

#

True to his word, Damon carries her new TV into the bedroom and places it on top of Lake's dresser. It sits at an angle, but she can maneuver it better once she decides on the best placement for it. She hadn't planned to have a television in her bedroom, but now that it was here, she kind of likes the idea of watching a romantic movie in bed.

Standing back to admire his handiwork, Damon says, "I like it."

Lake drapes an arm around his waist and says, "I know I was against having a TV in the bedroom before, but maybe this will be good."

Placing his arm around her shoulder, Damon says, "What's that I hear? Could it be my little chicklet admitting her handsome best friend was right?"

Lake lets go of his waist and pushes Damon playfully. "I didn't say you were *right*. I said maybe it will be good to have the option to watch TV in here when I'm not feeling the living room."

"You can phrase it any way you want, Mary. The fact of the matter is, Damon knows best."

Lake laughs and hugs her goofy friend. "Thanks for helping me get a great deal on the TV. I do love the combo built-in DVD player."

"You're welcome, love. I had fun tonight. And now that you have some time off from school, you, me, and Bruno can all pile into your bed and watch movies together."

"I'm not sure my bed can handle all that," says Lake.

"You never know until you try," he says. "Tomorrow night! I'll bring the popcorn."

"Fine, but I get to pick the movie," says Lake.

#

After Damon leaves, Lake locks up and grabs a DVD from the entertainment center in the living room. Damon had plugged the TV in when he placed it on her dresser, and it turned on, but she wants to make sure the DVD player works. She pushes EJECT to load the DVD and discovers there's already one it.

Without thinking, she hits PLAY and begins watching her first gay porn movie. It's like a train wreck. She wants to look away, but at the same time, she's so intrigued and into it that she can't bring herself to stop watching.

Ten minutes later, the movie ends. She rewinds it, planning to watch it again—soon. She's wanted to ask Damon questions about his sex life, but she hasn't had the nerve. What she just watched answered most of them.

The next morning, she gets a call from none other than James, the guy who sold her the DVD player. She wonders how he got her home number, and then she remembers it's printed on her checks.

"I think I might have left one of my discs in the player. Do you mind checking real quick? I'm happy to stop by and pick it up this morning," he says.

"Sure, hold on a sec. I'll check."

Lake sets the phone on her kitchen counter and waits thirty seconds or so before picking it back up.

Selfishly, she lies when she speaks, "Hey, James, I checked, and there's no disc in the player. It's empty."

James lets out an audible sigh. "Are you sure?"

"Positive. You probably just misplaced it. Good luck on your move." Lake disconnects and places the phone back in its cradle.

No hot man-on-man action here, James. Sorry. Not sorry.

#

Damon and Bruno are sleeping over again tonight, and all three are piled into Lake's bed watching a movie. "I have a confession to make," she says.

Damon picks up the remote and presses PAUSE while he waits for her to continue.

Bruno, used to the normal level of noise in the background, is confused by the silence. He stands, barks twice at absolutely nothing, paws incessantly at the bed, then spins around twice before curling up in a ball, smack-dab between them. Once he's settled in, Damon turns to her and says, "Well? What's this big confession? Out with it, girl."

Lake looks at the TV when she speaks, even though the picture is frozen. She's too ashamed to look at Damon when she says, "I think I'm addicted to gay porn."

Damon's head turns abruptly as his brows shoot up, "Join the club," he says. Then, in a softer tone, he continues, "C'mon, munchkin, why don't you tell me what's really on your mind. Is it Kingston? Did something else happen?"

Two days ago, Lake had been grocery shopping and spotted Kingston at the store, but she wasn't alone. She was with a woman. Lake didn't recognize the woman, but she looked to be about the same age as Lake. Petite, dark-blond hair, blue eyes, fit. If asked, Lake would use the same words to describe herself.

She'd known Kingston was dating again, but actually seeing her with another woman, joking, laughing, and picking out produce was another thing altogether. It was jarring and unpleasant to the point that Lake left her shopping cart half full of groceries in the middle of the aisle and walked out of the store. She was crying before she made it to the car, and she cried all the way home. The first thing she did when she walked in the door was call Damon.

"We're on our way," he said. "Give me a few to grab some essentials, and we'll be right there."

She has not one, but two amazing boys in her life. Damon and Bruno are safe. They love her unconditionally and ask nothing of her in return. Zero expectations, sexually or otherwise.

They've became her routine, and it works perfectly for all of them. Damon and Bruno spend more time at Lake's little bungalow than they do at their own apartment. Damon claims that being near her is an inspiration and he's never been more productive. He's created a makeshift studio in her backyard, and Bruno loves it. They're part of the family now, and she loves having them at her place.

"No, nothing more has happened with Kingston. She's obviously moved on. Bully for her. I hope she and the new chick have tons of screaming babies," she says.

"Wow, pumpkin, bitter much?" asks Damon.

396

Lake realizes what a brat she sounds like and feels the need to course-correct. "I'm sorry, that was petty, but dang! It hasn't even been a year."

"We've moved out of the Victorian era, Prudence. There's no hard or fast rule that says our ex-loves have to wait a year or more before engaging again. Sexually or otherwise. Just because you're too busy and irritated to put yourself out there doesn't mean Kingston isn't. Have you forgotten whose idea it was to split in the first place?" he asks.

"I know, I'm being a hostile witch, and I'm sorry. Thank you for calling me out on it," she says teasingly.

"Well, someone has to," he says.

Lake smiles and says, "I was serious when I said I think I'm addicted to gay porn. That was my actual confession before we got side-railed."

"What do you know about gay porn?" he jokes. "We ain't ever had that conversation, although I'm totally open to it."

Lake leans over Damon, opens the drawer of her nightstand, and is about to reveal her DVD of guilty pleasure when he grabs her arm.

"Now, hold up, Mary! If your nightstand is filled with the same things mine is, I ain't ready for any of what you're about to share."

Lake laughs and pulls out the DVD. Climbing back into her side of the bed, she tells Damon the story of how she came to be the current owner of her new favorite movie. Wiping an imaginary tear from his eye, Damon says, "I've never been prouder of you than I am right now. And don't worry about your watching habits. Just remember the old saying—everything in moderation—and you'll be fine."

Lake hugs her friend, refusing to let go.

"Alright now, enough of that," he says. "Can we please finish the movie? I need my winks. All of them!"

When the movie ends, it's only nine forty-five, Lake's not ready for bed, and Damon has gotten a second wind.

"What do you say we grab a glass of wine and wind down the evening out back?" asks Damon. "Bruno needs to go potty, and the firepit helps to settle my mind."

Jumping up, Lake says, "Sure. You let Bruno go out and get the fire going. I'll grab the wine."

The two of them sit quietly, watching the flames dance around the pit. Bruno is off in the far corner of the yard just outside the circle of light cast off by the fire. Neither of them can see him, but both can hear the jingle of his collar as his nametag bounces against the metal fastener. Reaching for his glass, Damon says, "Bruno and I love being here with you. You're the closest thing to family we have, and we're both just crazy about you."

Lake stretches wide, bringing her mind back to the present, and responds, "You know what's crazy? I was thinking the exact same thing earlier. You both came into my life at just the right time, and I'm so much better because of it."

"It's a wonderful world we live in, that's for sure," he says.

Lake looks across the fire at her friend. The moment is filled with love and emotion, and Damon's face has never looked more beautiful. He has a warm glow about him, angelic and peaceful. Lake smiles and watches the twinkle in his eye roll slowly down his cheek.

"Was that a tear? Are you crying?" she asks.

The peaceful look fades as Damon shifts in his chair. His face takes on a somber look, and he says, "I have a confession of my own to make."

Lake's never seen her friend act this way before, and it scares her. "What is it? Is everything okay? Why are you looking at me like that?"

Damon brings the wineglass to his lips, finishing off the last of it, then looks directly into Lake's eyes. "Before I met you, I was in a dark place. I know I put on a good show and talk a good talk, but I'm not a promiscuous guy. I dabbled a bit, trying to find my way, and yeah, I dabbled a lot when I finally arrived, but I've always been relatively safe."

Lake has no idea where this is going, but she's terrified nonetheless. She starts to speak and Damon's index finger immediately goes to his lips, the universal *shhh* sign.

"Please, Lake, just let me finish."

Damon rarely uses her first name when speaking to her. When he's cranky, it's "Mary," and when he's not, it's whatever pet name he's feeling in the moment. The use of her first name has her on high alert.

"A few months before you and I met, I spent one glorious evening with an amazing man. We met at the club and danced our asses off until last call. The chemistry between us was undeniable, and neither of us wanted the night to end. We went to breakfast at that spot on Ponce and talked until the sun came up.

"I had just come out of a semiserious relationship and had been playing it cool, tending to my gently bruised heart. I hadn't been with anyone in almost a month, and I had no intention of jumping into bed with this man I'd just met, yet that's exactly where we landed. It was everything, Lake. Hungry, passionate, tender, raw.

"We fell asleep in each other's arms, and when I woke up, he was gone. No note on the pillow, no call or text later that morning. Nothing. Hours turned into days, and I just didn't understand how or when the night went bad. I went to the club every night for a week, hoping I would run into him again, but he wasn't there.

I kept thinking about our night together, playing it over in my head again and again, and I realized I didn't know a single thing about the guy. I assumed he was local, but he never confirmed that. I had driven us to breakfast and back to my place. I don't know what kind of car he drives or where he lives. I don't even know his last name. I never saw or talked to him again, but I couldn't stop thinking about him. I romanticized our night together and imagined all kinds of happy endings.

Then one day, I went to my general practitioner for a routine checkup.

Damon stops talking but continues to look in Lake's eyes. She can see his chest moving in and out as he breathes deeply, like he's summoning up the courage to continue. There are a million questions running through Lake's mind, but she hasn't a clue where to start. She continues to watch his chest rise and fall, and after he exhales painstakingly through his shapely mouth, he says, "I'm HIV-positive."

It's a direct hit to her heart. Lake can't bear to lose him. Not now, not ever.

Damon knows his words are hard for Lake to hear. They're hard for him to say. It's the first time since his diagnosis that he's said the words out loud. When the doctor himself called to discuss his test results, he knew it was serious. He wasn't sure what type of cancer it could be, but he braced himself for the delivery of the dreaded C word. He was so wrapped up in his own thoughts and self-diagnosis that he didn't even hear the actual words spoken to him. When his doctor asked if he had any questions, he realized he hadn't caught all of what had been said, so he asked the doctor to repeat the information.

"The results of your HIV test came back positive."

Damon almost laughed out loud. This couldn't possibly be right. He got tested every six months and had been doing so for the past several years. His previous test had been negative, and he hadn't been unsafe with anyone except…no, it couldn't be. Was that why Mr. Wonderful had slipped away so quietly into the night and never looked back?

Damon didn't know what to say. His doctor was patient and offered all the right words, carefully laying out a plan for care while Damon embarked on his journey through the five stages of grief. He spent about a month working through the first four and was trying hard to claw his way out of the deep state of depression when he started hanging out with Paulette.

Her crew was pensive and dark, and they seemed a natural fit for this particular phase in his life. They were fine with his baby steps back into the world of social norms, and they let him be, for the most part. The night he opened the door for Lake was a decisive moment.

"I'm going to be okay, shug. Actually, I'm better than okay, and it's all because of you. You saved my life."

Lake is trying to grasp the reality of what she has just heard. Each day with Damon is a history lesson in being queer, but there's still so much she doesn't know. She definitely gets that HIV and AIDS are bad, but they aren't the death sentence they used to be. She has so many questions, but she knows she should probably let Damon get everything out before she starts in with them.

"I was stupid. I let my emotions get the better of me, and there's nothing I can do now to change that. I was angry for a while, and I wanted to hit things. I *did* hit things, but it didn't make me any less angry. Then I started having thoughts about killing myself, but those thoughts were short-lived. I became depressed and went through a few different prescriptions, hoping to get the right mix to come out of it. I just wanted to feel better. My doctor and I agreed on an alternative diet and a whole different set of prescriptions. I got on a new regimen, and I was slowly coming out of the fog when I opened the door to your sweet face. Being with you is better than any drug I've tried yet. You lift me up, buttercup."

Lake inhales sharply to keep from crying.

"I can see the tears you want to cry. Please don't do that," he says. "'Cause if you start, I may never stop, and I cry ugly. Like, no one wants to see that, especially you." Damon contorts his face in a way that makes Lake laugh, and she blinks back her tears. She needs to be strong for him.

"You know what time it is?" she asks.

"I don't know—late," is his reply.

Lake extends her arm to him and says, "No. It's time to dance."

Damon's smile is so big, his cheeks make his eyes look like little squinty beads of brown. Holding her close to him, Damon sways Lake in time to the leaves rustling overhead until the crackling fire beside them is nothing more than an insignificant pile of deep red coals.

Chapter 31

" *A*m I the first boy to meet your parents?" Damon asks.

Lake shakes her head and says, "I wish you were. Then I could pretend high school prom never happened. But if it's any consolation, you are the most handsome boyfriend of mine to meet Jack and Sylvia."

"Girl, you're lucky to have just the one backseat mistake you'd like to forget. I lost count a long time ago."

"Ew! No offense, but my mistake took place on a king-sized bed. I've never done it in the back seat of a car, nor do I want to," says Lake, all high and mighty–like.

"Okay, Mary Magdalene, not everyone from the Midwest is a saint like you. Some of us grew up getting it where and when we could. Even if that meant bending over a back seat."

"Wow! All this time I wondered if you were a top or a bottom. Now I know! Thanks for painting that rather explicit picture for me," teases Lake.

"Ha! That's rich coming from you, sweetheart. I didn't want to embarrass you by calling out the fact that I had to eject your favorite disc from the player last weekend to make space for our wholesome Christmas movie, but I just did! I know you enjoy the boy-on-boy action, so drop the innocent charade. It doesn't suit you."

Lake's face turns three shades of red in a matter of seconds. Damon's right, and she had no idea that he was the one who returned the disc to her nightstand drawer. It was there yesterday, and she assumed it was because she had placed it there. Oh my, what if he saw her treasure trove of toys when he opened the drawer? Is it possible that her face is now a deeper shade of red?

"And besides, you know how I hate labels. I'm not one thing or the other. If you must know, I'm a versatile kind of guy, my little gay voyeur, so no need to wonder anymore."

How does this man effortlessly pull double-duty twenty-four/ seven? One day he's her best friend; the next he's like the brother she never asked for. Her real brother, Pete, is always kind and never overbearing. This one is mostly kind and always overbearing.

"Can we just drop the topic of the movie and how often I may or may not watch it?" asks Lake. "I need to pick a place for my birthday dinner and make a reservation. Anywhere worth going is going to be booked soon."

Damon looks at her like she has a third eye. "I got you, my one and only. I say we go Midwest-big with your parents and take them to an iconic steakhouse that's been around almost as long as you. The service and food are legendary, and I happen to know one of the managers there very well. I will not only get us a reservation for the day and time of your choosing, but I will also guarantee one of the best tables in the house."

"That sounds expensive," says Lake.

"Normally, it would be, but since William and I still have play dates every now and then, I think I can get us a discounted rate. It ain't gonna be cheap, but we won't be paying retail, either."

"Alright, done. Make a reservation for four on the Saturday before my birthday. You know my dad's a rancher, right? Mealtime in the Myerses' house is no joke. Dinner is served daily between five thirty and six p.m., depending on the season, and that schedule remains intact no matter what," Lake says seriously.

"We are of the same soil, so to speak. Have no fear, my lovely. I will procure a dinner reservation between the hours of five thirty and six p.m.," he says.

#

James from the sixteenth-floor condo has sold almost all his furnishings before moving to Greece. But the one big item he hasn't been able to offload is his king-sized, overly masculine black-upholstered bed. Two days before he is supposed to leave, a few of his friends host an impromptu bon voyage party at the club, and Damon is invited. The two get to talking, and James mentions he is going to have to pay someone to come haul the bed away if he can't get rid of it before his flight. Of course, Damon, being the generous man he is, offers to come take the bed off his hands for free.

"You live in a studio apartment. Where do you propose to put this bed?" asks Lake. The two are sitting at her bistro table drinking coffee.

Damon uncrosses his legs and replies, "Well, here's the thing. You have a spare bedroom with basically nothing in it, and I'm here all the time. I love you lots, but I need a space of my own to lay my head. So, I was thinking, I could put the bed in your spare room."

It isn't a terrible idea, she thinks.

"I'll buy new bedding and a mattress for the frame, and it'll be great. A couple of the guys can help me move it over here, and when the new mattress is delivered, they'll haul away the old one. James's potentially costly problem is solved, and you get a stately bed for your guest room. I'll even save up for a nightstand and a dresser," he says, batting his eyes.

Lake knows she can't say no to him, and he does have a point. Her parents are coming for her birthday, and she'd also love for them to stay at her place. Having a furnished guest room for them to stay in would make that possible. "Okay. But my parents are staying here when they come for my birthday. So, you and Bruno will have to crash at your place that weekend. Seriously, why do you even pay rent? We need to talk about us being official roommates at some point. It doesn't make sense for both of us to be paying rent when you're here, like, four nights a week."

Damon shakes his head and says, "What do you think I'm doing the other nights? A boy needs his privacy, queen. I can't be bringing my dates back to 'our' place. Awkward!"

"That is a valid point you make. I hadn't really thought about it, but I don't want to be getting all cozy with a little cutie on the couch one day and have you walking half-naked through the living room," she says.

"Oh, right, because you entertain cuties all the damn time," says Damon.

"It could happen. I could get back in the game any day now. Chicks dig me, D. And at some point, I'll have time for the ladies again."

"For sure. But until that time comes, I think you're safe from the likes of all this chocolatey goodness," says Damon as he runs his hands down his body and does his best runway walk out of the room.

#

Standing in the center of Lake's living room, Sylvia turns slowly, surveying every inch of the space. "I love what you've done with the place, Lake, and the neighborhood is very cute. Your dad and I like that it's close to shops and restaurants. You don't really even have to drive if you don't want to."

"Yeah, this neighborhood is becoming really popular, and I was lucky to find this place. My favorite part of the house is the fireplace and hardwood floors. They remind me of home."

"Our house hasn't changed much since you moved out. Your dad and I have been kicking around the idea of sprucing up the kitchen, but nothing's been decided."

Lake loves the stark-white appliances and varnished wood cupboards of her childhood home. Sylvia walks toward the back of the house.

"I was thinking maybe we could start small and replace the linoleum in the kitchen and hall bath. Your dad never really cared for the turquoise. I think he might like a more neutral color tile, but I'm just not sure. It's a big decision."

"Well, it sounds like you have time, Mom. I'm sure whatever you decide will look great. Let me show you the rest of the house and the backyard."

Lake and Sylvia are in the backyard when her dad joins them. "Cute place, kiddo. The firepit is a nice feature," he says.

"Thanks, Dad. We can sit out here tonight if you and Mom are up for it. I thought we could eat here at the house since we're going out for a fancy steak dinner tomorrow night. We can take a walk around the neighborhood later and sit by the fire for a while."

"I like the sound of that. Your mom said you asked for her red sauce recipe. Are we having spaghetti for dinner?" asks Jack.

"Spaghetti and meatballs are a tradition on my birthday. I followed Mom's recipe for the sauce step by step. We all know practice makes perfect, but I had fun cooking it for the first time, and the whole house smelled delicious."

"If you followed your mom's recipe, it'll taste terrific."

#

Lake's first attempt at her mom's red sauce is a home run. After dinner, she shows her parents around the neighborhood, and they stop for ice cream on the way back to her place.

During the walk, her mom brings her up to speed on the latest family happenings. Pete and Deanna are doing great. Lucas has started pre-school and loves being Lila's big brother. Jeanne's killing it with her event-planner work, and she's met a new guy whom they like a lot.

Lake can't believe how her family has grown and flourished since she was last home. She's happy to hear her siblings are doing well, and she misses her niece and nephew. She's only seen Lila once. Just after she was born, she and Kingston had spent a long weekend in Cleveland. They had dinner with Jeanne, spent the day at Pete and Deanna's new place, and then drove out to the ranch for an early dinner with her parents. On Sunday they'd had brunch at a neat little place on the lake and then went to a baseball game. It was one of the best trips home she'd had since she moved away.

"How are the aunts, uncles, and cousins?" Lake asks.

Sylvia replies, "Your aunts and uncles are all good. Everyone's busy and doing well. All but one of your cousins have left the county for bigger and better things. Cousin Kate married that boy she dated in high school, and they're expecting. They bought a little place close to his parents, and she seems real happy. They just found out they're having a boy."

Lake's cousin Kate was the sweet, quiet cousin who always kept to herself. A year younger than Lake, she attended a different school, so the two of them were never really that close, but they did play together when the families gathered for holidays or the annual Myerses' family reunion.

It's hard to be away from family and the place she grew up, but when Lake does go back, she's always grateful for the life she's made for herself in the city. Lake's mind jumps to Damon and Bruno, and she reminds her parents that Damon will be joining them for dinner the next day.

"My friend Damon recommended the place we're going for dinner tomorrow night. He knows one of the managers, and he insisted on taking care of the reservations. I've never been there before, but people rave about it."

"It sounds wonderful, but you know your dad and I are fine with whatever place you choose," says Sylvia.

"I know that," says Lake. "I only have a couple nights with you, which is why I planned a casual dinner at home with just us tonight. Tomorrow you two can relax, maybe have a cup of coffee out here in the morning while I make breakfast. We can pretend that we're all locals and take the train downtown. I'll show you where I'm going to school, and we can walk by the Capitol Building, where I work. We can eat lunch in the area, or we can eat here at the house."

"It's a shame the Capitol Building is closed on the weekend. Your dad's been reading up on your city's history. Did you know the building you work in is the third of its kind? There were two others that served as state houses before they were torn down."

Lake looks at her mom, impressed that her parents care enough to learn about the city's rich history. "I have heard that. Maybe next time, you guys can plan to be here on a weekday, and I'll give you a tour of the building and the museum."

Jack perks up at the mention of touring the Capitol Building. "I think we could arrange for a weekday here if you promise to show us around," he says.

"I for sure will do that, Dad."

Sylvia's hand goes up to Jack's shoulder, and she gives it a squeeze. Lake has watched her mom do this since she was a little girl, and it never fails to make her feel warm and content.

Turning her attention back to Lake, Sylvia asks, "So, tell us again how you met Damon? You two seem to spend an awful lot of time together."

One day with her parents, and Lake has reverted back to being a thirteen-year-old girl. Solely for her mom's benefit, she rolls her eyes exaggeratedly and says, "I met Damon through a friend at school.

He's an artist who lives close by, and we're just good friends—best friends, actually."

Her dad rarely gets involved in these mother-daughter exchanges, but he feels the need to make his opinion heard. "You're a smart, attractive woman living alone in the city, Lake. I can tell you from experience that it's hard for men to have a friendship with girls such as yourself. When I met your mom, she wasn't interested in me one bit. 'Let's just be friends,' she said, and I agreed to play along because I saw it as a way to spend time with her. But don't you think for one second that I didn't want more. It took a lot of sweet talk and persuading, but your old dad eventually wore her down."

Her mom shakes her head and takes her dad's hand. The two stroll hand in hand along the sidewalk next to Lake, swinging their arms like a pair of schoolkids. The last time Lake held hands like that with a woman was when she and Kingston were still together. They had driven up to the mountains for the weekend and gone for a hike. They were on the way back to the car when it started to rain. Kingston took hold of her hand, and together, they ran to the little wood shelter at the head of the hiking trail. They were both soaking wet and laughing by the time they made it to the small patch of concrete under the shelter. As they stood there waiting for the rain to let up, Kingston tenderly brushed the clumps of wet hair away from her face, kissed her sweetly, and said, "I love you."

Her parents never asked about Kingston, which stung a little. They'd been together for more than three years. She'd spent time on the ranch, slept in their home, and met most of the Myers family.

When Lake confronts them on this, they beg it off. Looking to his wife for guidance, her dad sits quietly.

Sylvia responds, "Your dad and I respect your privacy, Lake. We know that you and Kingston split up, and there must be a reason why, but it's not our business. We figure you'll tell us if you want us to know."

Whatever. They're in front of her house now.

Shaking her head, Lake unlocks the door, and her parents follow her inside.

"I loved her," says Lake sadly. "And we split up because Kingston wants a family. She offered to build us a bigger home, and she wanted to have kids."

Sylvia says, "I'm sorry that it didn't work out for you and Kingston. But how would that work? You're both women."

Lake can feel the rage building inside her.

Louder than she means to, Lake says, "Exactly, Mom. It can't work. We are two women who love each other, but we can't get married, and we can't make a baby."

Sylvia chooses not to respond to that. Lake can see that she's made her parents uncomfortable, and she feels bad for reacting the way she did. None of this is their fault.

"I'm sorry for getting angry and yelling at you, Mom. Sometimes I just get mad at how things are. I saw Kingston at the store not too long ago. She was with another woman, and it hurt me to see her so happy with someone else."

Lake's dad has always been better at understanding her, and he speaks up. "I've never had to deal with heartbreak because your mom's always been there for me. But I can imagine how awful I would feel if something happened, and she wasn't there. I hope you're not too grown up for a hug, kiddo, 'cause I'm coming in."

Lake smiles and meets her dad halfway. His shirt absorbs the tears in her eyes, and she does her best to think happy thoughts and keep more from falling. The thing that pops into her head is an image of Damon painting in her backyard, Bruno sleeping at his feet.

Lake has never confided in her parents about Damon's sexuality. It's not her story to tell, and honestly, she's a little nervous that they'll pass judgment before meeting him. He's her plus-one for dinner tomorrow. Jack and Sylvia can form their own opinions of her best friend over a prime cut of birthday beef.

In an effort to smooth things over and avoid going to bed with any hurt feelings, Sylvia asks Lake if she has anyone special in her life now.

"School and work take up most of my time. I don't really go out much, but when I do, I hang out with Damon and his dog, Bruno."

Jack and Sylvia exchange a look, but she's too tired to acknowledge it or push back.

Lake's dad realizes she caught the look and says, "Your mom tells me school is going well. Says you have a real shot at making law review. That's amazing, kiddo. We're all so proud of you."

"Thanks, Dad. If it hadn't been for you and Mom, and the money that Kiki and Gramps left for me, I'd probably still be working for the senator full-time, trying to figure out my next move."

Jack gives her a slow, knowing wink and asks, "Do you have any kindling for that firepit? I'm ready to go sit out there and enjoy a beer by the fire."

Chapter 32

*D*amon is on his best behavior at dinner, and Lake's parents seem drawn to his Midwest charm. Unlike the version he shared with Lake when they first met, he only shares the fun, G-rated version of his life story, completely omitting any details that might lead them to believe he's not heterosexual and completely in love with their daughter.

The mischievous grin is a permanent fixture on Damon's face throughout dinner. And at the end of the story, he says, "I knew the first time I laid eyes on this little peach that it would only be a matter of time before she'd be my better half."

Lake rolls her eyes and says out loud, "You're killing me!"

Jack smiles and gives her a smug "dad look." *See, I told you, men have a hard time with friendship with women.*

It's been a delightful evening, and Lake sees no point in calling bullshit on Damon, so she doesn't. He hasn't lied once to her parents this evening. He simply omitted big, significant chunks of his life's story, but he's never fibbed. Maybe the next time she goes home, she'll invite Damon to tag along. Who knows what a few days with Jack and Sylvia will reveal?

When the meal is over, Damon is the perfect gentleman. He gives Lake a heartfelt hug and a kiss on the cheek before helping her in the truck.

"It was a pleasure meeting you both. I have to run home and let Bruno out, but I do hope to see you again."

Leaning forward in the truck, Sylvia waves and says, "The pleasure was ours, Damon. Take care now."

#

With her parents back in Ohio, life resumes to its normal state of high gear. Year two of school is kicking Lake's butt, and Paulette has become her new school bestie. At the beginning of the semester, Paulette forms a new study group and asks Lake if she wants to join.

"You were smart to steer clear of the last study group. There were way too many chefs in the kitchen, and we didn't get shit done. Most of the time we sat around bitching about class or the professors. One day I was complaining about Professor Ward and called him Professor Sketch—that was a big hit, it really stuck. Anyway, if you join, it will just be the four of us. Me, you, Cato from Sketch's class, and Olive."

Lake likes the sound of that. Olive is a brilliant student, and she'll be a great addition to the group.

"I could use a different perspective and would welcome the feedback. When do you guys meet?" asks Lake.

"I think to start, we'll for sure meet once a week on Thursday afternoons. If we need to meet more often, we might do Tuesdays, too."

"That works for me," Lake says.

"Cool. If we can stay on track and pull the grades we need, Cato's going to throw a small party at his parents' cabin up north. Just the four of us."

It's been too long since Lake has been to the mountains, and she misses it. A couple days of hiking and breathing the clean, cool air would be amazing, and knowing that she got there because her study group made the grades would be the best.

#

"It's not fair," whines Damon. "Paulette sees you practically every day, and now you tell me that you're going away with her for the weekend? We always spend the weekend after the semester ends together. This is total and utter bullshit."

"C'mon, Damon, you know I love you the most, and if I could stow you away in my duffel, I would. But this weekend is only for our study group. Cato's parents have a cabin up north, and they made him swear it will be just the four of us. Besides, there's only three bedrooms. Paulette and I are sharing a room with twin beds. I haven't slept in a twin bed or been forced to share a room with anyone since I was, like, ten. My sister, Jeanne, and I shared a room up until she was in middle school. After my grandparents were killed, Pete moved down to the basement, and Jeanne got his room. It's going to be weird sharing a room with Paulette. I hope she doesn't snore."

For a minute, Damon is quiet, and Lake can tell he's thinking about Kiki and Gramps. One night when he and Bruno were sleeping over, I'd told him the story about how I got my name, and he thought it was the coolest thing he'd ever heard.

"I love your mom and dad. Especially your dad! He's a silver fox, and he's a horse rancher, c'mon! I could name like five pornos right now where the main character is basically your dad, and he's way better looking."

"Okay, ew. This is my dad you're talking about."

"Whatever, Mary. Do I dare say what's in your nightstand drawer?" asks Damon.

"Now, that's crossing a line, and it's totally different. My movie basically takes place in an auto repair shop."

"Well, I still love your dad. He was the one who named you Lake. I have to love him by default."

"True. It is a great story, and he's the best dad ever. But the real protagonist in my life story is my grams, Kiki Adele Myers," declares Lake.

"Ooooh, I feel another good tale a'brewing. Tell me all about her."

An hour and a half later, I close the chronicles of my youth with the unexpected death of Kevin and Kiki Myers.

"What the F, Lake! That's way sadder than the lame-ass tale of my days on the farm! I'm pissed that you waited this long to lay all that on me, but in a way, not so much."

Seeing the hurt look on her face, Damon softens his tone and says, "It's not your fault, hon. I hate that you lost your grandparents at such a young age. That sucks, but it explains a lot, like why you're so driven and why there's very little room for gray in your life."

Sharing that story has drained every ounce of energy from Lake, and she wants to move on. "You're all the color I need, handsome."

#

"Well, I hope she does snore—loud! And I hope it keeps you up all night! You deserve it for abandoning me all weekend, leaving me to fend for myself." Damon has his tail in a tizzy, and Lake wonders if there's more to it than her going away for the weekend without him.

"What the hell is wrong with you?" she asks. "It's two days! And I deserve this time away, Damon!" says Lake in a loud voice.

Damon looks hurt, and she immediately feels bad. *Oh my gosh, what if he's sick and she's acting like an inconsiderate, entitled little monster?*

"Sorry, D. I shouldn't have gone off on you like that. Is everything okay?"

Damon looks like the kid who is caught with his hand in the cookie jar.

"Everything's good. I'm fine. I'm the one who should apologize, my little honey butter biscuit. I've really missed you, and I was looking forward to the end of your semester."

"Get over here, you big, beautiful goofball. I wasn't lying when I said I love you the most. I'm giving you and Bruno at least three nights next week, and we're going to tear it up," says Lake as she goes in for the hug.

#

Cato has a large SUV and offers to drive the group to the mountains, and since all four of them live in the same general part of town, he picks each up from their houses. Door-to-door service and a free stint in the mountains—all Lake has to do is kick back and enjoy herself!

Paulette brings a half-dozen donuts for the ride, and all four are soon hopped up on sugar and caffeine. Olive suggests a game of I Spy, and the drive up is amusing and scenic. As sweet as he is, Cato is also uber-competitive. He takes the game seriously and points at and guesses all kinds of crazy things, but it's a good strategy. When he pulls into the circular driveway, he's got more correct guesses under his belt than anyone else.

"I win!" he yells as he turns off the ignition.

Paulette is up front riding shotgun and says, "Damn, Cato. This place is amazing."

"Thanks. My mom and her twin sister, Helen, are very close. Aunt Helen and her husband, Jerry, live up in Tennessee, so the sisters don't get to see each other as often as they'd like. A few years back, my parents went in with my aunt and uncle and had this place built so the families could meet up here. Aunt Helen and Uncle Jerry have a son, and I'm an only child, hence, the twin beds in the one bedroom. C'mon, I'll show you around, and you all can get settled in your rooms."

414

When Lake enters the cabin, the first thing she notices is the view. The two-story cabin has a large set of sliding-glass doors off the main floor that provide an unobscured view of the greenery and mountains. She could sit out back all weekend staring off into the trees and be happy as a clam. It's easy to picture two families enjoying the holidays here. The main level has a nicely appointed kitchen with breakfast bar and a dining room with seating for ten. There's a great room with a TV and a whole wall of built-in shelves full of books, puzzles, and games. A massive, floor-to-ceiling stone fireplace is the focal point of the room.

Cato takes the main bedroom upstairs, which has a large, en suite bath. Olive takes the second bedroom, which also has an en suite bath. Paulette and Lake are in the third bedroom with the twin beds. No en suite for them, but there is a large hall bath with double sinks, which is nice.

"Let me show you around back," says Cato. "It's my favorite part of the property."

Out back is a flagstone walkway leading up to a small clearing in the woods and a private six-person hot tub.

"There's a trailhead about a hundred yards in that direction. It's just a loop a little over a mile long, but it's a pretty walk, and I always see interesting wildlife along the way."

The air smells like damp moss, wet tree trunks, and pine. Lake closes her eyes, takes a deep breath, and is transported back to the woods of her youth. Her early years might have been marred by a tragedy or two, but for the most part, her life on the ranch was independent and idyllic. Being surrounded by nature from an early age left an unerasable, good mark on her that will remain the rest of her life.

Lake jumps when Paulette interrupts the ephemeral sounds of their arboreal environment by blurting out, "What time is dinner?"

Paulette is a city kid.

"We need to make a run to the grocery store and get what we want for meals. If everyone's okay with it, I thought we could do chicken on the grill tonight, and tomorrow I'll grill up some burgers," says Cato.

Everyone nods in agreement.

"Cool, we can get some potato salad from the deli to go with the chicken and maybe some chips for the burgers," he says.

More nods from the ladies.

Cato looks relieved. "Alright. We're good to go for the dinner meals. We just need to pick up some breakfast foods, drinks, and snacks. I can grill some extra chicken to have for lunch. We can do chicken salad or something."

Olive seems excited. "I haven't had chicken salad since I was a kid. We need to get some veggies, too. We can throw them on the grill in some tin foil for a healthy side option."

Cato gives Olive a quick wink and seems embarrassed when he realizes Lake saw it. Aw, Cato likes Olive. Lake looks at Cato in a way that says, *Don't worry, buddy, I got you*, and he seems to get it.

It's still early when they get back from the store, and Lake decides to check out the trail Cato mentioned earlier.

"I'm going to take a walk. Does anyone want to come?"

Paulette says she's going to sit outside with a glass of wine and read. "I brought a trashy romance novel, and I intend to finish it before we get back."

"I'm going to stay and help Cato put away the groceries and get ready for dinner," says Olive. "You go explore the trail and let us know what you think. If you like it and you want to go again, I'll join you in the morning after coffee."

"Okay, I'll go and report back," says Lake. "Are there any bears up here, Cato?"

From over his shoulder, Cato says, "I've heard there are, but I've never seen one. I did see a coyote once, but that was years ago. I mostly just see squirrels this time of day."

"I'm okay with squirrels. Hopefully, that's all I see," says Lake.

Lake is careful to watch where she's going. The last things she needs is to get lost in the woods. Helpfully, the trail and the path leading up to it are well worn from years of Cato's family making their way around it. No longer concerned about losing her way, Lake lets go of all her worries and opens her heart and mind to the soft ground and delicate folds of nature and the forest that surround her. This is a world where time doesn't matter, and she's in no hurry to be anywhere but the present.

#

The cabin kitchen is fully stocked, and Cato makes a mean marinade for the chicken that makes it tangy and juicy. When Lake and Kingston were together, she rarely cooked, and she never learned to grill.

"This may be the best chicken I've ever had," says Lake. "Where'd you learn to grill like this?"

Cato takes a swig of his beer and says, "My dad and Uncle Jerry act like pit bosses when they're hear. You name it, they can grill it. I've spent a lot of time hanging out with them and have picked up a few things. I'm not much of an inside cook, but I do know my way around a grill."

"Yeah, you do," says Paulette. "This is some really tasty bird, man. Good job."

"It's cool to have you all here. Thanks for inviting me to join your study group. Here's to another semester of law school behind us."

"I'll drink to that," says Paulette.

They all take a drink, and Cato says, "I know it's kind of corny, but we have like every board game ever made here. You guys want to play a game of something after dinner?"

Olive says, "I don't think that's corny. I love board games."

"I like them, too," says Lake. "C'mon, I'll help with the dishes before I kick all of you all's butts."

Paulette shoots Lake and the others a look and says, "I'd love to help clean up, but I need to drop a bomb in the bowl. I'll meet you back here in ten."

Lake watches Paulette clomp down the hall toward the bathroom and thinks how lucky she is to be sharing a room with her.

#

To her surprise, Lake sleeps later than expected the next morning, and it takes a few seconds for her to adjust to the sights and sounds of the room. Paulette doesn't snore, but she does make a weird wheezing noise when she sleeps. Lake casually rolls over and almost falls out of bed. She silently curses her crib's lack of width as she quickly readjusts and calms herself.

She thinks of Olive having the queen-sized bed in the room next door all to herself and wonders if she actually slept in it. Paulette is completely oblivious of the blossoming romance between Olive and Cato, but Lake can see what's happening and is happy for them. They make a cute pair and if they're able to find love, happiness, or both together, who is she to question it? Still, it would be nice to call dibs on the bed if Olive isn't using it.

Shit! I have to get up and leave this room to go pee, thinks Lake. Dibs on the bed with access to an adjoining bathroom would be flipping brilliant right about now.

Careful not to rouse the wheezing beast, Lake eases her body from the miniature bed and tiptoes to the door. Standing by the frame with her hand on the knob, she presses her ear to the door. The house seems quiet. She turns the knob slowly and opens the door just wide enough to make it through. The door to Olive's room is closed, but Cato's door is open about a foot. When she passes by his room, she can see that he's not in his bed. Lake uses the restroom and walks lightly to the kitchen.

Cato is at the table drinking coffee. "Good morning," he says.

"Good morning. I thought I smelled coffee, but I wasn't sure," says Lake.

"I made a whole pot. Mugs are in the cupboard next to the sink."

"Are we the only ones up?" asks Lake.

Cato gives a nod toward the back of the house and says, "Yeah. I guess our late game night was just too much for those two."

"Could be. Or maybe they're feeling more stress-free here at your little oasis in the woods, and they just need to catch up on their sleep?"

"I hope so," answers Cato. "This place has that effect on most people, which is why I suggested it in the first place."

"Well, I'm glad you did. I'm having a great time."

"I know you and Olive talked about going for a walk after coffee, but I know some really great hiking trails if you want to do something different," says Cato.

Lake responds, "I'm always up for anything outdoors."

#

Lake was the last to get picked up, and she is the first to get dropped off when they get back to the city. Cato grabs her bag from the back and sets it at her feet. Unexpectedly, Lake hugs him tight, holding on longer than she means to, but he doesn't seem to mind.

"Thanks so much for this weekend," she says. "I hadn't realized I was wound so tight until just now. I feel a hundred pounds lighter."

"I'm glad to hear that 'cause in a week it's back to research and reading till our heads are about to explode." Cato uses his hands to illustrate simultaneous explosions on both sides of his head.

In response, Lake presses her hands together, fingers pointed up to express hope and gratitude. "I choose to hold on to the inner peace and will not think or speak of such matters until that day comes," she says. "Now, please, go and enjoy your week!"

Chapter 33

Lake tosses her keys in the bowl next to the front door and plops down on the couch in her absolutely quiet little bungalow. Soaking up the serenity like a sponge, she's full to the brim. Her eyes move around the room and land on the phone. She needs to call Damon—she's missed his silly mug!

She dials his number, but he doesn't answer. *That's odd. Maybe he's out walking Bruno.* Lake decides to unpack and start a load of laundry; she'll try him again in a little while.

Thirty minutes later, she dials Damon's digits for a second time. After an unknown number of rings, she clicks the receiver, and the fear starts creeping in. After a few seconds, she tries him again. No answer. *Where the hell is he?*

She hits redial and lets the phone ring ten times before clicking the receiver and hitting the redial button again. After a dozen more tries, she's no closer to reaching him.

With her anxiety level on the rise, she grabs her keys out of the bowl and makes the short drive to Damon's place.

She rings the doorbell, which sets Bruno off. From out in the hallway, Lake does her best to console him.

"Hey, buddy, where's your dad? Where's Damon?"

Bruno begins to whine, and Lake's heart breaks in two.

She pounds on the door and Bruno starts barking again. Shit! She can't keep getting him riled up like this, but she has no idea how else to get Damon to the door.

After a few minutes of talking to Bruno through the door, Damon's nosy next-door neighbor opens her door just enough to complain about the dog.

"Where's that boy been all night? That poor dog's been crying and barking on and off since early this morning. It started about four a.m., and it's been going on ever since," she gripes.

The woman's words create an immediate sense of doom in Lake's mind. Her high-stress response is activated, and the hair on the back of her neck stands up.

The spare key to Damon's place is hanging on a hook in her kitchen. She's so freaked out about what could be waiting for her behind his door, she's afraid to drive. The super's apartment is one floor above where's she's standing, so Lake yells to Bruno, "I'm coming, buddy. I'll be back for you in just a few minutes."

Lake is the annoying girl who rings the doorbell to the super's place impatiently while banging on the door. He finally answers the door, and she quickly explains why she's there.

The super has seen her going to and from Damon's place many times before, and he knows the two are close. He agrees to open the door for her, but he tells her she has to wait in the hall while he goes in. "I'll take a look around the place and let you know if I see anything suspicious," he says.

The moment he pushes the door open, Bruno runs into the hallway. He's got his leash in his mouth and is prancing around Lake. Damon taught him the leash trick, and Lake knows Bruno has to go potty.

"I'm going to take Bruno for a quick walk. I'll be right back," she calls to the super.

When she gets back, the super is standing in the hall outside of Damon's apartment. "He isn't home, and from the looks of it, he hasn't been here for a while." Pointing at Bruno, he says, "Your buddy there made a mess in the hall. I didn't want it to damage the wood floor, so I cleaned it up."

Lake is scared and confused. "Thank you for doing that. I'm sure Damon will appreciate it."

"No problem. I've known the little guy since he was a pup."

Lake decides to take Bruno back to her place until she figures out where Damon is. He would never leave Bruno home alone all night on purpose. Something is definitely not right.

When she gets back to her place, she sets out food and water for the dog. Bruno and Damon are here so often, he has all the comforts of home at her place, too. He even has a big, fluffy dog bed in the hall closet, which she pulls out for him.

It's a cool, sunny day, and Lake opens the back door, giving Bruno full access to the yard in case he needs to go potty again or wants to lie in the sun.

She feels completely helpless. She has no idea how to locate her best friend. His cell goes straight to voice mail, and she's already confirmed he's not at his place. Before she left his apartment, she asked the woman next door for a Post-it Note. She wrote a quick note to let Damon know Bruno is with her and that he needs to call or come over as soon as he sees her note.

She knows it's only been twenty minutes, but she hasn't heard from Damon, so she knows he hasn't been home to see the note.

Instead of sitting idle, Lake starts calling everyone she knows who may know Damon. No one has seen or heard from him. Tears form in her eyes, and then she remembers the guy from the steakhouse. The night of her birthday, Damon had mentioned something about hooking up with him on occasion. What the hell was his name?

She closes her eyes and tries to picture the man Damon introduced to her. *W*, it starts with a *W*. Winston, maybe? Wyatt? Then she remembers—it's William! Lake looks up the number for the steakhouse and makes the call. A perky young voice answers.

"Yes, William is working this afternoon. Please hold."

After what seems like an eternity, William picks up. "Good afternoon, this is William, how may I help you?"

"Hi, William. My name is Lake Myers. I had dinner at your restaurant a few months ago with Damon. I've been trying to get in touch with him, and no one seems to know where he is. I was hoping you could help."

"Does Damon have a last name?" he asks.

"I'm sorry, yes. His name is Damon Jackson," she says.

William is quiet for a moment. When he responds, his tone is softer, less formal. "You said you've been trying to reach Damon, and he's not responding?"

"Yes, but I'm worried. His cell goes straight to voice mail, and he wasn't answering his home phone, so I drove to his place earlier. When I rang the bell, Bruno, his dog, was really upset. The neighbor told me he had been whining and barking all night. I got scared and had the super check out the apartment. Damon wasn't there, and Bruno had messed on the floor. Damon would never leave Bruno like that. I took Bruno back to my place and left a note for Damon on his door, but I haven't heard back from him."

"When was the last time you spoke with Damon?"

"Friday, right before I went out of town. He was upset because I was leaving, and we made a plan to get together today, after I got back. I first called him around two o'clock this afternoon."

"It's been about a week since I last spoke with him," says William.

Lake's heart sinks. She'd really been hoping William knew something. Anything.

He asks, "Have you tried any of his friends?"

"I only know how to get in touch with a handful of people who might know where he is. I tried all of them before I called you. No one knows anything," says Lake.

"May I ask whom you called?" says William.

Lake rattles off a few names.

"I know all but one of those people. Damon and I have a few other mutual friends, and I know a couple of the bartenders at the club he likes. Let me make a few calls and see what I can find out. What's the best number to reach you at, Lake?"

Lake gives William her cell and home numbers.

"Give me thirty minutes or so, and I'll call you back," says William.

#

Twenty minutes later, Lake's cell rings. It's a local number she doesn't recognize. "Hello?"

"Hi, Lake. It's William."

His voice is flat, emotionless. This can't be good. Lake takes a deep breath and waits for him to continue.

"I spoke with one of the bartenders at the club. He said Damon was there last night. He was with a group of people dancing and partying. They left just before closing. He didn't have all the details, but he said there was a fight about a block away from the club and he thinks

Damon might have been involved. Someone called an ambulance, there was blood. He isn't sure who's blood it was or how bad the person was injured. He thinks they were headed to Grady."

"Oh no," says Lake.

"I'm sorry, Lake. I wish I had more information for you. I haven't called the hospital, but you might start there. It's almost time for the restaurant to open, but I want to know what you find out. Damon and I were together for a while, and I still really care about him. This is my cell. Will you call and let me know how he is when you find out, please?"

"Of course, I'll let you know. I had no idea what to do next. I really appreciate your help, William. Thank you," says Lake.

Her hands are shaking as she calls the hospital. After several transfers, Lake is able to confirm that Damon had been admitted early that morning. He's in the intensive care unit.

Lake is on the verge of a total breakdown, but now is not the time. She has to keep her shit together long enough to get to the hospital. She closes her eyes, takes a deep breath, and counts to ten.

When she opens her eyes, Bruno is next her. She forgot she left the door open for him to come and go as he pleased. The way he's looking at her, it's almost as if he knows she's upset.

Lake wraps her arms around him and nuzzles his neck. He's a big boy, soft and warm.

"I found your dad, buddy. I'm gonna go see him and tell him that you miss him, okay?"

Lake kisses Bruno's head before standing up. She checks his water dish to make sure it's not empty, then walks to the back door and shuts it.

When she turns around, Bruno is right there at her heels.

She pats his head, grabs her keys, and says, "Stay off the couch, okay, buddy?"

#

Lake has driven past the hospital more times than she can remember, but she's never had a reason to go inside until today. The place is massive, and there are people everywhere. She follows the signs to the reception desk and receives instruction on where to go and what to do. Lake feels like she's in a real-life version of the game Mouse Trap. After passing through a maze of corridors, two elevators, more long hallways, and several double doors, she finally arrives at Damon's room.

Peering through the small plate-glass window, she sees a badly beaten man lying in the bed. His eyes are closed. This can't be him, right? There's no way that's him.

Lake enters the room and approaches the bed. Standing next to the man, she's able to see both of his hands. Damon has a small, intricate tattoo of a compass on the back of his left hand between his thumb and forefinger. This man she doesn't recognize has the same tattoo.

Lake's breath catches, and she loses it. The tears come fast, and her nose begins to run. She wipes her face with the back of her hand and looks around for a tissue. *What happened to you, Damon?* Out loud she asks, "Who did this to you?"

She spots a box of tissues on the other side of the bed and is walking over to pull one out when she hears a weak voice. "Didn't catch their names," says Damon.

Relief floods through her body. When she turns to look at him, Damon is half smiling.

He's awake. He knows who I am. He's going to be okay.

For the next few hours, Damon is heavily sedated and is asleep more than he's awake. Visiting hours are over at eight, and Lake is forced to leave. She kisses him lightly on the shoulder and tells him she'll be back in the morning.

\#

Over the next couple of days, she gets bit and pieces of the story from Damon. She was out of town, and he was bored, so he went to the club. He was having a good time dancing, and he picked up a few late-night revelers to join in the hijinks. One of them, an artist friend of Damon's named Enid, is a trans woman who runs with the creative crowd. She's a master stained-glass artist, and several of her pieces are currently on display in one of the local galleries. Enid got hungry and suggested they go out for a bite.

They had settled their tab and were halfway around the block when a group of good old boys started in on Enid, taunting and calling her names. Damon stepped in to defend her, and fists started flying. He was basically wiping the floor with the lead fuckhead of the group when his buddies jumped in and pounded the ever-living shit out of Damon. Someone called the cops; the guy whom Damon got the better of pulled out a knife and his guys held Damon while the jerk stabbed him. They heard sirens in the distance, pushed Damon to the ground, and left him for dead.

It angers Lake to see Damon lying broken in this hospital bed for no reason other than being a standup guy.

"How's Bruno?" he asks.

"He misses you. But Auntie Lake is taking good care of him. He's having fun chasing birds and butterflies in the backyard," she says.

Damon smiles and asks, "Where is he sleeping? Please tell me you're not letting him sleep in the bed."

Lake has tried keeping Bruno on the floor, but she caved the first time he stood with his front paws up on the bed and stared into her soul with those big brown eyes of his.

Lake scratches her head and looks away.

"Damn it, Mary! You know I don't like him in the bed. I spent a fortune on his bed—he needs to sleep in it," says Damon.

Lake smiles when he calls her Mary.

"You think this is funny," he asks.

"Noooo. Don't be mad. Bruno's sad, and so am I. We both just miss you."

The scowl fades as his expression softens. He looks terrible. The bruises on his face are changing colors, which makes things seem worse than they probably are, but there's something else going on. His eyes aren't as alert as they have been.

She wants to ask if he's okay, but clearly, he's not. He's said more today than he has the past two days combined. He's probably just tired.

"Do you want to watch TV?" she asks.

"Sure," is all he says.

Lake turns on the set and flips through the channels. Damon offers no direction, so she chooses a talk show that neither of them is all that interested in. They sit together in silence through the news, through dinner, which he ate none of, and through more news.

It's an hour before visiting hours are over, and Damon is fast asleep. Lake kisses him lightly on the forehead, pulls the covers up over his chest, and leaves.

When she arrives the next morning, she's asked to wait outside of Damon's room. A few minutes later, a doctor and two nurses emerge from his room. Lake looks from one face to the other for any kind of news. She recognizes one of the nurses from earlier in the week and asks, "Is everything alright? Is Damon okay?"

The woman looks at her and replies, "Damon's developed an infection. We're keeping an eye on him."

Lake knows his immune system is already compromised. Can his body fight off this infection? She wonders if the staff here know that Damon's HIV-positive. It's strange to think about it. Surely, they're aware.

Lake begins to cry as she watches the woman walk down the hall. She stands there motionless, fixated on the woman's backside until she's so far away her limbs are no longer discernible. She looks like a slow-moving dot that eventually disappears.

Lake turns her head so that she can see Damon lying in his bed. As the salty droplets slip from her eyes and slide down her face, she thinks about the many sad tales they've shared and the tears that they've shed. Lost years and buckets of tears.

#

When Damon told Lake that he was HIV-positive, her first instinct had been to cry because she couldn't imagine living her life without him in it. Sweet Damon had assured her he was handling it and that he would always be by her side.

The confession about his diagnosis had been shared at a time when hundreds of thousands of gay men were still dying of AIDS each year. Damon opened a whole sad, new world of gay to Lake. Before meeting him, she had only heard of one or two friends of friends who were infected or had died of the virus. It was never anyone she knew personally—until now.

She can't let him see her crying like this. She takes another look through the small window in his door and can see that his eyes are closed. She decides to take a walk around the block to clear her head before she visits him.

#

When she gets back to his room, he's asleep. Lake pulls her chair as close to the bed as she can possibly get it. It hasn't even been twenty-four hours since she'd last seen Damon, but he looks as though he's aged ten years. His bruised, black-and-blue face has started to turn a horrible greenish color, and it is still badly swollen.

Lake is due back in class in just a few days, but she hasn't decided for sure if she'll return. She is still waiting to see if Damon will be discharged and what kind of care he will require. With everything up in the air, Lake is distracted and fidgety. She reaches into her bag, pulls out a thick text, and begins reading out loud.

Damon is out of it most of the day, so Lake keeps at it. When she looks up at the clock, it's quarter past one in the afternoon. Bruno needs to be let out, and she's hungry. She studies Damon's face, watches as his eyes dance behind his lids, and wonders if he'll ever dance at the club again.

Lake quickly runs home, lets the dog out, and grabs a sandwich. When she gets back, nothing has changed. She gives Damon's hand a squeeze and goes back to her reading. After another hour or so, she's in the middle of a sentence when she hears him say, "That is the worst, most boring shit I've ever heard."

Lake laughs and looks at him. "Hey. How are you feeling?" she asks.

Damon doesn't answer, which tells her he's not good. He can be bitchy and short-tempered at times, but he's never deliberately cruel or evasive. He avoids answering Lake's question because he legit feels terrible and he knows telling her this will be hard for her to hear.

"So, you don't like hearing arguments about the law?" she asks. "I tried to smuggle in some smut, but they confiscated it at the door."

This elicits an attempt at a smile. Seeing him struggle at this simple response pains Lake.

In a barely audible voice, Damon says, "I need you to call my mom."

Without realizing it, Lake moves her head from side to side. It's the tiniest of movements, but it doesn't escape Damon. "Yes," he says.

Lake looks at him and thinks, *I have no idea how to get in contact with your mom. I don't even know her name*

As usual, he's a step ahead of her. Slowly, he raises his hand and points to the stand next to the bed. Tucked under a coaster is a folded sheet of paper. Lake opens it and can see that Damon has written down his mom's name and phone number.

Written below her information, it says, "Hey, honey pie. If anything happens to me, please take care of Bruno. And go back to class. I don't want you here feeling sorry for me. Damon." Next to his name, he's drawn a heart.

When she looks up at him, his head is turned toward hers, and he whispers, "Please."

Lake is about to lose it for the second time today. Blinking fast, she tilts her head up. This can't be happening.

Damon is lying there with his eyes glued to her every move. She looks at him and stands, tears streaming down her face. She squeezes his hand, walks out of the room, and heads for her truck.

She considers calling Mrs. Celine Jackson from her truck but thinks it will be better to call her from her house. During the short drive back to her place, she tries to come up with the right words to say. When she pulls into her driveway, she has no idea how the conversation will go.

Lake is on her couch, and Bruno's head is resting in her lap. She punches all but the last digit into the phone. She rubs the soft tip of Bruno's ear, and he raises his head to look at her. It's like he's saying, *"It's okay, I'm right here."*

She takes a deep breath and punches the last number.

#

Celine senses the urgency in Lake's voice and makes the trip to Atlanta the next morning. Lake is at the hospital when Mrs. Jackson arrives. With every hour that passes, Damon grows weaker. His body is not responding to the antibiotics.

Damon's mother is a stoic woman. She knows that her son had been beaten and stabbed while defending someone else, but that is all the detail Lake is willing to give. Damon's mom should know that her son is a good man who doesn't deserve the hand he was dealt as a result of being honorable.

Lake isn't sure if she should embrace the woman standing next to her or not. The woman says nothing to her, and she takes that as a no. Instead, she extends her hand while introducing herself. Mrs. Jackson is about to shake her hand but withdraws at the last minute. The reaction stings a little and makes her heart hurt for Damon. She can only imagine how tough his life was growing up with this coldhearted witch for a mother.

Lake leaves the room and isn't sure if she should come back later today or wait until tomorrow. Damon's mom has flown here to spend time with her son, and she'd probably appreciate an afternoon alone with him.

Lake picks up a pizza from her favorite place and goes home for the evening. She can't stop thinking about Damon, and she certainly doesn't have the patience or motivation to crack a law book. She's sitting on the couch, completely undecided about what to do, when Bruno walks over to her. He has his leash in his mouth. Decision made.

Lake follows Bruno along side streets and avenues she's never been down before, and when they finally get back to her bungalow, the sun has dipped below the horizon, and the moon is out. She runs a bath with bubbles and sits in the tub until the water turns cold. Bruno is curled up in a ball on the mat in front of the tub, and she almost steps on him when she gets out.

Wrapped in a towel, she lets him out back to do any final business before getting into bed. He barks to let her know when he's ready to come in. She walks through the house shutting off the lights and making sure the doors are locked. When she drags Bruno's bed into her room, he's already up in her bed.

She shakes her head and says, "Who am I kidding, buddy? Just like your dad, I can never say no to you. Hold on."

Lake returns to the living room, grabs the comforter off the back of her couch, and uses it to cover Bruno up, then climbs in next to him. With the blanket over him, he manages to scoot as close to her as his body can get.

The two sigh at the exact same time, and both fall fast asleep.

#

When Lake arrives at the hospital the next morning, Mrs. Jackson is gone. She assumes the woman will return at some point, but she never does. Why did she come at all? Did she come to say good-bye to her youngest son and then leave him to die alone?

What kind of mother does that?

Lake is so preoccupied with her anger that she doesn't notice a new machine next to Damon's bed. He has sepsis, and his organs are failing.

Screw his family, she's not about to call them again, ever.

Lake refuses to leave Damon's side all day, and no one comes to make her go, even when visiting hours are over. Paulette is at her bungalow with Bruno, so there's no reason for her to leave.

In the end, Lake is there with Damon when he takes his last breath. His passing is surreal and absolute.

#

She calls Kingston multiple times but always disconnects before the first ring is complete. It's been well over a year since they last spoke— what would she even say to her? Instead, she calls her parents' number. Her dad picks up after the second ring, and before she can even say hello, Lake begins to cry.

In a shaky voice, she says, "Hi, Dad. Is Mom home?"

Concerned, her dad says that yes, her mom is home. "Are you okay, kiddo? What's going on?"

"I'm okay, Dad, I just need to talk to Mom."

Jack calls for Sylvia, who's close by. Before she comes on the line, he says, "I know you want to talk to your mom, I love you, kiddo."

"I love you, too, Dad."

Lake tells her mom the same story she shared with Damon's mom, and Sylvia listens quietly. Her parents only met Damon the one time, but they know the two were close. Jack and Sylvia both express sadness at his passing and are concerned for their daughter's safety.

"I'll be okay, Mom. I'm rarely out past midnight, and I'm always cautious. Oh, and I have a dog now—a big one. His name is Bruno."

#

The guilt for going away that weekend and the regret Lake carries for how Damon passed sits with her for a long time. She's angry about gay life in this moment, a life that neither she nor Damon chose. Like who in the hell would ever knowingly choose to be gay? Sadly, it's often a life that separates people like her and Damon from so many they love and care for. Without warning, they are the enemy, the hated, the less deserving.

Coming-out stories are like a quilt of many colors. Some of the patches are brilliant, optimistic and depict happy endings; some are neutral, earth tones that illustrate a life placed on hold. Suspended in time. Deferred to another day. Others are light and bright-colored, favorable for continuing, a patch for when those whom we choose to share with are in a better place. As if that will change the outcome or help to make the situation more acceptable. For those who press on, the chances are 50/50 that the story will end well, and the quilt will emerge lively and comforting.

The story ending well is half the battle, a compelling push to continue down the road to acceptance and love for oneself. Although each had been in a different place, Damon and Lake were on the journey together before he died. Now she's out here alone again, and she isn't sure she has any fight left.

Chapter 34 — Bishop

After Damon dies, Lake wanders aimlessly through the days. No matter how much sleep she gets, she's exhausted by the time the sun goes down. Even Bruno is conditioned to get his business done and head for bed when night falls. The two climb into bed, their sides marked by the faint indentions their bodies made during the prior night's slumber.

Damon's dying wish for her had been to return to class, and she has, but her grades are slipping.

Lake should still be awake, reading and preparing her arguments for class, but it's easier to lie down in the dark with Bruno and hide from the world.

Staring up at the ceiling, Lake isn't sure if she should consider it a good thing that in all her years, she's only had to suffer through the loss of three people who were close to her. But in her mind, that's three too many.

#

Paulette and Lake have become close, and because of this new-found, elevated friend status, she feels justified in being unpleasantly honest with Lake, as if she wasn't already.

"I know he was your best friend, but you have got to move beyond the rage stage, bypass depression altogether, and get on with the upward turn. Your grades suck ass, and you'll never make law review if you keep this up."

"You're a sentimental, shining beacon of hope, Paulette. Meeting you was like being given the golden ticket of friendship," says Lake sarcastically.

"You bet your sweet ass it was. You know as well as I do that Damon was the only person in your life with balls big enough to go toe to toe with you. And now that he's gone, I have to be that person."

Lake cocks her head to convey her skepticism, but in her heart she knows Paulette is right.

Everyone else, including her parents, tiptoe around the obvious and continue to blindly support her, even though she's royally screwing things up.

"We all miss him, but nothing will change the fact that he's gone. But you know what? His words live on in that note you have stuck to your refrigerator. He asked you to take of Bruno and you are."

At the mention of his name, Bruno runs to the kitchen from his spot in the sun out back. He circles the table like a shark, pausing for just a second each time he passes by Paulette.

"What the hell is he doing?" she asks.

"He was lying in his spot catching some rays when you blurted out his name. Usually, when we interrupt his sunning, it's time for him to come in and get a treat."

Paulette watches Bruno circle the table a few more times before saying, "For the love of dogs, where do you keep the treats?"

"They're in the cookie jar next to the stove," is Lake's reply.

Paulette acts like it's a huge bother for her to get up, but Lake knows she has a soft spot for Bruno.

"This cookie jar is weirdly phallic and ugly as hell. Why have I never noticed it before?" asks Paulette.

"I have no idea. It's been there in that same spot for as long as I've lived here. It's a vintage, hand-painted mushroom cookie jar from the seventies. My mom gave it to me."

"She probably gave it to you because she couldn't stand to look at it," says Paulette. "I mean, what is up with this lid? These mushroom caps straight-up look like dickheads."

Lake has never really thought about it before, but the mushroom caps do resemble penis heads.

"C'mon, Lake. The handle of this lid is made to resemble dickheads that you pull on to get to whatever goodies you have stored inside the giant shaft. I guarantee a man designed this," she says.

"You're probably right," says Lake. And then she starts laughing.

Paulette takes a treat from the jar and hands it to Bruno. Tail wagging, he takes it gently from her hand and scampers off to eat his treat in the sun.

"What's so funny about this dick jar?" asks Paulette dryly.

"Damon loved that cookie jar. He told me if I ever decided I didn't want it anymore, it was his and no one else could have it," she says between giggles.

Paulette looks up at the ceiling and says, "Thank you, my good man. Even from the heavens, you got my back. You've proven the point better than I ever could." Standing next to Damon's note, she continues, "So you came through here on the first ask and his fur child has officially been adopted. Next, he told you to go back to class. Damon knew how important school is to you, and he supported your choice to pursue the law one hundred percent. He'd be freaking pissed if he could see you now. You're abandoning your dream of straight As and being in control of your future. You need to pull up your big-girl panties and get your head in the game—today!"

Lake wants to hug Paulette for being so candid and real, but she's not an affectionate kind of girl. They've never discussed her personal life, but Lake is under the impression that Paulette is asexual. She's never heard her mention being attracted to anyone—like, her interest in any type of sexual behavior is a negative five on a scale of one to ten. Maybe one day she'll get Paulette to spill the beans about what she does or doesn't like.

"You're a kooky chick, Paulette, but I love ya," says Lake. "You call me out on my shit, just like he did, and you're both right."

Paulette pats herself on the back and says, "I know. Now, do me a favor and show up for study group this week. I'm tired of feeling like the third wheel with Cato and Olive."

#

After her grandparents were killed, Lake had months to work through her grief and anger. Now she's an adult, living on her own, with more responsibility than she'd like, and her healing timeline has been significantly shortened.

When she was eight, her diversion was school. It was the one activity at her disposal that forced her much-needed distraction and sense of connection and normalcy. Normalcy meaning routine, regularity, and the illusion that she is just like everyone else.

Now she's twenty-six, and the diversion of school remains the same. Lake's being is not prepared to move on and accept all that's happened, but it will.

#

She's all-in again. Lake throws herself into school and manages to finish her most difficult semester and earn better-than-satisfactory grades in all her classes. Her accomplishments should make her feel fulfilled, but instead she feels nothing. After she and Kingston broke up, Lake's vision was distorted. Her view of love and the world was broken and glossy, as though she were peering through a kaleidoscope. She was actively working through her split from Kingston when she'd been pressed to deal with Professor Sketchy McPutrid, an experience that left her feeling even more jaded. Lake had been tired and had no interest in dating or intimacy.

Then she'd met Damon. The time she spent with him had been an extraordinary journey through different layers of friendship and deeper levels of affection. Now he's gone, and Lake yearns again for the touch of another woman.

The plan Lake has laid out for herself leaves little room for relationships; they require too much time and energy. No-strings dating and sex are worth considering if it can help her cope with the wicked ways of the world, the pressures of school, and the hole in her heart where Damon used to reside.

Unfortunately, being out means involuntary limitations, and that can be a challenge.

Lake thinks back to how she met the girls in her recent past. She'd met Margot, the college student by day and call girl by night, in a gay bar. She'd met Amy at a bar during a lesbian concert, and she'd met Kingston when she'd accosted her for mowing the grass too early on the weekend. The latter two meetings will be difficult to replicate, which leaves her with only the bar option.

Lake fiercely loves lesbian bars and has had numerous titillating, fun firsts in them, but it stinks to think they're now her best opportunity to find physicality with an attractive, intellectual equal.

Lake channels her sexual frustration and uses it to do a deep clean on her place. Owning a big dog deposits more dirt and hair on the surfaces of her home than she could have imaged. Bruno seems content to watch her scour every inch of the bungalow, but he shifts to astounded and annoyed when Lake confiscates his puffy bed and blankets and tosses them in the wash.

With the house organized, sparkling clean, and fresh smelling, Lake tackles the truck next. Most everything she does is within walking distance, so she rarely drives it, but it's been a while since she'd kicked the tires or had the oil changed. There's a Sears auto center not too far from where she is. For the guy behind the counter, it's love at first sight.

"Your truck's a beaut. They don't make them like that anymore," he says.

"That's what I hear," is Lake's reply. "I've had her since I was sixteen, and I don't take her out much anymore. She mostly just sits in the driveway collecting dust."

The nametag sewn into his gray, one-piece mechanic's uniform displays his name in cursive letters.

"Would you ever consider selling her?" asks Mack.

"You're not the first to ask me that, Mack. Is it okay that I call you that?" asks Lake.

"Of course, it is, young lady. That is my name," he says.

"Cool. You see, Mack, I'm a student on a fixed budget. My truck's paid for, and it's in pretty good shape, so I don't really see any reason to sell her," says Lake.

He fires back at her, "That's smart thinking, which is hard to come by nowadays. People tend to think new is automatically better, and that's not always the case."

The guy reminds Lake of her uncle Rick, an honest, hardworking man. "I couldn't agree with you more, Mack."

Mack grins and pushes a piece of paper across the counter. "This here's an estimate for your services today. We should have you out of here in less than an hour. You're welcome to have a seat in the waiting room. There's a TV and some bad coffee there, if you're interested."

Lake takes a seat by the wall and zones out completely while her truck is being worked on. She's out of projects once this is done, and she is already bored out of her damn mind. She hasn't been out to a bar solo since Savannah, but she needs to satisfy her sexual desires, and the goodies she keeps in the drawer next to her bed aren't enough.

On the drive back to her place, Lake devises a way to meet quality women at the bar. She'll go early, before the clubby strobe light scene kicks into high gear. Her favorite spot has a piano lounge and a chill patio area for women who prefer a less rambunctious space to partake of a beverage and have an actual conversation.

It's a perfect plan, really. Lake can eat dinner, let Bruno have his time in the backyard, get herself ready, and still make it to the bar by nine.

The first few times she goes, the pickings are slim. A lot of the women are couples, out for a drink with their mates in a place where they can be themselves. Lake isn't interested in being with a couple, so she keeps to herself. There are a few other single women at the bar, but none to whom she's attracted. She drove herself to the bar, and she'll need to drive herself home, so she limits herself to two drinks, tops.

Her window to meet someone she's willing to take home is small. She only has two hours to nurse two drinks before the vibe in the place changes completely. Her perfect plan has gone to hell in a handbasket, but she clings to it like a life preserver in rough seas.

When the leaves begin to turn, she has four months' experience with her less-than-perfect plan, and her stats are in the shitter. She's two for twenty-three, which is really, really bad no matter how you slice it. It could be that she's too selective, or maybe the lady bar buffet isn't the right venue for her.

She chose the first woman she brought home because she was charming and witty at the bar. The conversation flowed effortlessly, and she was easy on the eyes. Lake pictured the conversation continuing at her place, wine in hand, a fire in the fireplace casting a warm, sexy glow. She envisioned the tension building to the point they could no longer stand it, forcing them to retreat to the bedroom for hours of hot, passionate sex. But that didn't happen.

Apparently, their banter at the bar was all the woman needed to get her motor going. Once they got to her place, Lake's date didn't utter a single word until an hour later when she said good-bye. Instead of talking to her, the woman stripped, pulled Lake's clothes from her body, pushed her down on the bed, and had her way with her. Then, she rolled off Lake and pushed her down south, her way of communicating the oral part of the evening was now upon them. It was, without a doubt, the worst sexual experience Lake had ever had.

Lake's second experience with a woman she brought home was slightly more satisfying, but overall, it rated well below par. Lake had seen Bambi—not her real name—at the bar a couple times before, and they'd exchanged looks and a few words before Lake invited her back to her place. Things were going well—more like she had imagined the first time going—and Lake was having a terrific time. Bambi was cute, had a great body, and could carry an intelligent conversation. She was four months out of a long-term relationship and hadn't been with anyone since the breakup. Eventually, the two made their way to the bedroom, and the transition was quite pleasant. Bambi was sponta-neous and nimble, a commendable combination in the bedroom.

The night was going better than expected—until the part when Bambi began warming up for her high-pitched orgasm wail-o-rama. At first, Lake thought she might be in pain, but then she realized Bambi was moaning in pleasure. A positive response, so Lake kept going, but the moaning got louder and more annoying. By the time Bambi was climaxing, the moan had turned into a full-on scream, and it was the worst sound Lake had ever heard. Bruno, who was passed out in his bed, in the living room, began howling in concert with the screaming.

Lake was worried that her neighbors might call the cops because they believed someone was being murdered and the only thing she could do to make the screaming stop was kiss Bambi—so she did. Bambi interpreted the move as one of tenderness, and she latched on to Lake's face like there was no tomorrow. Lake went with it, happy to have restored the peace. But then, the next thing she knew, Bambi was sobbing uncontrollably.

Lake went to the bathroom and brought Bambi a handful of Kleenex, but this seemed to intensify the crying, which made Lake super uncomfortable. She didn't want to come across as a heartless shrew, so to get away from the weeping, she kissed Bambi on the forehead and told her she was going to make some tea. Bambi was wearing Lake's favorite robe when she waltzed into the kitchen. Her eyes were swollen and red from all the crying, and her nose was running. While Lake stood there fuming about her robe, Bambi proceeded to tell her how thoughtful and wonderful she was.

"I know this is our first time together, but it was amazing, and I've definitely caught feelings for you," Bambi said.

Lake choked a little on her tea. She didn't want to do or say anything that could be misinterpreted by Bambi, so she just smiled and nodded. To herself, she thought, *I need to get this woman out of my robe—and my house*.

"I don't know about you, but I'm starving. How about you let me buy you a late-night snack? There's a great little pub just a few blocks down," said Lake in her sweetest voice.

"I am kind of hungry," said Bambi with a wink.

"Great, let's get dressed. It's such a nice night, we can walk," said Lake.

The snack ploy worked, but Lake did end up having to spend another two hours with Bambi that night. When they finally got back to her place, Lake made a big show of stretching and yawning.

"Thanks for coming out with me," Lake said. "I have a lot of reading to do tomorrow and a paper to write, so I'm going to hit the hay."

Bambi looked disappointed but didn't push. She added her name and number to Lake's phone contacts, kissed her, and said she looked forward to seeing her again.

Lake smiled and nodded. She had no intention of calling Bambi. The whole point of going to the bar was to meet women, have sex, and possibly date, occasionally.

For Lake, the evening could have ended sooner, but clearly, Bambi wanted more.

Time to lie low and stay clear of the bar for a while.

#

With the Bambi incident burned into her brain, Lake reverts to serious student mode and picks up where the scholastic foursome stopped before she'd gone off in search of some summer "V." It's a less-stressful, more-rewarding role, and she plays the part well.

First week in, and study group is veering off-topic. None of them are anxious to talk shop.

"I heard a new restaurant just opened near the park. Someone was saying the brunch menu is awesome. We should check it out this Sunday," suggests Olive.

Brunch had always been Kingston's thing, but Lake loves it, too. There's something about day drinking on a Sunday that makes it appealing and fun. And the food at brunch always seems to taste better, almost decadent.

"We could use more brunch places near the park. The ones we have are always packed, and the wait for a table is so long. By the time you get seated, you're closer to dinnertime than brunch," says Paulette.

"I don't have any plans for Sunday. Do you know if the place is dog friendly? Can I bring Bruno?" asks Lake.

"I'm sure it is," says Cato. "If it's the place I'm thinking of, they have a huge patio."

"I'll call and ask," says Olive. "If they take reservations, I'll make one for twelve thirty on Sunday. Does that work for everybody?"

They all nod in agreement. With that settled, the group reluctantly shifts the conversation back to the law.

#

The restaurant Olive suggests for brunch is destined to become a favorite of theirs. Lake has been looking forward to brunch all week, and the weather is perfect for an afternoon meal outside. The atmosphere of the relaxed tavern overlooking the park is sophisticated and mellow.

Olive is excited, and her voice goes up an octave when she says, "Check out this brunch menu. They have biscuits served a dozen different ways, the classic chicken and waffles, farm-fresh omelets, and for the health-conscious, house-made granola with yogurt, fruit, and berries. It's going to be tough to decide."

Cato reaches under the table and gives Olive's knee a squeeze. "I like all those things. Why don't you pick your top-two favorites to order, and we'll share?"

Olive smiles and kisses Cato on the cheek.

"Ugh! Can we please just have one day where you two aren't so syrupy sweet on each other? It's really annoying," whines Paulette.

Cato and Olive both sit up straight in their seats, hands on the table, like they've done something wrong.

"Okay, Miss Fuddy-Duddy. These kids have done nothing wrong. What do you have against love, anyway?" asks Lake.

"I'm not against love, I just think it's stupid," says Paulette.

"I know there's a story behind that statement, and I'd love to hear it sometime, but not today. We came here to drink, eat, and have fun."

Paulette rolls her eyes and says, "Where's our server? I'm ready to get the drink part started."

Determined to keep it light and do what she's set out to do, Lake says, "That a girl. And here she is, right on time."

In a chipper voice, their server says, "Good morning! Can I get you all started with a drink?"

Two mimosas later, Paulette has a belly full of food and is much more pleasant to be around. Swooshing the liquid inside the pitcher around, she says, "We still have mimosa here to drink. Who's ready for a refill?"

Setting her napkin on the table, Lake says, "I'm good, you guys finish it off. I need to pee."

The inside of the restaurant is jammed wall to wall with people waiting for a table, and of course, the restrooms are in the far back corner. Lake is doing her best to maneuver through the bodies that are two and three deep in places.

"Excuse me, pardon me. Excuse me."

She's almost made it to her destination when she feels a light tap on her shoulder.

"Hi, excuse me. I think you dropped this."

The man next to her is holding a small gold coin purse.

"That looks like it belongs to a five-year-old. It's not mine, sorry," says Lake as she scurries off to the ladies' room. She's had two glasses of water and two mimosas, and she really has to pee.

When Lake returns to the table, her study buddies have the check and are ready to settle up. They agree to split it equally four ways. Bruno's been a perfect gentleman throughout the meal, adjusting his body to settle in the sliver of sun as it passed slowly by their table. Patting him on the head, Lake says, "You're a good boy, buddy. Let's go walk off some of the delicious calories we just consumed."

Chapter 35 - Bishop

Lake is as comfortable at the park as she is in her own home. She and Damon had spent a lot of time here walking Bruno and just hanging out. There's always something going on, and it's a great place to people-watch.

Having been here hundreds of times himself, Bruno takes the lead as they pass through the gate, and Lake follows along happily, ready to walk as far as he'll take her. The two are deep inside the park when Bruno decides he'd rather be horizontal in the cool green grass than upright on the blacktop that radiates heat from every angle.

Lake looks around for a park bench, a large rock, or anything other than the ground to sit down on, but there's nothing close by, so she sits down on the grass alongside Bruno. She knows it's against the rules, but since she doesn't see any people or dogs nearby, Lake unsnaps the leash from his harness and allows him to roll around and drag his body freely through the grass. He's having a grand ol' time, and she loves that he's so into it. Damon would have loved it, too. Being able to spend every day with Bruno is like having a small piece of Damon with her all the time.

"You know it's basically illegal to have your dog off the leash in the park, right"? The man's voice startles her, and she jumps a little. Bruno, still rolling around in the grass, is a good six feet away from her and completely oblivious to the man and his schnauzer, who came out of nowhere.

Lake's hand goes up to her face to shield her eyes from the sun. From this angle, she can't tell for sure, but she thinks it's the guy from the restaurant.

"You were right, by the way. The owner of the mini-purse *was* a five-year-old. But it was boy, not a girl," he says.

It is the guy from the restaurant, and he's brought reinforcements.

"It was a coin bag, not a mini-purse, then," says Lake.

"Well, I looked inside, and there was no money in it. Only Pokémon cards," says the man.

"And your point is?" asks Lake.

"I don't have a point. I just thought you'd like to know the bag was returned to its owner, and he was very relieved to have his card collection back."

The man's dog is pulling on its leash, eager to join Bruno in the grass. Lake looks at the dog and then back at the man standing next to her.

"I won't tell if you don't," says Lake.

"I don't let Tucker run willy-nilly through the park. It's irresponsible and against the rules," he says with a smile as he drops the leash and joins Lake in the grass. Tucker runs over to Bruno, and the two get to sniffing.

A rule follower herself, Lake appreciates his humor, even if it's bullshit.

The man extends his hand to Lake and says, "I'm Bishop, by the way. It's nice to officially meet you."

Lake ignores the hand and says, "I'm Lake. Nice to meet you, too."

Up now and fully alert, Bruno is ready to move on. Lake snaps the leash back onto his harness, then stands and brushes the dirt off her backside.

"Tucker and I are new-ish to the city, and he doesn't have a lot of friends. Mind if we walk with you? And what's your dog's name?" asks Bishop.

Lake takes a hard look at the man seated next to her. He's well groomed, handsome, tan, and fit, and he has a schnauzer, for goodness' sake. She assumes he's gay, and she is okay with him tagging along.

"It's Bruno. Most everyone in his circle of friends is human, so he could use a dog friend," she says.

Bishop and Lake talk nonstop on the walk back, and she learns that he's a financial attorney who has moved here a few months ago from Chicago to work at a bank.

"That's crazy. I can't believe you're an attorney. I'm a law student, second year," says Lake.

Bishop looks surprised and says, "Second year? That's when I fell in love with finance, regulation, and tax-related law. Hang in there, it only gets better."

"How long have you had Tucker? He looks and acts like he still has a whole lot of puppy in him," says Lake.

"He's a couple months shy of his first birthday. I got him just after I moved here. My office is close enough to walk to, so I'm able to run home at lunch and let him out most days. I have a retired neighbor who's sweet as can be, says I remind her of her grandson. When I'm in a bind and can't get home, she takes Tuck out for me."

Lake pictures the retiree next to Bishop as the typical Southern woman—tastefully dressed, appropriate, and pretty. One he can count on to be kind, thoughtful, and genuinely interested in the handsome young man next door.

"She sounds like the best kind of neighbor to have," says Lake.

"She is. I lucked out with Mrs. Jamieson."

Bishop takes his sunglasses off and places them on top of his head. His eyes are a gentle, beautiful brown, just like Grandma Kiki's.

"Will you look at those two?" he asks. Lake turns to see Bruno and Tucker sitting butt to butt, staring off into space.

"Fast friends," Bishop says. "We should plan a playdate for them."

"Sure," says Lake. "Why not?"

"Cool, how about next Saturday morning?" he says. "We can grab a coffee and walk through the park."

"Okay. Is seven thirty too early for you?" she asks.

"Tuck and I are early birds. Seven thirty is great for us. We can meet there on the corner and walk over to the coffee shop. It's just around the block."

Lake bends down and gives Tucker an affectionate pet on the head. "See you next week, Tuck. Later, Bishop," she says as she and Bruno head toward home.

#

Lake doesn't give Bishop a second thought until Friday night. She and Paulette are sitting by the fire in the backyard when she says, "Bruno has a playdate tomorrow at the park."

446

At the sound of his name, Bruno raises his head, looks at Lake, then lowers it back down on his crossed front paws. *Oh, my goodness, how sweet is that*, she thinks.

Lake waits for Paulette to say something, but she doesn't.

"Don't you want to know who it's with?" asks Lake.

Paulette takes a swig of her beer and says, "No. Not really."

"Well, I'm going to tell you anyway," says Lake.

Paulette shoots her a look that says, *Great, I can't wait to hear it*, then takes another pull from her longneck bottle of beer.

Lake gives Paulette the rundown of how she and Bruno met their new walking buddies after Sunday brunch at the park. "And he's an attorney at a bank downtown. I looked him up just to make sure he wasn't lying."

In typical Paulette fashion, her single word response to Lake's story is "Bitchin'."

Lake shakes her head and says, "Good talk."

#

The playdate goes pretty well. The dogs get along great for the most part. There is one skirmish, though, when they both go after a random tennis ball at the same time. Lake sees teeth and the distinct sound of Bruno growling. She's about to jump in when Bishop puts his arm out. "Wait, give 'em a chance to work it out."

Bruno has at least twenty pounds on Tucker, and Lake's worried he'll hurt the little guy. What she doesn't count on is how fast Tucker is. The two are going at it full-bore, and during the tussle, Bruno drops the ball. Before he's able to scoop it back up, Tucker wraps his little teeth around it and takes off. Bruno chases him around the dog park for a good ten minutes before he passes out in the grass.

With Bruno down for the count and panting hard, Lake says, "I feel like you knew that was going to happen."

Bishop chuckles and says, "We come here every weekend. Tuck's a speedy little guy, and he doesn't take shit from any dog. I had a feeling he'd end up with the ball."

"Tuck's a freaking dog park ringer. You knew his speed and agility would beat out my Bruno, and you played it off like conflict is normal, let 'em work it out." Lake pretends to frown.

"Are you seriously upset that your big galoot couldn't hold his own with a little guy like Tuck?" he asks.

"I'm not upset, but I can be pretty convincing, huh?"

"Are you hoping to be a trial lawyer one day?"

"No. I'm leaning toward environmental law, but it never hurts to be a persuasive communicator. I think it's a skill we all need to hone. Especially women."

"Why do you say that?" asks Bishop.

"Because I believe women have to work harder to overcome bias. The power to persuade is an art that's crucial to success in business and in our personal lives. When we're able to master the art of persuasion, it puts us in a better position."

"Well said, Lake. Whatever type of law you end up practicing, you're going to be great," he says.

#

Bishop is contemplative and respectful to his core. He and Lake make a standing doggie playdate for the pooches, and she looks forward to those days. He doesn't pry or inquire about private matters, which makes Lake feel more comfortable and free with select details of her personal life.

One Saturday at the park, she tells him the story of Damon being badly beaten for defending a friend and that he later died due to complications from his injuries.

"Just before he passed, he asked if I would take Bruno, and that's how I ended up being his mom," says Lake.

Bishop looks at Lake with genuine concern in his eyes and says, "That's a really terrible story. I'm so sorry for your loss."

Lake thanks him and looks away so he can't see the tear in her eye.

"Hey, random question, do you like jazz music?" he asks.

"That is a random question, and yeah, I guess I like jazz, why?" asks Lake.

"The Jazz Festival is in a couple weeks. I thought maybe we could go together, if you want," he says.

Lake's heard good things about the Jazz Festival, which is huge and free, but she has never been. "Sure, that might be fun. But let's leave the dogs at home," she says.

"I wasn't planning on bringing them. I need to be dog free when I listen to the smooth sounds of jazz, in case I feel like bustin' a move."

"Wow, is it too late to back out?" jokes Lake.

"Hey, I'm a pretty good dancer—you might be surprised," he says with a wink.

For some reason, the wink makes Lake feel like she needs to set a boundary with Bishop to alleviate any future misunderstandings. "Bishop, I think you should know I'm gay."

Bishop has an incredible poker face. In a very matter-of-fact manner, he says, "I was not aware of that, but it makes no difference to me who you're attracted to."

What a refreshing response! Lake has shared the news of her queerness with several men in the past, and not a one of them has ever responded the way Bishop just did. One guy actually asked if she was sure. Another guy told her she didn't have to lie, that if she didn't want to go out with him, she should just say so. And the stupidest response to date: "You just haven't met the right man yet." Some guys are real jackasses.

Lake is hoping her personal admission will ring a bell with Bishop, and he'll confirm that he's gay, too, but he doesn't say anything else.

"Thanks for that very accepting response, Bishop. I appreciate it."

"What are friends for?" he asks.

#

Try as she might, Lake cannot get a read on the guy. Jazz Fest is the first of their dog-free outings, and things progress quickly from there. Bishop suggests a supper club so the two of them can try a new restaurant every Wednesday night, and Lake loves the concept. Together, they try nearly every type of ethnic food available in the city, which is wonderful. She develops a love for Indian food, now her favorite, and he discovers a fondness for Mediterranean cuisine. Occasionally, depending on which is closer, they'll swing by his condo or her bungalow for an after-dinner drink. Regardless of the locale, Bishop is always a perfect gentleman, and never once does he overstep.

One night, they end up at her place, and she can't help but think how handsome he is. If they were to walk down to the neighborhood pub right now, Bishop could have his pick of women and probably most men, so why is he here spending his time with her?

Looking back, this has been essentially the longest courtship of her life. For months, the two have dedicated countless hours of their free time to a union built on self-imposed monogamy. Lake simply has no desire, and Bishop seems content to continue as they are—until the day when everything changes.

#

They're at his place watching a movie, some old action/comedy flick he'd been after her for weeks to watch with him. "I can't believe you've never seen this movie. Arnold is fucking awesome in everything he does. Please tell me you've seen *The Terminator*," Bishop pleads.

Of course, she's seen *The Terminator*. Lake's brother, Pete, had been obsessed with the movie for months, and Linda Hamilton is totally hot in it.

"Sorry, no. Never seen it," she says.

"Oh my God! I'm going to pretend I didn't hear that. Next time it's my turn to pick the movie, we're watching *The Terminator*!"

"Okay, but it had better be awesome. I wouldn't want you to waste your pick on a mediocre flick," says Lake.

"Blasphemer! Stop talking right now, or you will be punished," he cries.

Lake's tossing around the idea of coming clean and telling him the truth about already having seen the movie, but she decides not to. His reaction to her saying no is too entertaining.

"Wow, talk about hero worship. He's just an actor," she says.

Bishop stumbles backward as though he's been stabbed in the stomach. With his hand on his belly, he pretends to pull out a rather large sword before falling to the floor. He lies there perfectly still for a few seconds.

When Lake walks toward him, he starts convulsing and making an odd gagging noise. After a couple seconds of this nonsense, he goes limp again. Lake kicks his leg just to be sure he's dead, then says, "Good. Now I never have to watch the stupid *Terminator* movie."

Bishop is up in a flash. He grabs hold of Lake's legs, causing her to lose her balance and fall on top of him.

"You're a heartless wench, Lake Myers. Just for that, I call double feature! You have to watch *The Terminator* and *Terminator 2: Judgment Day*. You can thank me later."

"I'll just thank you now. I've actually seen them both."

Bishop looks confused, then he begins to laugh. While he lies there laughing, Lake stands and offers her hand to him. "C'mon, fool, we have a movie to watch."

Using her hand for leverage, he stands and says, "Get high with me."

Lake's never been much of a smoker, but Bishop likes smoking weed and she likes his company, so on occasion, she indulges him and takes a few hits. The downside is that his fat-ass blunts hurt her throat, so now when she smokes, he insists on giving her shotguns, which, for some reason, are less painful but at the same time, weirdly sexual.

Lake is munching away on her popcorn watching the movie and trying to get into it, but the scene between Harry and the used car salesman totally harshes her high with his comment: "The 'vette gets them wet." When he blurts that out, she looks directly at Bishop and gives him her very best *what the F* look.

It might just be paranoia, but the look on his face is one of total panic, which she finds hilarious, and they both start laughing hysterically.

Lake's face hurts from laughing so hard that she has to look away in order to stop. They both go back to watching the flick, and Lake is like, *Damn, why am I just now seeing Jamie Lee with the slick-backed hair, dancing in a black bra and panties? This movie is incredible.*

Just then, Bishop taps her on the shoulder. When Lake turns to look at him, his face is within an inch of hers. He leans in to give her another shotgun, his eyes locked on hers.

Lake inhales, holding the smoke in her mouth for a few seconds, and doesn't look away. When she exhales, Bishop kisses her, and she lets it happen.

Bishop is kind, safe, and a really great kisser.

When the kissing stops, Lake sits motionless, trying to make sense of what just happened.

In the silence, Bishop pulls his T-shirt over his head, exposing his tan, smooth chest. He has a six-pack. His eyes are on hers, and he realizes she's looking down, staring at his hair-free torso.

"I swam in college, and to be the fastest, I had to shave, like, my entire body. I still swim at least four days a week just to stay in shape. Old habits die hard."

"Take your clothes off. I want to see," she says.

Bishop stands and strips down to nothing. His entire body is smooth, sinewy, toned, like a woman's.

Lake touches his leg, runs her hand up the inside of his thigh and down the front of his other leg. His legs are smoother than her legs are right now.

"You shave your entire body?" she asks.

"I shave what I can. I have the rest of it waxed," he tells her.

Lake looks his body up and down. She's never seen him without a shirt, much less naked. His body is beautiful. The muscles in each of his limbs are quite pronounced. His collarbone is high and well defined. The bone structure of his face is exquisite. And his eyes are so dark and expressive.

She can feel the wetness between her legs, and the urge to kiss him is overpowering. He takes hold of her hand and leads her to the bedroom.

Bishop and Lake have sex for hours, exploring each other's bodies, kissing, licking, tasting every inch of each other.

"Please stay," he says after.

"I can't. I have to let Bruno out. I should be home already." Lake can't explain what has just happened. It wasn't planned, and it wasn't terrible. It just was.

Pushing the covers back, Lake crawls out of Bishop's bed, gathers her clothes, and takes them into the bathroom to get dressed. She has just gotten naked and made whoopie with her best boyfriend, and *now* the modesty kicks in.

When she comes out, the bedroom is empty. Bishop is sitting on the couch in the living room. She kisses him lightly on the lips and says, "Good night."

Bishop takes hold of her hand and looks at her as if he's about to say something, but then he doesn't. Letting go of her hand, he says, "Good night."

#

On the short ride home, Lake thinks about how she's tried to let go of her anger over how gays are treated, the rate at which they are dying, and on a deeper, more personal level, the resentment she feels for holding back, forced to watch from the sidelines.

She's been trying to resolve her attraction to women her whole life, because the world in which she lives isn't set up for her five percent of the population. Society fervently enforces codes of behavior regarding sexual orientation, and Lake has received the message that she should be heterosexual and act according to society's definition of her gender. She lives an imposturous life on the daily for fear of being different or not fitting into the role expected of her by family, friends, work colleagues, or greater society. Each time she comes out or attempts to explain her unnatural attraction, she's forced to confront societal response and attitudes toward queers. It's a breathless waiting game fueled by shame and isolation.

With Bishop, though, life is no longer an obstacle course of hate coming at her from every angle. When she's with him, Lake breathes without difficulty and is present in every moment.

With Bishop, the world is easy-peasy, light and breezy.

Lake can slip her hand into his and kiss him anytime and anywhere she wants. She's never experienced that freedom before. Not one single time.

No more late-night strategic planning sessions, trying to pinpoint the right hours to meet an acceptable match in a setting that's already narrowed the field of players considerably. Her dating prospects are no longer restricted to just one building between the hours of 9 and 11 p.m.

With Bishop, it's like she's been given the gift of time.

#

Lake reaches across the bed to turn off the lamp on her nightstand and sees the photo of her and Kiki. Reluctant to look her in the eye, she turns the photo facedown, shuts off the light, and goes to sleep.

The next morning, she moves the photo to the living room, eventually replacing it with a photo of herself and Bishop.

A few days later, he asks, "Where's the photo of you and Kiki?"

"I moved it to the living room bookshelf so that your handsome face is the last thing I see before going to sleep," she says.

"I know how much that picture means to you. You didn't have to move it—there's room for both," he says.

No, there isn't, Lake thinks to herself. She feels defeated but free. Disappointed but optimistic.

Lake gives in and stops fighting. What a shitty lesbian she is.

Chapter 36 – Bishop

*B*ishop proposes to Lake exactly one month after their first night together, and she says yes. She's never visited his hometown, nor has she met his family or any of his childhood friends. When push comes to shove, there's a lot she doesn't know about the man, really, but still she says yes. Lake Myers has agreed to become Mrs. Lake Myers-Anderson.

Aside from Bishop, Lake's study group has never been introduced to anyone she's been with, so his gender is never in question. The same is true for most of her friends and family.

Her parents seem genuinely happy for this turn of events. Sylvia is excited to help plan the wedding, but Lake declines having a big ceremony in her home state.

"We're both just so busy, Mom. Bishop is swamped at work, and I can't miss class. We've decided on a small ceremony here in the park."

"Whatever you think is best, dear. Wild horses couldn't keep your dad and me away," says Sylvia.

An accommodating response with a dash of humor.

It's hard to tell if her mom is sincerely supportive of her choice to be with Bishop or relieved that she's no longer living such a questionable lifestyle.

#

The entire next year of her life is a blur.

Lake's adoring husband encourages her to keep being awesome and finish law school, and notwithstanding his own sixty -hour work-week, he sacrifices countless waking moments to help her prep for and pass the bar exam. It's official. Lake and Bishop are a two-lawyer, dual-income, no-children household with an abundance of disposable income.

To celebrate their winning lifestyle, they purchase a fully restored charmer in the Highlands, set back from the road on an ultra-private lot. The perfect blend of farmhouse chic and contemporary cool, it checks all the boxes, and it's right down the street from the park.

If she's being completely honest, there have been a couple of insignificant red flags that have popped up, but they were more a light pink than red, and therefore easy to ignore.

#

It's crazy to think that one curious night has changed her life completely. It was Lake's decision to stop making time for friends, especially those on the fringe. No lazy Sunday brunches with her former law circle friends, drinking mimosas to the late afternoon. Definitely no more clubs.

She is now a wife to a man, living the dream. Two cars, a fine-looking house, and of course, two perfectly playful pups.

The years go by with little change. Looking back, she can now see the subtle shifts and how they played out. But at the time, she didn't notice.

Lake, the lesbian, wife, and mom, has fallen prey to the embedded, alternate image and thought of what a real woman should be. *Anatomy is destiny, damn you, Freud.*

Every year that passes, she hears at least one person spout off, "It's 200_ [fill in the blank]. For Pete's sake, no one thinks that anymore." Sadly, though, yes, they do.

Blips on a screen, in one case, a stage.

Lake is driving to work one morning, listening to the radio, and she wins tickets to see *Angels in America.* Her first thought is, *Damon would have loved this play!* And she would have loved to have seen it with him, but it's not possible. She's treated all her friends from the past so terribly, she has no one else to go with but Bishop.

#

Lake spends the better part of the afternoon shopping at three different stores to get all the ingredients for his favorite dinner. Admittedly, Bishop is the designated cook in their house. Not only does he enjoy it, but he's better at it. But she really wants to see this play, so she does her best to follow the recipes closely, and to her surprise, the meal turns out well.

Turning the knob of the front door, Bishop detects the aroma of a home-cooked meal, and it catches him off-guard. He takes a step back and does a double take on the door before passing through. Yep, this is his house. Standing in the foyer, he has a clear line of sight to the kitchen. He can see movement in the room, but no bodies. Bishop deposits his briefcase on the bench near the door, and as he's walking down the hall, he calls out, "Who's in my kitchen? And what have you done with my wife?"

Lake emerges from behind the pantry door. "Call me silly, but I was looking through some old photo albums this morning and got a little emotional. I probably don't say it as often as I should, Bishop, so I thought I'd show you how much I love and appreciate you. Please be considerate as you're eating dinner—lambchops are not the easiest to prepare."

Bishop beams at his wife and sidesteps to the archway that leads to the dining room. The table is beautifully set. "You're using the Waterford crystal candlesticks and glassware my parents gave us when we got married. We only use those things during the holidays. Are you trying to butter me up before dropping a bomb on me? Did you wreck the car or something?" he asks jokingly.

Lake shoots Bishop a look of utter disbelief. "No, I didn't wreck the car. I told you, I just felt like doing something sweet for my amazing husband, and I wanted to make it special."

Bishop squints one eye as he loosens his tie.

"I've almost got everything ready," says Lake. "I want you to just sit back and relax."

Bishop pulls out the chair at the head of the table and sits.

"I'll be right back," she says.

Lake returns two minutes later with plates of roasted lambchops, garlic mashed potatoes, and sautéed broccoli rabe. She looked at several different cookbooks before settling on the presentation she felt was best. Lake adjusts the plate so that the bone is up and leaning away from him.

She bends toward Bishop, gives him a lingering kiss, and asks, "Would you like wine with dinner?"

"A glass of wine sounds perfect," he says.

The Oregon pinot noir she's chosen is the best part of the meal. After they've finished eating, Lake clears the plates. Then tugging lightly on his sleeve, Lake leads Bishop to the living room, bottle of wine in hand.

Bishop's smile takes over his face, extending from one ear to the other. He's a good man, her husband. Smiling back at him, Lake feels her breath catch involuntarily because she knows she's not made for this life. She wasn't entirely ready when she committed. She should have been.

She lives a heavy, terrifying, ugly lie every day, but she is too far down the rabbit hole to claw her way back out. So, she persists.

With their smiles still in place, she asks, "So, you had a good day, babe?"

His smile remains as he replies, "I did, actually. I'm almost done with a case I've been working for months, and the outcome looks like it'll be better than expected. Traffic was light coming home, and I walked into this! I'm the luckiest man in the Highlands."

Unintentionally, his words twist the knife deeper, and it hurts. Lake has to look away or risk giving herself up. Pouring the last of the wine into her glass, she says, "I'm going to grab another bottle of wine." From the kitchen, she casually mentions winning a pair of tickets to an upcoming show.

"You won tickets to a concert? That's awesome, babe. Who are they for?"

"Actually, it's for a play called *Angels in America*."

"Never heard of it," he says. "What's it about?"

Topping off his glass, she says, "From what I gather, it's a play about politics, sexuality, religion, AIDS, race, and a few other hot topics. I thought it sounded interesting, and it's free. But we don't have to go if you're not up for it."

"I guess that depends on when it is," he says.

"It's next Saturday at a venue downtown. I thought it could be a fun date night for us. Dinner and a show…"

"It's no risqué leg lamp, but you're a major award winner, babe. We have to go. Maybe you can wear that sexy blue dress you wore to my sister's engagement party last year?"

Lake agrees to the dress and dinner at Bishop's favorite restaurant because it's the path of least resistance. She doesn't want to wear the blue dress, but she will. The restaurant isn't her favorite, either, but it's easier to agree than it is to debate. To win the smallest of battles, she presents options in the most unassuming, innocent way possible. All she really wants is to sit in a dark theater surrounded by queer men and women watching a play about gay men and AIDS. It's a horrible disease that devastated her best friend's body, rendered him helpless, and left him to die. Seeing this play is a way for her to connect with other gays and lesbians without actually having to speak or interact with anyone.

#

Less than an hour into the play, she can see that Bishop is uncomfortable with the story, but she chooses to ignore it. Still, he fidgets in his seat, crossing and uncrossing his legs multiple times before squeezing her hand. When she finally looks at him, his eyes plead, *Can we please leave?*

She's pissed that she won't get to see the end of this play. She's a fucking lesbian, and this story means something to her! What a senseless woman she is. Her husband has no idea why she identifies so closely with the story, and she sure as hell doesn't want to tell him. Admitting anything at this point will do nothing but open the door for failure and heartbreak.

She squeezes his hand and tries to refocus on the actors on stage. Bishop is still until the anonymous gay sex scene in Central Park plays out. The conversation and actions between the two men onstage are graphic and harsh. He leans over and whispers in her ear, "Babe, can we please leave?"

Reluctantly, Lake nods and stands. Bishop follows her out to the lobby, trailing behind her as they walk to the car. Neither of them says a word during the drive home. This is the first time in their marriage that the gay elephant in the room is sitting right beside them and neither of them is ready to acknowledge it.

#

Feeling restless, Lake grabs a beer and heads outside to the front porch swing. When Lake and Bishop were looking for a home to buy, walkability and proximity to the park were at the top of their list. They looked at so many houses that fit the main criteria, and then they came here.

Their house sits back off the road and has a huge front yard, a side deck, a fenced backyard for the dogs, and the best feature, a screened front porch. Lake didn't grow up in a home with a screened porch, but ever since she moved to the South, she's admired the architecture and the idea of intentionally connecting the inside of the home to the activities happening outside. And what better way to watch the world go by than from their own porch swing? The simplistic, wood bench supported by heavy metal links is her happy place, and she comes here often to clear her head and heal her heart.

Tonight, the crickets are loud. They help drown out her otherwise-shrill thoughts. *Make a move, Lake. What is it that you really want?*

That's a loaded question. She wants to feel true happiness and contentment in her marriage and her life, but as long as she stays in the marriage she's in, those feelings will never be within reach.

Lake finishes her beer and spends several minutes patiently peeling the label off the bottle in one piece. Walking away from her relationship with Kingston was hard, but leaving her life with Bishop will require a lot of unraveling and far more bravery. She's not going to solve the problem or make any life-altering moves tonight. She considers getting another beer but isn't really feeling it. She could stay out here and fall asleep on the swing, but eventually she'll have to face her husband and another day with him.

The house is quiet when she goes inside, and she knows that Bishop has gone to bed.

Feeling like a failure, trapped and ashamed, Lake trudges up the stairs to the room they share. Motivated more by duty than desire, she climbs into bed, kisses her husband gently, then turns away from him just as a tear slides down the side of her face. Lost years and buckets of tears.

#

It's year number six of her marriage. Lake and Bishop are a fine example of love and success, the envy of all their acquaintances. The two work hard to maintain an impressive portfolio of wealth, and they attend countless dinners and holiday parties with his friends and work colleagues to prove that what they have is real.

"You're never going to guess what it is. Open it," says Bishop excitedly. Lake is still in her pajamas, working on her first cup of coffee. The box in front of her is medium-sized—not too tall, not too wide. She picks it up, and it's heavier than it looks. She shakes it and hears a dull thud when the item inside it bounces off the sides of the box.

"Babe, you're not going to figure it by shaking the box," he says. "Would you just open it already?"

Lake sets the box back down and takes a sip of her coffee. "Did you wrap this yourself?" she asks.

"I'd like to take credit for the wrapping, but no, I did not wrap it. But I did pick it out myself and I'm really freaking proud and excited about it, so would you just open the box already?"

Lake appreciates the beautifully wrapped package; she is terrible at wrapping presents. She's happy to pay extra every year to have her gifts wrapped at the store. It's deeply satisfying to know you're done with the holiday shopping ritual when you walk through the door. When she pulls her packages out of the bag, they're ready for the tree. *Voila!*

The box in front of her is neatly wrapped in a heavy-gauge brown paper with a puffy white, traditional Tiffany-style bow on top. Lake tugs on the end of the ribbon and watches one loop after the other collapse onto the box before turning it sideways so that she can tear into the fold of the paper. She spins the package around and releases the tape from the other side. Bishop watches closely as she lifts the folded corners of the paper to expose a plain white box.

Lake rode the struggle bus for days trying to come up with a suitable gift for their anniversary this year. She finally settled on a high-end set of golf clubs. Bishop and his associates from work have taken up the game of golf, and he needed a set of his own, so she purchased a gift certificate from the local pro shop. It's enough for clubs and a lesson with a pro. A gift that shows she cares deeply but still hides her hideous stonewalling face. The time will come to lay all her cards on the table, but their anniversary is not the time.

Lake lifts the top off the box and finds the gift inside is wrapped in white tissue paper. Tearing the tape away from the paper, she sees the edge of something metal. She tears the remaining paper away, and there it is.

"It's a personalized anniversary plaque for the house, and it's made of iron—for strength," says Bishop. "It signifies a long-lasting and solid marriage. Isn't it cool?"

Lake is suddenly eleven years old and can hear Sylvia's voice as plain as day: *"Be grateful for every gift, even if you don't like it. Find one nice thing to say about it and always say thank you."*

"It's very thoughtful, Bishop. Thank you," she says.

The plaque reads, *House of Anderson, established October 21, 2006,* the day they were married. He left off her last name altogether. Her choice to hyphenate has always bothered him.

"I thought it would be good by the front door, inside the screened porch, but I can hang it wherever you want," he says.

"That's a great place for it," she says. A constant reminder of the one day that haunts her mounted right on the wall of her happy place. Hard to think of a better spot for it.

"Cool, I'll hang it today, right after breakfast," he says.

#

A few days later, Lake wakes to the smell of coffee brewing. It's a scent that brings her happily to the kitchen day after day, but today, the powerful smell of dark-roast java makes her feel queasy and sends her running to the bathroom. Leaning over the commode, the wave of nausea subsides, and her heart rate begins to slow down. She stays still for a few moments, giving her body a moment to calm.

Lake is rarely sick, but for the occasional cold or when her allergies are acting up. Dinner last night was tame. Bishop made a roast chicken with broccoli and rice, bland, nothing spicy or overly herby.

Then it hits her. No. She can't be. There's no way she can be pregnant.

She takes the pill every day and is very serious about it. The only time she's ever forgotten to take her pill was right after they got back from vacation. The week after their trip to Hawaii. She had such a difficult go adjusting to the time difference after ten full days of island-hopping and an even harder time getting back to the routine of life at home. Two nights in a row she fell into bed so exhausted she skipped her nightly pre-sleep routine entirely. No face washing, flossing, or pill taking.

But it was just those two times. Last month.

Lake waits for Bishop to leave the house before making a quick trip to the drugstore. Unsure of which brand to get, she buys both at-home pregnancy tests available and drives back to the house.

The one stick reveals two bright pink lines; on the other, a dark red plus sign appears. She's positively pregnant.

Chapter 37 – Bishop

*L*ake is taken aback, and Bishop is over the moon. It hasn't been a topic of conversation in their marriage because they exchanged I dos with the understanding that the two of them, the dogs, work, and the house are enough to keep them busy.

Motherhood. The state of being a mother. Lake is far from having a motherhood mindset, but as her belly grows bigger, she becomes more and more excited. There's no getting around what's happening inside her belly.

Bishop agrees to wait until she's twelve weeks into the pregnancy before either of them spill the beans to the family or any of their friends. This gives Lake time to process and plan. After the tests confirmed the pregnancy, Lake bought the holy grail of motherhood books to help grasp the concept and understand what to expect now that she's expecting, and she's all in.

She reads the book from cover to cover and is amazed at what the human body can do. Her OB-GYN is her new best friend, and she recommends a slew of prenatal vitamins. The first few weeks of pregnancy are crucial to fetal health and development, and since she's carrying a future superstar, she needs to get onboard now.

The families are pleased about a new baby entering the ranks, and their friends are happy and supportive, as well. Lake's position as an environmental lawyer provides more flexibility than her husband's, and the firm she works for is accommodating from the start. "Take as much time as you need," says her boss.

Lake begins a nightly ritual of reading to the baby in her belly. She joins a children's book club and begins filling their shelves with nursery rhymes, the classics, and everything in between.

At the start of her third trimester, Lake enrolls in birthing and baby care classes. Bishop plans around them and never misses a one.

The day Paige is born is the happiest day of her life. Seven pounds, five ounces, twenty-one inches—Mom and baby are healthy and doing well. This is the call that goes out to everyone on their phone tree.

Sold on the benefits of nursing, Lake is committed to breastfeeding. She has twelve weeks of maternity leave to get to know her daughter. As hard as it is, she puts the outside world on hold for the time being and enjoys all the time she has with Paige. Together, they explore the neighborhood and connect with other new moms. Bishop is a terrific coparent and steps in to help with meals and bath time. The husband-wife team fall into a pattern, and four years pass before their very eyes.

When Paige turns four, she starts Pre-K at a nearby private school, and Bishop takes a position that requires intermittent international business travel.

"Are you sure you don't want to hire someone to help with Paige?" he asks. "I'm going halfway around the world, Lake. I need to know you two are okay if anything happens."

"We're fine, Bishop, I got this," says Lake. "She'll go to after-school care while you're gone, and I'll be there to pick her up every day by five. She likes after-care. She gets to play and have fun with her bestie. It's good for her."

"It's a long day for a four-year-old," he says.

"Lots of kids her age have long days. She's in a wonderful class-room setting the majority of her day, and then she gets to blow off steam until I get there. We have a sitter we trust if I need her and plenty of people who can help in a pinch."

Hesitantly, he says, "Okay, if you're sure."

Lake gives him a quick kiss and says, "I am," before turning off the bedside lamp and going to sleep.

#

Bishop is out of town for two weeks. At first, it is strange not having him there, but with all the parental duties falling to her, Lake is too busy to dwell on his absence for long.

On Saturday, she and Paige meet up with another mom and her daughter at the children's museum. The next morning at breakfast, she asks Paige if she'd like to go to the farmers' market.

"What's a farmers' market? Is that where you go to buy a farm?" Paige asks innocently.

"Not exactly," says Lake. "A farmers' market is a place where local farmers sell fruit and vegetables and sometimes cheese, your favorite, and all kinds of other stuff."

Paige shrugs her shoulders and says, "I like cheese."

"I know you do. I think they have ice cream, too. And you can play on the swings," says Lake.

"Okay. Can we go now?" asks Paige.

"We'll go in just a little bit, after you finish your breakfast," answers Lake. Motherhood and the predictability of marriage have mellowed her feeling of unrest, but they haven't caused her to forget the feeling entirely. Lake loves her family and her life, but it's not complete. *She's* not complete. Lately, she's felt wistful, not to the point of uncompromising regret, but a change will do her good.

The market Lake remembers has been transformed into a bustling home for all kinds of interesting stuff. It's three times the size she remembers, and the variety of produce and goods is overwhelming.

Paige is anxious to locate the ice cream tent and Lake has no idea where to begin, so they roam the sidewalks and pathways, zigzagging from one area to the next. Lake is just about to stop and ask for help when she hears someone calling her name.

She stops and looks from side to side but doesn't recognize any of the faces she sees.

There it is again. Tugging on her sleeve, Paige says, "Mom, that lady back there said your name."

When Lake turns around, she sees a woman who seems vaguely familiar to her. Waving, the woman calls out her name again, "Lake. Hi!"

Tara. It's been many years since she's seen or thought of the woman. Coming out from behind the table full of baked goods, Tara embraces Lake, hugging her tightly.

She smells wonderful. Clean and fresh, like home.

"My gosh, Lake. Where have you been? I thought you'd fallen off the face of the earth," says Tara.

Lake opens her mouth to speak, but no words come out. The words are jumbled in her mind and her mouth.

More tugging. "Moooom, you said we could get ice cream."

Now it's Tara's turn to stumble over her words.

"Wait. What? 'Mom'?" she asks

"Tara, this is my daughter, Paige," says Lake sheepishly.

"It's nice to meet you, Paige. How old are you?" Tara asks.

Paige battles to hold up the appropriate number of fingers on her right hand and says, "I'm four. How old are you?"

Lake shoots Paige a look, and Tara says, "I'm older than four. Do you like cookies, Paige?"

"Yes," says Paige.

Tara steps aside and says, "I sell cookies and pastries. Do you see anything here you want to try?"

Paige points to a thick, chewy-looking chocolate-chip cookie that's at least six inches in diameter. With a smile, Tara says, "Excellent choice, a classic. Babe, can you please give my friend Paige here that cookie and a napkin?"

Lake hadn't noticed the other woman behind the table until Tara addressed her. Babe?

The woman smiles at Paige and gives her the cookie, which keeps her busy just long enough for Lake and Tara to have a couple minutes of adult conversation.

"Thank you," says Lake.

"Of course. How have you been?" asks Tara.

"Good," says Lake. "Busy. How about you?"

"Really good." Tara winks at the woman she'd called "babe." "Steph and I have been together for a few years now. Work is work, which is fine. Steph owns a small bakery, and I help out here at the market on the weekends."

"A bakery? I can't believe you're in such good shape. If my partner owned a bakery, I'd be twice this size," jokes Lake.

The comment opens the door for Tara's next question.

"When we first got together, I gained a few pounds. After a while, I learned to restrain myself, no matter how good the things she bakes smell. What does your partner do?"

Lake answers truthfully, "He's a financial attorney."

If Tara is surprised, she doesn't show it. "That's great," she says. "And what about you? Did you finish law school?"

Still sharp and attractive, thinks Lake. She doesn't remember telling Tara about law school, but she must have mentioned it the last time she saw her.

"I did graduate from law school. I practice environmental law," says Lake.

"Do you have any milk?" asks Paige.

Both women look at Paige. She has chocolate on her fingers and the corners of her mouth. What's left of the cookie is still in her hands.

"I don't have any milk, but I know where you can get some," says Tara.

Lake picks up the napkin that Paige has dropped on the ground. "Are you done with the cookie?" she asks.

"No, I'm going to finish it. I'm just thirsty," is Paige's response.

"C'mon. Follow me," says Tara.

Lake and Paige walk with Tara to the end of her row of tents. A food truck there sells cartons of milk. She buys a carton for Paige, and Tara says, "Hey, I've got to get back. Do you want have lunch next week?"

"I'd love to," says Lake. "My Thursday is pretty light, if that day works for you?"

"Thursday works for me," says Tara.

#

Lake looks forward to Thursday and lunch with Tara. What was meant to be a quick meal to catch up turns into a leisurely sit-down with plenty of sweet tea refills. Lake notices the ring on Tara's finger, and Tara catches Lake up on all that's happened since the day she told Lake about her and Kingston's past. The high point? She and Steph are legally married.

Lake is elated to hear this and fills in the gaps between their last meeting and now.

"I'm sorry about you and Kingston. I hope what I told you wasn't the cause of you two splitting up," says Tara.

"It wasn't, but it did force me to face my future with her. We wanted very different things," says Lake.

Tara nods her head in understanding. She knows exactly what Lake is talking about. "I'm sorry about what happened to your friend Damon," she says.

Hearing Tara say his name strikes a chord deep in Lake's chest. She misses him. Tara reaches across the table, and Lake takes her hand.

In a soft voice, Tara says, "Living a queer life isn't always easy. But living a lie day after day will eventually take a toll. It can be toxic to your body and soul."

Lake has been careful to keep her distance from people like Tara, away from situations like the one she's in now. It's a dangerous meeting with potentially stark side effects, but she's like a moth to a flame burned by the fire.

Lake says Tara's name out loud, and it sounds like "Tarot." Tara the divine has just put Lake back on track, gently forcing her to realize how much she misses her former life. The ball has been set in motion, and there is nothing she can do to stop it.

#

All the attempts to make like she's happy in her heart no longer work. Their careers, the travel, the beautiful home, and the gifts, they are just lipstick on a pig.

Lake has an amazing job, and she knows she is capable of taking care of herself and Paige. Bishop is back from his travels abroad. With Paige fast asleep in her bed upstairs, Lake arms herself with a beer and asks Bishop to join her out front on the porch swing.

He knows what she's going to say before she even has the chance to say it. Over the years, their roles have become reversed. With new life blown into her sails, he's now the tired one. He gives up as easily as she did when she said "yes" to his proposal. He wants what's best for their daughter and for Lake to be happy. She wants the same for him.

Their split is irksomely amicable.

Bishop keeps the house, a familiar home base for Paige. Lake buys a house in a nearby city, just a few miles from the home she'd once shared with Bishop, and they raise their daughter together. Separate, but equal partners.

The coparenting arrangement Lake and Bishop create works well. Their established boundaries and predetermined schedules allow both of them to plan and take precious time for themselves. Paige is a loved, well-adjusted little girl, and the trio is happy.

Lake spends the next few years growing and learning to love herself.

With time to travel and explore gay life outside of the clubs, she attends pride parades, discovers a few gay-centric coffee shops and restaurants, and stumbles onto a lesbian-oriented campground. Lake is back in a big way! She misplaced a chunk of time, years actually, but now she's back and is having so much fun getting to know herself.

Lake is selective with those she brings home. She isn't physical with women in front of her daughter, and she doesn't allow women to sleep over when Paige is home. The weekends when she doesn't have Paige with her are a different story.

One evening, Lake is at dinner with a few friends when someone suggests popping into the bar for a drink after. Lake is hesitant but agrees to go. A nice-looking woman she's never seen before offers to buy her a drink, but Lake declines. As she continues to have a good time, though, she reconsiders the woman's offer. Spontaneity is not a normal part of Lake's life, but there is a mutual attraction there, and she has the house to herself this weekend. She invites the woman back to her place and ultimately takes her to bed.

Early the next morning, Lake hears someone at the front door. She rolls over to look at the clock and is face-to-face with the woman from the night before. The sex had been more than satisfying, and Lake smiles as she reminisces over the events of the evening. The doorbell rings again and again. It's seven fifteen in the morning.

Careful not to wake her bedmate, Lake crawls out of bed, grabs her robe, and tiptoes out of the room.

Whoever's at the door rings the bell again insistently, forcing her to pick up the pace. She can see a head through the leaded glass, but she has no idea who it is until she cracks the door open. Lake is surprised to find Bishop and Paige standing on her front porch.

"Hey, what are you two doing up so early?" she asks.

"Paige threw up in her bed and is running a low-grade fever. She asked me to bring her here," Bishop explains.

Lake's mind jumps to the woman in her bed. She wants to be upset with Bishop for dropping in unannounced, but when she looks at Paige, her negative feelings fade away. Lake takes Paige by the hand and says, "C'mon, pumpkin, let's get you cleaned up."

Bishop holds Paige's backpack out and asks, "Do you want me to put this in her room?"

Lake glances toward the hallway leading to the bedrooms and says, "No, I've got it. You can just set it there by the door. I'm going to give her a cool bath, then throw all her clothes in the wash. Thanks for bringing her home."

"I can stay and help," says Bishop.

"We're good. I got her. It's Saturday morning, go back home and have some coffee. I'll call you later and let you know how she is."

"Okay. Bye."

After Bishop leaves, Lake runs a cool bath for Paige and starts a pot of coffee. She's in the bathroom with Paige when the woman pops her head in the door. Paige and Lake both turn their heads at the same time.

"Hi," says Lake.

The woman smiles, glances over at Paige, and says, "Good morning."

Lake doesn't want to make the situation weird. "I made coffee. The cups are in the cupboard by the sink. Help yourself."

"Okay," says the woman before popping back out.

Having witnessed the exchange between her mom and the woman, Paige perks up and asks, "Who is that lady?"

"She's just a friend of mine," Lake answers.

"Did she spend the night?" Paige asks.

This is a question Lake wasn't expecting this morning, but there it is. Out of the mouth of babes. Lake's house has three bedrooms: her room, the primary bedroom; Paige's room, and a third bedroom that she uses as her home office.

"Yes, she did. We had a sleepover," replies Lake.

There are life-defining moments she will never forget; this is one of them. Rather than make up a story, Lake decides to tell Paige the truth, no matter what question she asks next.

In a concerned voice, Paige asks, "Did she sleep in my bed while I was at Daddy's house?"

Shaking her head, Lake tells Paige, "No. She didn't sleep in your bed."

Puzzled, Paige continues with her line of questioning. "Did she sleep on the couch?"

Again, Lake shakes her head and says, "No. She didn't sleep on the couch, baby. She slept in Mommy's bed."

This seems to end the ask-and-answer part of the morning. "Oh," is all Paige says.

Lake helps Paige rinse her hair and then pulls the plug from the drain. Watching the water swirl down the hole, through the tub pipes, out to wherever tub water goes, Lake makes the choice to keep the conversation going.

"You know Mommy's friend, Miss Tara?" asks Lake as she helps her little girl get out of the tub.

"Yes," says Paige.

"Do you remember her friend, Miss Stephanie?" asks Lake.

"You mean her girlfriend?" says Paige.

Lake hands Paige a towel and says, "Yes, that one. Miss Tara and Miss Stephanie aren't just girlfriends. They're married," says Lake. "Paige, do you know what 'gay' means?"

In her know-it-all tone of voice, Paige says, "Yes, Mom, I know what 'gay' means. Terrence from my school, his brother is gay."

Lake is a little shocked that Paige is familiar with the word "gay" and that she has a classmate who has shared that his brother is gay. Kids in second grade today talk more freely about these things than when she was Paige's age.

"Okay, so Terrence has a brother that's gay. What does that mean?" asks Lake.

Again, in the same tone, Paige replies, "It means that Terrence's brother likes boys. 'Gay' is when girls like to kiss girls and boys like to kiss boys."

472

Lake is combing Paige's wet hair and smiling. "You're such a smart girl, Paige. That's exactly what 'gay' means. That lady who spent the night, she stayed over because I like to kiss girls."

Lake is waiting for Paige to freak out or ask more questions, but she doesn't. Instead, Paige hugs Lake and says, "It's okay to be gay, Mom. I'm hungry. Can I have pancakes for breakfast?"

With that simple question, Lake looks into her daughter's big blue eyes and knows there is hope. Not just for her, but for Lake too. Her sweet, wonderful daughter is looking at her through innocent eyes, waiting for her to answer a question about breakfast. An unassuming question requiring nothing more than a simple, one-word answer. No hidden agenda, no judgment.

Lake gives her a smile and hugs her back. "I love you, Paige, and yes, you can have pancakes for breakfast. Go put on some clean pajamas. I'll be in the kitchen."

She's done it. Lake has raised a strong little girl, self-assured, funny, and capable of accepting her mom's innate desire to kiss and love a woman.

She wants to high-five herself.

Chapter 38

After her guest leaves and Paige is asleep on the couch, Lake calls Bishop to give him an update.

"I gave her a bath and a dose of children's Tylenol. Her fever has gone down, and she had a big breakfast. She's asleep on the couch now."

"I'm glad to hear she's feeling better. I tried working my best dad magic on her, but she wasn't having it. Sorry if I messed up any of your weekend plans bringing her home early. I can double up and take her next weekend if you want," says Bishop.

"It's part of being a parent, Bishop. This morning she wanted me. One day, she'll ask me to bring her to you for comfort, and I will. You don't need to take her next weekend, but I appreciate the offer."

"No problem, Lake. We're still a family, even though we're divorced and live in separate houses."

Lake looks over at Paige's sleeping face and says, "There is something else I wanted to talk to you about. Do you have a minute?"

"Sure. What's up?" asks Bishop?

The boundaries Lake and Bishop have set transcend the parental aspect of the triad. They are legally divorced, and neither of them asks the other about their private lives. What goes on behind closed doors is off-limits, unless, of course, Paige is affected.

"When you dropped Paige off at the house this morning, I had a guest here. I was just so surprised when you showed up. She was asleep when you rang the bell, and nothing inappropriate happened after you left." Lake stops there, giving him a moment to absorb her words.

Bishop clears his throat and says, "It was your weekend to do as you please. You had no way of knowing the two of us would be on your doorstep so early in the morning."

If this conversation was happening in person, Lake would hug him. She's heard the ex-spouse horror stories and is beyond thankful for man she chose and who is now her ex.

"My friend did wake up when I was helping Paige with her bath. She stayed for coffee and pancakes, but that's not my point," says Lake. Bishop knows her well enough to know she has more to say about the situation. "Paige asked where my friend slept last night, and I told her the truth. I said that she slept with me in my bed, and I asked her if she knew what 'gay' meant."

"What did she say?" asks Bishop.

"In true Paige fashion, she acted like I was the dumb one for even asking. She told me that Terrence from her school has a gay brother and that gay means that Terrence's brother likes to kiss boys. She said gay is when girls like to kiss girls and boys like to kiss boys."

Bishop laughs and says, "Of course she did."

Lake is relieved to hear his laughter. At least she knows he's not pissed about the situation. "I would have talked to you about it first, but when the opportunity with Paige presented itself, I took it."

"I remember the day you told me you were gay, and I told you it makes no difference to me whom you're attracted to. It still doesn't. You have every right to love freely whomever you want."

A tear of happiness rolls down her cheek. "There's more," says Lake. "I told our daughter that I like to kiss girls."

In a playful manner, Bishop says, "Oh no. What did she have to say about *that*?"

"She told me it's okay to be gay and then she asked for pancakes."

They both laugh, and Lake says, "The gay world today is very different from when I was a kid. The community is growing and assimilating to the positive changes. I never thought I'd see the day when same-sex marriage would be a constitutional right, but that dream's been realized. National monuments are being erected in honor of lesbian, gay, bisexual, and transgender rights, and the Pentagon has lifted the ban on transgender people serving openly in the military. I would like to expose Paige to LGBTQ+ friends and families and teach her that diversity and inclusion of all people is the expectation."

In a sincere voice, Bishop tells her, "Paige is old enough to understand that this family celebrates and supports LGBTQ+ people and same-sex relationships. I will always have your back, Lake."

Lake can feel the waterworks are about to start, and she doesn't want Paige to wake up and see her crying. Before she disconnects, Lake says, "I will always love you for that. Thank you, Bishop."

#

Now that Bishop and Paige are onboard with Lake's lesbianism, it's time to begin the more selective portion of her comeback to the coming-out process.

Lake's Monday morning commute to work is light. One morning, operating on autopilot, she enters the parking garage, eases into her designated spot, and enters the building with a push through the turnstile. She catches the elevator on the ground level and is the only face in it until the doors open on the lobby level. Two and three feet deep, the many faces staring back at Lake catch her by surprise. She moves to the far right of the elevator cabin and does a double take to confirm the button she pushed earlier is still illuminated. The bodies attached to the faces flood the cabin, each vying for their sliver of space.

"Do you mind pushing eleven, please?" asks an anonymous voice from the back of the cabin.

Lake scans the faces more to assess than to confirm. No one on the elevator is a friend, colleague, or acquaintance. She has spent some time over the weekend running through the faces of people she knows, doing her best to correctly guess who needs to know her truth and whom she can trust with this very personal information. The building is home to her company and place of business. It's where she spends her days and how she earns a living. It's a wage that pays for private school, a mortgage, car, utilities, clothing, sustenance, and the occasional family vacation.

Positive progress within the gay community has made things easier, but she's learned not to judge a book by its cover, and she usually errs on the side of caution when speaking out.

#

When Lake started working at the firm, she had been married to Bishop and the nameplate outside her office read Lake Myers-Anderson. A few years later, they had a baby. The child grew older, and the couple got divorced. She dropped the "-Anderson" and ordered a replacement nameplate, but few people noticed. Multiple life events, both public and private, eventually all become known by those closest to her, but that isn't always by choice.

The overwhelming majority of people at her place of employment know and refer to her as married Lake, wife to Bishop and mother to Paige. One or both images are etched into their brains, triggering the same questions each time they run in to one another: *"Lake, so good to see you. How's Bishop doing?"* or *"Nice to see you, Lake. How's Paige? Has she started school yet? Is she playing any sports?"*

Although it tends to make things awkward, most days, her truthful response goes something like this: *"Bishop's well, we're divorced now. Paige is doing great. She's playing soccer and learning to play the violin. She prefers soccer over the violin but is coming along with the instrument. It helps that I give her an extra five dollars a week in her allowance money if she practices."* There's usually a smile and wink before she adds, *"Well-rounded kids, right?"*

On the likelihood that any conversation turns to dating, Lake avoids the truth for fear of the pronoun trap, because once it's out there, there's no going back. She does her best to size up the asker in those split seconds before answering, but it could really go either way. Her reasoning boils down to appearance.

She looks openminded; surely she can be trusted with the truth, or, *He's dressed in Brooks Brothers from head to toe and is wearing a red striped bow tie, there's no way I'm telling him anything.* It's a constant "queer struggle," and she's left straddling the fence, hesitant to lean one way or the other. But it's not Lake; it's them. She has to take into account how they will react. Will it come back to bite her in the ass the next time she's in line for a raise or seeks a promotion? The short- and long-term consequences are very real, and Lake highly doubts straight people have the same thoughts before they choose to answer a simple question about their dating life.

Atlanta is often referred to as the LGBTQ+ capital of the South due to its progressive reputation, but it's a liberal city full of transplants in the heart of the Bible Belt, and Lake could never know which side of the Mason-Dixon line a person was from until she put herself out there.

Lake takes her cue from Paige, a brilliant seven-year-old. It's her weekend with Paige, and they're up and out early on Saturday to beat the late-morning shoppers at the DeKalb Farmers' Market.

"Mom, can I go look at the lobsters?" asks Paige. "They're right there, Mom. You can see me from here—please?"

Paige is familiar with the market and knows to stay within eyeshot of her mom. "Yes, but please come right back to where we are now when you're done, okay? I won't leave this aisle without you, and don't you wander off, either, promise?"

Paige gives Lake her word and skips off in the direction of the giant lobster tank.

Lake is making her way through an array of hot sauces for sale when she hears her name. "Lake? I thought that was you. How are you doing, darlin'?"

Lake turns to see the wife of an attorney at her firm. An attorney whom she's not at all fond of. An A-one douchebag, for lack of a better term.

"I'm doing well, Mary Beth. You look fabulous! Where's Kurt?" asks Lake.

Mary Beth replies, "I told him I deserved a morning to myself. Kurt ran off to play golf with his buddies, and I dropped the boys at Little League. My sister is bringing them home later for me."

"Well, good for you," says Lake. "All us moms need and deserve personal time; I think it makes us better parents."

"I couldn't agree with you more!" says MaryBeth. "Kurt told me you and Bishop are divorced. I'm so sorry to hear that."

"Oh, don't be. The split was totally amicable. He's very involved with Paige, and it's nice to laugh with him again. We were always better friends than lovers."

Mary Beth steps closer to Lake and leans in. "Do tell! How'd you manage to get away and keep things going for the better? Did you catch him cheating? Sorry, that was rude, you don't have to tell me, but I am curious..."

A sporty and attractive older woman, Marybeth has a good fifteen years on Lake. She is dressed in luxury casualwear, her hair is perfectly coiffed, and her make up is well done, simple and understated. Her body language is screaming for Lake to trust her, but it's not that simple.

Lake cocks her head to the right and assures her that no one cheated.

Mary Beth is determined to get to the truth. "So, what was it? You can tell me. Is he secretly married to someone else?"

"No, it was nothing scandalous. We honestly just grew apart. The marriage wasn't healthy for either of us. It was my decision to leave," Lake tells her.

"C'mon, Lake. It's never quite that simple and hygienic. There's something you're not telling me. Wait—is he gay?"

Oh my gosh, Lake can't believe she's asked that. "No, Bishop is not gay."

A familiar little voice pipes in, "Dad's not gay, Mrs. Armstrong, Mom is. She likes kissing girls more than she likes kissing my dad."

Lake doesn't see Paige standing behind MaryBeth until she shares this tidbit of information.

MaryBeth doesn't miss a beat. "Hello, Paige. I didn't see you there. Where on earth did you come from?"

In her confident Paige voice, she replies, "I was looking at the lobsters, but I got bored, and Mom said I had to come right back. So here I am."

Nodding her head in affirmation, Mary Beth says, "Indeed, here you are."

Lake looks at Paige and can't help but love her, she's so stinking cute and brutally honest. She feels her cheeks getting warm. She looks back at MaryBeth while speaking to Paige, "If you're done looking at the lobsters, we should get going. We still have a few more stops to make."

Paige grabs hold of Lake's hand and says, "Okay. I'm ready, Mom." Lake smiles sheepishly.

Mary Beth squeezes Lake's free hand and leans in for a hug. "So nice seeing you, Lake. I do hope to catch up with you again soon."

#

The remainder of the weekend is quiet. Paige has a playdate with a neighbor friend, and Lake spends the afternoon outside in the yard. Monday traffic is heavy for the start of her workweek, and Lake uses the time in her car wondering how much of her conversation with Kurt's wife was repeated to him. Kurt's a sixty-hour-a-week man's man. He'll be on his second cup of coffee by the time Lake settles in, with plenty of time to share her life choices with a few of the other douchebags at work. It's high school all over again.

As she approaches the office, Lake's heart is racing, and she can feel the perspiration from her armpits and cleavage seeping into the fabric of her new blouse. She thanks the voice in her brain that suggested she wear black today. She rounds the corner and slows as she passes Kurt's office. He's leaning back in his chair, talking to someone on the phone when he sees her. Kurt's all smiles this morning. He waves and mouths *"hi"* to her, and Lake smiles and waves in return.

It's a busy day, and it's almost over before Lake realizes no one has looked at her funny and no eyes were averted to avoid contact as they passed in the hall. Gossip is a given with most women, especially upper-middle-class Southern women, and Paige had handed Mary Beth a mouthful. Lake imagines the amount of self-discipline required for a woman like her to keep something juicy enough to make Kurt's head explode all to herself. Then she remembers how giddy Mary Beth was to have Saturday morning to herself. Lake doesn't wish an unsatisfying marriage on anyone, but in her case, it seems to work in her favor. For all she knows, MaryBeth blabbed to all her society friends, but it would appear the buck has stopped there. Withholding information from Kurt likely gives Mary Beth the upper hand.

The week flies by, and it's like the conversation with Mary Beth never happened, with not a peep from anyone. Thank you, Mrs. Armstrong. Lake had obviously misjudged her.

#

Lake is in a good place. The two most important people in her life are privy to her truth and love her unconditionally. Work is going well, and the people in her circle are healthy. For the first time in a long time, she can breathe easily. When left alone with her thoughts, Lake thinks of the ranch, her family, and Kiki, solace and motivation when times were hard. Conviction leads to confidence.

It's rare for her to travel, but Lake's firm has asked her to handle a case for them in Los Angeles, and it's an opportunity for her to shine and prove her worth. Bishop will pull extra dad duty this week shuttling Paige to school, soccer, and violin practice, more proof that she married and divorced one of the best men out there.

The case in Los Angeles involves a chemical company that has been named in a civilsuit. It's a straightforward case of noncompliance, resulting in huge fines and the need for tighter scrutiny on how they do business. Lake and her team could have handled the case from home base, but the senior leaders at both companies have a strong personal tie, thus the need for cross-country travel and the posh, yet highly impersonal hotel room.

Lake adores Los Angeles. The city is one of the most diverse she's ever visited in terms of culture and food, and the weather is outstanding—perfect for lazy days at the beach or hike in a lesser-known park. But she's here to work, not play or explore the outdoors. She spent enough time listening to Bishop complain about his business travels to know that travel of this type is highly overrated. The idea that a career that sends you to new places is way to explore the world is simply not true. What it's really like is a whole new level of exhaustion, and when the day is done, sitting in a room that looks just like a room in any other part of the world.

The first night away from home is always the worst. Lake fell asleep fast the night before, but she woke up before the sun because of the time difference. For a while, she lay in bed watching bad TV, which became so bad that she switched over to her computer screen to get a jump on her morning meeting. Thirty minutes in, and she was ready to go back to sleep, but now it was time to get up—ugh!

She moves through her morning routine and is at the office early. Running on fumes, Lake bellies up to the lobby juice bar and opts for a concoction of fresh fruit and veggies with a shot of spirulina, gingko biloba, and extra B vitamins for a healthy boost of energy to get her through the day. The fat straw aids in helping her drain the cup full of vitality in record time. Ducking into the ladies' room, she does a quick check of her teeth for seeds or leftover specs of leafy greens—all clear. She's energized and ready to get on with it.

Chapter 39 – Anne

*L*ake steps up to the cheerful front desk clerk and checks in. Her badge is secure, and she has a clear understanding of where it is she's going. The suite of offices is on the twelfth floor—she will take a left off the elevator and it's the first door on the left.

A nice-looking young man is waiting for her by the entry doors. "Good morning, Ms. Myers. Mr. Boyd is expecting you. Follow me, please."

Lake follows the young man down a hallway that veers to the right and continues for some distance past several well-appointed offices, until finally they reach the desired space. The massive wood door is cracked just enough for her to hear voices. A woman pops out of nowhere, sees Lake's escort, and opens the door for them. The corner office with floor-to-ceiling windows and a view of Los Angeles' financial district belongs to the man Lake has spoken to multiple times but has never actually met. He's leaning against the front of his desk speaking to someone when they walk in.

"You must be Lake. It's great to put a face to the name. We're happy to have you here in the office, welcome."

The person seated in front of the man turns to see whom he's speaking to. Lake has had conversations with most of her host's team, and she prays that this woman is one of them. She's a beautiful new addition to Lake's world.

"Thank you, Mr. Boyd. It's my pleasure," says Lake.

Don Boyd, senior vice president, shakes her hand firmly, his face smiling warmly, perfect white teeth glistening brightly. Lake likes him instantly.

"Call me Don. Let's move over to the conference room. I want to introduce you to the team."

Yes, please get on with it, Don. I'm dying to know her name.

The unidentified, piping-hot woman takes a seat at the farthest end of the table, facing Lake. Her sunny blue eyes bore into Lake's, and Lake doesn't hear a single name until Don gets to her.

"Lake, this is Anne Waits. You'll be working closely with her while you're here. If there's anything you need, anything at all, please let Anne know."

Anne. Lake's never met an Anne before.

"Yes, sir, I will," says Lake. "And thank you. It's very nice to meet you, Anne."

The meeting drones on as one of Don's top associates walks the group through a PowerPoint presentation with the details of what should be known, the findings, the key players, and a working agenda for the week. Twice during the meeting, Anne excuses herself from the table and leaves the room. It takes every ounce of Lake's willpower not to run after her.

The team powers through a working lunch with a full review of the formal dossier. Don has an important call come in, and they break for the day just before 3 p.m.; it's almost 6 p.m. at home. Paige is at her violin lesson right now, sneaking peeks at the ancient wall clock, patiently waiting for the big hand to be on the 12 and the little hand on the 6. Paige knows how to tell time and express it in the right terms, but she insists on calling out the positions of the hands on the clock when it's an actual clock she's looking at. Thinking about the peculiarities of her daughter makes Lake smile.

She's busy shoving the file and notes into her already-full briefcase when a hand appears out of nowhere. It's attached to the knockout from the far end of the table.

"Hi there. Jack's set you up in an office down the hall. May I take you there?"

Lake will follow this woman anywhere she wants to go. *Please let there be a comfortable sofa in her office.* She' thinking about the possibilities of the space when she catches Anne checking out her chest. Yes, she's definitely looking at her girls. Lake can't help but smile as she turns to follow Anne to her lair. The office set aside for Lake has a nice view of the surrounding buildings, but no comfortable sofa, damn!

"The closest ladies' room is just around the corner here, and the breakroom is two doors down from there. My extension is two-three-eight, it's on a Post-it Note next to the phone. Please let me know if you need anything else," says Anne.

Lake's mind jumps to any number of things this woman could do for her if given the chance.

"Thank you, Anne. I'll be fine."

Anne hesitates at the door, her piercing blue eyes looking directly at Lake's. Lost in the moment, neither speaks. Lake would give anything to know what Anne is thinking right now.

Anne blinks and then says, "Open or closed?"

A million miles away, Lake doesn't hear a single word.

In a slightly louder voice, Anne asks, "Would you like the door open or closed?"

"Open. Open is good," says Lake. Four words that mark the close of her first day with Anne Waits.

#

Lake spends the next two days working alongside Anne, but neither woman is outwardly aggressive with their feelings for the other. There's no denying the attraction, but somehow keeping each other at a professional arm's length helps the sexual tension grow, adding to the suspense of what it would actually be like to kiss and explore.

On Lake's last day in the office, there's a lot of work to get done before she boards the plane back to Atlanta. The team orders lunch in, as the sun passes by the windows and begins to set. Don and her boss back in Atlanta are pleased with the outcome of Lake's week in Los Angeles.

Don's hand rests lightly on Lake's shoulder. "Terrific job, Lake. You've accomplished a lot while you were here, and I'm grateful for the time you put in. Do you have any plans for dinner this evening?"

Lake glances at Anne and responds, "No, I haven't really thought about dinner."

"I know a great place close by, I'll have Tobin reserve a table for six," boasts Don. "Anne, you know the place. Can you see to it that Lake finds her way there? I have a couple things to take care of, so I'll meet you all at seven thirty."

Anne and Lake's eyes meet, and Lake's heart skips a beat. She cannot let this night end without getting Anne's story. The lack of a wedding ring on her left hand doesn't necessarily mean anything. It seems unlikely that the comely Anne is not tethered to a partner, but Lake chooses to remain optimistic.

"Of course, Don. I'll take care of Lake," says Anne with a smile.

Please do, thinks Lake.

"I need to finish up an email, and then we can head over. Give me twenty minutes?" asks Anne.

Lake can use the time to organize her notes and freshen up. "Twenty minutes is perfect."

"Great. I'll come by your office and get you," says Anne before disappearing down the hallway.

#

Lake is shutting down her computer when Anne pops her head in the door. "Ready to go?" she asks.

Lake closes the lid of her computer and responds, "Ready."

Lake and Anne are the only two people in the elevator. The ride is quiet as the cabin drops a full five floors. They're halfway to the lobby before Lake asks, "How long have you worked for Don?"

Without turning her head, Anne replies, "I've been with Don about a year. I'm originally from northern California and was with a company just outside of San Francisco for about five years. When the opportunity here came up, I was ready for a change, and so I took it."

The *ding* of the elevator bell confirms their arrival at the lobby level, and the two women pause the conversation as they wait for the door to open.

Anne steps out first. "The restaurant's just a block away. I hope you like seafood. The place is known for their wild spiny lobsters, but they have other options if you're not into that," she says.

Lake doesn't care for lobster—the meat is too rich and buttery for her taste—but she does love other types of seafood.

"How about you?" asks Anne. "What's your story? How long have you been with your firm?"

Lake eyes Anne and gives her a half smile. She's fishing. The amount of time she's been with the firm is only a part of her story. Anne is curious about her personal *and* professional life.

Lake has come a long way since her early days in the city. She allowed Amy to walk away because she wasn't ready for everyone to clock her as a lesbian from minute one whenever they were together. Kingston was everything to her, but she ran that relationship into the ground when the topic of children and family was discussed to the point of exhaustion. The idea of two women building a family together had been pushed so far that it was, in effect, dead and buried, along with any connection they had ever shared.

Law school had given her purpose, and Damon had given her unconditional love. Her marriage to Bishop was the result of her vulnerability, and Paige was the best gift he'd ever given her.

Things are beginning to fall into place for Lake, and her only option is to move forward and be unforgettable.

"It's hard to believe, but I've been at the firm for almost ten years now. I interned there when I was still in law school, and they offered me a job when I graduated. I love the work, and I'm fortunate to be where I am now. I have a wonderful life, a beautiful daughter, a happy home, and a very supportive ex-husband, whom I recently came out to after telling my daughter, Paige, that her mom prefers kissing women to kissing men."

Anne's hand is resting on the front door of the restaurant when Lake finishes the last sentence. She stops and turns to look Lake dead in the eyes. With a twinkle in her light blue eyes, Anne says, "I love that story. Can I buy you a drink, Lake Myers?"

#

Lake and Anne spend the next few minutes at the bar chatting about work and family before Don and the rest of the crew arrive. Dinner takes longer than either woman wants it to take, and the two reconvene at the bar as soon as they are able. It's past midnight when Lake is forced to face what's left of the evening. She really likes Anne and wants nothing more than to invite her back to the hotel, but this woman is special. She has no idea how a relationship could work, but she's willing to give it a try.

Lake looks at her watch and says, "I don't want to stop learning about you, but I have an early flight. Can I call you this weekend?"

Anne smiles and says, "Yes," before looking away.

"What?" asks Lake.

Anne laughs softly and says, "I wrote my cell number on a Post-it Note next to my name and stuck it to the inside of your folder just before we finished up today."

Presumptuous, but precise, thinks Lake. *Look who's unforgettable now.*

#

On the flight home, Lake spends the time when she should be looking over her notes to think about Anne. She hasn't been this excited about a woman in a very long time. It's a great place to be.

She and Anne are two adults with the same desires. Lake has been given the okay to move forward, and she wants this. Lake texts Anne to let her know she'll call after Paige has gone to bed, and she can hardly stand the anticipation of hearing Anne's voice again.

In the beginning, the distance works for them. The phone is their lifeline, forcing them to talk and listen for hours, and Lake learns more about Anne than she ever thought possible. It's electrifying and strangely gratifying.

#

"Bishop has Paige next weekend, and I have no plans to speak of. I want to see your face, Anne. If you're not busy next weekend, come visit me in Atlanta. I can ask Bishop to keep Paige on Sunday night, too, and drop her off at school the following Monday. Let me buy you a ticket. I can pick you up Friday night and drop you off at the airport on Monday afternoon." Lake holds her breath waiting for Anne to say something.

It's a sweeping, romantic gesture, very Kingston-esque. It worked on Lake; will it work on Anne?

She can hear the intake of Anne's breath. "I want to see your face, too," she says. "I can plan to leave work early on Friday to catch the flight out. I'll take the day off on Monday."

Lake jumps up in excitement and silently shouts, *"YES!"*

#

Lake's heart stops, and she struggles to breathe when she sees Anne standing at the curb outside of baggage claim. Dressed in jeans and a sheer white blouse, she's eye-catching. Lake maneuvers the car close to where Anne stands and beeps.

She pops the trunk and steps out of the car. "Hey you," she says.

Anne swoops in for a hug, and Lake embraces her fully. Her scent is feminine and warm, floral with a hint of freesia. No matter how the days go, Lake will never forget the way Anne smells today, in their first embrace.

Lake helps Anne with her bags. Once they're inside the car, Lake leans over and gives her a quick smooch on the cheek. "Hi," she says.

Anne smiles and says, "Hello."

"Are you hungry? I didn't make plans for dinner because it's already so late, but we can stop somewhere if you need something to eat."

Anne reaches out and rests her hand on Lake's shoulder. "I ate a big lunch before I left. I'm not really hungry at all, but I could use a drink."

"Sure," says Lake. "There's a bunch of places within walking distance of the house."

Anne's hand moves across her shoulder, her fingers resting at the base of Lake's neck. "Do you have anything to drink at your place?" she asks.

"I have beer," says Lake. "And I have bourbon."

Lake can feel Anne's fingers creeping up to her hairline, drawing circles there. "Two of my favorite beverages. Let's stay in tonight," she says.

Anne's response sends a quiver through Lake's body to the crown of her head and back down, making her shudder involuntarily. Her reaction makes her think of the carnival game that requires people to heave a large mallet and hit the base to ring the bell. *Ding, ding, ding.*

Lake has a considerable variety of beers at her place, and both decide on a light lager to ease the tension building between them, but neither makes it to the bottom of a bottle before giving in.

Every minute of Lake's first weekend with Anne is erotic, easy, and destined to be.

#

Lake and Anne take turns flying back and forth between Atlanta and Los Angeles for a long weekend once a month for seven months. Lake is ready to take the next step in their relationship, but her support system and her life is here, in the city of Atlanta. She can't take Paige away from her father, and she doesn't want to. She thinks back to when she asked Kingston the question of where she had envisioned they would be in five years. That conversation didn't go the way she planned, so Lake remains silent in the situation. Afraid to rock the boat, she accepts her one weekend every four weeks.

Eight months into their far-reaching romance, Anne is in Atlanta for three days with Lake and Paige. It had been month six when Lake introduced her to Paige on Friday and Bishop on Saturday.

"I can see why you love her, Lake. She's great, and Paige has really taken a shine to her. Anne could be the one," says Bishop sweetly.

"I think she is," says Lake. "And I'm glad you got to meet her, Bishop. I want you to know that Paige and I aren't going anywhere. I don't know for sure where this thing with Anne is going, but I hope that she's open to moving here, for good."

"Have you talked to her about it?" he asks.

"Not in so many words, but she knows that my life here is very involved and that I can't just pick up and move," says Lake.

Bishop nods and squeezes her hand.

#

It's a beautiful spring day in late April, and the dogwoods are in full bloom. Lake has agreed to pancakes, Paige's favorite, and she is in the kitchen stirring the batter when Anne comes in.

"Mmm, pancakes, my favorite," says Anne as she kisses Lake.

Lake smiles and says, "I was looking forward to the day when Paige's tastebuds matured and she moved from pancakes to omelets as her go-to breakfast request. Now I have two of you to battle with over the morning meal."

"As long as you're cooking, I'll eat whatever you make, babe," jokes Anne.

Rubbing her eyes, Paige enters the kitchen, pulls out a chair, and sits down at the table.

"It's going to be a few minutes before the pancakes are ready. Did you sleep good last night?" asks Lake.

Paige nods her head.

"It's a pretty day outside," says Anne. "What do you say we have a picnic in the park later?"

"Can we have marshmallow and peanut butter sandwiches?" asks Paige.

Anne's eyebrows shoot up, and she defers to Lake on that one. "When do you eat marshmallow and peanut butter sandwiches?"

"Dad makes them for me sometimes and puts them in my lunch," is Paige's reply.

Lake rolls her eyes and says, "I don't think we have any marshmallows, but we do have grape jelly and strawberry jam. You could have one of those with peanut butter—what do you think?"

Paige scrunches up her face and says, "I like marshmallows, but I guess grape jelly would be okay. Can we have wavy potato chips, too?"

"You can pack whatever you want with your sandwich," says Lake.

After breakfast, Anne and Paige pull out all the fixings for a picnic at the park while Lake cleans up. Paige is standing across from Anne at the island when she asks, "Why don't you live here?"

Lake turns to look at Anne. Neither of them knows how to respond.

"Mom loves you, and you love her. You should live here," says Paige.

Anne winks at Lake and says, "You're right, Paige. I should live here."

Lake gives Anne a sweet smile and turns back to the sink. *My love just said she should live here.* Lake's heart is happy.

#

Anne returns to Los Angeles and contacts a headhunter to help with a job hunt in Atlanta. She's a well-respected CFO, and she receives two job offers in no time. Don is happy for her and Lake, but he is sad to see her go. Anne had bought her condo in West Hollywood shortly after moving to Los Angeles, and she has loved living there. It's a corner unit in a beautiful building that sells in less than a month.

"One-way tickets are crazy-inexpensive," says Lake. "I get in early Monday afternoon. We get one last night together in West Hollywood, and then we're off on our fabulous cross-country road trip back to Atlanta. We'll be like Thelma and Louise!"

"I love you, babe, But I'm not driving my car off the edge of the Grand Canyon for you," jokes Anne. "I'm looking forward to a long, crazy, beautiful life together—on solid ground."

"Okay, so not like *that* part of *Thelma and Louise*, but the adventurous part, for sure. I have this coffee table book of great quirky roadside attractions for every state we're driving through. You're going to love it."

In a snide voice, Anne says, "That *does* sound adventurous, can't wait."

You can learn a lot about a person during a weeklong road trip. Lake had no idea she could love Anne any more than she already did, but that's her big takeaway from the trip. The world's largest cedar rocking chair pales in comparison.

#

Anne taking the step to move to Atlanta is huge, and neither woman wants to mess up what they have by going too far, too fast. Their long-haul courtship is almost a year old when Anne is handed the keys to her short-term rental.

"You know I have plenty of room for you, Anne. Paige loves you, and Bishop is fine with you moving in with us," Lake says to Anne when she calls to tell her the sale of her condo is final.

"I know, and I'm ready to wake up to your face every morning, but this is just one more step to our forever," says Anne.

Lake knows that she's right. They have the rest of their lives to be together. There's too much at stake not to do this right.

In a very un-lesbian-like move, Anne has signed a six-month lease at a new high-rise in town close to where she's working. The fully furnished corporate unit gives her time to acclimate to the city and her new full-time surroundings.

"I found a storage unit close to your house. I'll have what I'm bringing delivered there to make it easy when I move in. You can use my apartment as your downtown getaway on the weekends when Paige is at her dad's, and I can get settled in at work."

Anne's place is centrally located to coffee shops, restaurants, shopping, and night life. It really is the perfect downtown getaway. The couple spends more nights together than apart, but it's nice having the space available when they need to retreat to their separate corners of the city. The trial run to their forever allows Lake and Anne to establish healthy, respectful boundaries.

When her lease is up, Anne drops the keys with her doorman and walks out of the building to Lake's waiting car. Now when someone asks what her husband does, Lake is proud to say, "My wife, Anne, is a chief financial officer."

Lake's life today is an open book, predictable and reliable. Perhaps because the first half of her life had been so hidden and capricious.

Sink or swim.

Push or pull.

Butch or fem.

Top or bottom.

Kiki is a distant memory, a blip in her life, but the indelible impression she made is unmistakable. Her presence remains, even though her body disappeared so many years ago. The way she and Gramps died made closure nearly impossible. It fractured Lake's family, leaving irreparable damage and deep, ugly scars that are impossible to hide.

But her grandmother told her time and again that she was special, a strong girl, a force to be reckoned with. It was Kiki who planted the seeds of confidence and Lake's acceptance of herself.

Grandma Kiki knew. She saw Lake, every part of her, and she used the years she had to gently guide and coax without making Lake feel self-conscious or ashamed.

\#

This morning, Lake is up and out of bed before her alarm goes off on a quest to steal a solid thirty minutes of quiet reading pleasure before Anne is awake. She grabs a cup of coffee and settles into her favorite corner cozy chair. Earlier in the week, she had agreed to join a yoga session with friends at one of their homes. It sounded like a good idea at the time, but now the day is here, and she's feeling a little selfish.

What she wants is to stay here in her chair and get lost in her book. Feeling nostalgic, she's rereading Judy Blume's *Summer Sisters*. But being the responsible adult that she is, she closes the book at the thirty-minute mark and heads upstairs to wake Anne.

After breakfast, they load their yoga mats in the car and head over to Beth's. Walking up to the house, Anne and Lake comment on their friend's wall-to-wall potted plants and how comfortable and inviting her home is. As soon as Lake walks through the door, she's happy to be there. It reminds her of when she was little, walking into her grandma's home and being enveloped in a cocoon of warmth and happiness—a special place for a girl like her. To those who helped to create her true identity, who love who she is, and who embrace the life bestowed upon her, *Namaste.*

The class is beautiful. Lake can hear someone in the kitchen offering to pour her a mimosa, and in a loud voice, she says, "Hell, yeah!" She's exactly where she should be on this warm Saturday morning.

Book Club Questions

1. What was your reaction to this book? How did it make you feel when you were reading it? What were the lasting impressions and takeaways from Lake's tempestuous road to happiness that you found yourself thinking about hours, days, or weeks later?

2. What character or chapters stood out to you the most? Why?

3. From her earliest memory and throughout the story, Lake's North Star is her beloved grandma Kiki. Even after her passing, Kiki's presence is strong enough to hold Lake up in the toughest of times. Who is your source of support and strongest ally?

4. Do you have a LGBTQ+ hero or role model in your life? What have you learned from them?

5. This book touches upon many provocative topics: sexuality; lack of acceptance; fear of persecution; masturbation; pornography; and access to LGBTQ+ safe spaces. Did this book spark awareness or change your perspective about any of these topics?

6. Members of the LGBTQ+ family are often marginalized, ignored, or shamed by friends and family. Lake demonstrates the importance of separating from the negative and surrounding yourself with those who will have the most positive influence on your life. Compare some of the people in Lake's birth family with those in her chosen family. Which faces represent the positive relationships in this book?

7. There are numerous examples of "The Pink Divide" in this book. Discuss the significance of the title of this book and how it relates to the circumstances of Lake's life. Why do you think the author chose to use this title?

8. As a child, Lake leaned heavily on her love of the outdoors, the discipline and comradery of sports, and academia as coping mechanisms to ignore her true sexuality as she plotted and planned her great escape from life in a small town. What are some examples from your own life of how you cope with denial or difficult situations? Have they proven successful? If not, what were your course corrections?

9. What surprised you the most about this book?

10. Lake made the decision to leave her family, home, and friends to cultivate a judgment-free space in which her sexuality could take root and blossom. Can you think of a situation in your own life where you had to make a difficult or painful decision in the best interest of your personal growth?

11. If you are LGBTQ+, do you have access to LGBTQ+ education, counseling, and safe spaces? If not, how do you talk about or discuss your feelings with others? Do you discuss your feelings with anyone?

**The Pink Divide is a fictitious establishment, but during the time the author lived in Atlanta, there was a women's bar called The Otherside Lounge, which she frequented. The Otherside had distinct areas carved out, designed to accommodate a large, diverse group of gays and lesbians. Depending on the night, it might be loud, or quiet and intimate, but most nights it was simply a place for friends to gather, have fun, and be free. LBGTQ+ safe spaces are pivotal to our communities. The loss of these places is heartbreaking, especially when it's due to violence.

"February 21, 1997. A nail-studded pipe bomb explodes at The Otherside Lounge, a local gay and lesbian nightclub, and injures five people. Investigators later charge Eric Rudolph with the bombing, along with others (including the January 16th bombing at an abortion clinic and the bomb that killed a visitor to the 1996 Olympic Games). Rudolph is eventually sentenced to five consecutive life terms in prison" (outhistory it's about time, outhistory.org).

In the late 1980s, there were an estimated two hundred lesbian bars across the country. In 2022, the number was thought to be just twenty two.